# THE MAN WHO WAS VOGUE

# THE MAN WHO WAS
# VOGUE

## THE LIFE AND TIMES OF
## CONDÉ NAST

# CAROLINE SEEBOHM

THE VIKING PRESS                    NEW YORK

# FOR MY MOTHER AND FATHER

LIBRARY OF CONGRESS CATALOGING IN PUBLICATION DATA
Seebohm, Caroline.
    The man who was Vogue.
    Includes bibliographical references and index.
    1. Nast, Condé, 1873–1942.    2. Publishers and
publishing—United States—Biography.    I. Title.
Z473.N28S43        070.5′092′4    [B]        81-14689
ISBN 0-670-45366-8                            AACR2

A selection from this book appeared originally in *Vogue* magazine,
in slightly different form.

Printed in the United States of America
Set in CRT Bodoni Book
Designed by Beth Tondreau

*Acknowledgments*

Photographs/illustrations on pp. 4, 49, 59, 74, 75, 78, 87, 93, 98, 108, 109, 113, 117, 154, 155, 160, 176, 177, 192, 202, 205, 210, 219, 243, 250, 251, 322, 337, courtesy Condé Nast Publications. Copyright © 1922, 1923, 1925, 1926, 1927, 1928, 1930, 1933, 1934, 1935, 1937, 1941, 1960 by The Condé Nast Publications Inc. Copyright © renewed 1950, 1951, 1953, 1954, 1955, 1956, 1958, 1961, 1963, 1965, 1969. All rights reserved. Photographs on pp. 22, 34, courtesy Mrs. Gerald F. Warburg. Photographs on pp. 11, 49, 129, 145, 313, 350, 358, courtesy Iva Patcévitch. Photographs on pp. 297, 346, courtesy The Hon. Mrs. Mark Bonham Carter. Drawing of Frank Crowninshield on p. 105, courtesy Jeanne Ballot Winham. Drawing of the Gibson Girl by Charles Dana Gibson on p. 167, courtesy the author. Illustration of Dr. M. F. Agha in *P/M Magazine* on p. 230, courtesy Mary Jane Pool. Photograph of Brodovitch's revolutionary spread of Munkacsi, appearing on p. 267, © 1935 The Hearst Corporation, is used by permission of *Harper's Bazaar*. Photograph on p. 284, courtesy Samuel H. Gottscho. Photograph on p. 347 by John Phillips, *Life* Magazine, © Time Inc.

The black-and-white line drawings used on the title page, chapter headings, and endpapers are unattributed artwork from *Vanity Fair*.

# ACKNOWLEDGMENTS

My thanks go first to Condé Nast's family, Mrs. Gerald F. Warburg, The Hon. Mrs. Mark Bonham Carter, the late General C. Coudert Nast, and the late Lady Benson, for their wonderful cooperation and patience during the writing of this book.

I could not have completed the project without the generous help of Alexander Liberman, editorial director of The Condé Nast Publications Inc. His support, and the blessing of the late Mary Campbell, made it all possible. I also owe a special debt to two other colleagues of Condé Nast's, Iva S. V. Patcévitch, former president of the company, and Harry W. Yoxall, former managing director of the London office, whose advice, sought time and again, was invaluable. Other Condé Nast people who made the work easier were Benjamin Bogin, Paul Bonner, Robert J. Lapham, William P. Rayner, Perry L. Ruston, Jeanne Ballot Winham, Pamela Van Zandt, and Lucy Lewis in New York, Daniel Salem and Susan Train in Paris, and Alex Kroll in London. Diana Edkins was my expert guide through Condé Nast's enormous photographic archive.

## ACKNOWLEDGMENTS

Alan Williams was my eagle-eyed editor at Viking, and with Nanette Kritzalis and Beth Tondreau helped produce the book to a standard of which Condé Nast might have approved. My undying gratitude also to Patrick O'Connor for effortlessly providing the title.

I must also thank Theo Tarter, Leslie Prouty, Dianne Spoto, and Cynthia Cathcart of the Condé Nast Library for looking after me and putting up with my shrieks and groans while I wrote the book—and afterward.

The following people have also greatly helped me in various ways:

Constantin Alajálov, Andrew Alpern, Brooke Astor, Toni Frissell Bacon, Eduardo Benito, Linda Blandford, Frederic Bradlee, Francis Brennan, L. Llewellyn Calloway, Jr., Eileen Cumming Cecil, Ferdinand Coudert, Baroness Edwina d'Erlanger, The Hon. Millicent Fenwick, David V. Foster, Victoria Glendinning, Marcel Guillaume, Dorothy Hirschon, Horst P. Horst, Anne Horton, Mary Lasker, Elinor Wurzburg Lawrence, Helen Lawrenson, Liza Leinbach, Eleanor Lippincott, Clare Boothe Luce, Lydia McClean, Joyce MacCrae, Edward McSweeney, Marya Mannes, Grace Mayer, Mabel Morrison, Thomas Naegele, Ewart Newsom, Thomas Phipps, Mary Jane Pool, Steven Ruskin, Rosamond Bernier Russell, Carmel Benito Semmes, Dorothy Sherrill, Barbara Stanwyck, the late Marie H. Stark, Allene Talmey, Constance B. Thayer, Helen Valentine, Hugo Vickers, Diana Vreeland, the late Dr. Richard Wallace, Mary Warburg, Lewis and Joan Wechsler, Charlotte Wilson-Young, Allen Young, Rosalie Smith Zimmermann.

Finally, I bow to the inspiration of my husband, Walter H. Lippincott, who came up with the idea for this book in the first place.

# CONTENTS

# CONTENTS

# THE MAN WHO WAS VOGUE

# PRELUDE
## "THIS IS A CLASSY JOINT"

O n Sunday, January 18, 1925, Condé Nast gave a housewarm-
ing party in his new apartment, at 1040 Park Avenue in New
York City. It was a large dinner dance, and among the guests were
Richard Barthelmess, Herbert Bayard Swope, Efrem Zimbalist,
Alfred Lunt, Lynn Fontanne, Gilbert Seldes, Rube Goldberg, Edna
St. Vincent Millay, Katharine Cornell, Fred and Adele Astaire, Ina
Claire, Jascha Heifetz, George Gershwin, Frank Crowninshield,
Edward Steichen, Philip Barry, Arthur Hammerstein, Frank Case,
Ralph Barton, Laurence Stallings, and George Jean Nathan. Apart
from the uninvited and unlamented President Calvin Coolidge, a
group more representative of the beau monde could hardly have
been assembled.

The apartment was a thirty-room duplex/penthouse decorated
with an opulence that befitted the publisher of *Vogue, Vanity Fair,
House & Garden,* and *Jardin des Modes.* These magazines, after
all, spoke to the richest, most fashionable, most amusing people in
America and Europe—and in the twenties, they were very rich,
very fashionable, and very, very amusing. The building had been

1

designed by the distinguished firm of Delano and Aldrich, and in the original 1923 drawings there were three apartments per floor, with the penthouse devoted to servants' quarters, as was customary at that time. (With no air conditioning, no one else would contemplate inhabiting the heat-collecting top floor.) By 1924, the plans had been changed to accommodate a special apartment for Condé Nast, who decided, daringly, to use the roof for a spectacular entertaining space—cooled, he trusted, by lingering crosstown breezes.

Nast's specially designed apartment had ten entertaining rooms on the roof and a suite of sleeping and domestic rooms on the floor below, the two floors connected by a main staircase. A glassed-in conservatory or solarium was added later, sometime between 1926 and 1928.

The interior of the apartment was decorated by the current darling of the design world, Elsie de Wolfe, a former actress who became the first professional female interior decorator in America when she "did" the rooms for the Colony Club, the famous women's club on Park Avenue. She covered American living rooms with chintz, after seeing it in England, where they had been doing it for years. But her undying passion (if passion she knew) was for the French Look. Every room in Nast's penthouse reflected this enthusiasm—Louis XV furniture upholstered in pale green damask, Chinese screens, Régence needlepoint sofas, grisaille walls, gilt-framed mirrors, Savonnerie rugs, organdy curtains, ceilings covered in silver tea-paper. The floor of the solarium was made of a fascinating waxed blue-green slate, laid in a random mosaic.

Of course there were the obligatory amusing touches, too—the *chaise percée* in the mirrored penthouse powder room, for instance, which came from Gloria Swanson's apartment; or the trompe l'oeil railing at the top of a small staircase which Lord Birkenhead, three sheets to the wind at a party in his honor, mistook for the real thing. (His subsequent tumble down the stairs was fortunately not fatal.)

The pièce de résistance of Miss de Wolfe's extravagant vision was the ballroom, which was decorated with an eighteenth-century Chien Lung wallpaper, salmon-pink moiré curtains edged with blue-green fringe, silver gauze undercurtains trimmed with Chinese-blue ribbon and silver banding, and a parquet floor made in France and laid by specially imported French workmen. The solarium, entered from this shimmering room through French doors, was a glass-enclosed bower of flowers and greenery where guests sat at tables and admired the view of Park Avenue by night, or waved to Moss Hart, who lived opposite.

Wonderful copy, all in all, for a spread in *Vogue,* where, naturally, photographs of the apartment ultimately appeared. And that, as far as Condé Nast was concerned, was the point. This thirty-room duplex was not acquired to house his wife (divorced) or his children (both almost grown); a middle-aged bachelor hardly needed thirty rooms to play in, even if one of them boasted a Chien Lung wallpaper. Nast's apartment was designed as a mise-en-scène, a production center for the publisher's creations. Like Jay Gatsby, he had created a palace of hospitality "where he dispensed starlight to casual moths," a milieu whose purpose was not entertainment but the fulfillment of an obsession, a painstakingly constructed dream.

His parties were fast and fabulous—but they were business. Into his sumptuous stage set Nast lured the fashionable people who briefly illuminated their age, for they were the stuff, the matériel, of his magazines. From the beginning of 1925, when he moved into the apartment, until a few months before he died, in September 1942, Nast threw at least two parties a month—enormous ones like his housewarming, cocktail parties, buffets, after-theatre suppers, and intimate sit-down dinners, many of which appeared later in gossip columns. "Publisher Condé Nast gave a fabulous Grace Moore party to which most of the Somebodies in town gladly went" was the sort of thing. Most of the guests had appeared, or would appear, in the pages of *Vogue.* Many of them contributed to *Vanity Fair.* Many of their houses had been or would be featured in *House & Garden.* The parties were, in a sense, *tableaux vivants,* the magazines come to life, with Nast the omniscient, omnipresent editor.

Even the most expert chroniclers of class aspirations would have been impressed by the preparations that preceded these parties.

Elsie de Wolfe photographed by
Nickolas Muray shortly after her
marriage to Paris-based diplomat
Sir Charles Mendl. Her clothes
were frequently the subject
of comment. *Vogue,*
October 1, 1927.

Perfect setting
for a party—the
glass-enclosed terrace
of Condé Nast's apartment
at 1040 Park Avenue, with
French doors leading into
the ballroom. Photograph
by Mattie Edwards Hewitt.
*Vogue,* August 1, 1928.

Each occasion was coded, checked, budgeted, and analyzed. Each was documented, with notes on table arrangements (plus drawings), menus, flowers, and entertainment. The percentage of shows and no-shows at each party was recorded, and reasons for same. For instance, for a bon voyage cocktail party for British photographer Cecil Beaton in 1936, 147 guests showed up, or 44 percent of those invited—"5 days notice (very bad weather)." At a cocktail party for Lady Mendl (as Elsie de Wolfe became), "168 guests arrived—39 percent. 8 days notice. In looking at this low percentage account must be taken of the fact that the party was held in Thanksgiving week and many people had gone out of town for the Thursday to Monday holidays."

For that party, the complete breakdown looked like this:

|          | MEN | WOMEN | TOTAL |
|----------|-----|-------|-------|
| COUPLES  | 162 | 162   | 324   |
| SINGLES  | 60  | 42    | 102   |
| TOTAL    | 222 | 204   | 426   |

Flowers by Armstrong & Brown—$107.10
Food by Edith Huntenen
22 small tables
86 green-and-gilt chairs
4 coatracks, hangers and checks
10 waiters
1 dishwasher
2 buffet tables [the one in the ballroom 8 feet long]
Liquor used—$98.79
   [This was in the thirties, when whiskey cost $1.87 a quart.]
4 bottles vermouth
6 bottles gin
17 bottles whiskey [rye and scotch]
1½ bottles sherry

(No champagne was listed, which perhaps explains why the amount of liquor consumed appears small for 168 people.)

Prohibition merely added to the excitement of the evenings: during the years of bootleg liquor, on entering the elevator to the apartment one had to volunteer a password. And in an upstairs bathroom, unsuspecting visitors might sometimes encounter a tubful of bottles of whiskey or champagne. Post-party breakdowns show that rye and scotch were the most popular drinks, with champagne, gin, Bacardi, vermouth, brandy, and sherry regularly on the list.

Before the big parties, instructions were given to remove the Chippendale chairs, hall runners, and the dining-room rug ("disconnect electric bell and replace when rug is put back"). The solarium was stripped of everything except four green-painted chairs, lamps, and a glass table, and the Ping-Pong room of everything, to make room for a cocktail table. The solarium floor was washed and waxed; the rug in the Ping-Pong room was cleaned. All chandeliers were cleaned, as were the mirror walls in the powder room.

On the morning of the party, buckets of fresh flowers were brought into the apartment and massed in every corner, on every table. "I have never seen anything like it," reported the Spanish artist and *Vogue* illustrator Benito. "The staircase was literally covered with roses. Thirty thousand dollars' worth of roses, I was told. One million, eight hundred thousand pesetas' worth of roses." This was surely an exaggeration, but about Nast's parties one could believe almost anything.

Also on the day itself, Garvin, the building's head porter, was notified so that both main elevators and sometimes the service elevator were alerted for duty.

The service elevator was presumably not necessary for the small dinner party Condé Nast gave on April 24, 1935, for Princess Nathalie Paley. Twenty people were invited (including Cecil Beaton, the Thomas Hitchcocks, and the Harrison Williamses). Thirteen people sent their regrets, and eight people were listed as reserves. The flowers were furnished by Armstrong & Brown and arranged by Mr. Monis on April 23. Service was by Welch (three waiters, canopies, sandwiches, green-and-gilt chairs). The cocktails and wines came to $34.60, and the food, catered by Longchamps at $4.75 per cover, consisted of:

Shrimps
Consommé Bellevue
Cheese straws, celery, nuts, olives
Suprême of Sole Marguery
Heated Fleurons
Individual Baby Guinea Hen boned, stuffed with wild rice
Fresh new peas    Fried hominy
Whole tomato stuffed with  Waldorf Salad
Lemon Sorbet Kirsch
Petits fours    Mints
Demitasse

After the party was over, the list of liquors consumed included half a bottle of vermouth, two bottles of whiskey, four of champagne, and one and a half of sherry. (No other wine list survives, probably because Nast served champagne with his meals, a fearful faux pas in the eyes of the Old World but evidently enjoyed by the palates of the New.) Further notes were made of bills for the butcher, grocer, waiters, service, wine, cigars, flowers, and invitations, both per person and totals for the group.

The guest lists were just as meticulously documented. The host divided them into A, B, and C groups—society, people in the arts, celebrities—with subdivisions for foreigners, singles, couples, and so forth. The lists had constantly to be adjusted and brought up to date. Was Mr. du Pont still married? Who was Cary Grant's new lady friend? Should Esther Williams be included? There were lists for married people, separated people, shortly-to-be-divorced people, people living with people. It was one of the duties of Nast's staff to keep the lists in order. Who, after all, would be more au courant than a *Vogue* feature writer? "I knew *everything*," said Allene Talmey, one of Nast's last list-updaters. "I knew about separations before the people themselves did." There were not many mistakes after such scrupulous surveillance.

Dinner place cards, handwritten on gold-edged paper by *Vanity Fair* assistant Jeanne Ballot, whose hand was fair, were regarded as treasures by their recipients. Such stiffies placed Mrs. Cornelius

Vanderbilt, whose devotion to the headband as a form of personal decoration invited a redefinition of the headache, at the left hand of Mr. George Gershwin, the musician, a revolution in entertaining etiquette that accounts for Nast's title as the founder of café society. No one before had dared to mix society with show business. The parties often took place on Sundays, another departure from form that added to the spice of the evening.

For women, Nast's parties were a special sartorial challenge. The publisher of *Vogue* knew the most beautiful and elegant models in the world; his standards were impossibly high. Diana Vreeland remembers Josephine Baker at one of Condé's parties in 1927, "wearing a dress by Vionnet in floating bias, with white silk butterflies decorating her hair, which was carved in flat curls tight to her head by Antoine."

If the women were chic, they were also often outrageous. At the party for Clare Boothe (Luce) after the opening of her play *The Women* in 1937 (Nast's analysis reads: "902 invited; 602 appeared—66 percent—very bad, stormy weather"), Tallulah Bankhead picked up her skirts and danced the Charleston. Another demonstration of this fashionable dance was given by Bessie Love at a party attended by Benito, a man quick to respond to female charms. "She was deliciously young and enchanting," he sighed in recollection. "Regrettably, Elsie de Wolfe, angry and wanting attention, herself subsequently took to the floor with her version. It was a danse macabre." This kind of abandoned exhibition was evidently customary; instructions to the staff included, "Be sure there is a powder can in a place *where the butler knows* if there is to be dancing so that it can be sprinkled on the floor later." There were to be no slips for overenthusiastic Terpsichoreans.

This was perfectionism in its most extreme form, a perfectionism that ran through Condé Nast's personality like a steel spring, dominating his life. Like the other great magazine publisher of the twentieth century, Henry Luce, Nast, although a brilliant businessman, was driven by a vision. But whereas Luce's vision was political and patriotic, Nast's was purely aesthetic. He approached his parties in the same way he approached his magazines—with the intent to produce the most beautiful and tasteful creation it was possible to produce, and to make no error that could possibly be avoided. He wanted stylistic perfection, and the parties were an expression of his ambition.

In an America for which Europe was still the cultural *fons et origo*, he wanted to give women a sense of their own identity and style. His magazines showed Americans how to appreciate modern art, music, photography, and illustration, and in making an intellectual standard of art acceptable to society, he elevated American taste. "What is charm to an American?" once wailed the outrageous French dress designer of the Belle Epoque, Paul Poiret. "Everything is utility or necessity. They do not know how to invent the superfluous, which, for us, is more indispensable than the necessary." At an exhilarating moment in history, Nast invented the superfluous in America. He showed Americans how to spend their money on the embellishment of life, and carried his standards of taste to England and France in a triumphant reversal of form. He cultivated a social world that may have been glossy and frivolous at heart, but whose members were encouraged to appreciate some of the most dazzling forms of aesthetic excellence, and to improve their own lives, through the pages of his magazines.

"You may say that Condé Nast's was a trivial field compared to Harriman's and Morgan's transformation of the United States with railroads," former *Vogue* editor Millicent Fenwick has said. "But it was part of the same enthusiasm, verve and zest that developed this country."

By insisting on the best-quality paper and printing, Nast paved the way for the success of the art magazine; his publications proved that a connection between fashion and art was not only plausible but promotable. While Derain decorated textiles and Chanel designed theatrical costumes, Condé Nast's magazine covers disseminated the latest fauve and cubist forms of art. It was largely owing to Nast's vigorous interest that fashion photography later found its way into the galleries and museums. Whether such art is worthy of the name remains debatable: but it was Condé Nast who first provided the basis for the argument.

"Does the young woman in Fort Smith, or San Antonio, or Birmingham, or Topeka," asked the *New York Herald Tribune* in Nast's obituary notice, "dress somewhat better than her ancestors, and does she have a surer appreciation of the world of manners and decorum and what might be called the art of gracious living? Then much of the credit must go to Condé Nast."

But it is the parties that people remember most. "The parties of Condé Nast," F. Scott Fitzgerald wrote, "rivaled in their way the fabled balls of the Nineties." Going up in the private elevator to the penthouse at 1040 Park Avenue, jammed together with Astors, Vanderbilts, and other personages of consequence, Groucho Marx was overheard by the writer Helen Lawrenson to remark to his brother Harpo: "This is a classy joint." It was indeed. For a brief moment, while parties such as Elsa Maxwell's and the de Polignacs' became legends of fantasy and extravagance, Condé Nast's exquisitely orchestrated evenings outdid them all.

Yet to most of the guests who so freely accepted his hospitality, the publisher was a remote and mysterious figure. He was not a tall man (about five feet eight) and had penetrating brown eyes, a fine straight nose, and an elegant, dapper manner. He continued to wear a pince-nez long after the fashion had given way to spectacles, a habit which, with his stiff collars and three-piece suits, gave him the appearance of a nineteenth-century banker. He walked with small steps and a rigid gait, perhaps owing to his shortsightedness. (His poor sight led him into some awkward moments, particularly during his visits to the *Vogue* office in London. When he left the office in the evening, after his customary long hours at his desk, the local prostitutes would be starting to emerge for duty around Bond Street. Nast, accosted by one of these night ladies, would enthusiastically return the greeting, courteously murmuring, "Where did we meet?" until nudged into realization by a colleague. This happened every year.)

Nast was a devotee of good deportment, keeping his own back so upright that grace was sacrificed to rigidity. ("Keep your back straight," he would say briskly to the secretaries as they sat hunched over their typewriters.) The effect was one of dignified

Condé Nast at the height of his career in the twenties.

austerity, which in truth concealed an acute shyness. On the fortunate ones he bestowed a radiant smile which transfigured his face.

Not a party man, this famous party-giver hardly ever drank. There are only two known occasions when he succumbed to liquor: once in Paris, when he learned that his most promising and trusted employee after Edna Chase, an Irish talent named Carmel Snow, had defected to his rival, Hearst's *Harper's Bazaar*; and once on his honeymoon with his second wife, Leslie Foster. His young bride had ordered a round of martinis before dinner and then, believing the old axiom that there is no such thing as one martini, cheerfully ordered another. Nast demurred, saying he could not take a second. "Oh, come on, Condé," she urged, and Nast, not wishing to appear an old fuddy-duddy, complied. The subsequent dinner was for one, and the new Mrs. Nast learned a lesson.

Shyness induces reserve, formality, a kind of tension. Even the Jazz Age failed to penetrate Nast's inhibitions. Once, at the notorious Quatre-Arts Ball in Paris, for which everyone was supposed to dress in the style of "Scenes from Old Pompeii," he arrived at the door attired, as was his wont, in correct white tie and tails, only to be turned away by the police, who assured him that no one so respectable could survive the saturnalia within.

Nast was immortalized in the early thirties in an MGM movie entitled *Wife vs. Secretary,* in which a fashionable magazine publisher's loving wife (Myrna Loy) is threatened by his zealous secretary (Jean Harlow, in an early appearance), while the publisher attempts to take over a series of mass-market publications owned by his Hearst-like rival. The film openly admits its debt to Nast by showing the fictional publisher walking in and out of his apartment—at 1040 Park Avenue. There the resemblance ends; for contrary to public belief, Nast could hardly have differed more from his swashbuckling, self-confident screen persona, played by Clark Gable.

As his guests cavorted in the Park Avenue penthouse, Nast was often to be seen standing apart, isolated, ill at ease. He had a chronic forgetfulness of people's names—even those he knew well—and was always whispering in an associate's ear for help in greeting his friends. He did not dance, or if he did, it was stiffly, without pleasure. He was more frequently glimpsed in another part of the vast apartment, playing bridge, smoking a cigar with a colleague, or drifting through the gilded rooms alone, checking on lighting, traffic flow, waiters, liquor, ventilation—monitoring the machinery of his famous evenings, "while in his blue garden men and girls came and went like moths among the whisperings and the champagne and the stars."

Condé Nast's story is of a man who had little personal glamour, yet who understood glamour, surrounded himself with it, and projected it to a world eager to pay for it. He reached the apogee of success, as did so many others, in the twenties, a period romanticized into stardust by Scott Fitzgerald in his voguish novels. (The comparison with Fitzgerald is tempting. Both came from the Midwest; both were brought up Catholic; both were raised in genteel poverty; and both were preoccupied by, and based their careers on, the implications and consequences of class, money, the East, and sophisticated, unattainable women.) The twenties are now considered frivolous and irresponsible. Revisionist historians say the decade was not much fun. Maybe not. After all, the best representatives of the younger generation had been decimated in the trenches. "It was a time of escape from reality," wrote John Lardner, "of stunts and swells, of midnight bathing parties at the Plaza fountain, of skies filled with confetti that took $16,000 to clean off the streets of New York. In an age of artifice and exhibitionism, everybody had a 'line,' a come-on, a stylish facade."

Not least Condé Nast. His life was as riddled with paradoxes as was the age. Behind the urbane, sophisticated front lay a man who liked nothing better than ice-cream sodas or lunch at the Automat. Like a Medici, he was an enlightened patron of artists, writers, and photographers; yet he never understood or cared for the Picassos, Matisses, and Braques that *Vanity Fair* so impudently published. He never originated a magazine until three years before he died— his three great successes, *Vogue, Vanity Fair,* and *House & Garden,* were all founded by others; yet he is regarded as the father of them all. Though his publications projected a life of frivolity and fun, his own days were devoted to a ceaseless flow of analyses, critical evaluations, long-range plans, charts, comparisons, summaries. Behind the glamorous models featured in *Vogue,* the witty, artistic spoofs in *Vanity Fair,* the grand mansions photographed in *House & Garden,* lay an uncompromising underpinning of facts and figures. Surrounded all his life by women of unsurpassed beauty and wit, he never enjoyed a long-lasting relationship with any of them. He desired the company of young women until the day he died, yet the role of Lothario ran oddly counter to his ascetic, fastidious, statistical mind.

The final paradox was perhaps the most cruel. Long considered one of the most successful and wealthy businessmen in America, Nast lost control of his company after the 1929 Crash and lived the last years of his life mortgaged, in hock, a ghost at his famous parties, a stylish facade.

Almost no one knew this last strange tale—but then nobody ever knew much about this impenetrable figure, so often photographed and so rarely revealed. To most of his acquaintances, he offered no past, only a glittering present—like fashion itself—and he played out the brave extravaganza to the end.

# ONE

# A TIDIER GARDEN

They said he was many things. They said he came from a fine New York family. That he was descended from Louis II of Bourbon, the "Great Condé." That he was a relation of the political cartoonist Thomas Nast. That his background was wealthy Huguenot stock. The truth, as in many aspects of Condé Nast's life, was simpler.

His grandfather was interesting enough to have had several books written about him. Wilhelm Nast came from a long line of Swabian clergymen of the Lutheran Church and public officials in Württemberg. Born in Stuttgart in 1807 and left an orphan at seventeen, Wilhelm studied to be a Lutheran minister in the tradition of his forefathers, but suffered a traumatic crisis of religious doubt, and at the age of twenty-one left Germany for New York to start a new life as a teacher. Still tortured by religious scruples, he traveled through the States as far as Ohio, where he joined a Methodist class at Kenyon College, and was converted to Methodism in 1835. That year he was appointed by the Ohio Conference as a missionary to the Germans in Cincinnati, then a growing city with a population of

38,000. By 1840 the city was 23 percent German, providing a receptive audience for Nast's message.

Wilhelm Nast was a shy and introverted man, but his sturdy Methodist preaching gained him converts throughout Ohio. In 1839 he started a German Methodist paper called *Der Christliche Apologete,* which he edited for more than fifty years. It was this that really allowed his talents to flourish. Nast was an excellent editor, gathering news of a general nature as well as disseminating Methodist teaching, declaring the magazine to be "a defender of evangelical truth, a courageous representative of church interests, and a guide to conversion." The *Apologete* became required reading for German Methodists in the United States, and by 1869 its circulation had reached 15,000. Nast directed the journal into increasingly wide-ranging fields, including paid advertising that reflected the needs of its foreign-born readers. It also published a children's column, poems, and recipes.

Nast himself wrote many of the columns, urging abstinence from alcohol and observance of the Sabbath, and attacking the Roman Catholic priesthood, which he regarded as too influential in American political life. Reflecting his intellectual upbringing, he wrote and spoke in a scholarly fashion, which gained him respect and influence throughout the Methodist Church. He became President of Wallace College, a German Methodist affiliate of Baldwin University in Berea, near Cleveland, and won other honors. In spite of these secular successes, however, he was never free of the torment of religious doubt, which plagued him throughout his life. He died with a prayer on his lips in Cincinnati on May 16, 1899, a year after the death of his wife of sixty-two years.

In 1836 Wilhelm Nast married Eliza McDowell, from Fulton, Ohio, a former Scottish Presbyterian who had converted to Methodism before she met Nast. She bore him five children over ten ears—Ernst Theodore, who died early of cholera, William Frederick, Josephine Pulte, Albert Julius, and Franzeska Wilhelmina (Fanny). The marriage was a reasonably happy one, although Eliza would have preferred wider horizons than Cincinnati. She also found her husband's frequent bouts of depression difficult to understand and live with. A further difficulty was her lack of sympathy with his German origins; she never learned to speak German with any fluency and considered his background dull and unsophisticated.

Condé Nast's father was the second son, William Frederick, born on June 14, 1840, in Cincinnati. After his brother's premature death, he became the eldest, a role for which he was singularly unsuited. William seems to have suffered a violent, if classic, reaction to the rigid German Puritanism and austere moral values preached by his father. The boy was good-looking, high-spirited, and charming, attributes that were hardly likely to endear him to the preacher but, not surprisingly, made him his mother's favorite. His schooling was minimal, largely because at the time the Nasts could not afford it. Later they regretted this failure—they felt that a more "German" or structured approach to his studies might have formed his character better. To compensate for this mistake, they sent their other son, Albert, to be educated in Germany by himself for four years, without returning home—a severe discipline indeed for a young boy. (It seems, however, to have been effective; Albert later turned out to be all the things that William was not.)

After a series of short-lived jobs that started when he was sixteen, William wangled a place on the reception committee for President Lincoln when he passed through Cincinnati on his way to Washington for his inauguration. This connection, aided by letters from his father and other contacts, secured him the post of American consul in Stuttgart, his father's home town. It was a great coup for the twenty-one-year-old Nast, who responded to the elevated social life and ceremonial occasions with such enthusiasm that his father wrote increasingly cautionary letters: "I am tormented with the fear that it will be your ruin . . . with your notions of life." His mother, on the other hand, who visited him in Stuttgart with her other children during his term of office, was delighted by her son's success in Württemberg social circles, and wrote excitedly that William had had three suits made in Paris, because he considered

German tailors inferior craftsmen, and that one was "a court suit, hat and sword."

William had little time for the stuffy Stuttgart relatives, responding, like his mother, to the sophisticated European way of life as though to the manner born. Gradually the bureaucratic restrictions and diplomatic limitations of his job began to take their toll, and carried away by the temptations to luxury on every side, he began to spend considerably beyond his means, and to send his family rich presents—silver cigar cases, jewelry, and for one of his sisters, a dozen pairs of custom-made kid gloves. This perhaps accounts for the rumors of suspicious financial dealings that began to leak from the American Consulate in Stuttgart back to the United States. Finally, charges were brought against the young consul and the reports, which appeared in local German newspapers, were picked up by the American press.

Poor Wilhelm Nast was mortified by these attacks on his son, which he took to be indirect assaults on the Methodist Church. William calmly denied any wrong-doing, and filed a libel suit against one of the Stuttgart papers. In America the incident died down and the consul returned to the United States in 1864 without any legal action having been taken against him, but without the offer of another posting. The diplomatic experience had, however, given him a taste for luxury that was to haunt him for the rest of his life.

In 1865 he tried to get rich in railroads. In 1870 it was Florida real estate. By 1875 he was a stockbroker in New York. It was during the relatively stable decade he spent in the United States that he married and had his children.

On January 14, 1868, William Nast married Esther Ariadne Benoist, a devout Roman Catholic whose well-to-do French family lived nine miles outside St. Louis. It would be hard to imagine anything more calculated to distress his father than William's decision to marry a Catholic. It was the culmination of years of disappointment and rebellion. The more dogmatic and earnest the father became, the more flippant and irresponsible the son. Sometimes one feels more than a flicker of sympathy for William, whose approach to life was so much more light-hearted than his father's. For instance, when William once wrote home that a little whiskey might improve his mother's health, the answer he received was a sermon on the wickedness of liquor—this was the depressing level of their communication. But his marriage to a Catholic was indeed a bitter pill for his father to swallow.

All credit to father Nast, then, that he conquered his abhorrence of the ceremony and went to the Catholic wedding in St. Louis. This time it was Mrs. Nast who pointedly stayed home. The service was conducted by a Catholic priest who, sensitive to Nast's scruples, performed it with the greatest tact, according to Nast. Nast liked the handsome, red-haired bride and in the end was partially reconciled to the union, although he wrote to his son Albert that she "will always remain a stranger to us." Eliza Nast, however, made little attempt to be accommodating. Like many mothers whose favorite sons marry, she found it impossible to enjoy her daughter-in-law's presence, and although Esther obligingly participated in the family devotions when she visited the Nasts, her mother-in-law was described by Wilhelm as being "unfit to deal with this power of darkness."

The marriage meant, of course, that William and Esther's children would be brought up as Catholics, an idea repugnant to the Nasts, who were terrified that all William's daughters would become nuns and his sons priests—a fear that appears to have been oddly prophetic, though not in the way they imagined. William's four children were all born in New York: Louis, born October 7, 1868; Esther Ethel, on May 31, 1870; Condé Montrose, on March 26, 1873 (not 1874, as *Who's Who* has it); and Estelle Josephine, on January 21, 1875. Shortly after this, William, again lured by the promise of bigger and better fortunes to be made elsewhere (and perhaps daunted by the prospect of four small mouths to feed), took himself off to Europe, and this time vanished for thirteen years. So at the age of three, with his elder brother and two sisters, Condé was taken to the Benoist family and St. Louis, where he grew up. Occasionally a letter or package arrived from Paris or London, but rarely did William send money. At one point he claimed he was about to make a fortune building a machine to dry straw; at another it was a company making paper out of manure. In 1890 the wanderer returned to his faithful wife and wrote a long letter of justification to his father, explaining how his attempts to make a living had left him "struggling, pushing, persevering against impossible odds." When his father finally returned home, Condé was seventeen. Three years later, on April 7, 1893, William Nast died and was buried in Calvary Cemetery in St. Louis, not even in a Methodist grave.

Marrying Esther Benoist was one of the few sensible things poor William Nast did in his erratic life. She was a forthright, strong character, well equipped to bring up four children entirely on her own.

Her great-great-grandfather, the Chevalier Antoine Gabriel François Benoist (later known as the Chevalier de St. Louis), was the first of the Benoist family to leave France, sailing for Canada in 1735. He was aide to General Montcalm in the campaigns against the British, won many advancements from Louis XV, and returned to France to die. Her grandfather, François Marie Benoist, born in Canada in 1764, joined the Indian fur trade up the Missouri River and became active in the city of St. Louis after the Louisiana Purchase. There he married Marie Catherine Sanguinette, who was the daughter of one of St. Louis's first physicians, Dr. Auguste Condé, surgeon to the French army before the ceding of Louisiana to the British. Louis A. Benoist, Esther's father, was the second of seven children born to François and Marie.

Louis was born in St. Louis in 1801, and studied law and medicine before opening the first private bank in St. Louis in 1832, under the name of Louis A. Benoist and Company. In 1838 he opened a branch in New Orleans, Benoist & Hackney, which later became Benoist & Shaw. An additional bank was opened in San Francisco. From these banks Louis Benoist amassed a considerable fortune, some of which was used to build a magnificent summer house called Oakland, nine miles south of St. Louis, which still stands today. Designed by George I. Barnett in 1852, it looked like an Italian Renaissance palace, with marble floors and an arched porch; it was surrounded by extensive grounds, including a lake. Louis lived there with his enormous family until his death in January 1867.

Louis Benoist was married three times, first, to Eliza Barton, who died after eleven months of marriage; then to Esther Hackney of Virginia, who also died, after bearing him six children (the fourth of whom was Condé's mother, Esther); and after her death, to Sarah E. Wilson, who bore him nine more children. (A game Condé used to play with his children was to try to name all his uncles and aunts; he always ended up saying, "Tom, Dick, and Harry.")

The Benoist family was an old and cultivated one—ancestors included Guillaume Benoist, recorded in 1437 as Chamberlain to Louis XI, King of France, and Antoine Benoist, court painter to Louis XIV. Louis, Esther's father, helped found the St. Louis Philharmonic Society in 1859. They were culturally sophisticated pillars of the community, and Esther's dowry, along with a fortune estimated to be $300,000, was a guaranteed position of bourgeois respectability.

It was just a little perverse of her, to be sure, to fall for a dashing Protestant reprobate, but she seems to have stoically borne the treatment he subsequently dished out to her. Her four children were brought up with the very best she could afford out of her dwindling fortune. The young Nasts, with the exception of Condé (for reasons unknown), were fluent in several languages, including French. They played music in a family chamber orchestra, with Condé on the flute and Louis on the piano. Religion also played an important part in their lives, for their mother's Catholicism never flagged.

Condé's maternal grandfather, Louis A. Benoist, had died before Condé was born, but the mansion, Oakland, became the symbol to him of wealth and material success, and when he went to play there with his many cousins he must have been conscious of the emotional and financial gap created by his father's absence. There is no doubt that the size of old Mr. Benoist's family caused additional economic hardship to the Nasts: his money had to stretch a distressingly long way. Condé went through the St. Louis public school

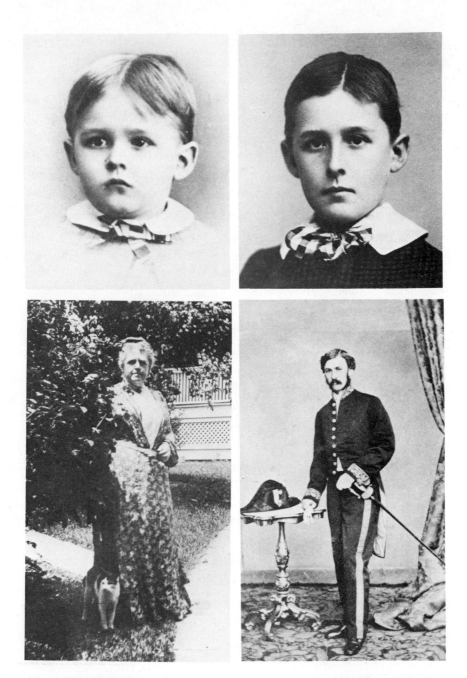

Condé Nast as a boy growing up in St. Louis; his father, William F. Nast, dashing in his dress uniform as U.S. consul in Stuttgart, about 1860; and a late photograph of his formidable mother, Esther Benoist Nast.

system, and faced the bleak prospect of hard work ahead to help support the family. But one of his Nast aunts had done well for herself by marrying William A. Gamble of Procter and Gamble—this was Fanny, William's younger sister. (She was generous with her gifts to the Methodist cause, and in 1901 contributed $10,000 to a Children's Home near Wallace College, where the dining room and chapel were named after her mother.) Childless herself, and ashamed of the way her brother ("Mr. Disappoint," as she called him) had deserted his wife and children, she promised to help out when the time came.

It came soon enough. When the two boys were old enough to think about university, Aunt Fanny told her sister-in-law that she would help send *one* of them through college. But which one? Obviously Louis, the elder. But family legend has it that an incident swung the vote in favor of the younger. Fanny went to visit the Nasts in St. Louis, and on walking up the path to the house, observed two patches of garden, one tidy and the other a disorganized mess. "Whose is that?" she asked. The messy garden, it turned out, was the responsibility of Louis; Condé's garden was the immaculate one. "Then I'm not educating that boy," Fanny said, pointing to the elder brother. "I'm educating Condé." So tidy Condé, already demonstrating his perfectionist tendencies, was given the opportunity to progress further—an opportunity he seized with vigor.

This stroke of good fortune for Condé did not endear him to his brother, who seems to have had a strong streak of his vanishing father in him. In 1891, when Condé went to Georgetown University, Louis went off to Europe and settled in Paris as a pianist. He never went back to America. Condé later painted a romantic picture of his artist brother living in a garret, perhaps to hide the guilt he felt for his leap over his brother's head. Unlike his sisters, Louis never accepted any money from his brother after Condé had become successful. And when Condé later made his annual visits to Paris, at least on one occasion Louis refused to see him. It was a sad comment on an ancient rivalry. Louis died in Paris, alone.

As for his sisters, convention-flouting set in early. Esther (known as Ethel) wanted to become a nun, just as her Methodist grandparents had feared, but failed to find an order that suited her, so she went to Rome and attempted to found her own religious order, without much success. She did a lot of traveling, and wrote about her experiences most vividly, to the delight of the readers of the *Catholic World,* where some of her articles appeared. Her story "From Jerusalem to Nazareth on Horseback," written in 1900, was full of adventures and heart-stopping moments, described in the following vein: "We passed a restless night, haunted by discordant cries and phantoms of murderous Turks . . ." A year later, she published in the same periodical a short story entitled "The Buried Casket," a bloodcurdling melodrama about family dishonor and buried jewels, containing such sentences as, "He took the paper from my nerveless grasp."

This was only the beginning of a wonderfully eccentric life, later supported by her successful and indulgent brother Condé. Before the start of the First World War she came back to the United States and decided to see America, persuading her brother to build her a sleeper-bus in which she could tour the country. This she did, saying a merry Hail Mary at every stoplight. Finding West Palm Beach the place she liked best, she simply parked her bus and lived there. Later, she had a house built to her specifications (again with Condé's money), and later still, invented an electric car to get around in, and had a console for charging it installed in her bedroom. She used to swim in the surf until her late seventies, when she began to find the undertow too strong, at which point she designed a water tank to stand in the garden, into which she climbed to take her exercise. A combination of simple tastes and deep religiousness, after Sunday mass she would have coffee at the local truck drivers' café. When Condé and his second wife went to visit her and wished to take her out to some fancy restaurant, she insisted on being taken instead to the new Horn & Hardart, which she'd never seen.

Estelle, the other sister, became a painter. She fell in love with a married man at an early age and ran off with him. This was a severe shock to the Benoist family, and her mother, in a dramatic bid to save her daughter's name, went to the man's wife and begged her to divorce him. It is an indication of Esther's powerful personality that her pleas succeeded and the divorce went through. But Esther had not bargained for the independent nature of her daughter. Estelle refused to marry the man; she moved to Florida and late in life married the widower of her best friend. Estelle, like Ethel, designed and built her own house (it was raspberry pink), thanks to Condé, in West Palm Beach.

Occasionally the sisters came to New York to visit their glamorous brother, looking endearingly out of place in the Louis XV drawing room, surrounded by fringed lampshades and gilt rococo furniture. They died in their late eighties, within a few years of each other.

Condé's mother also visited him after he became famous. He used to go to mass with her when she came to New York, though he went at no other time. She was not one to let him off lightly for such negligence. When he married for the second time, he was very much afraid of her disapproval and delayed telling her. Her sympathetic acceptance of the marriage and kindness to his young new wife were a great relief to him (although when their child, Leslie, was born, his mother made him promise that she would be brought up a Catholic). In later years, she had some difficulty moving about, but continued to make the trip East. It was on one of these visits that she died, in his splendid house in Sands Point, on July 1, 1929, at the age of eighty-four. The timing was felicitous; she just escaped witnessing the Wall Street Crash and the downfall of her hardworking, loving, dutiful son.

Freudians may see in Nast's life a case history of a child who successfully removed his father from, and supplanted his brother in, his mother's affections, thus bringing down a lifetime of guilt upon his own head. The fastidiousness, the formality, the perfectionism, and the inability to form a close relationship with a woman that characterized Nast's later life, all may hinge on subconscious guilt and suppressed aggression. Because he had no father with whom to identify, his mother loomed very large. Condé always sought the company of women. As he got older, they got younger. Perhaps this was his way of making up for the lack of a father in his own life—but as the women did not always want to be his children, the role of father was seldom satisfying.

The vividly contrasting individuals who formed his background are easily identifiable in Condé's personality. On the one hand, there is the strict, pious grandfather, who would have suffered several coronaries had he witnessed his grandson's Sunday night extravaganzas, with Prohibition liquor flowing and actresses lifting up their skirts, and yet whose editing genius surely found its way into the grandson's genes. On the other hand, there is the charming, ne'er-do-well father with an instinctive sense of European sophistication, good taste, fashion, and luxury, who would have matched Condé waistcoat for waistcoat in sartorial splendor and who would have adored his son's *Vogue* and *Vanity Fair*. As inheritor of this taste for the good life, what effect can it have had on the young Condé to have been brought up so frugally and carefully in the shadow of grandfather Benoist's monument to material success, Oakland?

Early economies, a rigid Catholic background, and a middle-class Middle West upbringing, together with an eagerness for self-improvement and refinement, produced in Condé the necessary ambition to seek a brighter, more demanding world. It was precisely the experiences of his own past that made him later so acutely sensitive to what readers in Fort Smith, San Antonio, Birmingham, and Topeka wanted to see and learn about in the pages of his magazines.

# TWO

# FIGURE JIM

Aunt Fanny's investment was a sound one. Even though finances were still so stretched that Condé rarely went home for Christmas because he could not afford the fare to St. Louis, her gift of Georgetown University produced excellent dividends.

In his first year, Nast became the first student president of the Yard. The Yard was the university's athletic association, which organized the intramural and intercollegiate sports team. Prior to Nast's appointment, a Jesuit faculty member had always held the post. To be president meant controlling the scheduling and finances of the athletic teams—and for Condé Nast, it also meant raising money for them, publicizing them, making the university sit up and take notice. It turned out that Nast was a born promoter; for this undergraduate at least, a college career was the foundation of a life's work.

Although not himself a committed sportsman at Georgetown (he played a respectable game of squash), Nast nevertheless dominated the college sporting world, becoming head of the tennis association and manager of the baseball team in addition to his other duties. A classmate who particularly appreciated the talents of this energetic organizer was Robert J. Collier, whose father owned a flourishing book business in New York and a magazine called *Collier's Weekly*. Collier and Nast became close friends. When Nast's father died, it was Robert Collier, class president, who signed the letter of condolence that appeared in the *College Journal*.

Their college life reads like a double act. Nast followed Collier as class president in their senior year. Together they were associate editors of the *Journal*, of which Collier later became editor in chief. They also performed together in musical events, with Nast showing his expertise on the flute. (A *Journal* review of one of their concerts in 1894 says, "The flute solo by Mr. Nast, appealing as it did to the most musical audience, won him much applause.") Condé's career at Georgetown was crowned with success when he delivered the bachelor's oration at the seventy-fifth commencement in June 1894. His friend Robert Collier gave the class poem. In his final examinations, Nast gained a "distinction" in rational philosophy and mathematics, two natural disciplines for a tidy gardener.

The friends separated after graduation. Collier went back to New York, and Nast stayed on at Georgetown to take his master's degree. Having decided that law was the most sensible occupation for a young head of the family, he returned to St. Louis in 1895 to obtain an LL.B. from Washington University.

The law, however, failed to excite Nast's enthusiasm, and he dragged his feet about committing himself to a career as a lawyer. He found himself far more interested in the small printing plant that his family had invested in to the tune of $2,000. It was doing very badly, and in the summer of 1897 the printers asked for his help in building up their business. This was an assignment the former president of the Georgetown Yard accepted with alacrity.

Nast went the rounds of his friends and acquaintances in St. Louis in an attempt to direct printing jobs to the struggling firm, but he received little response. He looked around desperately for inspiration. People were preparing for the annual St. Louis Exposition and suddenly Nast realized this was precisely what he needed.

He quickly made up a list of all the exhibitors from the Middle West and South who would need small printing jobs done in connection with their displays at the fair, and offered them an advertising and marketing deal with the printing plant. The strategy worked, and the firm's business was established on a firm footing.

Later that summer, Robert Collier, who by this time was running his father's rather feeble *Collier's Weekly,* paid a visit to St. Louis and heard about Nast's little campaign. Collier realized that his friend's marketing talents should not go to waste in a law office, so he invited Nast to come to New York and join the staff of his magazine. With hardly an overcoat to his name, Nast agreed. His salary was to be $12.00 a week.

In the 1890s, *Collier's Weekly* was a slim, dull-looking journal offered as a premium to buyers of Collier's books. It called itself "an illustrated journal of art, literature and current events," and cost ten cents. Considerably more editorial space was devoted to current events than to art and literature—indeed art hardly made an appearance at all. The editors were keen on photographs: of war (the Boer War was a fruitful source), of football (for instance, Princeton in a poor play against Lehigh, "illustrating Princeton at a poor period of her development"), of prominent singers of the Metropolitan Opera (Mlle. Calvé, Mme. Eames, and Albert Saléza), and of such pioneering acts as the building of the Panama Canal. Short stories were published, and a few departments, such as "Round the Hearth," catered to women.

There was no contents page, and the paltry advertising was in the form of a classified insert in the back, carrying small-print messages concerning typewriters, vapor baths, Pears Soap, Rae Lucca's olive oil, a plated silver tea service ($5.00), Harderfold Hygienic Inter-air-space underwear, and a promise to cure your opium or liquor habit in ten to twenty days.

"In 1897, Robert Collier developed a new kind of weekly—the 'fiction-with-public-affairs' formula—which resulted in *Collier's Weekly,*" Condé Nast wrote thirty years later about his friend. He omitted the fact that in 1900 he became advertising manager of the magazine, and that his contribution was nothing short of miraculous. In 1897, *Collier's Weekly* had a circulation of 19,159, and its total income from advertising was $5,600. When Condé Nast left ten years later, its circulation was 568,073, and its advertising income was more than $1,000,000.

They called him Figure Jim. He produced sworn audits of circulation. He produced promotional material full of facts and statistics. He composed an entirely new form of aggressive and provocative solicitation letter: "I am the Advertising Manager of *Collier's,* but I don't expect you to give me any business. Most manufacturers don't believe in weeklies; and it has only taken three months' canvassing to prove to my perfect satisfaction that the few who do won't use *Collier's.* However, I accept the situation, I don't want to argue with you. I merely want your residence address: We want to send *Collier's* to you regularly. Certain things are going to happen; things that you have neither the time nor inclination to inquire into . . ."

And the advertisers loved it. They began to find the time and inclination to look at *Collier's* with some care. By 1904 the magazine had been redesigned; it had a contents page and five large-space advertising pages before the lead story. The advertisements were more male-oriented—fewer vapor baths, more shaving sticks and beer. The editorial content was far livelier, with the work of distinguished writers and artists such as Upton Sinclair and Frederic Remington appearing weekly. There was still an emphasis on war photography ("Liao-Yang—the Greatest Battle since Gettysburg"), photographs of the season's most successful plays, and fiction by fashionable writers (Booth Tarkington, Jerome K. Jerome, Agnes and Egerton Castle). Color ads appeared on the back page, and the cover designs, now in color, were for the first time credited to artists.

Circulation figures and advertising revenue were rising fast, and Nast thought he knew why. Top writers and artists attracted readers, particularly if you promoted their appearance in a particular issue. Stories on the latest shows and performers were always successful. The appearance of color, which involved making four-color-process plates for printing on specially coated stock, in a largely black-and-white publication created a dramatic effect. Regularly presenting the most fashionable topics of the day was a sure-fire winning strategy. For instance, Nast knew and admired Charles Dana Gibson, creator of the Gibson Girl, whose face and figure enhanced every periodical in which she appeared. Knowing that Gibson was paid $500 a drawing by Edward Bok's *Ladies' Home Journal,* Nast persuaded the artist to provide *Collier's* with one hundred drawings at $1,000 each. The effect on circulation was invigorating.

But perhaps the most interesting innovation that Nast introduced during his years at *Collier's* was the "special number"—that is, an issue devoted to a particular topic or individual. In February 1904, *Collier's* put out a "Gibson Number," which boasted twenty drawings and a double-page spread created exclusively for *Collier's* by the famous artist. It is worth quoting a portion of the advertisement relating to this issue. It has the mark of a vintage piece of Nast's promotional writing:

SPECIAL DE LUXE EDITION
COLLIER'S GIBSON NUMBER

Printed throughout on heavy plate paper. Every picture suitable for framing. A separate art-proof of the double, "Telling His Fortune." The largest and best collection ever published outside of his annual book selling at $5.00.

He was claiming exclusivity, affordable luxury, and the highest quality. These three elements were to be the foundation stones of the marketing strategy for his own magazines.

In 1905 Nast was promoted to business manager, and by 1907 he was earning a salary in excess of $40,000, an astronomical sum in those days. At this pinnacle of success, Nast told his friend he was resigning. Collier was dismayed. "You know perfectly well, Condé," he said, "nobody else is going to pay you that much money. You're not worth it. I give it to you because I want you around and I like to see people happy." Nast agreed. "I'm not worth forty thousand of your money and I know it. I'm going out to see if I can't make more than that."

In ten years, Nast had carried *Collier's Weekly* from last place to first place among all magazines that carried advertising. He pioneered color pages, the double-page spread, and the special number. He divided the United States into marketing areas, realizing that goods could be promoted more effectively in some areas than in others. This led to his conclusion that you did not have to have a very large circulation to influence people's behavior or develop an active audience for specific goods. He was well on the road to his theory of "class" publications.

Nast had learned valuable lessons at *Collier's,* but *Collier's* was not the place where he could practice what he had learned. He was anxious to move on—and he had already decided on the field that was to make his fortune.

In 1904, as a personal venture while working at *Collier's,* he became vice-president of the Home Pattern Company, manufacturers and distributors of women's dress patterns franchised by the *Ladies' Home Journal.* Women's dress patterns had become big business since the invention in 1846 of the sewing machine, which gave millions of women access to styles and fashions hitherto restricted to the very rich who lived in the capitals of Europe and the United States and who could afford the very best dressmakers. The Buttericks were the first to market paper patterns, starting in 1863, and by the end of the century, magazines and catalogues such as *Godey's Lady's Book, Mirror of Fashion, Ladies' Home Journal,* and *Demorest's Magazine* were all publishing patterns for fashions that could be made at home.

Early in 1899 a woman named Rosa Payne had called at the New York office of a small society journal called *Vogue* and suggested that they run a pattern she had made. The editors saw no objection, and printed it in the February 23, 1899, issue. It was for a modified Louis XV coat, plain satin, appliquéd or embroidered, to be worn with fancy fronts of chiffon or plaited lace—and it was the first of a weekly series. The reader snipped a coupon and sent it in with fifty cents and received Mrs. Payne's creation, hand-cut by the author on her dining-room table. ("At that time and for several years after I joined the staff the problem of pattern sizes was simple," Edna Woolman Chase, later *Vogue*'s editor in chief, reported. "There was one, and it was a thirty-six.")

The Home Pattern Company published its patterns in a series of catalogues, of which the two most important were the *Quarterly Style Book* and the *Monthly Style Book*. Nast was responsible for finding advertising for these publications—probably the most difficult medium of all to sell to space-buyers, since most of the copies were given away free in department stores and usually thrown away by customers. "The *Monthly Style Book* not only sells patterns," Nast boldly argued, "it brings the *other fellow's* customers into your store." It was an altogether new departure for the advertising and business genius of *Collier's,* but he sensed that patterns were a potentially explosive market. The Home Pattern Company was merely a sprint. Nast was marshalling his energies for something else to run with; and by 1905 he had settled on one publication in particular for the long-distance race.


On September 20, 1900, *Vogue*'s weekly editorial grappled with an unfamiliar problem: "As the leisure-class girl is increasing in numbers as the country grows in wealth, the question as to what she shall do with her life becomes ever more vitally the concern of the community."

Before this date, questions of what she should do with her life had never, thank goodness, arisen. Women were the expression of what social historian Sheila M. Rothman has called "virtuous womanhood," confined within corsets, Victorian morality, and, if upper class, the boundaries of what was Done and Not Done in Society. But things changed rapidly after 1900. In that year, some 85,000 women were enrolled in colleges; by 1920, the figure came to a quarter of a million. The technological innovations that transformed domestic life in the early 1900s lightened the burden of household drudgery; both mistresses and maids took advantage of

A rare portrait of Condé Nast without his pince-nez, at the beginning of his career at *Collier's*.

the convenience offered by electric cookers, irons, vacuum clean-
ers, and packaged foods. (One of the most frequent advertisers in
*Vogue* in the twenties was Campbell's Soup, which might seem an
odd client for a fashion journal until one realizes the impact the
simple act of opening a can had on women who previously had to
make all their own soup, and preserve all their own vegetables and
fruit.)

Homemakers became absorbed with the problems presented by
new appliances such as the telephone, considered unsightly and offensive ("because of its present unprepossessing appearance, the
object should be heard and not seen"), or the "barbaric" radiator, a
blissful solace to chilblained limbs but deeply disturbing to contemplate in one's drawing room. The wealthier families began to enjoy
the innovations in plumbing and design—shower baths, constant
hot water, hygienic tiled walls and floors in bathrooms and kitchens.
Along with these novel installations came accessories. Bombarded
with information about new, mass-produced objects for their
homes, women began to discover the delights of shopping for them.
Department stores responded by presenting wares in enticing new
ways; they became glittering palaces of seduction to tempt a new
economic class—the female consumer.

The wave of European women who became notorious spenders
of great fortunes at the end of the Belle Epoque—Princesse Ed-
mond de Polignac, Marchesa Casati, Princesse Jean Louis de
Faucigny-Lucinge, Vicomtesse Marie-Laure de Noailles—was followed by an even larger tide of Americans who, presented for the
first time with the concept of leisure, and with money made by the
new millionaire husbands of the tax-free century, became an important part of the booming capitalist economy. These American fortunes, created largely by the exploitation of land and forests, gave
women the opportunity—with the right kind of guidance—to as-
pire to a kind of European aristocracy, as expressed in their houses
and their clothes. While the great tycoons such as Carnegie, Frick,
and Morgan collected art as a monument to their wealth, their wives
learned how to address a royal personage at a reception, how to set
a table with Georgian silver and Sèvres porcelain, and how to

choose the right dress for a garden party at Newport. The image was born of the fashionable female—the sophisticated, urbane woman who knew how to converse amusingly, how to handle servants, and how to keep up with the Mode.

The Mode—the word alone was enough to send frissons down the spine of an ambitious young lady at the turn of the century. If one was not au courant with the Mode, one might as well stay in Hammond, Indiana, for the rest of one's life, doomed to provincialism like Madame Bovary. The importance of the right clothes to aspiring womanhood in those years cannot be overestimated. One has only to remember the desperate efforts of the tragic Lily Bart, in Edith Wharton's *The House of Mirth,* to raise money for the right clothes to realize how easily a woman's fortunes could rise or fall on the quality of her gowns.

For the silent majority of American women, the ready-made-clothes industry, thanks to the sewing machine, was able to provide millions of reasonably priced machine-made suits, skirts, and blouses. Aided by the often brutal exploitation of immigrant labor from the 1850s on, the women's-wear industry flourished. In 1900 there were 1,600 houses listed as "waist and dress factories" (600 were in New York), and their production was valued at $50,000,000. By 1920, the number of factories had almost doubled.

For the moneyed class, what one wore was dictated by two things—one's proximity to Paris and the dexterity of one's dressmaker. For the less affluent, ready-made copies were becoming easily available at home. For both, everything depended on information about the Mode, and by the early 1900s fashion journals had become required reading.

Fashion journalism originated in France, or at least the first magazine devoted to the publication of fashion plates was French—*Le Mercure Galant,* published in 1763. Other French and English examples followed in the eighteenth century, the short-lived but elegant *Gallery of Fashion* being the most notable, in that it consisted entirely of hand-colored aquatint plates designed by the distinguished artist Niklaus Wilhelm von Heideloff. The publication of fashion news became firmly established in the nineteenth century, although most European journals lasted only a short time and were distributed to a very small audience.

In the United States, eighteen fashion magazines existed in 1880, reflecting the first wave of women's liberation and the consequent interest in dress reform, and also the growing social aspirations of the new industrial millionaires. Economics also tended to encourage magazine publishers—in the late nineteenth century, speedy distribution methods and special second-class-mailing privileges greatly enhanced the commercial prospects of national magazines, which could reach a wide audience of increasingly literate, college-educated readers.

By 1900, there were at least ten major women's magazines in America that covered fashion: *Good Housekeeping,* the *Ladies' Home Journal,* the *Woman's Home Companion* (these three being mainly family magazines); *The Delineator,* showing Butterick Patterns, probably the most fashion-conscious of them all; *Pictorial Review,* which published serials by Edith Wharton, Booth Tarkington, and Joseph Conrad as well as fashion news and patterns; *McCall's; Modern Priscilla; New Idea Women's Magazine; Harper's Bazar* (sic; the second *a* was not added until 1929); and *Vogue.*

Of all these, only *Vogue* specifically set out to interest an elite; the rest were what would now be categorized as mass-market magazines, aimed at unrestricted audiences. (The *Ladies' Home Journal* was the first to declare over half a million subscribers, in 1891; that number rose to a million in 1903. *The Delineator* claimed one and a half million in 1906.)

In 1905, Condé Nast entered into negotiations to buy *Vogue.* It was at that time owned by Arthur B. Turnure, a wealthy Princetonian with publishing interests, who unfortunately died the following year, leaving the magazine in the hands of his sister-in-law, Marie Harrison. She had been working for Turnure as the magazine's editor but had few clear plans about *Vogue*'s future, and the negotiations with Nast lingered and stalled. In 1907, when he left *Collier's,* his ambition to own the chic little journal remained a pipedream.

He turned his attention full-time to the Home Pattern Company, installing in his advertising department a brilliant *Collier's* advertising man, Thomas H. Beck, and hiring another, Kenneth M. Goode. The three of them transformed the company. In 1907, the annual advertising patronage of the *Quarterly Style Book* was $1,500. Less than three years later it was $180,000. By 1908 the Home Pattern Company as a whole was bringing in advertising revenue of about $400,000.

For Nast, the lesson was clear. He saw how women responded to his call, and how a publication aimed at their special interests not only sold well but also provided excellent bait for advertisers. His promotional writing for the Home Pattern Company remained a model of its kind for the rest of his career. He had discovered, unlike most of his competitors, that a high circulation was not necessarily profitable, or even desirable. "If you had a tray with two million needles on it," he explained, "and only one hundred and fifty thousand of these had gold tips, which you wanted, it would be an endless and costly process to weed them out. Moreover the one million, eight hundred and fifty thousand which were not gold-tipped would be of no use to you, they couldn't help you; but if you could get a magnet that would draw out only the gold ones, what a saving!"

Nast, who had struck gold with his advertising ideas at Georgetown and later at *Collier's,* had found a formula he was sure would work. Through publishing the pattern books, he had accumulated valuable experience of women and the fashion world; he had a market to whom he wished to address his message. All he needed was a product.

In 1909, after four years of negotiation, he acquired *Vogue.* It had then a falling circulation of 14,000, an annual advertising revenue of $100,000, and a readership that included some of the richest and most socially prominent members of New York society.

*Vogue* was to be the magnet that drew out the gold. It was also to transport Nast forever out of his midwestern bourgeois background and into the vortex of the struggle between an exclusive, hidebound, aristocratic society and the new wealth, glamour, and social ambition that were impelling America into the twentieth century.

# THREE

# THE REQUIREMENTS OF CLASS

Most people think that the line around Society, as Americans liked to call their upper classes, was drawn at the famous "Four Hundred" ball given by Mrs. William Astor in 1892 in New York. The number arose from the fact that her ballroom could accommodate only that number of guests, and it was left to Ward McAllister, the disproportionately influential arbiter elegantiarum modeled on Beau Nash, to choose from her list the four hundred personages most worthy to grace the ball.

Eighteen years previously, however, Old New York had already seen the writing on the wall. The event in question was a fancy-dress ball at Delmonico's, which both Society and newcomers (known as bouncers) attended, thus bringing to an end 250 years of aristocratic exclusivity. "Social prominence," wrote Mrs. John King Van Rensselaer, a chronicler of the day, "as the city understood the term, was to be expressed henceforth in terms of millions rather than lineage." This milestone in American social history was known as the Bouncers' Ball.

These were minor skirmishes, however, as far as the rest of the

world was concerned. Society at the turn of the century seemed secure enough to the nouveaux riches industrialists knocking on the
door. Old New York might be foundering, but its facade was built to
last. Edith Wharton's Mr. Rosedale had no doubts on that score.
"It's this way, you see," he explained to Lily Bart. "I've had a
pretty steady grind of it these last years, working up my social position. Think it's funny I should say that? Why should I mind saying I
want to get into society? A man ain't ashamed to say he wants to
own a racing stable or a picture gallery. Well, a taste for society's
just another kind of hobby. Perhaps I want to get even with some of
the people who cold-shouldered me last year—put it that way if it
sounds better. Anyhow, I want to have the run of the best houses;
and I'm getting it too, little by little." In the 1900s, New York was
flooded with people wanting to have the run of the best houses, and
the lengths to which they were prepared to go to achieve this goal
were sometimes positively embarrassing. Mrs. Van Rensselaer
gleefully tells the story of the young matron, new in town, who
wanted to impress New Yorkers by riding every day along the new
bridle paths in Central Park. People indeed remarked on her expertise as a horsewoman, until one day it rained and the lady was mys-
teriously unable to dismount. It turned out that she had never
ridden before she came to New York and had strapped herself into
the saddle.

Frank Crowninshield, social observer, wit, editor, and later
Condé Nast's mentor and friend, called the years 1901 to 1914 the
boom or bonanza period in New York's social progress, "ushered in
by the sale of the Carnegie Steel Company to Mr. J. P. Morgan and
his associates for approximately half a billion dollars (a tenth of the
national wealth)." A group of six or eight steel merchants from
Pittsburgh, Mr. Crowninshield explained, had divided those five
hundred millions and had proceeded to invade New York. "Others
followed. It was estimated, during that period, that more than a
thousand men in America amassed a million dollars between the
years 1898 and 1907, and that three hundred of these captains of
industry gravitated to New York."

In the face of so many millions, one can see how vital it was for the Old Guard to preserve the values of lineage. (As early as 1877, the society rag *Town Topics* had asked, "Where were the Vanderbilts socially, even 5 years ago?") The Van Rensselaers, Stuyvesants, Astors, Whitneys, and Jays, who took their social responsibilities very seriously indeed, were resolved to maintain the standards of morality and taste so carefully nurtured over the years since the British took their own aristocrats home. What could be more timely than the appearance of a magazine to reflect their concerns, to report their activities, to set an example and encourage a sense of unity among the leading social figures of New York?

And so it came to pass. Arthur B. Turnure, who founded the Grolier Club, and his friend Harry W. McVickar, great-grandson of Stephen Whitney and an accomplished artist, had precisely that idea, and in 1892 they launched a little gazette entitled *Vogue*. As well as the five first families mentioned above, other distinguished personages who rushed to back Turnure's venture included Cornelius Vanderbilt, Mary M. Heckscher, Harold Brown, Frances M. Pell, Alice Lippincott, Mrs. A. M. Dodge, Henry Parish, Jr., William Jay, Peter Cooper Hewitt, Pierre Lorillard Ronalds, Jr., Cornelius R. Cuyler, and, of course, Mrs. Stuyvesant Fish, the current darling of the dinner-party circuit.

The first issue appeared on December 17, 1892, as a weekly costing ten cents. It had 250 shareholders and a list of annual subscribers, with Arthur Turnure named as publisher, Harry McVickar as art director, and Mrs. Josephine Redding as editor. "The definite object," declared the publisher, "is the establishment of a dignified authentic journal of society, fashion and the ceremonial side of life, that is to be for the present, mainly pictorial."

Its first editorial discussed at length the meaning of society, fashion, and the ceremonial side of life:

A foreign critic of American society has said that in no monarchical country is the existence of aristocracy so evident as in the republic of the United States. That with us class distinctions are as finely drawn, social aspirations as pronounced, and snobbishness as prevalent as in any nation that confers titles and ignores the principle of equality. This assertion is undoubtedly true.

The author then examined the meaning of aristocracy ("the strength which comes from the union of what is best") and concluded:

American society enjoys the distinction of being the most progressive in the world; the most salutary and the most beneficent. It is quick to discern, quick to receive and quick to condemn. It is untrammeled by a degraded and immutable nobility. It has in the highest degree an aristocracy founded in reason and developed in natural order. Its particular phases, its amusements, its follies, its fitful changes, supply endless opportunities for running comment and occasional rebuke.

The ceremonial side of life attracts the sage as well as the debutante, men of affairs as well as the belle. It may be a dinner or it may be a ball, but whatever the function the magnetic, welding force is the social idea.

The Van Rensselaers, Stuyvesants, Astors, Whitneys, and Jays must have been gratified to read those ringing words.

The first issue also contained cartoons drawn by Harry McVickar, and a "Society Supplement" which began, "The fashionable season is well under way, the first Patriarch Ball of Monday, supplying to the 'buds' the decisive change from the dancing class, where early hours and simple gowns had been the rule . . ."

Jokes were also scattered through the pages, such as this one:

CRUMMER: "Some men have wonderful courage."
GILLELAND: "I should say so. I have known men to buy cigars in Brooklyn and then smoke them."

Walter G. Robinson was hired by Turnure and McVickar (they all belonged to the same clubs, such as the Union and the Calumet) to write about men's fashions under the heading, "As Seen By Him." Whatever was amusing society at the moment made good material for his articles, as Robinson described later:

> Harry McVickar, who belonged to the Meadowbrook hunting set, used to spend the winter at Aiken [South Carolina], the club's exclusive annex, then unknown to the reading public. I remember he sent in some characteristic sketches one winter, and I wrote a "Him" about them. *Vogue* in those early days was, like society, "very New York." We followed all the traditions. We dined, when en ville, at Delmonico's and later at the Waldorf. A few of us remained faithful to the Brunswick. If we wanted to be Bohemian, we went to Martin's on University Place. . . . Men bought their haberdashery at Budd's, and their ready-made garments at Brooks'. . . . We had Slater for boots, Dunlap and Knox for hatters, and a half-dozen other ultrasmart Fifth Avenue tailors for our clothes.

Walter Robinson's columns were the most popular and controversial part of the magazine. His approach was uncompromising:

> A word about the treatment of servants. One should always be kind to them. I am never familiar, never allow them to bring tales to me and I always keep them at a distance. I, however, occasionally encourage them with a bit of commendation. In fact, I always make it a point to be scrupulously civil to inferiors. I say make a point, but it really comes to me naturally. I frequently stop in the street to pat a vagrant dog upon the head or to say a kind word to a horse. Every man who feels assured of his position would do likewise.

On another occasion, he discussed the unfortunate impression made by Americans abroad:

> A very odd thing about this class of Americans, and, in fact, about nearly all our country people, except those who have been in the habit of going abroad for years, or who have lived over there, is that, no matter what their morality may be at home, the moment they arrive in Paris they imagine that they must mingle with the very worst and most disreputable assemblages and visit the most

extraordinary places. In other words, they want to do "the sights. . . ." In spite of this mob abroad, and with such representatives, there are some who still deny that there exists in America both the upper- and the lower-middle class.

Mrs. Van Rensselaer could hardly have put it better. No false modesty about American democracy here. Why, one only had to poke one's nose outside one's town house to see the most vulgarly appointed carriages, carrying women dressed in undesirable toilettes, in from the provinces with a million dollars to spend and expectations to match. On *Vogue*'s third anniversary in 1895, Arthur Turnure explained his position quite clearly: "Two leading ideas control [*Vogue*'s] career," he wrote. "One, the constant recollection that improvement and development go hand in hand; the other, that its readers are gentlemen and gentlewomen and that to the requirements of this class its energies and resources shall conform."

Turnure divided the magazine up into departments, the readers themselves dictating what would most please them. "Seen in the Shops," "*Vogue* Designs for the Seamstress," "Smart Fashions for Limited Incomes: The Paris [or London] Letter," "Society Snapshots," "For the Hostess," and "Answers to Correspondence" were some of their favorites. Reviews of the season's new plays, music, art shows, and books also appeared. Since the magazine was run by people in the vanguard of society, it had an advantage over most other journals in the same field. Who else could have got into the new Vanderbilt house at Fifth Avenue and 57th Street and published photographs of its interior? The Society Snapshots were all of *Vogue*'s friends. Notes for the Hostess came fresh from *Vogue*'s most recent dinner parties. Designs of what everyone was wearing went straight to *Vogue*'s Seamstress. *Vogue*, in short, was the dernier cri of the week, thanks to the people who published it, who happened to know better than anyone else what was going to be accepted by the people who mattered.

Of course *Vogue* was not entirely devoted to these matters, pressing though they were. Equally diverting for the editors were the weekends at their country clubs (Tuxedo, Westchester, Shinnecock), where golf was all the rage by day, and bridge by night. And then there were all the little details of life that made *Vogue* so amusing. One simply had to know, for instance, who was at the party on the *Nourmahal,* John Jacob Astor's yacht, after the America's Cup races (Mrs. Cornelius Vanderbilt, of course, Mrs. Stuyvesant Fish, of course, and heaps of Burdens, Iselins, and Hitchcocks), or what, if any, were the changes in the cut of the morning coat for the winter season ("For street wear a morning coat suit of plain smoke or dark gray is rather smart"). And female readers would rather have died than have missed reading about the current style ("Not to have an all-black or black and white Chantilly gown this season is to declare oneself out of the mode").

Whether this made *Vogue* a commercial proposition for advertisers was less certain than its popularity with Mrs. Stuyvesant Fish. At the turn of the century, advertising was largely a mail-order business, with varied novelty items being offered on a small-scale, one-time-only basis to a limited market. *Vogue*'s advertising for its first issues in the 1890s, therefore, was restricted in scope, unambitious, and very eclectic. Announcements of other magazines figured largely—*Scribner's, Cosmopolitan, Harper's Magazine, Harper's Bazar,* the *Art Interchange Monthly.* Gorham Silver, Gunther Sons (Furriers), W. & J. Sloane, Veuve Cliquot Champagne, B. Altman's ("importers of the Tasso Corset"), Crouch & Fitzgerald, Marsh Mallow Hair Tonic, Remington Typewriters, Knox Fashionable Hats, Johannis Table Waters, Linene Reversible Collars and Cuffs, and Howard & Co., Silver, also took space.

In 1900, the total advertising revenues of all American publications amounted to $95,000,000. In 1905, the figure stood at $145,000,000—a 50 percent increase. With the rapid increase of mass-produced goods, in particular the introduction of the automobile, and with the rise of women as spenders of the new wealth, advertisers shed their modesty and rapidly took on an aggressive consumer orientation that transformed the business.

In contrast to the national trend, however, very little change could be discerned in *Vogue*'s advertising. If anything, by 1902 volume had dwindled, with Venus Hose Supporters, Frederic Jewelers, Mme. Gardner's Corsets, and Colgate's Cashmere Bouquet Toilet Soap representing some of the few who bought full pages. The magazine also published an interesting advertisement for *The Smart Set,* "a Magazine of Cleverness," published by Ess Ess Publishing at twenty-five cents a copy, declaring an "unparalleled list of contributors, including from both hemispheres the brightest men and women of the literary and social world," which prefigured another magazine that was destined to overshadow every other publication in this field, Condé Nast's *Vanity Fair.*

Turnure and McVickar, it may safely be ventured, preferred not to sully their hands with the commercial elements of their slim journal; their interests lay several city blocks away from the advertising department of *Vogue.* The Meadowbrook set simply never thought about such vulgar matters. Nor, in spite of the burgeoning passion for the Mode, was *Vogue*'s fashion department encouraging to space buyers. This, perhaps, was not entirely unconnected with the fact that in charge of the fashion pages in *Vogue* was Arthur Turnure's first editor, Mrs. Josephine Redding, a rather unlikely choice for such a position in that she was a square little person given to wearing sensible shoes and a large hat. She is credited, however, with coming up with the name *Vogue,* no mean accomplishment. She was responsible for the regular fashion columns and also for the *Vogue* patterns. Since the rest of the magazine was in the hands of Turnure, McVickar, and friends, it is hardly surprising that fashion got short shrift beside the men's interests, such as sports and club news.

Mrs. Redding was not interested in sports, nor in club news, nor in fashion. Her real passion was animals. Pets were not quite what Mr. Turnure had in mind for his readers, however, so in 1900 Mrs. Redding was let go, and the magazine was editorless. Harry McVickar had also drifted away, so, ten years after its inception, the magazine depended almost entirely on Turnure's efforts. Luckily, his sister-in-law, Marie Harrison, agreed to help out, and in 1901 she became its second editor. Turnure also hired Tom

McCready, a bright young man from *Scribner's* magazine, to take over the advertising department, which by that time was practically nonexistent.

In 1906, Turnure died suddenly at the young age of forty-nine, leaving Marie Harrison and a young assistant named Edna Woolman Chase in charge, and this was the state of affairs when Nast bought the magazine three years later.

Condé Nast's name first appears on *Vogue*'s masthead on June 24, 1909. It reads: "The Vogue Company, Condé Nast, President, M. L. Harrison, Vice-President, Theron McCampbell, Treasurer, W. O. Harrison, Secretary." Having bought out the Turnure/Harrison interests, Nast signed a contract with Marie Harrison under which she would remain as editor for five years. Theron McCampbell, who had been Nast's president at the Home Pattern Company, was now his treasurer. The man who might have been a St. Louis lawyer was finally master of his own business.

Condé Nast was thirty-six years old when he became the publisher of *Vogue*. He was riding high on his stunning success at *Collier's* and the Home Pattern Company, and he had plenty of the ideas and ambition to go farther. He had been in New York for twelve years—long enough to know that when en ville, one dined at Delmonico's, or maybe the Brunswick. Long enough also to know that one bought one's haberdashery at Budd's, one's boots at Slater's, one's hats at Dunlap and Knox, and one's ready-made garments at Brooks'.

But was that enough? It was not enough for Edith Wharton's Mr. Rosedale, even when his name began to appear on municipal committees and charitable boards and his candidacy at one of the fashionable clubs was discussed with diminishing opposition. Arthur Turnure and Harry McVickar had gone, but Walter G. Robinson would have spotted Condé Nast at once as an outsider. For Nast's "set" was not New York, Newport, or even Southampton (where "more than one . . . had no American forebears whatever," sniffed Mrs. Van Rensselaer). The Midwest traditions Nast followed had very different origins from those described in "As Seen By Him,"

*Vogue*'s first-ever cover, announcing a very pretty new debutante, whose conversation "is very instructive on all points of fashion and topics of the day." *Vogue*, December 17, 1892.

In the publisher's seat, surrounded by layouts—Condé Nast's career is assured.

and his forebears would hardly have stood up to Mrs. Van Rensselaer's scrutiny.

According to Edith Wharton, all Mr. Rosedale needed was a wife "whose affiliations would shorten the last tedious steps of his ascent." Condé Nast had been brought up a good Catholic, and his interests were professional rather than social. Such a calculating approach to love as Mr. Rosedale's was never his way. But there is no doubt that the chance meeting that took place soon after his arrival in New York between the young advertising manager of *Collier's* and Jeanne Clarisse Coudert, and their subsequent marriage, had a most felicitous effect upon his standing in the eyes of those who cared about these things—the same people who were later to make him a millionaire several times over.

# FOUR

# CLARISSE COUDERT, SOPRANO

**"S**lender, suave, and frighteningly chic." That is how a young *Vogue* editor described Clarisse Coudert Nast at the time Nast purchased the magazine.

The Coudert family were members of the Four Hundred. Their names were listed in the genealogies of American Society. Clarisse's grandfather, Charles Coudert, born in 1795, became a Napoleonic officer and was sentenced to death for pro-Napoleonic plottings during the Bourbon Restoration. After Madame Recamier, among others, pleaded for his life, his sentence was commuted and he fled to London. At the urging of a friend, General Lafayette, in 1823 he moved on to the New World, where Lafayette promised him good fortune.

Charles started a French school in New York, and in 1826 married a French Royalist, Jeanne-Clarisse du Champ, who died of tuberculosis at the age of thirty-six. Four children reached maturity—three sons and a daughter. The first immigrant Coudert died in 1879 at the age of eighty-five, one year after his granddaughter Clarisse was born.

His second son, Charles, born in 1830, was Clarisse's father. In 1853 Charles cofounded an international law firm, the Coudert Brothers, with his elder brother, Frederic René, and his younger, Louis Léance. It later became one of the leading firms in the United States.

In 1859 Charles married Marie Guion, and they had seven children—six daughters, Claire, Léonie, Aimée, Grace, Constance, and Jeanne Clarisse, and one son, Charles Dupont. Clarisse, born in 1878, was the youngest, and like most youngest siblings, particularly in a large family, she was both spoiled and highly competitive. Brought up in affluent circumstances in Middletown, New Jersey, she was doted on by her father, was infatuated with her only brother, and longed above all to be a boy.

Her father died in 1897, at the age of sixty-seven. Clarisse was nineteen. An unpleasant incident occurred at his death that indicates the extent of the divisions in the Coudert family—divisions that must have become increasingly troublesome as Clarisse grew up.

On July 22, 1897, a week after Charles Coudert died, his will was published; in it he left the bulk of his estate to his wife, Marie. Frederic, his brother, was named as executor. A few days later, rumors began circulating of another will, and sure enough, on July 29, a second will was filed for probate. This one, dated a month and a half after the original one, left all the money to the children, and only personal property (books, furniture, silverware, and jewelry) to his wife. The testator said his wife had been otherwise provided for. Frederic was again named as executor.

The lines of a classic family feud were quickly drawn. The widow charged that a large sum of money was due the estate from the firm of Coudert Brothers; that her husband had owned a farm at Middletown, on which he had erected a dwelling that largely increased the value of the property; and that this estate was now being claimed by Frederic by virtue of an unrecorded deed made to him by her husband for the consideration of one dollar; that the second will was made when her husband was weak and subject to influence from other members of the family; that she was being cut off without a penny; and that her brother-in-law was a prejudiced executor and should be replaced.

Stories began to reach the press that the widow had for years been an object of persecution, that conspiring relatives had continually attempted to precipitate an estrangement between Charles and Marie, and that their marriage had been regarded with disfavor from the start by other members of the family.

The children sided with their uncle against their mother.

This bitter alliance was spearheaded by the youngest daughter, Clarisse, who, as a minor, allowed her name to be used by her guardian in the application to the court to appoint Frederic Coudert as temporary administrator of her father's estate, in opposition to her mother's allegation of prejudice.

Since Charles Coudert had specified that his brother was to be executor in both wills, the judge concluded that Frederic was trusted by the testator to be an impartial administrator, and so named him executor. After intense and desperate negotiations behind the scenes, Mrs. Coudert was persuaded to withdraw her petition. In view of the potentially sensational nature of the case, the Couderts must have brought irresistible pressure to bear on her; the provisions and terms of the settlement were not made known.

There is always something painful about children rising up against a parent, particularly in public. However difficult Marie Guion Coudert may have been—and there is reason to believe that she had some mental instability—it did not augur well for Clarisse's own future that she felt hostile enough toward her mother to support a court case against her.

All the Coudert girls, except Grace, who died in her thirties of tuberculosis, made good marriages with an international flavor. Claire, the eldest, married the Duc de Choiseul and lived in Paris. Léonie, known as Daisy, married Franck Glaenzer and also lived in Paris, where her singing voice enchanted the French composers Fauré and Debussy, for whom she sometimes performed in private. Aimée married McKenzie Semple and then Frederic Brennig; Constance married William R. Garrison and after her divorce also moved to Paris.

Clarisse married Condé Nast on August 19, 1902, in St. Patrick's Cathedral, New York. They had met on a horse-riding expedition in New Jersey, near Clarisse's home. He was with his old friend Robert Collier, who provided a better introduction than Nast's horsemanship, which left something to be desired. She, of course, was an accomplished rider. This small detail of equestrian inequality was to become emblematic of the marriage.

Twenty-four years old and the last sister to marry, Clarisse Coudert was not a classic beauty, but she had striking features, full lips, an eighteen-inch waist, great physical grace (she looked marvelous on a horse), and an instinctive elegance that immediately set her apart from the crowd. Her Frenchness and her Catholicism were bonds with Nast; her stylishness and quality were more immediate attractions to him. As for Clarisse, she saw in Condé a lean, dark, dashing figure with French blood (which she cared greatly about), good taste, and ambition. Although not the prize of French aristocracy her elder sister had captured, he nevertheless promised a stimulating life in New York. He was six years older than she, but older than that in experience and manner. The element of paternalism in his nature found a quick response in her.

In the eyes of Clarisse, his friendship with Robert Collier, a man of considerable social prominence, compensated for his lack of horsemanship. In the eyes of the interested parties of New York society, they made a handsome couple. And as for those extrasensitive monitors of the Mode, a huge sigh of relief went up all round when Condé Nast's name, along with those of his mother, his brother Louis, and his sister Estelle (Ethel was hors de combat, hunting for nunneries), appeared for the first time in the 1902 *Social Register,* in consideration, naturally, of his marriage to a Coudert.

The Coudert in question never let him forget it.

Things started out smoothly enough, although he was to say later that intimations of disaster were apparent as early as the honeymoon. Their first house was at 66 West 11th Street. Their first

Clarisse Coudert Nast, fashionably languishing for a photograph by Baron de Meyer that was never published.

child, Charles Coudert, was born on July 23, 1903, in Tuxedo Park, where they spent their first summers together, and their second child, Natica, was born on January 5, 1905, in New York. Those first years were reasonably settled. Clarisse was busy having babies, and Condé, moving rapidly up *Collier's* ladder in a shower of titular and financial rewards, had embarked on his independent venture, the Home Pattern Company.

In 1905 they moved to 9 East 12th Street, the first of the moves, gravitating uptown as the city grew, that occurred with increasing frequency during the marriage. The Nasts changed address seven times in fifteen years—that means a move almost every two years, a reflection of Clarisse's energy and restlessness. In 1906, she made her first major gesture of independence.

Showing some of the same talent as her sister Daisy, she had been studying singing with some success for several years, and now decided to go to Paris for more advanced coaching. Paris was her favorite city, and also the home of two of her sisters, who were apparently having a dashing and romantic existence there. So in 1906, after four years of domesticity, Clarisse took her two young children to France, leaving their father alone in New York. Accompanying them was a nurse, Cora Jane Richards, known as Dicky, the daughter of a Welsh customs officer living in Canada. Dicky was not, strictly speaking, however, the children's nurse. She was sent, on the recommendation of the family doctor, to keep an eye on Clarisse.

Clarisse's mental instability is not documented, but Dicky's presence in Paris indicates that her condition gave some concern. Clarisse had in fact shown symptoms of what was then called hysteria—emotionalism, erraticness, neurotic behavior. Dicky was indispensable, both for the mother and for the children. "I don't know where I would have been without her," Natica admitted much later.

In Paris, Clarisse flung herself into the sophisticated and artistic social life that her sister, the Duchesse de Choiseul, had created for herself. Claire de Choiseul had become an intimate friend of Rodin's, as well as a model for his sculpture. She introduced

American patrons to the aging and world-famous sculptor, accompanying him everywhere. (It was she who urged the American millionaire Thomas Fortune Ryan, whose bust Rodin sculpted, to donate funds to the Metropolitan Museum in New York to buy Rodin's work.) Paris, in 1906, cast few aspersions on her and her complaisant husband because of her well-publicized attentions to Rodin, although later Judith Cladel, Rodin's last amanuensis, wrote a stinging attack on the duchesse in her biography of Rodin. Mlle. Cladel identified Claire only as "the Duchesse de Ch——," presumably to avoid a libel suit. She describes the duchesse thus: "When we left the studio I was aware of a little thin woman in a wide-brimmed hat dressed with an elegance that was spoiled by the violent make-up on her faded features [make-up was not fashionable in those days], and a coiffure of thick red curls." Mlle. Cladel goes on to say that the duchesse threw herself at Rodin, "running her diamond-laden fingers through the white hair on his handsome head, simpering, 'I am your Muse.'" According to Mlle. Cladel, the duchesse believed she was Rodin's Egeria, and also that she was a reincarnation of his dead daughter, Maria. She also liked her brandy and chartreuse altogether too much.

Even allowing for the bitchy Mlle. Cladel's slanderous jealousy, Claire de Choiseul seems to have exhibited an excessive temperament similar to her younger sister's. At any rate, Rodin dramatically broke from his Egeria in 1912, causing the de Choiseuls much distress. The duchesse even sent a relative (probably her sister Daisy) to plead for a reconciliation, "emphasising both the financial as well as the sentimental aspect of the situation." Mlle. Cladel's prose fairly hums with delight at the downfall of her rival.

(In spite of their eccentricities, the Coudert sisters did not lack courage: Grace, one of the first nurses to serve behind the lines, was decorated for her services to the Red Cross in the 1914–18 war, and Claire had a distinguished war record with the French. She died suddenly of pneumonia in 1919.)

Clarisse obviously found this world stimulating for a while. Rainer Maria Rilke was then Rodin's secretary, and artists and writers flocked to his studio. After a year, enchanted by the bohemian life, Clarisse sent Dicky and the children home, while she remained in Paris and continued working on her singing. Sometime in 1907, Claire mentioned to her sister that there was a very talented young painter and photographer in Paris who was a friend of Rodin's. Why didn't Clarisse go and have her picture taken for Condé?

The photographer was practically penniless and unknown outside Rodin's circle. His studio was unheated and on Clarisse's first visit she found it too cold to consider a sitting. They made another appointment, and this time Clarisse sent her maid on ahead with fuel to warm the studio before she arrived. The photographer took her from several angles, using a vase of flowers and a fan as props. Her low-cut dress belied the winter temperature.

It turned out, however, to be worth the discomfort. The photographer's name was Steichen.

Finally Paris, too, palled. After a two-year separation from her husband, Clarisse returned to America, to the town house on Gramercy Park where the family was now living. There she found Dicky firmly ensconced, running the household well—too well, perhaps. After Clarisse's return, Dicky left almost immediately, and never came back on a permanent basis. The children missed her dreadfully. Condé, too, realized what he had lost, aware that hers was the most loving and reliable presence the children had ever had; so he did not lose touch with her completely. Whenever the children were sick Dicky was called in. During a polio epidemic in 1917 Natica was sent to Dicky's farm on the St. Lawrence River, where the young teenager, who at that time had never been to school (Clarisse's ideas about education were idiosyncratic, to say the least), learned about animals, seasons, and the careful disciplines of nature, during a pastoral summer. (Nast never let Dicky go. Twenty years later, she came to stay at his house in Sands Point and he entertained her royally. His affection for and loyalty to those who had served him well lasted a lifetime.)

Meanwhile, Condé had left *Collier's* and bought *Vogue,* which offered Clarisse a milieu very different from that of either *Collier's* or the Home Pattern Company, and one in which she was much

Fifteen-year-old Natica Nast modeling a wedding veil by Thurn under the direction of her mother. (The dress was what caused the trouble.) Photograph by de Meyer, *Vogue,* January 15, 1920.

Natica as the epitome of childish innocence in this never-before-published portrait by Steichen, dated 1918.

more at home. She immediately threw herself with characteristic brio into her husband's fashionable new acquisition.

Her first inspiration was to redecorate all the offices at *Vogue*'s new address, 443 Fourth Avenue. Editor Edna Woolman Chase was presented with a pale yellow desk with grooved legs picked out in blue, a tall, very narrow chest of drawers, and a gray marble-topped table. The furniture bought wholesale from office-equipment stores was replaced by bleached-oak writing tables and chairs, with raw-silk curtains and original art hanging on the walls. Later, Clarisse added to her interior design portfolio by turning her hand to the creation of a plush new reception room, complete with fake books. Dorothy Rothschild (later Parker), arriving at *Vogue* in 1915, took one look at this vision of grandeur and gasped, "Well, it looks just like the entrance to a house of ill-fame." (Dorothy Parker did not stay long at *Vogue*—Frank Crowninshield quickly kidnapped her to work on his own periodical, *Vanity Fair*—but she wrote several memorable fashion captions before her departure, such as "Brevity is the soul of lingerie, said the petticoat to the chemise," and this one, which never proceeded further than the proof stage: "There was a little girl and she had a little curl, right in the middle of her forehead. When she was good she was very, very good, and when she was bad she wore this divine nightdress of rose-colored mousseline de soie, trimmed with frothy Valenciennes lace.")

Clarisse also tried to get involved with the magazine, "turning the pages with her immaculately white-gloved hands," as Mrs. Chase warily observed. Mrs. Chase could not resist adding a tart comment about the bright red lipstick Clarisse favored, "used more freely than was customary among women of her social standing at that time. She was the cosmetic manufacturers' best friend." Clarisse must have got that habit from Claire de Choiseul.

Clarisse also decided that it would be a good idea for the office to have afternoon tea, "and for a time," Mrs. Chase said, "the smartly uniformed maid who dusted our desks and arranged fresh flowers in the editors' offices would arrive around half past four propelling her little wagon with its service of tea and sweet cookies." The editor soon dispatched the little wagon, as she did Mrs. Nast's other impractical ideas.

Not all Clarisse's contributions were so ineffectual. She worked closely for a time with photographers, in particular with Adolphe de Meyer and Steichen, who, since that first meeting with Mrs. Nast in his unheated Paris studio, had come to New York to work for *Vogue.* Her innovative and imaginative suggestions helped enliven their photographs for fashion stories. Some of her most effective efforts, published in 1919, brighten a series of new shoe fashions photographed by de Meyer. Each photo has a little story (tying a lace, an impatient little dog, a fallen rose)—quite a change from the normal, pedestrian method of showing footwear. During this period of productive work at *Vogue,* Clarisse also used her fifteen-year-old daughter to model wedding veils, arguing that no professional model looked innocent enough to create the right virginal effect. (The couturier Tappé complained about having to make the gown small enough to fit Natica, saying he would not be able to sell it afterward; but a few months later it adorned the dainty figure of Mary Pickford in a radiantly lit *Vogue* portrait by de Meyer; Miss Pickford wore the dress for her marriage to Douglas Fairbanks.)

At home, there were governesses, French and German governesses, who were instructed to make the children speak French for two days and German for two days each week. Clarisse was determined that they should learn languages as she had done, and succeed where her husband had failed. They traveled a lot, as most upper-class families did at that time, taking ocean liners to Europe for three months at a time. Clarisse often took the children to England, where her beloved brother lived, and rented a house near his. In 1909 Clarisse was abroad from June until November; in later years she stayed away from home even longer. For Coudert and Natica, it was not an easy childhood.

The summer after Nast bought *Vogue,* the family rented a house in the one place where the appearance of family solidarity counted—Newport. Newport was then, as *Vogue* put it, "the summer society capital of this country. Its so-called cottages are, many of them, veritable palaces, and its season is always punctuated by entertainments of the most lavish description. Existence at Newport is, for some women, a carnival of dress, a parade, for, as a rule, success at Newport opens the gates of New York society to the aspirant, and a fixed position there is a passport to the inner and even royal circles of Europe." How could Condé Nast afford *not* to summer at Newport?

There he watched the Vanderbilts frolicking on their torpedo-boat-shaped yacht; he listened to the Iselins and the Goelets complain about their servants; he examined the Vanderbilts' latest summer cottage, "The Breakers," as the seventy rooms were built, stone by grandiose stone; he escorted his children, dressed in the latest Paris bonnets and organdy frocks, to the Wideners' birthday parties; he heard Mrs. Stuyvesant Fish declaim to her friends about the evils of women's suffrage; he inspected in the minutest detail the uniforms worn by Mrs. Hermann Oelrichs's footmen.

He played golf, as everyone else did, but Nast played with more devotion and concentration, taking lessons, asking for criticism after a game, later even having a motion picture made of himself so he could improve his strokes. With equal thoroughness he learned how to swim and dive, accomplishments he sadly lacked from his St. Louis childhood. "It took real guts for him to execute the awful belly-floppers with which he disciplined himself every day," commented a young Harvard graduate, Harford Powel, in 1910. (Powel was watching Nast's social progress in Newport with admiration—so much so that a few months later he found himself working in *Vogue*'s new and sparky advertising department.)

Newport, for Nast, was business. Pleasurable business, but business nonetheless. That summer of 1910 was for him an anthropological field trip. He was the outsider, objectively observing; and at the same time he was also, by a form of social osmosis, taking on the characteristics of the observed. The sharp-eyed, serious, charming young publisher was soon a well-known figure around Newport, along with his elegant wife and pretty children. William G. Roelker, one of the resort's most distinguished summer residents, remarked that Condé Nast was the smartest man who had come to Newport in years. The natives, it seemed, were prepared to accept him.

In 1902, the year of his first appearance in the *Social Register,* no club was listed after his name. By 1910, there were three—Racquet & Tennis, Riding, and Piping Rock. By 1916, it had risen to eight, including the Metropolitan, Republican, City, Garden City, and Golf. Like mollusks attached to a host organism, the clubs gave Nast a protective shell and augmented his exterior shape to fit the world in which he had chosen to swim. Having worked out most meticulously the business goals of his publishing venture, he was in the process of becoming what his magazine extolled—a person of social prominence, refinement, and the Mode.

Photographs reflect this adaptation: Impeccably dressed, stiff-collared, pince-nez firmly in place (he was always adjusting it), the publisher cuts an austere, stern figure. The charming smile his friends remember was, sadly, never caught by the cameras. His children found his face comfortable enough, however. On one occasion, Nast was about to leave the office with a group of bankers, with whom he had been having a conference, when he picked up his small son, who was waiting to go home with him. Nast, the bankers, and little Coudert all traveled down in the elevator together. As it started to descend, there was silence for a moment and then Coudert piped up persuasively, "Father, make a face like an elephant."

With his children, the hard surfaces dissolved. He was a cozy, down-to-earth father, a calming influence amid the emotional flurries and erratic outbursts exhibited by his strong-willed, high-strung wife, and the cold discipline required by the French and German governesses. "When we were young he would often treat us to ice cream sodas," Natica remembers, "which he enjoyed every bit as much as we did. And every weekend, on returning to Newport, he would bring us little gifts and surprises, and always take back with him, 'for the art editor,' my wax crayon drawings for *Vogue* covers.

"He carried a press pass all through our childhood, and this to us was a very exciting thought, for when we lived near the firehouse, on one occasion or another, whenever it was possible, he would take us to watch the big horses race out with fire engines. Years later, when in my twenties I lived with him at 1040 Park Avenue, we would get up in the middle of the night to watch the most spectacular blazes—the burning of the Sherry-Netherland before it was completed, the scaffolding falling as it burned; and the Greek Orthodox church with the steeple ablaze.

"I also recall very vividly that Coudert and I had breakfast with Dad every morning in the dining room, and that it was always a happy time, full of jokes and tricks and sharing, such as games with the gold bands from his cigar.

"Mother always slept late and had her breakfast in bed."

Nast loved giving people presents, and after he made his millions the presents became legendary. But he always liked to give them in a subtle, indirect way, indicating a form of tact, of delicacy, that was one of his endearing qualities.

"By the time I was fourteen," Natica recalls, "my mother had already seen to it that I was possibly on my way to becoming a fine horsewoman, and I longed for a jumper of my own in preference to the mounts available by appointment at the Riding Club. That year, under the Christmas tree I discovered a little toy horse with my name on it, with saddlebags which I found to be stuffed with gold pieces, and a card reading 'The makings of an Irish hunter—lock, stock and barrel.'

"I had absolutely no idea what it was all about. The phraseology was quite beyond me. I realized that I was being eagerly watched for some very special reaction, and sat there deeply humiliated until Dad finally explained. Then, of course, I was overjoyed and soon became the owner of a lovely little dappled mare."

These were good times, but they grew harder and harder to sustain. Nast used to come home from the office and go round the block several times before plucking up courage to enter the house and face the latest *crise de Clarisse*. As the marriage faltered, they could not find the wherewithal to make peace.

In 1914, Clarisse made her first venture into theatre design, creating rooms and sets for Owen Johnson's new play, *The Salamander*. At that time *The New York Times* reported that Mrs. Nast's interest in the field was so great that she hoped to make it a

This superb photograph by de Meyer of Clarisse, never before published,
shows the Coudert profile that Rodin captured in his busts of Claire
de Choiseul.

full-time career, thus, as the newspaper put it, following other society women's example: "Mrs. J. Borden Harriman took up the idea of using her Mount Kisco place as a kind of sanitarium for women: Mrs. Lawrence Waterbury, before she married, dealt with artistic clothing for infants."

But stage design, like Clarisse's other career efforts, was doomed to failure. It was recognized that she had artistic talent, imagination, and great taste. She was hired by Mary Pickford, for instance, to give her decorating and entertaining advice in Hollywood; she also selected Miss Pickford's clothes, favoring, at the film star's urging, the models of Lucille (Lady Duff Gordon). Clarisse continued to take singing lessons, appearing in photographs in *Vogue* as "Clarisse Coudert, Soprano." But none of these ventures added up to anything.

Poor Clarisse. In another age she might have found a real focus for her energies and used her considerable sense of style and visual gifts in an authentic career, despite her evident temperamental difficulties. But she was born into a time when women of her class thought a career meant offering their houses to charity or dealing with "artistic clothing for infants," and serious commitment to work was almost impossible.

Like Zelda Fitzgerald, she envied men their careers and women their youth and beauty (she continued to dress her daughter in child's clothes—except for her modeling—long after they ceased to be appropriate), and she resented the fact that her husband loved his work more than her. Casting about wildly for something, anything, to do, every year plunging into something new and ephemeral, she ended up not as certifiably mad as Zelda but a disappointed, frustrated woman.

By 1919 the marriage was to all intents and purposes over. Condé had been seen in public with other women, in particular the lively opera star Grace Moore, and Clarisse finally packed her bags. Nast continued to live at their last address, 470 Park Avenue, and she moved to an apartment farther up, at 1000 Park. In 1920, Nast set up a trust fund guaranteeing his wife an annual income of $10,000. There is no record of any larger settlement. The Nasts remained married, partly owing to religious and social pressures, until 1925, when Clarisse divorced him to marry Victor Onativia, a stockbroker, who was younger than she. The marriage did not last. Nast generously continued his payments to her after her marriage and for the rest of her life.

In later years, long after their divorce, Clarisse continued to engulf him in family matters, for which he patiently accepted the responsibility. It may have been a marriage of promise for the young publisher, but it ended in bitter regret.

# FIVE

# "WHAT WERE THE CHAUFFEURS WEARING?"

On January 6, 1911, Mrs. Hermann Oelrichs gave a dinner party for two hundred people before a fancy-dress ball at Sherry's. Twenty-seven of these guests were photographed by Marceau for *Vogue,* including Mrs. Condé Nast, as La Tosca, in a gown of white satin embroidered in gold, carrying a staff decorated with gardenias. Of particular interest were Miss Maria de Barril, who wore a large black bird with jeweled eyes for a headdress; Mrs. Harry Lehr, who wore a Turkish outfit complete with loose red satin trousers and a white veil over her face; Miss Elsie de Wolfe as a Dresden shepherdess; Mrs. William Jay as Brünnhilde; and Mrs. Oelrichs herself, a generously proportioned lady, who was covered from head to foot in a costume of pearl-covered gold-and-blue fabric and a dangling gold headdress, representing Amneris.

Dressing up was very much the Mode in 1911. At a theatre benefit in aid of the Equal Franchise Society in February, Mrs. Clarence Mackay brought together her rich socialite friends in a series of *tableaux vivants,* which included Mrs. W. Bourke Cockran as Mary Wollstonecraft, Mrs. George Gould as Queen Catherine of

Russia, and Mrs. James Stillman as "The Spirit of Liberty" (wearing a helmet, Grecian-draped gown, and sandals).

To show that *Vogue,* which published these splendid pictures, was not *entirely* committed to the ideas promulgated by the Equal Franchise Society, however, an editorial on the subject in the same issue declared firmly: "One reason for sex antagonism is the virulence of the attacks that suffragists make in newspaper columns and from platforms upon any man who comes out into the open and opposes 'Votes for Women.' Such tactics argue ill for the reasonable discussion of public questions if ever women are enfranchised."

The most exciting social news of the spring season in 1911 was undoubtedly the March wedding of Miss Vivian Gould (it was her mother who had looked so good the previous month as Catherine of Russia), to John Graham Horsley Beresford, 5th Baron Decies, of Sefton Park, Slough, England. It merited four full pages in *Vogue,* plus a full-page portrait of the new Lady Decies sketched by Ernest Haskell. Lord Decies was photographed in the full-dress uniform of the Seventh Hussars; Lady Decies wore a five-yard-long train embroidered in silver lilies, with a long chain of diamonds and a diamond bowknot. "Never in the history of nuptial events in New York have we had so many of the old British nobility represented at one fell swoop," *Vogue* gurgled.

As for fashion, lavish use of lace was the extravagant note of the season, along with foulards carrying new bordered treatments. Hats were high, almost entirely decorated with colored plumes, tinted, spotted, or painted in the very latest shades. Round necks, polka dots, and dainty bows imparted a youthful charm to the newest frocks, which were basically simple in line, with high waists and long straight skirts.

To show that Society still took its role seriously, however, *Vogue* was proud to announce in its March 15 issue a new department, "Noblesse Oblige": "Under this title it is planned to publish a series of articles showing the various methods that women and men of social distinction employ in relieving the conditions under which the less fortunately placed exist."

The first person of social distinction so honored was Mrs. Henry Villard, whose husband had built one of New York's finest houses. A somewhat daunting gray-haired lady in black chiffon and pearls, she was president of a "unique and efficiently managed philanthropy," the New York Diet Kitchen Association. (The Association, founded in 1873 to relieve the destitute sick, was largely a distributor of milk to the poor.) "Certainly the Association is a great boon to thousands of the poor, who but for these Kitchens would go on ignorantly murdering their babies and as ignorantly spreading tuberculosis."

By the beginning of 1911 the new Nast *Vogue* had taken shape, and this was the prototype—a richly embellished frieze of society, fashion, social conscience, and frivolity, picked out in gold by the confident and stylish hand of its new publisher.

For a few months after Nast bought the magazine, nobody on the staff caught even a glimpse of their employer, which was something of a relief, because the *on-dit* was that he was very shrewd, remote, and a penetrating interrogator. *Vogue*'s only tactful nod to Nast's existence was the publication of a photograph of his children at a party, which appeared in a September 1909 issue.

His first move came after six months, when he cut the magazine's publication schedule back from weekly to fortnightly. (He said later that when he had originally tried to buy the magazine in 1905, he had determined that *Vogue* should be published only twice a month.) The price of each issue went up from ten to fifteen cents, the yearly subscription remaining at $4.00. More changes quickly took place: color covers, more pages of advertising, a build-up of *Vogue* patterns, more society pages, and more fashion.

Nast retained departments such as "As Seen By Him," "Smart Fashions for Limited Incomes," "Seen on the Stage," "Seen in the Shops," "The Well-Dressed Man," "What They Read," "Concerning Animals" (Mrs. Redding's legacy), and "Society." On June 1, 1910, the first new department was introduced—a "Sale and Exchange" page. "Every English publication for women we find has two or three pages each issue given up to a swarm of tiny advertisements—personal messages from reader to reader—private notices of their personal wants. . . . We have long felt that *Vogue*'s readers would welcome such a clearinghouse.'' (*Vogue*'s readers indeed welcomed such a clearinghouse. Sample advertisements: ''Wish to sell my black Russian lynx shawl collar, and large muff, for $25. Cost $55. Not worn, as black does not become me.'' ''Chaperon for girls or children. Refined gentlewoman will give care in country home to two children whose parents are to travel. Highest references.'' ''Pair very handsome Sheffield plated candelabra. Have just been replated by Tiffany. $75.'')

Each issue was packed with society news. The August 1, 1910, issue, for instance, contained an article on ''Society by the Sea'' (Newport, Bar Harbor, and Southampton), accompanied by photographs of the ladies who attended these resorts (Mrs. Robert Goelet, Mrs. John R. Drexel, Mrs. Philip Lydig, et al); the Acheson-Carter wedding (''The second of this season's fashionable Anglo-American marriages''); an ''As Seen By Him'' column on ''Newport Weighed in the Balance with Private Country Seats and Increasingly Found Wanting''; and articles entitled ''Where Europe's Varied Society Seeks the Sea'' (Trouville, Baden-Baden, Scheveningen, Biarritz); ''Newport Folk at a Charity Fete Given . . . at Mr. Alfred Vanderbilt's Home in Portsmouth''; ''Contestants in the Women's National Championship Lawn Tennis Tournament'' (in Philadelphia); ''Hurlingham, the Most Fashionable Country Club near London''; ''Riding Equipment and the Care of the Horse''; and ''An Attractive Summer Home'' (belonging to Mr. Charles P. Searle of Boston). The August 15 issue told readers ''What A Girl Will Need for a Year at a Fashionable Boarding School.'' There were photographs of ''Some of the Younger Members of English Society'' and of the ''Baby Prince of Greece''; ''Two Splendid and Wide-Spreading Country Seats in the Rolling Hills of Northwestern New Jersey'' and ''Flower-Garden Clubs for Matrons and Maids''; and a double spread on the Fish-Dick wedding at Garrison, New York.

This was weighty stuff, and so were the magazines—an average of 100 pages an issue compared with about 30 when it was still a weekly. Advertising poured in: full pages from Armour Toilet Soap

("The gardens of the world pay tribute"); J. M. Gidding & Co. Women's Apparel ("To establish a permanent institution in which the women of New York will place their confidence"); Goodyear Welt shoes ("brings within the reach of millions one of the comforts of yesterday's millionaire"); Franklin Simon & Co. ("Smart Coats"); Athena Underwear ("the fitted seat—the most important feature ever devised for use on undergarments"); Renard Millinery ("exclusive foreign models"); Forsythe ("the largest waist house in the world"); Plexo Cream ("You need it for a perfect complexion"); and Reiling & Schoen ("The poplin by which all others are judged").

These all appeared during 1910, Nast's first full year as publisher. The competition (fifteen-cent monthly women's magazines that covered fashion) included *Ladies' Home Journal* (whose big story in 1910 was a serial by Mrs. Humphry Ward, the Barbara Cartland of her day), with a circulation of 1,305,030 that year; *The Delineator,* edited from 1907 to 1910 by Theodore Dreiser and hence more literary during that period than the others, with a circulation of 750,000; *Woman's Home Companion,* carrying practical sewing and house-building articles as well as the lively food columns of Fannie Farmer, with a circulation of 698,568; and *Harper's Bazar* (still without the second *a*), more markedly slanted toward Society, with a circulation of 140,000. (*Good Housekeeping,* which also covered fashion, was the only one of these published in a small format, and therefore attracted different advertisers.) The circulation of all these magazines, apart from *Harper's Bazar,* placed them in the mass-market category. And yet, during the first six months of 1910, *Vogue* carried 44 percent more pages of advertising than its closest competitor, *Ladies' Home Journal;* 78 percent more than *Woman's Home Companion;* 138 percent more than *The Delineator;* and 292 percent more than *Harper's Bazar.* This is all the more amazing when one considers that *Vogue's* circulation that year was only 30,000! (It did not reach 100,000 until 1918.)

Moreover, Nast's advertising did not come cheap. He charged

advertisers $10.00 per thousand readers (a marketing formula based on the circulation of a magazine to establish its advertising value) for the privilege of buying a full page in *Vogue*. This was a staggering fee in the early 1900s—most mass-market magazines, such as *McCall's,* charged $2.00 or at the most $3.00 per thousand. Nast argued that the power of his page, which was read by precisely the audience the advertisers wished to reach, was worth the extra money. *"Vogue,"* he explained in 1933, "is the elimination of waste circulation for the advertiser of quality goods. I determined to bait the editorial pages in such a way as to lift out of all the millions of Americans just the 100,000 cultivated people who can buy these quality goods."

The competition was decidedly rattled by these alarmingly successful tactics, so much so that in September 1910, *Ladies' Home Journal* decided, like *Vogue,* to publish twice a month.

Nast was unmoved. In the last quarter of 1910 he added three new services to *Vogue*: an educational bureau, a Christmas Shopping bureau, and a Reader's Correspondence Service, an expanded question-and-answer column. His vigorous promotion included subscription campaigns in all the Junior Leagues across the country. One of his boasts was that every name in the *Social Register* was a *Vogue* subscriber.

On January 3, 1911, he sent his advertisers a letter:

> *As for progress in the periodical itself,* there are many who say that *Vogue*, in its unique influence over its readers, in its editorial selection, in the very intelligence and artistic quality of its make-up, and in the superiority of its physical appearance, dominates its field as does no other periodical.
>
> *As for advertising*: In the year 1910, *Vogue* has carried 573,075 lines of advertising—184,075 more lines than its nearest competitor. Its increase alone for this month [December 1910 over December 1909] is 90 percent and this increase is larger than the entire December patronage of any other woman's publication!
>
> *As for circulation*: *Vogue*'s subscription list has doubled; its newsstand sales have tripled.

MEN and women who appreciate quality and distinctive richness wear McCallum Silk Hosiery. They find it the most trustworthy silk hosiery manufactured today. In all grades upwards from $1, at the best dealers everywhere. Send for booklet "Through My Lady's Ring."

McCallum Hosiery Company
Northampton, Mass.

Mc Callum Silk Hosiery

*Vogue*'s advertisements were carefully geared to the magazine's upscale demographic profile. *Vogue*, April 1913, January 1914.

Those who used *Vogue* on my first invitation eighteen months ago did so largely through faith in my ability "to deliver the goods." Those who came in five months ago did so on a mixture of faith and fact. *Now I ask you to come in on fact alone. . . .*

And they did. As evidence of the confidence exuding from every corner of the *Vogue* offices (which had moved to 443 Fourth Avenue in the first flush of success), March 1911 saw the announcement that Condé Nast, who had already bought an interest in two other magazines, *House & Garden* (circulation: 24,000) and *Travel* (circulation: 30,000), was entering into a new partnership with his old friend and colleague Robert Collier. Together they purchased a monthly periodical called *The Housekeeper,* formerly published in Minneapolis and now to be published in New York under the firm name of Collier & Nast. *The Housekeeper* had a circulation of 375,000, and a yearly advertising revenue of $200,000. It is possible that Nast, with Collier's financial help, acquired *The Housekeeper* only to obtain its subscription list for his fledgling *House & Garden*—a common practice among publishers of expanding magazines—since he closed it down a year later. Of his other two acquisitions, *Travel* reverted to Nast's copublisher, Robert M. McBride, in 1915, and *House & Garden* went on to become second only to *Vogue* in Nast's great publishing empire.

Behind the dramatic rise in circulation and advertising claimed by *Vogue* lay a strategy carefully mapped out by Nast four years before he took possession of the journal. His policy was expressed in typically simple, direct terms: "*Vogue* is the technical adviser—the consulting specialist—to the woman of fashion in the matter of her clothes and of her personal adornment."

In fashion, until the decline of haute couture after the Second World War, everything that happened, happened in Paris. The first duty of *Vogue*, therefore, was faithfully to report the fashion news from Paris—the new season's modes from the great couture houses, with drawings (later photographs) and fabric descriptions. Obtaining this material was complicated. All the sketches were done by French artists in Paris and had to be shipped, with accompanying copy, to New York in time for appearance in the earliest possible issue. Every two weeks there would be the familiar sight at the New York docks of several elegant young women, hatted and gloved, waiting agitatedly for the artwork to be unloaded and then rushing back to the office to prepare the material for publication.

In addition to reporting on the couture, *Vogue* felt an obligation to report to the woman of fashion what other women of fashion were doing and wearing, which necessitated in every issue a series of pages covering Newport, Southampton, Aiken, Tuxedo Park, Palm Beach, and the other places where people played and were rich together. ("Oh, good," Nast would say when a *Vogue* editor blew in from a weekend in Newport. "What were the chauffeurs wearing?") London news was always important, since the English were considered the height of fashion, particularly if they had titles. Features on parties, theatre news, summer menus, and views "As Seen By Him" all helped the woman of fashion keep up with the fast pace of New York society. No fiction ever appeared; publishing it would have been against Nast's policy of restricting circulation, as fiction tended to attract an indiscriminate audience suitable to mass-market periodicals.

One of the most controversial items retained by Nast was the Vogue Pattern Service. Many people, including members of the staff, felt that Vogue patterns were really a little infra dig in this class-conscious magazine—paper patterns lowered the tone, implying that *Vogue* readers were too poor to buy a Poiret or a Vionnet gown.

Nast passionately disagreed. After all, he knew the magic to be conjured up from dress patterns. "It is the avowed mission of *Vogue*," he wrote, "to appeal not merely to women of great wealth, but more fundamentally, to women of taste. A certain proportion of these readers will be found, necessarily, among the less well-to-do cousins of the rich—women who not only belong rightfully to society, but who may in fact lead very fashionable lives, and, with their limited incomes, such women must look as well dressed as their affluent companions."

Nast knew enough about upper-class women to know that, how-

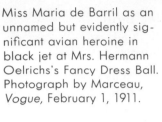

Miss Maria de Barril as an unnamed but evidently significant avian heroine in black jet at Mrs. Hermann Oelrichs's Fancy Dress Ball. Photograph by Marceau, *Vogue*, February 1, 1911.

Vogue Patterns sold smartness, exclusivity, and value—"the royal road to economy as well as style." *Vogue*, October 1, 1912.

ever rich they were, they enjoyed practicing thrift, or rather, the clever management of their resources. Indeed, sometimes the greater the wealth, the greater the frugality. The fashion rightness of Vogue patterns appealed to their taste as well as to their pocketbooks. When people criticized his retention of the pattern service over the years, Nast liked to tell this story: He was about to leave a party one evening when he was stopped by Mrs. Theodore Roosevelt, who said, "Do please wait a minute. You must see the evening wrap that I am about to put on—it was made from a Vogue pattern." Then she proceeded to tell Nast that Vogue patterns had played an important part in the wardrobes of her children and of herself.

More important than all of this, however, was the role of patterns in the lives of women who lived outside of New York. Vogue patterns were an essential concession to provincial subscribers. Copied slavishly, they allowed these women to feel that they, too, were people of fashion, in tune with the Mode.

*Vogue*'s early success was due largely to its unique power as disseminator of fashion to a class readership, aided by Condé Nast's energetic and innovative promotional work. After all, he had been planning it for four years. No advertising material had ever before spelled out so many percentages, linages, or circulation figures. Some space buyers were dazzled by the impressive statistics with which Nast peppered his letters; others were shocked by these tactics. In 1920, the business manager of *Century* magazine, then the most successful class publication outside of *Vogue,* told Nast he was making a big mistake in publishing circulation figures, and that he was lowering *Vogue*'s dignity by doing so. The man was off the mark by several zeros—*Vogue*'s profits increased from $5,000 in 1909 to $150,000 in 1915, $400,000 in 1920, and $650,000 in 1929. Circulation had risen from 30,000 in 1909 to 141,424 at the end of 1928.

In June, 1913, an article by Condé Nast appeared in the *Merchants' and Manufacturers' Journal,* a Baltimore trade publication; it was entitled "Class Publications," and in it, Nast spelled out the

testament that turned *Vogue* into one of the great publishing successes of the twentieth century:

> Even if we grant for the sake of argument that "all men are created
> equal," as the Declaration of Independence so bravely sets forth,
> we must admit in the same breath that they overcome this equality
> with astonishing rapidity. Among the 90,000,000 inhabitants of
> the United States, as a matter of fact, there is a lack of "equal-
> ity"—a range and variety of man and womankind—that simply
> staggers the imagination; every degree of learning from the man
> who prefers to read his Testament in the original Greek to the man
> who can't read anything in any language, every degree of wealth
> from the readers of *The Wall Street Journal* to those of *The War
> Cry* [the Salvation Army's magazine].
>
> Moreover, this vast population divides not only along the lines of
> wealth, education, and refinement, but classifies itself even more
> strongly along lines of interests. . . . And a "class publication" is
> nothing more nor less than a publication that looks for its circula-
> tion *only* to those having in common a certain characteristic
> marked enough to group them into a class. That common charac-
> teristic may be almost anything: religion; a particular line of busi-
> ness; community of residence; common pursuit; or some common
> interest. When I say a class publication "looks" to one of these
> classes for its circulation, I state it very mildly; as a matter of fact,
> the publisher, the editor, the advertising manager and circulation
> man must conspire not only to get all their readers from the one
> particular class to which the magazine is dedicated, *but rigorously
> to exclude all others.*

Nast himself underlined the last words, knowing full well how
they flew in the face of the principle adhered to by the most important and successful magazine publisher in America prior to Nast's
arrival on the scene, Cyrus H. K. Curtis. Curtis, publisher of the
*Ladies' Home Journal* and later *The Saturday Evening Post,* believed in circulation, more circulation, and still more circulation. In
1925, he made a profit of $17 million on circulation. But Nast knew
it was not the only way.

Today, his words seem so obvious as to be trite. The proliferation of special-interest, restricted-circulation magazines in the twentieth century is powerful evidence of Nast's remarkable insight.

Not everybody understood immediately what he meant by "class." Because he selected as his class the upper classes, people thought "class" publications meant "classy" publications, and hence attributed to him merely the bright idea of aiming advertising at the upper classes. This, of course, he did, and it turned out to be just as good an idea as all his others, since the class he chose was a large, hitherto untapped market of people who had more money to spend on consumer goods than any other group. But it was the idea of class *qua* restricted readership that expressed most accurately his revolutionary theory.

The clever corollary of class publishing was that it enabled his magazines to attract readers *who did not yet belong to the class which he had chosen, but who aspired to it.* Just as people who wanted to buy a car but did not yet own one might subscribe to *The Automobile and Motor Age,* so people who wanted to enter Society but had not yet the wherewithal to do so would read *Vogue* and take instruction. Nast, unlike some of his fellow Americans, never doubted that class (in the social sense) existed in the United States. By publishing a periodical for people of breeding, he was defining—for himself, for his advertisers, and for a generation of Americans—precisely what constituted the American upper class. The fact that advertisers responded as they did is proof enough that such a class was anthropologically and sociologically identifiable, and that their behavior, manners, clothes, and customs could be accurately chronicled in the pages of a journal.

Even the briefest glimpse at *Vogue*'s advertising in the 1910s confirms this conclusion: "Fleur de Lis: handmade blouses—the certain choice of the gentlewoman of aristocratic charm in dress"; "What beautiful paper! I didn't know George had such good taste"; "Who were her people? Amidst any amount of expensive display, the quiet refinement of good breeding stands out loud and clear"; "The new perfume by Houbigant, La Belle Saison, is the odeur of the patrician taste."

In the first decade of Nast's ownership, the most important

words in *Vogue* were "taste" and "breeding." In the twenties and thirties, the only word that counted was "smart." *Vogue* quickly assimilated the changes that took place in the social hierarchy. The one standard that remained constant—that made his class publications continue to appeal to the right class—was the standard of excellence. Nast may have been the first to invoke that ideal, but it was his editor, a woman as remote from Society, in the class sense, as an Eskimo, whose integrity and pursuit of the highest quality embodied *Vogue* as Nast had envisioned it.

# SIX

# WAR À LA MODE

Edna Woolman Chase was displeased. She was displeased with the French couture, a frequent occurrence during the early days of her editorship of *Vogue*. France had become the dominant force in European fashion since Worth (an Englishman) founded the first modern haute-couture firm in Paris in 1858. While the mass-produced clothes industry was flourishing in both Europe and America, couture—individual models created, for the most part, by male dressmakers and shown as a collection to prospective buyers—was an exclusively French notion.

This emergence of two fashions—capitalist couture from France and proletarian ready-mades—received quick acceptance in the United States, and nineteenth-century American fashion magazines such as *Godey's Lady's Book* and *Demorest's* used French fashion illustrations almost exclusively. Most New York houses imported their gowns; home-grown couturiers struggled in vain to gain acceptance for their designs, competing with the brilliant extravagances of Worth, Doucet, Redfern, Vionnet, and the great Paul Poiret. Their unquestioned supremacy did not make them easy to work with. The French couture, in Mrs. Chase's candid opinion, was "wearing, complex and illogical." French designers before 1914 were obsessed by one fear—that other people would copy their fabulous, unique, and absolutely exclusive designs. Yet they naturally craved fame and recognition throughout the world, which meant having their fabulous, unique, and absolutely exclusive designs published in *Vogue*. It was an impossible situation. Paul Poiret, the outstanding genius of French couture at the time, had recently visited New York and had seen his precious models being sold in American stores, with or without his label, at ridiculously low prices. *Quel horreur!* "No more reproduction of our designs," went up the cry in Paris.

Of course *Vogue* without Poiret was as inconceivable as Mrs. Vanderbilt without her headband. The magazine would expire instantly. So Mrs. Chase, Condé Nast, and their new European representative, Philippe Ortiz, got together with Poiret to see what could be done about the problem. The result was Le Syndicat de Défense de la Grande Couture Française (The Protective Association of French Dressmakers), which was officially formed on June 14, 1914, with Poiret as president, Jacques Worth as vice-president, and Paquin, Chéruit, Callot Soeurs, Rodier, and Bianchini among the members. The association aimed to "bring to an end the counterfeiting of the labels and the illicit use of their names, thereby protecting the American public and honest importers from the false representations made by unscrupulous merchants and manufacturers." The members could not prevent individual dressmakers from copying their designs—nobody has ever been able to do that. But they could prevent their labels being indiscriminately attached to mass-produced clothes sold at bargain prices. French couture was mollified.

Edna Chase had done it again. Throughout her long career at *Vogue,* her energy, quick thinking, toughness, and high standards cut through the emotional bureaucracy that dominated the fashion world, and earned her lasting glory as Defender of the Mode.

Edna Chase, like Condé Nast, came from less than grand beginnings. Born Edna Alloway in Asbury Park, New Jersey, in 1877, she was raised there by her Quaker grandparents. Her ancestors on her mother's side were the Quaker Woolmans who landed in the United States in 1678, and they included the author John Woolman, of whom she was very proud. When she grew up, Edna joined her mother and stepfather in New York, and found her first job in the circulation department of Arthur Turnure's *Vogue* in 1895, when she was eighteen. By the time Condé Nast bought the magazine, Edna Chase was one of the longest-serving members of the staff. In those days, she was referred to as Mrs. Francis Dane Chase, in view of her marriage to a charming but irresponsible Bostonian, from whom she was soon divorced. They had one daughter, Ilka Chase, who later became famous as an actress, writer, and wit.

One of the terms of the magazine's sale was that Mrs. Turnure and the Harrison family should take a number of shares in Nast's Vogue Company. They decided to take only preferred stock, but when the common stock paid a 20 percent dividend a few years later and *Vogue* profits were seen to be accumulating, Mrs. Turnure (who had since married Frederick Stimson), brought a suit against Nast for "lack of consideration." Nast hired a young lawyer called MacDonald DeWitt to take his case, and shortly afterward the suit was dismissed. Two good things came out of this unpleasant experience. Nast found a new friend in his lawyer, DeWitt, who joined the company and stayed for the rest of his life; and it precipitated the departure of the editor, Marie Harrison, who naturally enough had sided with her sister, Mrs. Stimson, in the legal battle. The way was thus left clear for Edna Woolman Chase to take over the reins, and on February 1, 1914, she was listed for the first time as editor of *Vogue.*

It was not necessarily an obvious choice. Mrs. Chase had no previous editorial experience; there were other people on the staff who were possibly as well qualified; and she had no social prominence whatsoever.

Condé Nast, however, knew exactly what he was doing. His instinct for hiring the right person at the right time was unerring, and Edna Woolman Chase in many ways *became Vogue.* She was its firm and constant guiding light for fifty years. In 1923, the thirtieth anniversary of the founding of *Vogue*, Condé paid tribute to his friend and colleague:

> There are few women, I think, whose character and tastes are more essentially feminine; and yet there are few men who bring to the solving of business problems keener insight, broader vision or clearer thinking than the woman who has stood so diligently watching over the pages of *Vogue* during the passing years. . . . Few people realize the variety of talents required in an editor. It is not only a literary or journalistic problem, or one dependent on good taste in the selection of drawings and photographs. It is a problem involving all of these qualities, to be sure, but added to them there must be a genius for organization, a practical knowledge of advertising, and unfailing tact in the management of the personnel. I am satisfied that in Mrs. Chase are combined these rare and seemingly contrary qualities, and it has been because of her ability in all of these special directions that we have been able to build up a periodical that appears twice a month on four continents and in three different languages.

Edna Woolman Chase was a small, birdlike woman with prematurely gray hair that was dyed a delicate shade of blue and frizzed on top of her little head like a powder puff. This, however, was the only soft part of her. Employees remember the hard parts better. "She had emerald-green eyes that saw through you and rejected what they saw there." "When she was with a man, she was always the one who got the taxi." These were the kinds of comments she inspired. Her editorial meetings were battlegrounds, where she confronted editors with their inadequacies and failings. (Whether this is what Nast meant by "unfailing tact" is doubtful.)

Mrs. Chase made great demands on her staff. They had to wear black silk stockings, white gloves, and hats—and never, never open-toed shoes. (She once made a speech about the horrors of open-toed shoes that sent tremors through every shoe manufacturer in the country.) When she hired Marya Mannes, at eighteen, she said to her, "You have a very fine pen, my child, but we must do

Edna Woolman Chase looking properly dignified in a portrait by Steichen after being honored as a Chevalier of the Legion of Honor by the French Government. *Vogue*, November 15, 1935.

something about your clothes." (When Marya Mannes left, rather abruptly, to follow a romance to Italy, her father, the musician David Mannes, wrote to Mrs. Chase, thanking her for her kindness to Marya and for developing her character and resources. "A fine letter," Condé Nast noted. "I got along well with Mrs. Chase," Miss Mannes said later. "She was properly demanding and precise, and had stability, calm, and judgment.") An editor once tried to commit suicide by throwing herself under a subway train. When the woman finally went back to work, Mrs. Chase summoned her. "We at *Vogue* don't throw ourselves under subway trains, my dear," she told her. "If we must, we take sleeping pills."

Her treatment of outside contributors was equally uncompromising, and her rejection letters would have made the toughest spirits wilt. Here is her reply to Caroline Duer, dowager society reporter who wrote the first *Vogue Book of Etiquette*: "At last I have gotten around to reading your 'Wine at Table' and 'Tell-Tale Tongues.' We can use the 'Wine at Table,' but the 'Tell-Tale Tongues' does not seem to me to be terribly interesting material. All the youngsters say it is a little preachy and that the examples are not very well chosen for their generation. . . ."

And to Howard Greer, a well-known Hollywood photographer, she wrote the following little note: "I have taken one look at the photographs of my daughter and am returning them to you, with my shudders! I do not think that they are good enough for publication. The clothes look interesting, but the photographs, no."

It is possible to guess at the causes of Mrs. Chase's forays into sadism. She suffered all her life from the age-old problem of class inferiority, and working in a world constructed on elitism, luxury, and money only aggravated the affliction. Although in private life she was a warm and fair-minded woman, the sight of a series of well-born, well-bred, well-heeled young editors lounging languidly over their typewriters at *Vogue* must have irritated her intensely. Quaker roots go deep.

None of this, of course, detracted from her genius as an editor. Like Harold Ross of *The New Yorker*, she demanded clarity at all times. If she couldn't understand it, she said, how could her readers? The fashion writing had to be as thorough as possible—you described everything, including what the reader could not see. If a dress and jacket were shown, the dress sleeves and waist had to be explained; if only the front view of a dress was shown, then the buttons down the back had to be described.

Mrs. Chase's editorials were unsparing, even stern: "The cloche is preeminently a hat for the youthful face—a hat for the woman who can afford to have her hair hidden, her eyes played down, her mouth and chin and the structure of her head emphasized at the expense of everything else. . . ." Or, "*Vogue*—surely as sophisticated, as modern, as shock proof as one can well be without sacrificing good taste—has come to a place where it actually holds up its hands in horror. And the place, to come directly to the point, is the knee of the woman of today. . . . *Vogue* does not insist that skirts should be long, since long skirts are not the mode. But *Vogue* does insist that, before buying a [new French] frock, one should look oneself squarely in the legs and temper the length of one's costume to the shape one sees."

Woe betide the less-than-youthful woman who had bought a closetful of cloche hats, or who allowed *Vogue* to catch a glimpse of a less-than-perfect knee!

Mrs. Chase's eagle eye missed nothing. Not even the most dignified of social personages escaped her judgment. "One notices that the cloche holds its own for sports at Palm Beach," one of her editorials ran, "that both Mrs. Frelinghuysen and Miss Byrne are wearing the Peel model shoe in brown leather or in white; that the universal parasol at Palm Beach is still Japanese in feeling despite those of black velvet or of taffeta launched by Paris." How many mortified Palm Beachers consigned their Japanese parasols to oblivion at Mrs. Chase's words! Poor Mrs. William K. Vanderbilt, Jr., photographed for a 1922 story entitled "Society Wears Clothes Like These In the Country," resembled a New York bag lady, wearing a shapeless old hat and *two* coats, "the under one of tweed with a raccoon collar, the outer one of broadcloth." Having used up her inspiration thus far, the caption writer, evidently at a loss, was reduced to finishing with, "Her felt hat is simple."

When Mrs. Chase met her daughter, Ilka, returning by train from her boarding school, her *Vogue* eye was as sharp as ever, even in her role as mother. Appalled by how poorly turned-out the girls from Farmington and Foxcroft appeared as they passed through the train station, she wasted no time in assigning a *Vogue* editor to the subject of what well-bred young ladies should be wearing at boarding school.

Like Condé, Edna Chase was a fast learner. She may not have belonged to the rich, fashionable world for whom she was editing the magazine, but she wasted no time in knowing everything there was to know about it. And throughout her reign, it was her taste (and Condé's) that dominated the magazine. "I cannot control the taste of our readers," she declared, "but I will not show editorially merchandise that I myself do not think is correct."

In later years, this position became more and more difficult to maintain as department stores and manufacturers, who spent large sums of money advertising in *Vogue*, expected a generous quid pro quo in the editorial section of the magazine. When the magazine fell on hard times during the Depression, this tacit agreement became particularly important; in 1934, for instance, Bergdorf Goodman spent $16,065 for 15¾ pages in *Vogue*, while *Vogue* gave Bergdorf Goodman 61¼ pages of editorial space, which represented, at current advertising rates, a value of $62,475. Saks Fifth Avenue spent $9,180 for 9 pages in *Vogue*, while *Vogue* gave SFA 66½ pages of editorial space, which represented a value of $67,830. But the separation of editorial from advertising continued to be one of the most strongly held principles of Condé Nast's staff:

"As I see the function of *Vogue*," Mrs. Chase said, "it is to produce a magazine of fashion, authority, information and beauty for our readers, and to make it as valuable a medium as possible in which advertisers may present their own messages to our readers. We are responsible for the merchandise that we select from the shops and we are responsible for the manner in which we present it to our readers, and we are equipped to do this work editorially, but we are not equipped in this capacity in the Advertising Department." This was Nast's view in a nutshell.

The working relationship between Nast and Chase was ideal. (If it was ever other than a working one, that was quickly sublimated to their real true love—*Vogue*.) She was painstaking, hard-working, and a perfectionist. "Whatever you did in life, Edna, you'd be thorough about it," he said to her once. "Have you noticed how in hotels, maids, if they dust at all, dust around things? You wouldn't do that. If a person moved anything in a room you took care of it would be dusted underneath."

This remark is as illuminating about Nast as it is about Chase. Their obsessions meshed perfectly—and the beneficiary was the magazine. No private life interfered with late-night conferences if such conferences were necessary for the health of *Vogue*. Their dinners together were countless—and thrifty. They used to go to the Automat, which he loved, or another favorite cafeteria. "Come on, Edna, let's go and have a quick and dirty," he would say as they trotted off happily together to line up at Horn & Hardart. In later years, their correspondence reads like that of a long-married couple fitting as comfortably together as a pair of old shoes. "Dearest Condé, I do hope you are having a chance to get in a few licks of fun and a little rest. . . . I send you worlds of love," runs a typical salutation from Edna.

Not that she had an entirely easy time of it with her employer. She may have had a flair for fashion, but he was a lawyer by training and cautious by temperament. She had to fight to get him to accept some of her more revolutionary ideas. One of the earliest—and perhaps one of the most far-reaching in its effects—involved the netting of Mrs. Stuyvesant Fish.

It all came about because of the outbreak of the First World War, that tiresome European engagement that threatened to close down French couture once and for all, sending ripples of panic into the drawing rooms of New York town houses and intimations of financial doom into the offices of *Vogue*.

Mrs. Chase, alarmed at the possibility of blank pages in her beloved magazine, cast around for alternative fashion editorial material, and lit upon the startling idea that New York itself might provide it. After all, New York had *some* designers—not of the caliber of Poiret, Worth, Chéruit, and the other Parisians, of course, but nevertheless designers who could at least produce a presentable frock.

Mrs. Chase went to Henri Bendel, whose shop was patronized by the most elegant ladies in town, and asked him if he would exhibit some original designs in a fashion show organized by *Vogue*. She knew that if he agreed, the other good houses would also agree. Bendel consented, so now Mrs. Chase had a list of New York fashion designers who would contribute to a fashion show. Her vision was that *Vogue* would organize it as a European war benefit, sponsored by all the great ladies of New York. The results, of course, would fill the pages of *Vogue* with wonderful local fashion copy.

Benefits of one sort or another were nothing new in New York society. But a *fashion* benefit was something else entirely. In those days one never discussed one's dressmakers, let alone appeared in public in their company. The idea of live models showing off clothes in front of ladies of breeding smacked somehow of commerce. And here was Edna Chase hoping to persuade a goodly number of these ladies to become patronesses of this dubious venture.

"You'll never get really smart women interested in this," Condé told her firmly. "They wouldn't dream of it; it has too much to do with trade." But he allowed as how he would support her idea if she managed to secure the names of enough patronesses to make the show a possibility.

Mrs. Chase, like all good fund raisers, decided to go straight to the top. And the top of New York society was indubitably Mrs. Stuyvesant Fish. Formerly Marion G. Anthon, after her marriage to Stuyvesant Fish in 1876 she took it upon herself to ginger up a society that had become so rigid in its rituals and etiquette that most members appeared to be either bored or dead. A witty, energetic, and strong-willed lady (one of the original backers of Turnure's *Vogue*), she displaced the old fop Ward McAllister as social arbiter and startled Mrs. William Astor out of her overstuffed seat by abandoning their rules of decorum and ceremonial. Mrs. Fish introduced society to the fifty-minute dinner instead of the interminable formal occasions previously insisted upon; she boldly served one

Mrs. Stuyvesant Fish, a substantial quality notwithstanding, courageously appeared as Queen of the Fairies at her famous Mother Goose Ball in Newport the year this portrait was taken. Photograph by Aimé Dupont, *Vogue*, September 1, 1913.

wine at the meal instead of the obligatory five; she replaced staid string orchestras with jazz bands; and she showed the world that living well could be fun instead of dull. (The house the Fishes bought in 1887, 19 Gramercy Park, redesigned by Stanford White to suit the owners' new brand of entertaining, was later owned by a twentieth-century purveyor of images, if not of class—the high priest of public relations, Benjamin Sonnenberg, who once said he wanted to be a cross between Otto Kahn and . . . Condé Nast. He became Nast's PR man in the thirties.)

Mrs. Fish's ability to bend convention according to her whim became legendary. At about the time Mrs. Chase was preparing to approach her, she gave a large dinner party at The Crossways, her cottage in Newport. Among the guests that evening were Bishop Darlington and the German ambassador, Count von Bernstorff. She seated the bishop on her right and the ambassador on her left. After the dinner, various social personages, pale with horror, asked her how she had the nerve to put the ambassador on her left. "Don't you know that Count von Bernstorff represents the Kaiser and all the German people?" "Perfectly," replied Mrs. Fish. "But please don't forget that Bishop Darlington represents God and all the angels."

Mrs. Fish lived in Garrison, New York—sometimes irreverently called The Fisheries or The Aquarium because of its association with the Fish family, and it was there that Edna Chase repaired with trepidation, to confront the woman whose lemon-sour expression and statuesque appearance confirmed her reputation as formidable. On arrival at the Fish mansion, Mrs. Chase was told by Mrs. Fish's secretary that Mrs. Fish was sorry, but Mrs. Fish felt that the subject at issue was not of interest to her and so Mrs. Fish did not wish to see the editor of *Vogue* at all.

Mrs. Chase was stunned, for she knew this message spelled the death of her plan. Without Mrs. Fish, there was little chance of attracting any little minnows. But by the greatest good fortune, it turned out that Mrs. Fish's secretary had a son who was an artist, and who happened to be frightfully keen on getting his work published in *Vogue*, and was there just the slightest chance that Mrs.

Chase might be able to help? Well, of course there was, and furthermore was it not a shame that Mrs. Fish was unable to see her way to
supporting her own national dress industry, and war-torn Europe, at
a time when they so desperately needed her? Indeed it was, said the
secretary, and she would this minute rush back to Mrs. Fish and
speak to her again about the matter.

Picture then, the unlikely but tender *tableau vivant* of Mrs. Fish
and Mrs. Chase eyeball to eyeball in Mrs. Fish's rose garden, during
which the smaller shrewd party succeeded in persuading the taller
shrewd party that the fashion show could be turned into a worthy
occasion for all New York society. At the end of the meeting Mrs.
Fish was already making plans to reach Mrs. Astor immediately.
"She will certainly be a patroness, and so will the others. Can't afford not to."

On November 1, 1914, *Vogue* announced that a fashion fete
would take place on November 4, 5, and 6, at the Ritz-Carlton
Hotel, New York:

> An exhibition of Original Models by the leading New York design-
> ers; under the auspices of *Vogue*. Heretofore, imported gowns have
> been so greatly favored that American designers have had little in-
> centive to create, and no opportunity to launch, their own designs.
> This Fete in New York will give these dressmakers a recognized
> occasion, equal in brilliancy to the famous Paris openings, for dis-
> playing their best new models of the present season. . . . Proceeds
> from this exhibition will go to the Committee of Mercy to relieve
> the women and children in every nation left destitute by the Euro-
> pean War. Price, three dollars for each exhibition.

The list of patronesses sounds like a roll call from the *Social
Register:* Astor, Belmont, Bishop, Bliss, Burden, Eustis, Harriman,
Hoyt, Iselin, Lydig, Mills, Peabody, Tailer, Townsend, Vanderbilt,
and Whitney were some of the women who jumped at Mrs. Fish's
summons, and found themselves for the first time mingling socially
with such commercial names as Bendel, Gunther, Tappé, Maison
Jacquelin, and Bergdorf Goodman. Since modeling as a profession
did not yet exist in America, models were taken from the dressmak-

ing establishments and had to be specially trained to walk the runway and show off the clothes.

Emily Post, who wrote an article about the event for *Vogue*, described the scene:

> Everyone leaned forward and talked to everyone else, and it was quite amusingly novel to bow on one side to a prominent hostess and on the other to Miss Dorothy, whom one had thought of hitherto only in connection with new gowns and as disassociated from anything in the least resembling the good-looking man she was presenting as "my husband . . ."
>
> As the procession of manikins, each announced by Miss Vogue, began, a dowager, whose own walk sways from side to side—but upon perfectly sound foundations—watched a particularly writhing dipper, fascinated by her collapsing progress. "Katherine," she whispered, "mark that model on the program. I think it is too sweet for words. I am going to get Félice to order one like it for me instead of taking that stodgy old model she wanted me to take."
>
> Each woman in the audience delightedly applauded her own dressmaker, heart and hand, and each had a rather protective feeling toward the Estelle, or Mary, or Rose, who wore the dresses of the establishment she patronized most, and Rose, Mary, and Estelle as they saw the faces of the women before whom they were accustomed to exhibit gowns, smiled a delighted recognition.

The fete took up eleven pages of the December 1, 1914, issue of *Vogue*, with fifty-seven models shown (others of the 125 designs appeared in the next issue), including a splendid ensemble of silver cloth and lace studded with pearls and rhinestones by Mollie O'Hara entitled "Vive La France." Three more pages were devoted to the fashionable people who attended the historic event, with the accompanying article by Emily Post, who declared: "It was an extraordinary achievement—all of it; for Fashion, meaning clothes, and Fashion, meaning the smart world, were represented, as they should be, together."

All in all, Edna Chase had garnered seventeen fashion pages for

*Vogue* out of her little idea. She had also invented the first charity fashion show, an event so familiar today that it is difficult to realize the sensation it caused all those years ago in the Ritz-Carlton Hotel, when client and dressmaker recognized each other in public for the very first time.

The New York fashion fete was also the first major recognition by the fashionable world that something unpleasant was really going on in Europe. In America, the war seemed remote. Once Mrs. Chase's fears about the disappearance of French couture had proved to be unfounded ("Women must have clothes, war or no war," announced Madame Chéruit, "and those who make them must have a way to earn their living. We shall keep open and make what we can"), such pressing matters as Isadora Duncan's latest tour, the arrival of the permanent wave, and Baron de Meyer's debut as an interior decorator were still the main topics of discussion.

Yet the mood of Paris, to which Americans so sensitively responded, was hardly one of idle gaiety. Poiret, Worth, and Doeuillet had joined the French army; the streets were full of soldiers; the terrible fact of wholesale slaughter was on everybody's mind. "When the head of a [couture] house was not away on affairs of war," wrote a *Vogue* correspondent in September 1914, "his assistants were; his designers were enlisting; his little sewing girls were with the Red Cross or he had set them to work in his ateliers making bandages; his vendeuses were with their families, helping in the preparations for war; approached on business, they could only weep." Condé Nast, his French blood aroused, perhaps, continued, with Mrs. Chase, to fill *Vogue* with articles about the terrible events devastating Europe: "American Women Who Are First in War," with photographs of such ladies as Mrs. Paris Singer, the Duchess of Marlborough, Lady Randolph Churchill, and Mrs. John Astor, who headed up the American Women's War Relief Fund in London; "War and the Social Map" ("Not by Neutrality, But by Patriotism for the Country of Her Husband Does the American Woman Who Has Married a Foreigner Meet the New Conditions"), which in-

A striking black-and-white-striped flowered taffeta gown by O'Hara entitled "Le Printemps," modeled at the first American Fashion Fete. The shiny cerise hat with bunch of grapes is from Waters & Co. *Vogue,* December 1, 1914.

"Lavish" was the word originally used by *Vogue* to describe this flaring broadtail coat trimmed with silver fox, also shown at the 1914 New York Fashion Fete, by Revillon Frères. *Vogue,* December 1, 1914.

cluded German as well as Allied wives; "C'est La Guerre" ("In the intensified darkness which now descends upon Paris at nightfall, people seldom venture out. The streets are too gloomy").

These constant reminders were hardly the kind of material that would have allowed Mrs. Stuyvesant Fish and her cronies to sleep easier in their beds. In May 1915, Nast wrote an appeal to the readers of *Vogue* to support the Sewing Girls of Paris Fund, in which he said, "In accepting, on behalf of *Vogue,* the direction of this fund in America, I have been impelled not merely by that general sympathy the call of distress always awakens, but rather by the strong conviction that *Vogue*'s readers who, perhaps, have worn more French gowns that any group of women in the world, will, in coming to the aid of the sewing girls of Paris, recognize not only a welcome opportunity, but a definite and peculiar obligation." On the page following this message, Edna Chase described the plight of the *midinettes* and appealed for help to be sent to the treasurer of the fund, Henry Rogers Winthrop. As a result of their efforts, a check for one hundred thousand gold francs was later presented to the head of the workers' organization in Paris by Philippe Ortiz.

Condé Nast's motives were sound. They were also sound business. For the French couturiers, complex and emotional as always, were not altogether thrilled at the news that *Vogue* had sponsored a hugely successful New York fashion fete. *Vogue*'s great rival, *Harper's Bazar,* fanned the flames, sending envoys to Paris with the news that *Vogue* was no longer interested in the French couture and that the *Bazar,* therefore, was a much better publication in which to show their work. Several Paris houses responded by refusing entry to *Vogue*'s editors.

Nast had to act quickly. In addition to making a conciliatory move with the Sewing Girls of Paris Fund, he also offered to sponsor a French fashion fete in New York to show that his faith in Parisian couture was just as secure as ever. So in November 1915, a year after the first one, the Paris fashion fete, given as a benefit for the widows and orphans of French soldiers, took place, also at the Ritz-Carlton. Roger Boutet de Monvel, the French author, who had been commissioned by Paul Poiret to write a little dialogue to be read as the eighty models were presented, wrote a piece about the experience in a twenty-six-page feature on the fete in *Vogue*:

> In the eyes of an inexperienced man, I must admit, it is the retrospective and imaginative side of these costumes which appears most important. There passes by a dull black mantle, silent, almost tragic; instinctively, I think of Beardsley. Then comes a house gown in bright colors, and I think of Rackham's drawings. So I recall Venice, or the frescoes at Siena. But how many details escape me, details clever and charming, which make the grace and charm of these little creations!

After this, de Monvel, with his Gallic literary flourishes, became a frequent contributor to *Vogue*.

The "little creations" included models by Worth, Poiret, Paquin, Callot, Doucet, Jenny, Chéruit, and Lanvin. The entire Lanvin collection was bought by Bonwit Teller. B. Altman bought the Callot, Jenny, and Doucet collections, and Poiret, closed since the war began, provided fourteen specially made models that were all bought by John Wanamaker. Henri Bendel bought several Chéruits. In spite of this major support from the New York stores, the French fashion fete was not nearly so successful as the American one, and Nast had to bear a large part of the expenses. "The financial results were galling to the Gauls," wrote Mrs. Chase, punning with pleasure at the recollection.

By the time America joined the war, such diversions had become the Mode. In July 1917, an "As Seen By Him" column declared, "Now Is the Time To Remember That Army Officers Are Equalled Only by Navy Men As Dancers and To Brush Up on Military Etiquette." Him also warned his summer readers: "Bar Harbor will not have as many celebrations as in former years; and from the present outlook, there does not promise to be much yachting there during the summer. The majority of people, in a truly patriotic manner, have placed their yachts and power boats at the disposal of the government."

Society, it may safely be said, carried on bravely, trying to put a good face on things, doing its bit, and contributing to general morale. Mrs. Condé Nast was one of a large number of socially prominent matrons photographed at a meeting of the members of the New York Honour System of Voluntary Rationing, and conservation, the newest national sport, was the topic of every dinner party. "The most entertaining woman," reported *Vogue*, "is the one who tells the most interesting anecdotes of fireless furnaces, meatless roasts, and eatless days."

*Vogue*, in short, made the war smart. Once one knew that even the chicest Parisienne was making ends meet by wearing simpler clothes, adapting last year's couture models, and adding belts and scarves, it was possible to breathe easier with one's own little problems of servant shortages, heating failures, and no caviar.

In October 1918, *Vogue* published an article entitled "What War Has Done to Clothes." "Now that all women work, working clothes have acquired a new social status and chic, and even formal evening dress takes a more serious and practical view of life." The article carefully described the new practical dresses that did not require changing during the day; the home dinner gown to be worn after a hard day's work (what would now be called informal loungewear); dresses made of warm materials with long sleeves for coalless days; and uniforms, which allowed women for the first time to wear men's clothes. This essay, modestly placed in the middle of the magazine with a few pen-and-ink illustrations done by an anonymous artist, chronicled a landmark in the history of fashion.

Between them, Edna Woolman Chase and the First World War finally dethroned the French couture from its long dominion over the world of fashion. The dynastic succession of the great Paris houses endured, and their influence continued to dominate in Europe and America. But their absolute hegemony was challenged when *Vogue* introduced New York designers to the public, and was destroyed when the war changed forever the way women looked at clothes. (Perhaps recognition should also be given to Gabrielle Chanel, who introduced jersey cloth to the Mode in 1917 and whose simple chemises and suits launched the new democratic couture of the twenties.)

Edna Chase continued to regard Paris as the main inspiration for fashion and for the fashion pages of *Vogue*. A considerable part of her work involved the maintenance of some semblance of civility with French couture, since so much of the magazine depended on the free supply of news from the Paris houses. But things would never again be as they had been before the war. By giving *Vogue*'s imprimatur to New York dressmakers, Edna Woolman Chase not only gave the fashion industry a much-needed injection of bright young talent, but also showed Americans that their taste could be independent of Europe's; that New York could be just as brilliant as Paris; and that American designers could create a Mode that was not merely a pale copy of French and English traditions. The 1914–18 war was the end of many things, but it was the beginning of America's stylistic coming-of-age.

# SEVEN

# "THE COCKTAIL WITHOUT A PADLOCK"

In February 1913, a show of paintings opened at the Sixty-ninth Regiment Armory in New York City. The paintings had been collected from America and Europe, and most of the European ones had never been seen by Americans before. The works caused a sensation. "A harbinger of social anarchy," the show was called. Matisse and Brancusi were hung in effigy by Chicago art students. But the painting that provoked the most passionate controversy was Marcel Duchamp's "Nude Descending a Staircase." "I remember trying, in my capacity of unpaid press agent at the show," Frank Crowninshield later recalled, "to stem the indignation which the picture aroused, by hinting that there could be no possible harm in aesthetic experiments of this sort, and that, if the spectators would only try to view it as a figure in motion, rather than as one fixed inexorably in time and space, they might possibly derive great pleasure from it. But such arguments were of no avail; visitors—thousands of them every day—continued to question Duchamp's sanity and to heap upon his intriguing lady epithets of the rowdiest possible order."

Condé Nast knew very little about art, modern or otherwise. If he went to an art show, it was because he was invited to the opening. He was more interested in his magazine empire, which was expanding. The year of the infamous Armory Show, he bought from Doubleday, Page a fashion magazine called *Dress,* which he saw as a possible rival to his four-year success, *Vogue.* Not satisfied with the title *Dress,* he also bought, for $3,000, the name *Vanity Fair* from a little social and political journal published in the eighties and nineties that somewhat resembled the *Police Gazette.* The first issue of the new *Dress & Vanity Fair* came out in September 1913, containing articles on fashion, art, music, theatre, and international news considered too specialized for *Vogue.*

It is not known at whose house Condé Nast and Frank Crowninshield first met. Since Frank Crowninshield's circle covered nearly all of New York and most of Europe, it would have been surprising had they not bumped into one another sooner or later. Indeed, "Crowny has introduced everyone in this country who has ever been introduced, and in many cases he has introduced them to each other," a friend of his said.

Crowninshield had worked in magazines since 1895, when he was publisher of *The Bookman.* In 1900 he became assistant editor of *Metropolitan Magazine,* then assistant editor of *Munsey's* magazine, and in 1910 joined *The Century Illustrated Monthly Magazine* as art editor. He had also published, in 1912, a frivolous little book of etiquette entitled *Manners for the Metropolis,* in which he explained: "The author feels that [the book] should prove of great value to those people who have been born and brought up in refined and well-bred families, and are, at the same time, desirous of entering fashionable society. To our newer millionaires and plutocrats it should be a very present help in time of trouble, for it is undeniable that many of these captains of industry—however strong and virile their natures—become utterly helpless and panic-stricken at the mere sight of a gold finger bowl, an alabaster bath, a pronged oyster fork, or the business end of an asparagus."

In short, Crowninshield and Nast were meant for each other. One

Frank Crowninshield, drawn by a famous artist of the day, James Montgomery Flagg, circa 1933. *Vogue*, August 15, 1960.

can imagine the conversation between the two when Nast voiced his concern about his new magazine, *Dress & Vanity Fair,* which he felt was not working well. Crowninshield readily pointed out its flaws. "There is no magazine that is read by the people you meet at lunches and dinners," he said. "Your magazine should cover the things people talk about—parties, the arts, sports, theatre, humor, and so forth."

The publisher brightened at this clear sense of direction expressed by a man whose wit, urbanity, and artistic sensibilities were already renowned. *Vogue,* after all, was a magazine devoted to society and fashion. Did not the arts deserve more thorough attention? With the astuteness in sizing people up that was one of Nast's most useful talents, he promptly invited Crowninshield to become editor of his new magazine. Crowninshield accepted, on condition that the word *Dress* be removed from the title, and that women's fashions be abolished from its contents. Crowninshield was then thirty-eight, two years older than Nast, and their collaboration turned into a friendship that, apart from Robert Collier's and Edna Chase's, was probably the most important and enduring in Condé Nast's life.

The first issue of *Dress & Vanity Fair* declared its policy thus: "We purpose in these pages to touch on all that is of interest in the Drama, the Opera, and Music, both at home and in Europe. We shall picture and record the manifold activities of the Great Outdoors. We shall discuss all that is new and worthy in the Fine Arts and Books. We shall not lack authority in those things which go to make the smart world smart. . . ."

Frank Crowninshield's first editorial, in March 1914, said in part:

> *Vanity Fair* has but two major articles in its editorial creed: first, to believe in the progress and promise of American life, and second, to chronicle that progress cheerfully, truthfully, and entertainingly. . . . Let us instance one respect in which American life has recently undergone a great change. We allude to its increased devotion to pleasure, to happiness, to dancing, to sport, to the de-

lights of the country, to laughter, and to all forms of cheerfulness. . . . Now *Vanity Fair* means to be as cheerful as anybody. It will print much humor, it will look at the stage, at the arts, at the world of letters, at sport, and at the highly vitalized, electric, and diversified life of our day from the frankly cheerful angle of the optimist, or, which is much the same thing, from the mock-cheerful angle of the satirist. . . . For women, we intend to do something in a noble and missionary spirit, something which, so far as we can observe, has never before been done for them by an American magazine. We mean to make frequent appeals to their intellects. . . .

At once it can be seen what Frank Crowninshield brought to the magazine—a sense of humor. Nast's private humor was quirky and tended toward the absurd; in business he was all seriousness. Crowninshield threw all traces of pompousness out of Nast's editorial efforts—and Nast loved it. The two men, just approaching forty, responded to the spirit of zest, enthusiasm, and affluence that was spreading across the country and expressed it in a magazine that for twenty years was to be the pacesetter of a new generation of Americans.

*Vanity Fair* had three great strengths under Crowninshield: (1) an extremely stylish and elegant layout; (2) an eye for the artistic avant-garde; and (3) some of the best writing being produced anywhere in the world at that time. *"Vanity Fair* has discovered more new writers than artists," Crowninshield wrote in 1928, when the magazine had been running under his editorship for fourteen years. "But revolutions in literature are never so conspicuous as revolutions in art, so that the new artists whom we have periodically presented have aroused the greater part of the criticism that *Vanity Fair* has had to combat from time to time."

The list of "new artists" included Rockwell Kent, Eduardo Benito, Marie Laurencin, Arthur B. Davies, Warren Davis, Kees van Dongen, Jacob Epstein, Miguel Covarrubias, Hunt Diederich, Nicholas Remisoff, and Pablo Picasso. Most of their early efforts in the magazine, as Crowninshield wryly noted, were greeted with abuse, distrust, obloquy, and indignation. By 1928, most of them were commanding astronomical sums of money for their work.

Always receptive to the avant-garde, *Vanity Fair* frequently profiled artistic innovators, such as the "enfant terrible" poet Jean Cocteau, photographed here by Delphi. *Vanity Fair* March 1922.

Another brilliant *Vanity Fair* contribution—Steichen's extraordinary portrait of Paul Robeson in the film version of Eugene O'Neill's *The Emperor Jones. Vanity Fair,* August 1933.

"Beginning in April, 1922," Crowninshield went on, "*Vanity Fair* published photographs and drawings of still-life—eggs, pots and pans, milk bottles, etc.—by Paul Outerbridge, Charles Sheeler, and others. It will be remembered that there was, at that time, considerable and violent controversy as to whether this kind of material was eligible for artistic treatment." *Vanity Fair* also employed Baron de Meyer and Edward Steichen "when their work was branded as wild and absurd. They are now the highest paid photographers in the world."

Writers first introduced to the magazine public by *Vanity Fair* included P. G. Wodehouse, Robert Benchley, Dorothy Parker, Nancy Boyd (pseudonym for Edna St. Vincent Millay), Corey Ford, Walter Winchell, Robert Sherwood, Elinor Wylie, Colette (in English), Aldous Huxley, Hugh Walpole, E.E. Cummings, Compton Mackenzie, Clive Bell, and Edmund Wilson. Crowninshield pointed out that "the Editor was not taking any sort of wild chances on these men and women. . . . They have already proved their place as masters when *Vanity Fair* first sponsors them. But the point is that the world at large has never even heard of them, and may normally be expected to disregard them for several more years. It is *Vanity Fair*'s function to continue resolutely and often, amid abuse and derision, to bring them to the attention of the world."

*Vanity Fair* not only made discoveries; it published already-discovered talents such as Ferenc Molnár, Paul Morand, F. Scott Fitzgerald, Paul Gallico, Heywood Broun, David Cort, Roger Fry, Carl Van Vechten, Alexander Woollcott, Wyndham Lewis, George Jean Nathan, and Anita Loos; and photographers such as George Hoyningen-Huené, Anton Bruehl, and Cecil Beaton. And in the realm of painting, *Vanity Fair* consistently and frequently reproduced, years before any other American magazine, and to loud cries of ridicule and disgust, Matisse, Maillol, Pascin, Derain, Kolbe, Laurencin, Despiau, and Meštrović.

These are all brilliant names, and there is no doubt that Frank Crowninshield exploited his material with consummate flair. Partly this was due to his knowledge of modern art (he helped found the

Museum of Modern Art in 1929 and his name is engraved on one of its walls; his own collection of Braque, Segonzac, Laurencin, and others sold for a small fortune shortly before he died) and of literature (particularly the off-beat or unexpected). Partly it was due to his wonderful sense of humor—Rabelaisian, Clare Boothe Luce called it. And partly it was due to his insatiable interest in people.

Jeanne Ballot, his long-time secretary and assistant, described him thus: "Mr. Crowninshield—he was always Mr. Crowninshield to me—was tall, grey/brown-haired, with a curly moustache and brown, brown eyes. He made everyone feel that he or she was the most interesting, most fascinating person. Someone once described him as, 'Frank Crowninshield—than whom no one could be than-whomer.' " When he hired Miss Ballot, he showed her a sheaf of photographs on his desk depicting lovely girls in revealing wisps of chiffon. "These," he said to her, "are the stenographers. On Saturday nights I take them up to the roof and photograph them." (The photographs were, as Miss Ballot remembered later, of the Denishawn dancers.)

He ran the office with the greatest informality. Actresses, models, photographers, and writers were always milling about in the reception room, under the impression that he had invited them to a personal interview. (He often had.) Weekly lunches were sent up from the Savarin, always consisting of the same things—eggs Benedict, kippered herrings and *café spécial*. (No martinis—Frank Crowninshield, throughout his long and social life, never touched a drop of alcohol.) These lunches usually turned into orgies of hilarity, some of which spread to the more staid offices of *Vogue*. The *Vanity Fair* people thought *Vogue* and its obsession with fashion boring and absurd. "Why not spend your summer under a black sailor?" was the kind of *Vogue* headline that sent colleagues on *Vanity Fair* into fits of laughter. *Vogue*, meanwhile, disapproved of *Vanity Fair*, regarding the staff as noisy and frivolous, always having lunch and publishing risqué articles.

Crowninshield was an expert staff-stealer. He was constantly prowling through the *Vogue* offices for bright young talent to whisk off to his merry lair—Dorothy Parker and Clare Boothe Brokaw (later Luce) were two of the most illustrious. This kind of thing did not go down well with Edna Woolman Chase, who regarded Crowninshield as a pest, and may sometimes have suspected he was laughing at her. One of Crowninshield's favorite diversions was to send people telegrams signed by famous people, and he once sent Mrs. Chase a particularly flowery poem full of expressions of "infatuation for your exquisite and incomparable self," and signed it— Boris Karloff. (He would send similar messages to his assistant, Jeanne Ballot, when she was on vacation, signed Rudolph Valentino or Ramon Navarro, much to the excitement of the hotel management and guests.)

Crowninshield had a notoriously soft heart. "Rejection does not necessarily mean lack of merit," he would say, and his rejection letters, unlike the no-nonsense negatives composed by Edna Chase, were often expressed with such delicacy as to seem like acceptances. When he fired people, which he hated to do, he always did it in such a way as to direct them into an alternative form of employment, as in the case of the office girl he was once compelled to dismiss:

"What are you really interested in, child?" he asked.

"Well, I like orchids," the employee answered doubtfully.

"Get me Max Schling," Crowninshield at once said to his secretary. "Max," he said into the phone, "I have a girl here who's very anxious to work in a flower shop."

His interest in people, from the highest to the lowest, was genuine and tireless. He often visited Miss Ballot's mother in Brooklyn (the trip to him was like going to Boston or Chicago; he took plenty of reading matter with him). He was a great sender of flowers, telegrams, and postcards, and showered them with equal profligacy on secretaries, cousins, stenographers, Tallulah Bankhead, and Isadora Duncan. His time at the office was often so limited by his devotion to his friends, office workers, and their relations that his absence could sometimes cause a little friction between Nast and his mercurial editor when the printing of *Vanity Fair* was at stake. "Once we held up the presses three hours," Nast related, "and

One of *Vanity Fair*'s favorite artists, Fish (an Englishwoman), sketches the season's opening at the Metropolitan Opera with what the magazine described as "the usual performance of Aïda." *Vanity Fair*, December 1917.

finally located Frank at the funeral of the mother of some messenger girl."

A typical Crowninshield evening would consist of a dinner party chez Mrs. Cornelius Vanderbilt to meet the Queen of Spain, followed by a visit to the Winter Garden Theatre, where Gypsy Rose Lee was performing. After bowing and conversing brilliantly with royalty, he would equally happily order in cases of soda for Gypsy Rose Lee and her exhausted colleagues.

Condé Nast once wrote about his friend: "A trait in F. C. which has always interested me is his concern over the aged, the sick, the underprivileged, and forlorn. His friendships with servants always seem as close as those he maintains with their employers." Nast went on to point out his most valuable talent of all to Nast and the magazines:

> He has a remarkable way of continuing an active contact with old friends. A happy result, for our publishing organization, of his wide acquaintanceship has been that if a friendly contact had to be established, he seemed certain either to know the men and women we were after or to sense exactly how to bring them into line. It was always, for example, easy for him to persuade Joseph H. Choate to write for us, or Irene Castle to pose for photographs, or John Sargent to permit our use of his sketches, or Aldous Huxley to work on our staff, or Joe Louis to pass on hour or two before the cameras in our studio, or persuade August Belmont and Harry Payne Whitney to cooperate in photographing their horses in their stables, or Isadora Duncan to help in a benefit dance recital, or Geraldine Farrar to do us any order of favor.

There you have it. Could there have been a better foil to Condé Nast? Of course, the accusation must instantly be faced that Frank Crowninshield was a snob. He confessed it himself, explaining that his interest in society "derives from the fact that I like an immense number of things which society, money, and position bring in their train: painting, tapestries, rare books, smart dresses, dances, gardens, country houses, correct cuisine, and pretty women." The things, in short, chronicled so meticulously in *Vanity Fair* and

*Vogue.* What Condé Nast conspicuously lacked, a long list of contacts, Crowninshield provided. What suited Crowninshield most, an agreeable platform for his interests and opinions, Nast willingly supplied. The mutual benefits were both financially and artistically gratifying.

Not that Nast either understood or approved of many of the things that appeared in *Vanity Fair.* There were regular monthly rows over Crowninshield's insistence on the inclusion of the latest Matisse nude, reproduced in four colors. "You're not looking at it in the right *light,* Condé," Crowninshield would say, turning the picture this way and that, to Nast's continued bewilderment. It was a broad-minded publisher who allowed his editor to publish an article written *entirely in French* by Erik Satie; a photograph of Jack Dempsey posing as Rodin's "Thinker"; an item entitled, "In the Race of Life, They Won by a Neck," consisting of photographs of the backs of famous people's heads; drawings made specially for *Vanity Fair* by Picasso, for which he never lifted his pencil from the paper; an Alajálov drawing of J. P. Morgan in his underpants; or articles such as "Dancing with One's Wife, by a Husband," and "A Problem for Freud: Why Do People Go to Cabarets?"

Nast admitted later that Crowninshield's passion for the modern art movement did them a certain amount of harm. "We were ten years too early (1915) in talking about Van Gogh, Gauguin, Matisse, Picasso, etc. At first people took the ground that we were (presumably) insane, and even as late as 1929 and 1930, our readers were still confused by the paintings we reproduced. Our advertising department, too, was greatly concerned because our advertisers (without much knowledge of the movement or of the men who headed it) thought the paintings distorted and, as they said, decadent. In time, however, as the movement grew, we derived a very considerable benefit from having published such pictures."

Crowny, of course, had not the slightest interest in the advertising department. He would sometimes show the advertising people on the magazine one of his more "decadent" art reproductions, and if they didn't understand it he would rush it enthusiastically into print. Nast constantly had to smooth ruffled feathers and hold hands in order to keep the angry advertising department from walking out. He knew what the problems were; he was an advertising man himself and spoke their language. Crowninshield, like Arthur Turnure before him, regarded advertising as a necessary evil—or, frankly, not even that, with Nast paying the bills.

Ewart Newsom, hired by Nast to write the "Well-Dressed Man" column for *Vanity Fair,* tells the story of how Crowninshield hated the column, indeed any merchandising column, as he felt it prostituted the magazine. He despised it so much that on one occasion he suggested Newsom just insert a page of the telephone book when he was late with his copy. For a while Newsom went to London to help edit *Vanity Fair*'s "London Letter," and while he was away Crowninshield cut the "Well-Dressed Man" column down to four pages a year. Nast said, "I want those pages back," and back they went. He knew such editorial material was the lifeblood of the magazine; the advertising depended on it.

Both advertisers and readers were sometimes driven to desperate measures by *Vanity Fair*'s outrageousness. The most famous case, one that even Nast was unable to prevent, took place in 1935, very late in the magazine's life. In a series called, "Not on Your Tintype"—"five highly unlikely historical situations by one who is sick of the same old headlines"—Gropper, the artist, drew a caricature of Emperor Hirohito of Japan carrying off a scroll of paper on a guncarriage. The caption, written by Helen Brown Norden (later Lawrenson) was "Japan's Emperor gets the Nobel Peace Prize." (Japan was currently invading China.) There was an international outcry, the issue was banned in Japan, the Japanese ambassador in Washington complained to the State Department, and Crowninshield had to write a letter of apology to Ambassador Saito. (Helen Lawrenson tells the apocryphal story that when the Japanese representative and his aide came into the *Vanity Fair* offices, "Crowny mistook them for some Japanese acrobats he wanted photographed and suggested that they show us their tumbling feats.")

Nast was in Europe when the cartoon appeared. On his return to America in September 1935, on the *Aquitania,* he made a state-

J. Pierpont Morgan, the world banker, whose hobby, my little readers, is gardening, but who also loves midgets, money and other "m" words, like muchness

INVESTIGATION SUIT, WITH MIDGET ATTACHED

OFFICE UNIFORM, NEAT YET IMPRESSIVE

J. P. MORGAN, THE MAN

GARDENING FROCK, FOR HORTICULTURAL MOMENTS

FANCY DRESS COSTUME, FOR FÊTE DAYS ON HIS YACHT

## Vanity Fair's own paper dolls—no. 1

JAPAN'S EMPEROR GETS THE NOBEL PEACE PRIZE

"J. Pierpont Morgan, the world banker, whose hobby, my little readers, is gardening, but who also loves midgets, money and other 'm' words, like muchness"— Helen Brown Norden's caption for Alajálov's paper doll. *Vanity Fair*, September 1933.

Gropper's scandalous drawing of the Emperor Hirohito and his Nobel Peace Prize, caption written by Helen Norden. (The drawing cost the magazine $25.) *Vanity Fair*, August 1935.

117

ment to the press: "Had we, Mr. Crowninshield and I, foreseen the feeling which our cartoon was to arouse in Japan we should not have published it; not that we believe in the divine origin of the Japanese Emperor, but because we do believe in the terrible horror of modern warfare. Every editor, every publisher of a newspaper or periodical has a solemn and sacred responsibility to respect the sensibilities of foreign peoples and avoid the publication of editorial matter which will offend these sensibilities."

This was 1935, a very different world from that in which Condé Nast had first introduced his new periodical in 1913. He had told his advertisers then that he had set a difficult task for himself in establishing a successful class periodical, particularly since he had two major editorial principles in mind: "(1) to accomplish it by devoting its entire editorial contents to the restrained, truthful and cultivated treatment of the arts, graces and humors of American life, *thereby strictly limiting its appeal to men and women of known means, and inferred high breeding and good taste.* (2) to accomplish it without the aid of that quickest of all circulation builders—fiction: a builder of large circulation, but because of fiction's indiscriminate appeal, a builder whose constant tendency is to dilute 'class' circulation."

In spite of these conditions, by the end of 1915, *Vanity Fair* was first in advertising linage of all American monthly periodicals (403,219 lines; the second-place magazine, *System,* rated 355,025 lines). Nast and *Vanity Fair* had turned the corner. From then on, the outlook was bright. There was, of course, a war, but Crowninshield kept it firmly in the background while concentrating on such pressing topics as "Hints on Social Climbing," "The Diary of a Newport Flapper," and "At last, the Vorticists!" Luckily, American involvement in the war did not last long, and in 1919 everyone was ready to be as full of laughs as ever: "Peace Reigns in the Canine World," "The Dullest Book of the Month" (Thorstein Veblen's *The Theory of the Leisure Class*), or "What Is Worse Than a House Party?"

The ominous note of political responsibility in Nast's 1935 statement was still a long way in the future. Sadly, it was to presage the end of the magazine. But *Vanity Fair* entered the twenties under a cloudless sky. "We are not going to print any pretty girls' heads on our covers," Nast and Crowninshield promised their readers. "We are going to spare you the agony of sex discussions. We shall publish no dreary serial stories. No diaries of travel. No hack articles on preparedness. No gloom. No problem stories. No articles on tariff, or irrigation, or railroad rates, or pure food, or any other statistical subject. . . . The world is moving, moving on all eight cylinders—some folks are even moving on twelve—and you might just as well move along with them. Don't stall yourself on life's highroad and be satisfied to take everybody else's dust. . . ."

*Vanity Fair* was signaling the arrival of what Crowninshield called the Period of Jazz, a period of devastating change that included: (1) an increasingly anarchic attitude toward authority in whatever form; (2) the liberation of youth to follow its own whims and devices; (3) the removal of every ritual of escort or chaperonage; (4) the scant attention paid to older people; (5) a blinking at supposed, or open, liaisons; (6) the sudden growth of drinking, smoking, dancing, and card-playing among women; (7) an increased neuroticism; and (8), a fantastic increase in the number of divorces among people of fashion. "These phenomena, naturally enough," wrote Crowninshield, "completely disorganized the social life of New York."

The cardinal sin in this new world of bootleg cocktails, the Castle Walk, cabarets, and women's suffrage was to be bored. "Do you, sir, bury yourself in the market page at breakfast?" demanded *Vanity Fair.* "Do you, madam, converse about the misdeeds of the cook and the modiste's perfectly unaccountable bill? Do you, sir, ever surprise her with a knowledge of a new dance or opera? Do you, madam, ever startle him with a clever story or a new slant on life?"

The answers were out there, in New York, to which all America looked for entertainment, style, the latest fad—New York, a brilliant, fascinating merry-go-round, where everyone ran madly to keep up with the latest art, music, theatre, sports, fashions, and gaieties; New York, a monument to the complexities of modern living; New York, the new national mecca of culture, excoriated by Babbitt, and courted by anyone looking for fun and money. And the voice of New York was *Vanity Fair*. However far from the city you lived, the arrival of *Vanity Fair* every month could make you feel there, living it, feeling it, loving it. Jack London once wrote: "I find that I really need *Vanity Fair*. It keeps me in touch with all the fripperies, insincerities, vanities, decadent arts and sinister pleasures of life." In those years of Prohibition, *Vanity Fair* was the only legal drink in town; the magazine's advertising claim that it was "the cocktail without a padlock" was no exaggeration.

*Vogue*, too, had become a prop for people who wanted to feel they belonged to the beau monde in action. Harford Powel, Nast's advertising man, who had observed his employer with such interest in Newport, visited Wichita Falls in 1917. "God must have loved this Texas town," he reported, "because he showered down upon its people incomes that averaged $1,000 a month, a week, a day. Oil gushed in their back yards. The ladies had two great festivals a month—the days when *Vogue* came. They met and tore it to pieces. It was their Magna Carta, their bible. They bought nothing from a thimble to a $15,000 automobile without the sanction—nay the permission—of *Vogue*."

Nor was it just society women who read *Vogue*. It was required reading for department-store buyers across the country, and for any manufacturer who produced the articles of fashion, fancy, and flummery with which women adorned themselves. (By the 1930s, Macy's in New York was buying one hundred copies every month for its staff.)

With the third jewel in his crown, *House & Garden*, which Nast took over outright in 1915 and shortly thereafter amalgamated with the old, established *American Homes and Gardens*, he promoted a magazine of interior design and gardening to the ranks of *Vogue* and *Vanity Fair*. Originally a male-oriented architectural journal, started as a lark in 1901 by two Philadelphia architects, *House & Garden* was transformed by Nast into an interior-design authority that encouraged women to believe that decorating their houses expressed just as much about their taste and position as decorating their persons. Richardson Wright, who had become editor in 1914 and remained at his post under the new regime, was perhaps the least avant-garde of Nast's three editors, remaining loyal to traditional European influences and "le style antique" (largely eighteenth-century French and English furniture and furnishings) that had so dominated American interiors in the early part of the century. Wright's report on the famous 1925 Paris Exposition, which presented art deco (or art moderne, as it was called in America) for the first time in a sensational display of sumptuous materials and futurist objects, positively quivered with disapproval. "As a people, we are not ready for such radical innovations as these," he declared, shortly before New York witnessed the apotheosis of art deco in the shape of the Radio City Music Hall.

If the decorative arts in the early issues of the magazine still looked back, *House & Garden* was also committed, as one by now had come to expect of a Nast publication, to the intriguing idea that interior design was the rightful domain of women, and of American women in particular. Edith Wharton had started the trend when she copublished, with Ogden Codman, a book entitled *The Decoration of Houses,* in 1897. Her successors, Elsie de Wolfe, Ruby Ross Wood, Rose Cumming, Nancy McClelland, Marion Hall, and Diane Tate, were some of the Americans propelled into the international spotlight by the magazine, and Nast once again showed that New York could offer just as much stylistic talent as the great centers of Paris and London. From a circulation of less than 10,000 in 1915, *House & Garden* gradually rose to 130,000 ten years later.

From the end of the First World War until 1929, affluence, the postwar cultural explosion, and the urbanization of America nourished Nast's magazines until they became as fat and sleek and glossy as cream-fed cats. It was not surprising that after the war was over, bringing to an end America's isolationism from Europe, Nast should capitalize on the new mood of self-confidence and international spirit, and look across the Atlantic for more worlds to conquer.

# EIGHT

# THE GRAND TOUR

L ong before the beginning of the First World War, Nast had begun flexing his muscles for a European campaign of his own. After all, since so much of American taste had been formed by exposure to European models, there was surely a mutual benefit to be obtained from putting manufacturer and consumer together in an international alliance. The most obvious place to start was the motherland, England, which claimed, at least in name, a common language. Moreover, things English, from hacking jackets to hairbrushes, continued to maintain a seemingly inexhaustible hold over the American upper-class imagination as the epitome of quality and style. It was only natural that Condé Nast should be hopeful of garnering English advertisers for *Vogue*.

But the response, at first, was sluggish. American *Vogue* was not at all well known in England, and certainly not by many commercial manufacturers. There was also the usual discreet English distaste for anything foreign, in particular for anything American. What, after all, could the English possibly learn from the Americans in the field of quality and style? The idea was ludicrous. Fortunately, Nast found just the person to change all that. He was William Wood, a young Englishman with some publishing experience and a great deal of energy. In 1912 Wood began to organize distribution of *Vogue* at selected central-London newsstands. Helped by his vigorous promotion, by 1914 *Vogue* was selling between 3,000 and 4,000 copies in England.

It is generally accepted by sociological scholars that such frivolous items as fashion goods and cosmetics sell well in wartime (escapism, morale-boosting, distraction, and so forth), and such was indeed the case after the outbreak of the First World War in England. With the immediate halt in distribution of French and Viennese fashion journals, hitherto the glossy reading-fodder of Englishwomen, the fashion-conscious public was forced to turn more and more to this strange American publication, *Vogue.* By 1916 sales had quadrupled. That year, however, saw a severe stepping-up of the war on all fronts. Paper supplies in the United States were restricted, and nonessential shipping between England and America was almost entirely banned. *Vogue,* suddenly, was stranded on the other side of the Atlantic, unable to obtain transportation to British shores.

It was at this point that Walter Maas, an Englishman of Dutch origin residing in Paris, head of the Paris office of the Dorland Advertising Agency and, since 1912, advertising representative for *Vogue, House & Garden,* and *Vanity Fair,* suggested to Nast that he produce a totally British edition of *Vogue.* William Wood thoroughly supported this idea, and assured Nast that he could get British advertising, and that with a supply of fashion pages from New York he could bring out a successful British version. Nast agreed, and on September 15, 1916, the first British *Vogue* appeared. "Nothing which had made *Vogue* what it is will be deleted," advertisers were promised. "On the contrary, each issue will be supplemented with carefully selected articles dealing with English Society, Fashions, Furniture, Interior Decoration, the Garden, Art, Literature and the Stage." A full black-and-white page was to cost £25, a color page £35 (£1 was then worth $4.75).

The first issue was a forecast of autumn fashions and cost one shilling. The advertisers included Waring & Gillow, Maison Lewis ("The smartest hats in town"), William Whiteley, Ltd., Peter Robinson's, Aquascutum, Gooch's Ltd., Selfridge & Co., and Spunella, Queen of Silks. The first society photograph was of Lady Eileen Wellesley, by Hoppé. Mrs. John Lavery was also photographed. War, of course, was an omnipresent subject in the editorial pages. "War Weddings and War Workers," ran one story, "are the topics of London's spare moments, but spare moments, of course, are few these days . . ." *Vogue* patterns could be ordered from Rolls House, Breams Buildings, E.C., the editorial offices. Color advertisements for Rolls Royce and the Gas Light & Coke Company completed the issue.

The first publisher, manager, and managing editor of British *Vogue* was, of course, William Wood. Dorothy Todd became the first editor, but she was rapidly succeeded by Elspeth Champcommunal, who came from the London office of Maison Worth with a strong fashion sense but no magazine publishing experience, an imbalance that was to prove costly. The advertising manager was George W. Kettle, principal proprietor of the British Dorland Company. (The publisher and his advertising manager did not get on, occasioning the office joke that there was too much Wood under the Kettle.)

The Great War, as well as changing forever America's cultural isolationism from Europe, also transformed Europeans' opinions of America. By 1918, drained of material from its own fatigued shores, British *Vogue* turned enthusiastically to things American— American cars, American parties, American mansions, American money. While American *Vogue* drooled over the cool English beauty Lady Diana Cooper, British *Vogue* breathed ecstatically over the vivacious, dashing figure of Irene Castle. While Americans still hankered for the perfection of a Rolls Royce, the English thought a new Stutz infinitely more amusing. If England still had class, America had, unquestionably—glamour. Fashion remained, in both countries, triumphantly French, and British *Vogue* sang the praises of Vionnet, Callot, Lanvin, and Chanel just as loudly as the Americans did, while the great postwar couture collections dazzled a new generation on both sides of the Atlantic looking for fun.

In 1922, the editorship of *Brogue* (as Condé Nast employees affectionately called it) changed hands. Elspeth Champcommunal's lack of publishing experience had not helped the magazine, whose circulation was well under 9,000. Dorothy Todd once more took over. Miss Todd was a woman of distinctly literary, as opposed to fashionable, leanings, and she hired such talents as Raymond Mortimer, Alan Pryce-Jones, Peter Quennell, David Garnett, Aldous Huxley, and other members of London's bright young literary set to write for her. She was also the first to show Cocteau's work in England, and to publish Gertrude Stein's verse, with commentary by Edith Sitwell. In short, she was a woman after Frank Crowninshield's own heart. This alone might have been enough to attract the censorious attention of Edna Woolman Chase; *Vogue,* after all, was a fashion magazine, not a British *Vanity Fair.* The morally rigorous Mrs. Chase also disapproved strongly of Miss Todd's personal proclivities, which were overtly homosexual. But the only thing that really mattered was *Vogue*'s financial situation, and it looked bad. To maintain advertising was a struggle under the new literary regime, and the magazine, for the first time, began to lose money. Things looked so bad that Nast thought of pulling out completely, prevented only by recollections of its unprecedented success during the war.

In 1923, Nast went over to London to attempt to reconstruct the flagging *Vogue* office staff. At that time a young *Vanity Fair* assistant called Harry Yoxall was also in London, home on leave. Albert Lee, the business manager of *Vogue* during this difficult period, was by all accounts a lazy sort of fellow ("allergic to work" is how Harry Yoxall put it), and he suggested to Nast that Yoxall be called in to help with the reorganization of the office. No sooner had this happened when Condé Nast fell ill with double pneumonia, a very serious illness in those days. Alarm was so great that his family was notified and Clarisse actually appeared at her estranged husband's bedside. Luckily the danger was averted, but Nast stayed several weeks in England convalescing.

The young Yoxall saw a lot of his employer at this time. The invalid invited Yoxall to accompany him on rides in Richmond Park, and together they discussed how best to put *Brogue* back on its feet. Yoxall learned about Nast's philosophy of publishing, and became deeply impressed with his grasp of business, advertising, and editorial matters. "He really taught me all I know about magazine publishing," Yoxall said later. "His system of accounts and budget projections was far in advance of his time. Years later, when I was engaging experienced men from other publishing houses, they would express amazement at the fullness of our knowledge of the financial and statistical side of our business—systems quite unknown in other firms."

Nast and Yoxall became quite intimate during the publisher's period of convalescence. They used to have tea and drinks together. Yoxall introduced him to gin and tonic.

"This is fascinating," Condé said, looking at the fizzy quinine water. "If you could manage to sell this in the Mississippi Valley you could make a fortune. I'll give up publishing and do it myself."

Yoxall declared that he had never met such an all-around publisher. But in the end it all came down to figures. "Harry," Nast used to say, "without full, accurate, and prompt figures, not even a genius can run a publishing business. With full, accurate, and prompt figures, anyone of reasonable intelligence can do so." This was a typically modest assessment by Nast of his achievements. He never regarded his success in anything but the most clear-headed, realistic, matter-of-fact terms—except perhaps in the last, crazy millionaire days before the Crash.

Toward the end of 1923, Nast and Yoxall returned to New York, leaving Albert Lee with a blueprint for resuscitating *Vogue*. In 1924, Nast again visited London, only to find that allergic Albert had not carried through any of the reconstruction that Nast and Yoxall had planned. In desperation, Nast cabled Yoxall to come over and take charge of the London office. It was on terms that Yoxall, although reluctant to leave New York, could not turn down.

"The offer was generous but Condé could be very inconsiderate," Yoxall said. "When I arrived, he'd gone to Paris, leaving me with no authority or a clear statement of my powers. He was very annoyed with me when I wrote to him about the problem, but he finally came back to London and my position was defined." Nast always hated the organizational details of personnel work and left them whenever possible to officers such as Francis L. Wurzburg, his trusty vice-president. In London there was no such useful functionary, and the lack was to become a serious problem. Meanwhile it was finally settled that the *Brogue* office was to be run as a troika—Yoxall as business manager, Lawrence Schneider, brought over from New York, as advertising manager, and Dorothy Todd remaining as editor.

At that time the London office was losing £25,000 a year. Yet Nast continued to run the business as he ran the New York office—in a way that completely bewildered Yoxall. "Continuous long memoranda and cables rained down on us from New York, the transatlantic phone not yet being available. These communications seemed to be wildly extravagant at this crisis in our fortunes, but that was his way of doing business. All important decisions were left to him, and he was a stickler for full information. So the cables and memos went on."

By 1926 everybody realized that Dorothy Todd had to go. Nast cabled Yoxall to fire her, which he reluctantly did. There was an immediate storm of protest from the editor's literary supporters. "We sat in the meadow [of the Woolfs' house in Rodmell] and discussed the future of Miss Todd," Vita Sackville-West wrote to her husband, Harold Nicolson.

> As Tray [Raymond Mortimer] has probably told you, she has got the sack from *Vogue,* which, owing to being too highbrow, is sinking in circulation. Todd, a woman of spirit, though remonstrated with by Condé Nast, refused to make any concessions to the reading public. So Nast sacked her. She then took legal advice and was told she could get £5,000 damages on the strength of her contract. Nast, when threatened with an action, retorted that he would defend himself by attacking Todd's morals. So poor Todd is silenced,

since her morals are of the classic rather than the conventional order. . . . This affair has assumed in Bloomsbury the proportions of a political rupture.

Thus was the brief and unlikely marriage between *Vogue* and Bloomsbury terminated. Dorothy Todd cannot have been altogether sorry. Nast, for instance, required each issue of *Vogue* to contain two full-page "society" photos. "In my early days with British *Vogue*," Harry Yoxall recalled later, "we kept a full-time assistant in the art department, air-brushing out the wrinkles and slimming the hips of our society." How the highbrow Miss Todd must have despised such observances.

Yoxall edited the magazine himself while he and Nast looked for a new editor. In the winter of 1926, Edna Woolman Chase was sent over to hold the fort. It could hardly have been a less propitious time. The General Strike had ravaged the country; food distribution was disrupted; transportation had come to a standstill; magazine circulation virtually ground to a halt. Yoxall had organized the staff to deliver copies of *Vogue* themselves to newsstands, and wryly reported a remark made by one of the dealers: "Gor bless you, now there ain't no newspapers they'll read anything, even *Vogue!*"

Nor was the arrival of Mrs. Chase taken in the best possible spirit. Nobody likes a foreigner coming in and telling him what to do, and the British less than most—particularly when that foreigner is an American. Resistance to Mrs. Chase's efforts at office reorganization was stiff. Politeness bordered on hostility. The typical male attitude of superiority that the British communicated so effectively was like a red rag to a bull as far as the feisty Mrs. Chase was concerned. Finally, she asked Nast to send them all a cable confirming her authority, which he duly did. The British executives nodded in the most affable manner, and then apologetically disappeared into a directors' meeting—leaving, of course, the American interloper, Mrs. Chase, outside the door.

But Mrs. Chase was made of sterner stuff. She quickly fired off another cable to Nast, who responded equally promptly, and within

Mrs. Chase appears only moderately amused at the editorial policy discussion she is conducting with Richardson Wright of *House & Garden* and
Frank Crowninshield of *Vanity Fair*.

a few days Mrs. Chase was sweetly accepting congratulations on becoming the newest director on the board of British *Vogue.*

Her first major change was to turn *Brogue* into a twenty-six-issue-a-year magazine (previously it had appeared only twenty-four times a year). This was in order to compete a little more effectively with the *Sketch,* and the *Tatler,* both society and fashion publications that appeared weekly. At least, with twenty-six issues, readers could look forward to their *Vogue* every *other* Wednesday, instead of "late June," or "early October," as the issues had previously been dated. Mrs. Chase also felt she had to raise the *ton* a little, which had become somewhat unkempt under the bookish Dorothy Todd. It must be remembered that Mrs. Chase's girls in New York were all expected to wear hats, white gloves, and silk stockings *at all times.* She hired a new editor, Alison Settle, and immediately set about transforming her into the correct image of a *Vogue* representative. *"Vogue* was snobbish to a degree," Mrs. Settle said later. "It was unbelievable how snobbish it was. I wasn't allowed to go into a bus and the fact that I lived in Hampstead and came down to the West End by tube they thought was very lowering. When Edna Woolman Chase came over she said Hampstead was no class at all, that I must not live there. I ought to live in a flat which had uniformed porters and a lift. This was an order. So I moved to a dreary flat in Upper Berkeley Street. That was 'class' until Edna came over and discovered there wasn't a uniformed porter on the ground floor. She said, 'That's not good enough, Alison.' So I had to move again."

In spite of these difficulties, Alison Settle had a good run—nine years. During this time she introduced Cecil Beaton to Nast and Chase, a valuable contribution. But in the thirties, magazine publishing changed and became more competitive. The Americans felt Mrs. Settle did not adjust sufficiently to the needs of merchandising, and also that she focused too much on London, instead of expanding into the rest of the country. She was finally removed in circumstances that reflected poorly on everybody. Nast, typically, was evasive and finally passed the buck to the long-suffering Harry

Yoxall. Mrs. Settle became ill under the stress, and had to be in effect frozen out.

This was not to be the last time Nast encountered personnel difficulties. He could arouse great loyalty in his staff, and he showed considerable flair in hiring people to work for him. But firing them was another matter. His inability to tackle the problem head-on and his dependence on others to do the unpleasant job for him became one of Nast's major weaknesses as an employer.

It was really thanks to Harry Yoxall that British *Vogue* survived. While the editorial crises continued, Yoxall quietly developed the Vogue pattern business, and built up the circulation of the *Vogue Pattern Book,* whose sales soon shot ahead of the magazine's. For years, profits on the patterns supported the diminishing losses on *Vogue.*

"Looking back," Yoxall wrote later to Edna Chase, "I am amazed at Condé's—shall we call it folly or far-sightedness?—in entrusting the London office to such inexperienced youngsters as Lawrence and me. I was genuinely convinced that you were going to ruin our recovery with your high-falutin' American notions. It really is amazing that we didn't ruin the show ourselves."

Not only did *Brogue* recover under the "inexperienced youngsters," but ten years later it was to be a vitally important factor in saving Condé Nast from financial and personal ruin after the Crash.

The editorial material was never a problem. Sometimes it was difficult to distinguish American *Vogue* from its British sister, since their interests were so similar. The covers were the same, sent over from New York. Frequently the same stories were run in both editions, with particular emphasis on English titles and American movie stars. Interesting personages in the British Isles were no less interesting to Americans, and vice versa. And of course the most inspiriting news of all was an Anglo-American love-match, joining titles and fortunes, or Diadems and Democrats, as a *Vogue* editorial inaccurately but catchily put it.

In 1920, Nast instituted an all-British *House & Garden,* also under the proprietorship of William Wood. It cost one shilling, and a carefully expressed editorial defined its market: *"House & Garden* does not cater for the wealthy alone. In that case its title would have been *Mansion & Park.* It is with the moderate, average house and the not too extensive garden of the moderate average Englishman that we propose to deal . . ."* As with the two *Vogues*, American material was used in the British edition, with local specials such as "The Town House of Lady Sackville," and "A Modern Topiary Garden at Brockenhurst." The local material, however, usually lost out to American features, which filled the pages—features which the moderate average Englishman found not remotely to his taste. With a small circulation and little, if any, promotional activity on its behalf, British *House & Garden* began to fail almost immediately.

Nast had a conversation with Harry Yoxall about the magazine's prospects. "It seems to me," he observed, "that English people are more interested in their houses than in their clothes."

"Yes, perhaps," agreed Yoxall, "but most of the English people of whom we speak have inherited their houses and the antique furniture inside them. Moreover, most of these English people have gardeners. Of what possible use, then, for them, is a magazine devoted to the furnishing of houses or the techniques of gardening?"

Yoxall's logic was irresistible. British *House & Garden* folded in 1923.

But it was not quite dead. In the mid-thirties, Yoxall began to bring out double numbers of *Vogue,* in combination with both the *Vogue Pattern Book* and what was called *Vogue's House & Garden Book.* These were quite successful, and continued until the outbreak of war, which brought with it paper rationing and the termination of any publications other than *Vogue* itself. In 1947 British *House & Garden* once again reappeared in its old guise as *Vogue's House & Garden Book* (restrictions on new magazine titles still obtained from the war years) and finally became British *House & Garden* in 1955, as it is today.

If England offered that old aristocratic magic, plus good tailors and stately homes, France, of course, offered the ultimate in feminine mystique. If you did not have something French in your wardrobe, you might as well retire from Society. Since Paris was the mecca for fashionable personages in Europe and America, a French *Vogue* seemed de rigueur. Condé Nast began his involvement with French fashion publishing in 1915 when he became copublisher of a special French-American issue of the *Gazette du Bon Ton* ("Art, Modes et Frivolités"), a small, exquisitely printed monthly fashion journal owned and published by Lucien Vogel. Vogel (pronounced Vo-jel) had harnessed a group of highly talented illustrators to work for him, and it was to ensure that he could make use of these artists in American *Vogue* that Nast first became interested in the *Gazette,* and considered publishing it in New York.

The *Gazette* had ceased publication, as had most de luxe publications, when war broke out, but in May 1915 a special issue was published to commemorate the Panama Pacific International Exposition in San Francisco, at which the Paris haute couture made a splendid showing. It was a highly patriotic issue, declaring, "Since the Latin races are fighting to uphold their taste against Teutonic barbarity, was it not to be expected that Paris fashion should once again take the lead this spring?" This was Condé Nast's first joint venture with Lucien Vogel, marking the start of a very successful publishing partnership.

After 1918, French couture revived in sparkling form, and the time seemed ripe for the launching of a French *Vogue.* At the beginning of 1920, the *Gazette* returned (on a rather more irregular basis); a year later Condé Nast bought a controlling interest in it from Vogel and began publishing it in New York. And on June 15, 1920, French *Vogue* (known, of course, as *Frog*), made its debut with a little fanfare and good notices from two important Paris newspapers, *Le Matin* and *Le Petit Parisien.*

Lucien Vogel had other publishing interests besides the *Gazette du Bon Ton.* His wife, Cosette, was also a talented editor, and came from an artistic family. One of her brothers was Jean de Brunhoff, a painter and the creator of the famous Babar storybooks for children. Her other brother, Michel, ultimately became editor of French *Vogue.* When French *Vogue* was launched, however, Nast asked Cosette Vogel to edit it. The two Vogels were also editing another French fashion magazine, called *L'Illustration des Modes,* a supplement to the famous magazine *L'Illustration,* which catered to a broader audience than *Vogue*'s. The publisher of *L'Illustration des Modes,* Marcel Baschet, wanted to sell it, since it had lost money heavily after the war, and the Vogels asked Condé Nast to buy it so they could keep their jobs. Baschet was even prepared to give the publication away, if Nast would take over the Vogel contracts. Mrs. Chase was fiercely against this purchase, since she was anxious to have Cosette concentrate on *Vogue.* But Nast was at that time, in Mrs. Chase's words, "hell-bent on expansion," so he took on Baschet's paper in 1921, renamed it *Jardin des Modes,* and in order to allow Cosette time to work on *Vogue,* brought in her second brother, Michel de Brunhoff, to help edit it. *Jardin des Modes* became another Nast success story, continuing to make money throughout the twenties which French *Vogue* continued to lose.

The reasons for French *Vogue*'s financial failure were simple enough. Fashion advertising was very weak in France, since most chic French women were dressed by the haute couture houses for next to nothing—a form of advertising they all found advantageous. The system worked like this: the dressmaker would select women who were both beautiful and socially prominent, thus ensuring that the gowns would be seen to the best advantage; and the clients would promise not to wear clothes from any other house. It was an exclusive deal, and woe betide the woman who reneged. Elsie de Wolfe knew a woman who was bound in this way to a couturier, and who turned up at a fashionable dinner dressed in a gown from a rival establishment. The couturier leaned across the dinner table and said, "How charming you are this evening in your latest model. It is so new that I have not seen it myself!" The next day she received a bill for the season's wardrobe—she had broken her part of the bargain.

Leone Blakemore Moats, a famous American hostess who lived in Mexico, was one of Madame Vionnet's most faithful customers in the twenties. She once asked the couturiere why she charged her so little for her clothes ($90 to $110 for a day dress; $110 to $150 for an evening gown, roughly half the price of a couture gown of the period). Vionnet answered: "For two reasons. First, I am an artist and it is a joy to have my work understood and set off to its best advantage. The second is because I am a businesswoman, and you are a good advertisement. I know that when you go to a Sunday dinner dance at the Ritz at least three women who see you there will be at my door on Monday morning asking for the model you wore."

In short, attractive Frenchwomen could not be persuaded to pose specially for *Vogue*. It was time-consuming, unnecessary publicity, and smacked of commerce. Advertisers were not interested in showing their modes in *Vogue* for the same reason; in America, yes, since they could not otherwise be seen, but in Paris, why bother? Moreover, the fashion business in France, international dernier cri though it indisputably was, was small and cliquish. Ready-to-wear clothes hardly existed in those days; dressmakers merely copied everyone else. Fashion simply was not a money-maker.

Already limited by these conditions, French *Vogue* was also very expensive to produce, given the high standards that Nast demanded. From 1920 to 1929 none of this mattered very much. Money was coming in fast enough elsewhere, and although *Frog* was not greatly successful financially, it was good for prestige and established "Les Editions Condé Nast" as a high-quality publishing name in France.

Nast was never deeply involved with French *Vogue*. It was a foot in the French fashion world and useful from that point of view. Since Nast never spoke a word of French, his communication with the staff was minimal. He enjoyed his annual trips to Paris, however, the main thing on his agenda being his visit to his hat-maker on the Place Vendôme. Indeed, a few eyebrows were raised back in New York when it was announced, on June 6, 1923, that the French government had conferred the Order of the Chevalier of the Legion of Honor upon Condé Nast, particularly in view of the reason given—"in recognition of his encouragement of French culture." Never mind. The publisher himself was delighted. (Mrs. Chase, perhaps a more worthy recipient, received hers in 1935.)

In spite of this, from the editorial point of view, Paris was an essential resource. What Paris said, thought, dreamed about, ate, listened to, were all as eagerly absorbed by American and English readers as what Paris wore. The most significant contribution made by the Paris office was the founding, in the mid-twenties, of a photographic studio for the exclusive use of *Vogue*; this meant that artists and photographers could work there, uninterrupted and with the best available equipment, previewing their most exciting experimental work exclusively for the eyes of the *Vogue* staff. It was a privileged position, and both editors and photographers made the most of it. The Paris studio became famous throughout the magazine world. Between them, the studio and the *Vogue* office provided American *Vogue* with almost all its central fashion pages.

It was amusing, too, to be able to tell American readers that *Vogue*'s Information Bureau in Paris was at their service: "They will tell you about the great Couturiers, and about the lesser dressmakers as well. They will direct you to the magnificent department stores—and at the same time give you the addresses of little lingerie houses and lace shops in the side streets. Say to the taxidriver, 'Numéro Deux, rue Edouard Sept.' Say to the doorman, 'VOGUE.' " French *Vogue* may not have made any money, but in the twenties everyone could afford to lose a little money to gain a little style.

In 1927, Main Bocher, a Chicagoan who had been fashion editor of French *Vogue* for several years, became editor. Bocher had wanted to be an opera singer, but he devoted his artistic talents instead to fashion, and for two years ran a highly charged but impractical shop as editor of *Frog*. He had frequent rows with the couturiers, who were always demanding too much, and finally Bocher himself demanded too much—a salary raise that both Nast and Chase found quite unconscionable. So the American left and two years later, as Mainbocher, opened his own couture house, which became very successful, culminating in his assignment to design Mrs. Simpson's trousseau for her marriage to the Duke.

Michel de Brunhoff, Lucien Vogel's brother-in-law, became editor of French *Vogue* in 1929. De Brunhoff was a chubby, cheerful, charming man who played the comedian and had a very soft heart. He loved the artists best, and was always full of encouragement when they brought in their work to show him. He understood them, supported them, and often was able to avoid a serious row by his tact and gentleness. De Brunhoff was happiest with a pencil and paper in front of him. When he discussed an issue, he would sketch it right there and then, the pages growing before the bemused editors' eyes.

Michel de Brunhoff was not, however, a good office administrator. Throughout the late twenties and the thirties, letters, cables, and memos poured into the Paris office with complaints of missed deadlines, muddled photographs, stories being filed late, artists' intransigence, and the other detritus of inefficient magazine editing. Mrs. Chase would send over smart young American editors to try to straighten out the mess, but nothing seemed to make much difference. Edna herself used to make periodic visits when the situation seemed to be completely out of control, and for a while things would return to a semblance of order. Then, after she had gone, leaving instructions for editorial planning meetings, for instance, there would be a typical post-Chase collapse, as described here by one of the many young Americans who worked in Paris, Bettina Ballard: "De Brunhoff would write things down in the cramped little spaces of a plan sheet with an unhappy, stubborn defiance on his face, knowing that before the issue went to press he would have blown all those stilted plans to bits."

One of the major problems for French *Vogue,* which neither the American nor the English editions had to face, was the overpowering presence of the couture houses. De Brunhoff and his aristocratic fashion editor, the Duchesse d'Ayen, spent much of their valuable time acting as diplomats and go-betweens, time that could no doubt have been better spent editing the magazine. There was intense, passionate competition among the major dressmaking establishments, and violent rows occurred if they felt that *Vogue* was giving one house more editorial credit or more advantageous page positions than the others. In 1933, for instance, Chanel, having promised de Brunhoff that she would give him everything he wanted from her new collection, then refused him his choice of models, saying that her day dresses (which everybody was buying) "did not show at all the spirit of her collection." Furthermore, she then said she would release no models at all unless they were shown alone on a page, with no models from other houses on the facing page. Marcel Rochas and Maggy Rouff also added to the list of real or imagined slights perpetrated by French *Vogue*. In 1934, Lucien Lelong cancelled his advertising contract with *Vogue* on the grounds that Schiaparelli and Molyneux had an undue amount of editorial space. It took a long and soothing letter from Edna Chase on this occasion, plus a promise of a special feature on Lelong's house, to bring the couturier back into the fold.

"It is not wholly possible to apportion editorial space purely upon the theory that each couturier must be given an equal amount of publicity in each individual number, or that those who advertise must be favored more than those who do not, et cetera, et cetera," she explained to the recalcitrant Lelong. "Our whole editorial integrity would be destroyed if we followed this policy."

But the couturiers remained argumentative, divisive, and demanding. The most classic eruption occurred in 1938. With the signing of the Munich agreements, a wave of nationalism started to sweep through France. The French couturiers, who had long been jealous of the success of Schiaparelli (Italian), Mainbocher (American), Molyneux (English), and more recently Balenciaga (Spanish), banded together to defend the rights of the native-born. They accused *Vogue* of conspiring against them in favor of foreign dressmakers, and thus ensuring the foreigners' success. At a meeting of the Syndicat de Défense de la Grande Couture Française (founded, it will be remembered, with the help of Condé Nast and Edna Chase), Chanel got up and made a vicious speech against *Vogue*. The effects of this were that many of the big houses refused to offer *Vogue* editors the usual viewing privileges, and many others threatened to withdraw their advertising. Naturally, the war quickly dissipated the impact of these petty squabbles and made the threats academic, but rancor remained.

During Nast's great years of "hell-bent" expansion, even Spanish *Vogue* made a brief appearance. The mistake was to choose Havana as its headquarters. This meant the magazine was translated into Cuban Spanish, which was considered an inferior form of the language, and therefore unable to communicate the quality and class of the other editions. The magazine lasted from 1918 to 1923 and the losses it incurred were easily absorbed.

Not so easy to absorb, however, were the losses incurred by German *Vogue*. This edition originated in an idea of Francis L. Wurzburg, who had been Condé Nast's business associate and vice-president since 1920. It was said that Wurzburg, whose business experience had come from department stores in the Midwest, showed Nast how to ring the cash register. Being of German parentage, Lew (as he was known) thought Germans ought also to be allowed to enjoy the fashion and social information imparted by the other *Vogue*s. Mrs. Chase, who disapproved of all Nast's efforts at expansion, found much to complain about here, the major problem being that she thought Germans had no taste. Condé and Lew agreed with this statement, but thought it was all the more justification for introducing them to *Vogue*. "Even in Germany, Edna, some smart women *must* exist," Lew urged. The men won the day; Nast's boom period was at its peak, he was making a lot of money, and it seemed perfectly logical to launch another international edition.

The man who was put in charge of the operation of starting German *Vogue* was Walter Maas, the same Walter Maas who had encouraged the birth of British *Vogue*. After the end of the First World War, Maas had returned to Paris to direct the French office of the Dorland Advertising Agency, which was advertising manager for French *Vogue* and *Jardin des Modes*. (In England, Dorland had also sold space for British *Vogue* until 1922, when Nast sent over Lawrence Schneider from New York to be advertising manager and set up his own staff. The custom of having an advertising agency act as advertising manager for a periodical, now fallen into disrepute, was not uncommon then.)

Maas went to the Dorland offices in Berlin and began his campaign. He opened offices for German *Vogue* on the Kurfürstendamm, with two gentlemen whose names he must have come to love, Dr. H. L. Hammerbacher, managing director, and Dr. L. O. Mohrenwitz, editor in chief. Dr. Hammerbacher had little publishing experience, and so he was brought to New York for a crash course with Nast, Chase, and Wurzburg. All seemed to go well, and the first issue of German *Vogue,* which appeared in April 1928 bearing the imprint of Vogue Verlag, Berlin, sold out in Germany, Austria, and Hungary in forty-eight hours.

But perhaps 1928 was not the most auspicious moment for a new foreign fashion journal in Germany. Inflation was raging; interest in fashion and society in Germany was minimal; and middle-class German women did not want to spend their meager savings on chic chitchat from New York, London, and Paris. There was no advertising, and no consumers, and no rich, aspiring middle class—in short, no constituency for *Vogue.* To add to these disadvantages, the Berlin office was run with mad extravagance under Dr. Hammerbacher, whose only lesson from his sojourn in New York, it appeared, was how to spend money. He equated luxury with promotional inventiveness; for Christmas he distributed 5,000 cocktail shakers filled with Martinis to newsstand distributors. (*Grog,* as the edition was called, was perhaps an apt name.)

Shortly after, German *Vogue* closed. Condé Nast lost about $300,000, just before he lost considerably more in the Crash of 1929. It was not a good time to suffer such a loss. But one great asset was rescued from the debacle. It was in the form of a swarthy, monocle-toting art director imported by Walter Maas from the Paris office of the Dorland agency to direct the artwork of German *Vogue.* The magazine may have been a flop, but the talents of Mehemed Fehmy Agha, for that was his name, were immediately apparent, and Nast quickly snapped him up and took him back to New York. This proved to be one of his most brilliant decisions.

By the end of 1929 three *Vogues* existed—American, British, and French. An elaborate system of communications had been built up among them, owing largely to Nast's predilection for sending long and detailed cables from whatever part of the world he might be in. Thus each issue of each international edition had a code word (to fool spies such as Hearst as well as to simplify messages). For instance, the January 1 issue of American *Vogue* was ACACIA, of British *Vogue,* ALMOND, and of French *Vogue,* EAGLE. There were also code words for Nast's major rivals, such as JUPITER for *Harper's Bazaar*. Other code words, generally used by editorial and art departments, included:

BLACKITE—a black-and-white page

TOCOL—a two-color page

BIGWIGS—important New York retail stores

LEADON—the London lead

IMMUTABLE—when used between the name of a model and the name of a store, indicated that the model had been bought for credit by that store and that credit, therefore, was immutable

CHERUB—cable reply

FOTOWINGS—rush photographs

MERCURY—followed by date, indicated date on which Paris was delivering material to French customs

SERAPHIM—cable immediately what issue

SOLOMON—use your own judgment

(Nast's passion for code words never abated. In 1934, when Lord Camrose, under conditions of the greatest secrecy, gave financial help to Nast, His Lordship, too, was given a code name, BARROW, after the name of his country seat.)

The most frequent interchange of cables was between New York and Paris, since it was news of the Paris collections, in considerable detail, that required the most speed and dexterity of communication. Rushing drawings, photographs, and descriptions of clothes through the French customs, on to the ship, and off again at New York was the most demanding duty of *Vogue's* editors. The international feature correspondents had an easier time of it. Contributors such as Cecil Beaton and John McMullin commuted from office to office with lightning speed, noses twitching with the latest social or fashion gossip, ready to file amusing stories for all three *Vogue*s. (One day in the London office, McMullin was overheard to cry to his secretary, "Cancel all my appointments; I have just heard of a white dress waistcoat with one button in a shop in Jermyn Street. I must fly!") They were foreign correspondents whose war zone was a ballroom instead of a bunker.

Nast was the first person to publish international editions of a magazine. While other magazines and newspapers had gained a limited export sale in lands foreign to their origin, *Vogue* was the first periodical to take root, not as an export magazine, but as a native periodical printed in the local language in the country of origin. "It has thus become," a *Vogue* advertisement declared proudly in 1928, "a living force in all of the civilized corners of the world."

The copywriter was a little grandiose perhaps, on this occasion, but there was a ring of reality to the claim. For a while, in the period between the wars, there was a community of standards, tastes, and interests shared by London, Paris, and New York. VOGUE KNOWS NO FRONTIERS, proclaimed the headline; and it was true. The rise of international celebrity socialites, such as Lady Mendl, Mrs. Reginald Fellowes, Lady Diana Cooper, Mrs. Harrison Williams, Princess Nathalie Paley, Mrs. William Randolph Hearst, and Madame Jean Ralli, all equally at home in an English country house, a Paris salon, or a New York nightclub, was as much attributable to increased affluence, easier travel, and faster communications as it was to the good offices of *Vogue*. But there was undoubtedly a connection. At a time when the most chic leisure activity in the world was to be a passenger on board ship, the three international editions of *Vogue* were able perfectly to chronicle the progress of these glamorous entourages in page after page of photographs and chatter about Americans abroad, Europeans in New York, and everyone of the beau monde on seemingly permanent vacation.

Condé Nast, too, became an international figure, taking trips to Europe every year to visit his foreign offices. With the elegant Frank Crowninshield on his arm as golf partner in England, translator in Paris, and social companion in New York, Nast represented *Vogue* in every sense of the word. Sustained by his suits from London, his hats from Paris, and his publishing fame from New York, he had realized, at least in external terms, the splendid mirage of which he had so determinedly dreamed. He finally belonged in the magic circle which had for so long fascinated him.

# NINE

# DROIT DU SEIGNEUR

In 1921, Frank Crowninshield moved into 470 Park Avenue, the apartment of his friend and employer, Condé Nast. Clarisse had moved out; the two men, buoyed by mutual success, had become almost inseparable. "I can get you in anywhere," Crowninshield assured his less well-connected friend—and he did. They became a familiar couple at parties, openings, theatres, operas, nightclubs, and the most exclusive Fifth Avenue salons. The gossip sheet, *Town Topics,* came right out with it and referred to the two as "Frank Crowninshield and his protégé, Condé Nast."

The stories about Frank Crowninshield's influence on Nast's social progress are probably exaggerated. It is undoubtedly true that Crowninshield was able to introduce Nast to almost any personage worth knowing in New York. It is also true that he helped Nast's passage into various New York clubs not previously penetrated by the publisher. He also encouraged Nast to join such new clubs as the Cavendish, an auction bridge club that daringly allowed women to become members. Crowny's own Boston Brahmin background made him an ideal Pygmalion. Nast's quick mind, personable appearance, and instinctive good taste overcame with ease the rain in Spain.

One of the most widely accepted canards is that Frank Crowninshield got Condé Nast into the *Social Register*. In fact, Nast's name first appears in the social bible in 1902, the year of his marriage to Clarisse Coudert. It was the connection with her, as we have seen, that facilitated his entry, not the good offices of Crowninshield, whose relationship with Nast was not established until considerably later. This may seem a trifling matter, but in those years when Society Counted (both metaphorically and literally), getting into the *Social Register* was about as difficult as getting into Heaven—and apparently as divinely rewarding. It was a *must,* and the fact that Frank Crowninshield is wrongfully credited in Nast's case indicates the extent to which observers rated Crowninshield's influence—and Nast's dependency.

In many ways they were dissimilar. Crowninshield was witty, charming, and malicious to his very bones. Nast was a verbal dullard by comparison. Crowninshield was a Brooks Brothers original—everything from his pink shirts to his black knit ties—whereas Nast favored English tailoring and French hats. Crowninshield had faintly amoral tendencies, at least on the occasion related by Edmund Wilson, when Crowninshield, who needed for some reason the text of a letter by Voltaire, borrowed a volume of Voltaire from Putnam's bookstore and simply cut out the pages he needed and sent the volume back, knowing that this would not be detected. Nast would never in a million years have done something like that; he was honorable to the point of naiveté. What they shared was an unabashed devotion to the pursuit of urbane, comfortable living—the kind of Edwardian Mode to which Crowninshield had been born, and to which Nast now belonged. "You go to the Twomblys' [she was a granddaughter of Commodore Vanderbilt] in Madison on a Sunday," Crowninshield explained, "—eleven acres of rolling lawn, twenty-five kinds of evergreens. It may be wrong to keep four men to mow the grass, but it does seem a pity all that has to disappear. It has to do with taste and elegance, and if

Condé Nast had his photograph taken at a joke photograph booth in Atlantic City on two separate occasions, so he must have enjoyed it—but you'd never know from his expression.

you don't have those things in the world, the results may be quite serious."

Along with this mutual pleasure in the refinements of life, Crowninshield and Nast shared a passionate interest in people of all kinds. The parties that later became the one thing anyone really remembered about Condé Nast were an outcome of this tireless interest.

Many people attribute the origins of "café society" to the sophisticated congruence of society and the arts created by Nast and Crowninshield at their parties. The guests were mostly culled from Crowninshield's eclectic circle of friends, whom Nast welcomed with reckless generosity. Typically, Nast himself described it in a more down-to-earth way. "Around 1922," he said, "I got a little money and decided to give a party. I thought, 'My God, I can't give a party; my friends are too mixed. I can't leave out George Gershwin and I can't leave out Mrs. Vanderbilt and I can't have them together.' But I did, and to my surprise, everyone liked it."

Nast and Crowninshield entertained together, traveled together, ate together, joined clubs together, played golf together, went abroad together, and lived together for six years.

There was talk, needless to say, of a sexual connection.

In New York in the twenties, homosexuality was a titillating topic, and to be an overt homosexual was very modern indeed. John McMullin, *Vogue*'s most frequently featured social columnist, and onetime menswear reporter for *Vanity Fair*, was as far out of the closet as one could be in those delicately perfumed days. Johnnie, as everyone called him, was a petit Californian with an unerring eye for the Mode and a penchant for the international life which prefigured the jet set. He was one of Nast's most loyal employees, and in the bad days of the Depression Nast wrote to him saying, "Thank you, Johnnie, your devoted loyalty is one of my treasures." In the late thirties, after a long, courtierlike association with Elsie de Wolfe and her husband, Sir Charles Mendl, McMullin left the Nast organization to live full-time with the aging decorator. (She was paying him an allowance of $5,000 a year and had promised him a great part of her fortune when she died.) In recognition of the close

ties between Nast and McMullin, Elsie wrote to Condé for his permission to take darling Johnnie away, which he graciously gave.

McMullin's predilections were such that, although Nast adored
him personally, the publisher was finally obliged to remove him
from his post as *Vanity Fair*'s menswear writer. By the late twenties, his reporting had grown increasingly mauve ("A complete jewelry kit is a most important part of a well-dressed man's wardrobe,"
and "Although the poets would have us believe differently, it is frequently his clothes to which a young man's fancy really turns in the
spring," were examples), and Nast found a young writer called
Ewart Newsom to resurrect the proper masculine *ton*. "I had been
sent to Exeter by my Canadian parents in all the wrong clothes—
tweed hat, green tweed suit, what a Canadian bumpkin would
wear," Red Newsom said later. "So clothing was a very important
factor in my early years. I think Nast must have had the same feeling, because his background was a simple one. He was as serious
about fashion as I was. I thought fashion percolated down from the
top, and that was all he needed to know."

As for the editor of *Vanity Fair*, he could not have cared less
about men's fashion, in spite of being impeccably dressed himself.
But this did not except him from sexual speculation. Well, was he or
wasn't he? Edmund Wilson, who worked for him briefly in 1920,
thought he was not. "In spite of his not very attractive habit of
seizing you by the arm in a way that seemed calculated to establish
some kind of sexual ascendancy, I do not believe that he was. He
once told me that he had a girl who came to see him once a week;
and this seems more in line with his cautious habits, for he was
careful in his personal relations and, in spite of his show of friendli-
ness, always managed to keep people at a discreet distance."

Crowninshield certainly liked pinching girls' bottoms in a playful,
and sometimes not very pleasing, way. He loved the company of
women and flattered them expertly. He wrote unfailingly amusing
letters to female relations and friends, such as this one to young
Lydia Sherwood (Robert Sherwood's niece), who had fallen from a
horse: "How could a horse conceivably want to part company with
*you,* of all women? I wish, dear, that I might aid you, in some *safe*

way, but long experience has taught me never to help a fallen woman." But his role as escort to innumerable society ladies, his faintly affected walk, his fascination with appearances, his commitment to "10,000 Nights in a Dinner Coat" (the title of one of his articles), his flowery attentions to the mothers of his staff, his love of club life, and his style of wit were all characteristics of the kind of elegant, urbane "bachelor" typified by Noel Coward. Jeanne Ballot, Crowninshield's personal secretary, recalls no evidence of the girl he conjured up for Edmund Wilson (who found the whole *Vanity Fair* world quite shocking). The only person Crowninshield seems genuinely to have cared passionately about was his sad, drug-addicted brother, Edward, an antique dealer in Stockbridge, Massachusetts, to whom his devotion was deep and constant until Edward's death in 1938. Another *Vanity Fair* (and later *Vogue*) colleague, Allene Talmey, used the word "eunuch" to describe him, which probably is as good as any to explain the significant fact that there was never a word proved, during his lifetime or after, about his enjoying a sexual liaison with *anyone*—of either sex. His discretion, if indeed it was necessary, was exemplary.

"They probably thought we were fairies," Nast remarked later to his then amour, Helen Brown Norden. The idea to them was as humorous as the latest *mot* by Dorothy Parker. It was not men who interested Condé Nast.

"He believed that all women everywhere should have the opportunity to have the prettiest clothes, the prettiest surroundings, and every known method to make themselves more seductive, knowledgeable, and attractive," Diana Vreeland once said.

In 1920, the year of women's suffrage in America, Condé Nast was forty-seven years old. For fifteen years he had been involved with women's affairs, and for the last eleven he had watched Miss Vogue change from a properly flounced young society matron to a smart, fast, emancipated flapper. The development had been slow. *Vogue* itself is the best witness of the steps women had taken since Mrs. James Stillman dressed up as the Spirit of Liberty at Mrs. Clarence Mackay's *tableaux vivants* party for the Equal Franchise Society in 1911.

In May 1912, a *Vogue* columnist reported: "The other day I heard a perfectly dressed woman at a reception ask who were 'the two dowdy ladies in odd bits of faded finery,' conspicuous among the guests. When told they were two most successful women novelists, she remarked only, 'I thought they looked as if they wrote.' "

In April 1913, *Vogue* considered the following:

> The daughter who has been destined to a social career cannot, from that point of view, spend time upon any occupation that does not conduce to the successful development of that particular mode of life. When she leaves the finishing school, she has usually arrived at debutante age, and if, instead of taking up the life of the average girl in society, she enters the freshman class at college, she defers for at least four years all participation in the events and interests which constitute the conventional life of young people of her class. One result of this, according to some observers, is greatly to lessen her opportunities of making an advantageous marriage. . . . It seems logical, therefore, for mothers who desire to secure brilliant social careers for their daughters, to hesitate in cutting them off from the intimate life of the young people of their acquaintance. . . . There is also the possibility, much feared by some mothers, that the point of view of the girl may be radically changed by her contact with the young women students who are drawn from all social grades. This influence often results in a girl's going in for philanthropic work to such a degree as greatly to lessen the time and attention she might otherwise devote to social duties.

In August 1915, the magazine sighed: "Social evolution, it is constantly being suggested, is about to eliminate the lady just as non-functioning organs of plants and animals are gradually atrophied from lack of use. . . ."

And finally, in May 1919, *Vogue* asked the question that all women faced who had lived through the decade: "DOES THE OLD ORDER RETURN?"

> Women have faced such novel experiences, entered upon such interesting work, will they ever consent to return to their old ways?

Many of them have had the experience of doing things women have never done before; some women have also experienced the trials of doing things that others once had to do for them. . . . It is hard to see why a young and daintily neat woman should prefer the peaked cap of an elevator boy to a bit of snowy lace and linen on her hair, why the factory surpasses the kitchen, provided work conditions are equal. Inevitably, it would seem, the work of woman must return to woman. . . .

While *Vogue* mused hopefully on *les temps perdus,* St. John Irvine wrote a forward-looking article in *Vanity Fair* on the New Girl, "a type of modern woman which is likely to bring the New Utopia to Ground."

I am perfectly sure that whatever revolutions may be coming in this country will have been brought about mainly, if not entirely, by the extraordinary change in the mental outlook of the young girl during the last five years. While men are arguing about Soviets and Socialism and Direct Action and similar doctrines invented by intellectuals who have learned to do everything but smile, and have studied everything except the common psychology of their countrymen, young women will be bringing about that state of society in which people will be ashamed to exist without accomplishing a definite job of useful work. . . .

Condé Nast's own career, whatever *Vogue*'s utterances, had been committed to this most modern incarnation. He had consistently and unhesitatingly hired women for most of the important editorial posts on his magazines (Frank Crowninshield and Richardson Wright being the only exceptions)—a policy that flew in the face of the conventional wisdom. In 1920, the doyen of women's magazine publishing and editor of the *Ladies' Home Journal,* Edward Bok, declared that full editorial authority of a modern magazine could not "safely be entrusted to a woman when one considers how largely executive is the nature of such a position." (Bok, one assumes, had not had the pleasure of an encounter with Edna Woolman Chase.) His position was rarely challenged, except by

Nast, and by this small voice, appearing unsigned, in *The Unpopular Review* (a socio/literary quarterly so aptly named that its circulation barely reached 2,000) in October 1916: "Why is it, I wonder, that the women's periodicals, always shrilly asseverating their noble ideals of woman, are nearly all carefully adapted in their text to infantile or arrested intelligence? Apparently this conception takes no heed of the women who can direct their households and manage their children with skill and grace and competence. No, we are all a flock of beautiful, but fat-headed little sheep. . . . Those [magazines] with the most glaring earmarks of their type—are edited by men."

Nast was only once heard to complain about his progressive hiring policy, when, after a particularly frustrating session at the office, he sighed to a colleague, "After a day like this, I feel that woman's place is in the home." For the most part, his respect for women was unshakable, and in 1937 his loyalty was rewarded with an award from the New York League of Professional and Business Women for his "liberal attitude toward women in business." He was convinced that women were the proper editors and writers for other women; he knew that male ignorance and arrogance would not build the readership he wanted. "Nothing that we can say is too clever for you," he told his readers in an anniversary salute in 1923: "Nothing we can print is too advanced for you. Making a magazine for you is like perpetually playing a first-night audience of a most astute and responsive character."

While the anonymous *Unpopular Review* writer might have found comfort in those words, Nast was subjected to a different kind of criticism. The accusation that he provided an agreeable finishing school to young ladies of good breeding (and private means) at the lowest salaries in town was only partly true. He divided his women employees into two categories—professionals and amateurs. The professionals—Edna Chase, Carmel Snow, Jessica Daves, Francesca Van Der Kley, Margaret Case, Allene Talmey—were paid a respectable salary. They put the magazines together and delivered them, complete, to the printers. The social types—Caroline Duer, Eleanor Barry, Ellin Mackay, Babe Cushing, and the hundreds of debutante editors who passed through *Vogue*'s office over the years—were amateurs. Nast paid them low wages and allowed them to drift in and out on their way to Newport, London, Biarritz, Rome. Their contributions, by mutual if tacit consent, were unreliable, ephemeral, and weighed nothing in their luggage. But they gave the publications chic, and their contacts provided vital entrée into the important ballrooms, dressmaking establishments, and country clubs of the day.

They also doubled as very high-class models.

Condé Nast knew nothing about fashion. Until the day he died, he could not tell you why a certain model was good or bad. But he was a connoisseur of women. His respect for them as colleagues was topped only by his appreciation of them as romantic inspiration. By showing in *Vogue* real women photographed in the latest Mode, which was his idea right from the start, he invested them with a new dimension of physical appeal. Society had always provided him with models. You were chosen because you were both upper class and also beautiful (such as Millicent Rogers, Mrs. Philip Lydig, and Mrs. Harrison Williams). Occasionally French mannequins were featured, protégées of the couturier and usually identified by first name only. Later, actresses became popular as models of the couture. By the twenties, photographers were using unknown girls with the right faces and bodies, for as fashion photography became more sophisticated, it required precision measurements on which to drape the designer's creations.

At this time French designers, anxious to woo American buyers, realized that French mannequins did not look like American women. So in 1924, the distinguished couturier Jean Patou held the first-ever mannequin audition in New York, sponsored by *Vogue*, to find American girls to model French fashions. ("Must be smart, slender, with well-shaped feet and ankles and refined of manner," ran the advertisement.) Over five hundred girls responded and five winners were chosen at the Ritz ballroom in New York by a jury consisting of Elsie de Wolfe, Edward Steichen, Edna Woolman Chase, Patou, and Condé Nast. (One of those selected was an eighteen-year-old Texas beauty named Edwina Pru, who was later to repay this favor to Condé Nast in a way he could not then have possibly imagined.)

Thus women all over America began to dream of a new kind of career, one that depended neither on brains nor on servitude, but on face and figure alone. Their looks became their passport to success, and the sensuous, glamorous, idealized photographs that filled Nast's magazines were the first socially acceptable erotic images ever to reach a national magazine readership. By the end of the decade, women were spending three quarters of a billion dollars on cosmetics and beauty aids. In Robert S. Lynd's Middletown, not one beauty parlor existed in 1900; by 1928 there were seven. Condé Nast's presiding spirit had contributed to the enshrinement of woman as sex object.

His personal favorites were not, as might have been expected, the refined offspring of the Fisheries or other compounds of good breeding. His association with Clarisse had weaned him of that. He preferred his women bright, lively, and independent, regardless of their bloodlines. His earliest serious involvement after Clarisse was with Grace Moore, the singer and opera star, who was the daughter of a traveling salesman and a Tennessee farm girl. Ten years later, his only significant attachment was to Helen Brown Norden, a *Vanity Fair* writer, whose father was an unsuccessful promoter and whose mother had been a provincial belle in Lafargeville, New York. He would have married both.

His separation from Clarisse signalled the entrance of a series of young and attractive women in Condé's life. Some were actresses, some were models, some were debutantes. Most had some connection with his magazines, which provided an enchanting and ever-refillable pool. Some were hired for temporary assignments, others were brought in by Nast himself. He was in the habit of meeting some pretty thing at a party in New York or Newport and inviting her to work for *Vogue.* A resigned Edna Chase then had to find these charming amateurs jobs for the duration of her employer's infatuation.

He always, without exception, responded to a pretty face. Benito first met Nast at a party Paul Poiret gave in Paris in 1921, and re-

The American woman as romantic ideal—posed by Steichen before a grand fireplace, wearing a bouffant tulle frock scattered with enormous flowers by Callot. *Vogue*, May 1, 1925.

The American woman as modern icon—this time placed by Steichen in a modernistic setting, draped in a Chinese silk scarf hand-colored in tones of red, purple, yellow, and orange by the Colour Studio. *Vogue*, June 1, 1925.

ports as follows: "I brought with me a young friend who was Scandinavian, like Greta Garbo, and as beautiful. As she did not own an evening dress, Poiret had lent her one of his gold lamé creations. It suited her marvelously. At our dinner table was also seated Condé Nast, and as my companion could speak English, the two of them carried on a conversation.

"When I came to New York about three years later, the first question Condé Nast asked me was, 'What happened to your Scandinavian girl?' "

A young male recruit, L. L. Calloway, who was employed in Nast's advertising department, remembers working in the office one Sunday and noticing a well-dressed man, "stylishly dressed, in fact, leaning out of the window, not far from where I was working. He was whistling to some woman in the nearby Commodore Hotel." When the elegant gentleman stopped his efforts, Calloway pounded vigorously on his typewriter to warn the whistler of his presence. "He came over to where I was sitting and in the most friendly manner asked me what I was doing there on a Sunday. I told him what my job was and he introduced himself. It was the great Condé Nast."

Nast's office life became inextricably entwined with his private penchants. In the washroom adjoining his office he had a private wire for beautiful women and stockbrokers. The office itself was in effect both an escort service and a feudal village, with Nast possessing *droit du seigneur*. Any unmarried woman drifting down the corridor was fair game. "Crowninshield's all right, but look out for Nast," mothers would warn. The staff disseminated endless stories: that the new model on the cover of *Vogue* was one of Mr. Nast's latest imports; that Mr. Nast made sorties to Grand Central Station and asked the prettiest girls arriving in New York from out of town if they wanted jobs on *Vogue;* that he had a separate apartment near the office where he spent romantic afternoons; that his socially prominent friend and banker, Harrison Williams, once said about Condé: "He hires them, sires them, and fires them." (No member of the staff complained that her job had been threatened in this way;

at least one, however, is known to have found the situation intolerable and resigned.)

At the beginning of his years of freedom, Nast's fixation was understandable and very much of the period. Everyone who had survived the Great War felt the same—both guilty and triumphant at being alive, and determined to make the most of it. Nast's first legitimate affair soon became public knowledge. He had started seeing Grace Moore before his marriage ended (this accelerated the separation as far as Clarisse was concerned), and the affair quickly blossomed. In 1922 they spent the summer in Paris together, and he introduced her to his friends Elsie de Wolfe, Edward Molyneux (the dress designer), and Millicent Hearst, the separated wife of Nast's rival William Randolph Hearst. He escorted her to Metropolitan Opera openings in New York, and although it had been a long time since he had played the flute, his musical instincts must have revived on hearing his loved one's Metropolitan debut in 1928 as Mimi in *La Bohème*. His devotion to the singer was such that on one occasion, when she was sailing to Europe without him, he arrived at her cabin carrying a whole orchid tree.

After Miss Moore's marriage to Valentin Parera, they remained good friends, and the Pareras were frequent guests at Nast's parties. In 1934, when Parera was working in Hollywood, Nast squired Grace to her fabulously successful film debut in *One Night of Love* at the Radio City Music Hall. They arrived too early and she asked him to drive her round the theatre so she could see her name in lights. "Well, Gracie," he said to her as they looked at the glittering signs, "I always knew it would happen. But from now on the worst is to come. Now you have to sit on top of the world and hold on. Take everything this brings and love it, assimilate it for all it means, but you're going to have to separate the rose from the sting and sometimes it's not easy. Your job is just beginning."

The generous message reflects the essence of Condé, wise and wistful behind the social facade.

Grace Moore was a vivacious, bubbly, energetic woman who liked to tease. She was also headstrong. On one occasion she interrupted a concert tour to join Condé in London. He was staying at Claridge's and had forgotten to prepare the authorities for her visit, so in the middle of the night the hotel manager knocked on the door and told him that his female companion must leave. Grace Moore turned on the flunkey and shouted, "I came three thousand miles to be with this man. Now you just get out of here and leave us alone." He did.

It may surprise some people (it no doubt did then) that Condé Nast, with his pince-nez, stiff deportment, and austere features, should be worth traveling three thousand miles for, but Helen Brown Norden (later Lawrenson, author of "Latins Are Lousy Lovers") has described in vivid terms the earthy sexuality the publisher exhibited with her when he was approaching sixty and she was twenty-four. Mrs. Lawrenson's recorded accounts of Condé's sexual enthusiasms reveal most clearly the basic paradox in his nature. He was sophisticated on the outside, childlike on the inside; the starched exterior belied the wanton will. With the encouragement of a pretty woman (the younger the better), the jack-in-the-box flew open to reveal the libertine.

This dichotomy characterizes much of Victorian life and literature. Men attempted to maintain a public pose of the highest rectitude while in private giving rein to their libidinous desires, a social and moral hypocrisy that lingered well into the twentieth century. William Randolph Hearst mercilessly chastised Mae West through his newspapers while carrying on an adulterous affair with Marion Davies. Nast, entirely lacking in self-righteousness, confronted a daily battle between his background and his desires; its unremitting severity gave him pain in place of pleasure. An episode described in a letter from Ilka Chase to her mother vividly illustrates his unease, which had clearly set in at an early date. Ilka was at a finishing school in Paris in 1921, and Nast, on one of his regular visits to the French capital, took her out to tea.

"While we were taking tea a woman passed our table whom Mr. Nast knew. Of course he spoke to her and I heard him explaining who I was, etc., and he told me afterwards that he had had to make it all clear or people would go round saying, 'Isn't that terrible? Condé Nast is a regular cradle snatcher.' "

This was in 1921, when his career with women had hardly started. His anxiety about his reputation then was as nothing compared with what it must have been by the end of the twenties, when he married a girl almost exactly the same age as his daughter. He took a gamble with his moral conscience, and he lost. Social and financial pressures defeated his desire. The marriage lasted barely three years.

Our psychohistorical century would interpret his behavior as a classic case of inability to achieve a close relationship with women, based on childhood guilt caused by having replaced his absent father in his mother's affections. This anxiety was compounded by the loss of a father with whom to identify. Thus his sexual identity was at risk, and the constant need for masculine authenticity drove him from woman to woman in an endless, frustrated quest. Nast's views of women were formed by those he knew in childhood—his admirable French Catholic mother, his two fiercely independent sisters, and his equally admirable Scottish Methodist grandmother (who, incidentally, was mortified by his occupation with "female" magazines; she wanted him to be a lawyer, the profession for which he had been trained). These powerful models gave him a respect for women that worked greatly to his advantage in his career, but in private life they ultimately defeated him.

Occasionally he was able to bring his warring selves into harmony. His involvement with Helen Brown Norden lasted from 1932 (when she was divorced from her first husband, Heinz Norden) until after she left *Vanity Fair* in 1936, in spite of the fact that he had to fire her and several others from the magazine in a last-ditch effort to save it from going under. The tactic failed, and *Vanity Fair* folded, but that does not seem to have affected their relationship. Nast once told Helen that she and Grace Moore were the two most glamorous women he had ever known. With Helen, he was a child again, or at least the child he would have liked to have been. They used to go to Atlantic City and ride in the boardwalk wheelchairs, or to Pali-

Nast's great favorite Helen Brown Norden. *Vanity Fair*, February 1933.

Singer Grace Moore, Condé Nast's first serious sweetheart after his separation from Clarisse, made frequent appearances in *Vanity Fair*. Photograph by Steichen, *Vanity Fair*, December 1923.

sades Park and drink beer and play pinball games. Even in his luxurious apartment at 1040 Park Avenue they abandoned decorum. "Condé had a book of exercises, *The Culture of the Abdomen*," Mrs. Lawrenson remembered, "and he insisted that we try the exercises, one of which consisted of rotating the stomach while holding onto the back of a chair; stomach in, up, over, out, down—as if turning like a chicken on a rotisserie spit—and while we were energetically doing this, the butler came into the room unexpectedly. His eyes almost popped out. 'Don't stop,' said Condé. 'You'll lose the rhythm.' "

In a way, Condé Nast was too old too soon. He reached the pinnacle of his success, and the height of his liberation, when he was already over fifty—an old man in the eyes of the debutantes and models he picked from the offices of *Vogue* and *Vanity Fair* to be his companions. As he grew older, his increasing loneliness was accentuated by the constantly shifting women at his side. There was a different one every night, called by his secretary to accompany Mr. Nast to an opening, a cabaret, a play. The *Vogue* girls sighed when Nast's office telephoned for "yet another boring date with Mr. Nast." They became younger and younger, less and less in touch with his world or his time. He gave them champagne at the Stork Club; they wanted beer at La Rue's. He lunged predictably in taxis; they worried lest his pince-nez fall off.

Nast had always felt comfortable in the company of men. Whether on the golf course, playing bridge, or talking business at a cocktail party, he could let down his guard and relax. With women he could not find this ease of manner. Unlike his friend Frank Crowninshield, he could not entertain them with wit and extravagant speeches. His shyness was a barrier. His severe manner must have seemed forbidding. To get to know him would have taken time and effort, commodities of little currency in those jazz-happy days in New York. What he offered was money, prestige, and fame, three well-known aphrodisiacs. Who *didn't* want to be photographed in *Vogue*? (Later, in the Depression, who *didn't* want to keep her job?) There was no shortage, therefore, of female attendants, whom he wore, in Ludwig Bemelmans's phrase, like boutonnières, to be quickly discarded when the evening was done. What Nast deprived himself of was a deeper understanding or affection that might have eased the difficult years to come. He did not want to be alone. It was as though he felt that life had passed him by and that he must, somehow, catch up. He wanted gaiety, vigor, youth. But what do you say to a twenty-year-old model?

"He had no hubris, no dishonest tricks, no vanity, and there was nothing mean, cruel, violent, vicious or bitchy about him," wrote Helen Lawrenson. His kindness, generosity and passions were all directed toward the sex to which he devoted his life, and which repaid him by making him a millionaire, but not a fulfilled human being.

In September 1928, the following announcement appeared in *Vanity Fair*:

### THE ERA'S CHANGED

Back in the days when young ladies sat stiffly on the hair-cloth sofa and embroidered antimacassars . . . when fainting was an accomplishment . . . NO girl would have dreamed of a career! But—times have changed! Women don't faint at the slightest provocation. Most girls, before they are twenty, become interested in the world in general and in some work in particular! They become artists or writers. They learn to be efficient secretaries, teachers, nurses, interior decorators, architects. Perhaps you have always had a secret longing to develop your ability along some particular line . . .

This was an advertisement for Condé Nast's Educational Bureau—another example of the publisher's unfaltering belief in women as people. He may have failed to live out that belief in private; his personal fantasies may have reflected an unrealistic vision of perfection; and his sexual Victorianism undoubtedly diminished his chances for personal happiness. But he never allowed his dreams to get in the way of the advancement of Miss Vogue. Frank Crowninshield and he never underestimated the intelligence of the women readers of *Vanity Fair* and *Vogue*: Nast's hymn to women in the pages of his magazines was a progressive testament for its time.

# TEN

# GIRLS WITH LONG NECKS

From the romantic, childlike creatures of the turn of the century to the graceful cubist sirens of the twenties and the earthy, knowing personages of the thirties and forties, *Vogue*'s covers reflected an image of women, as they progressed through the decades, against which many of them, consciously or subconsciously, measured themselves. Oscar Wilde once said that it was not until Burne-Jones and Dante Gabriel Rossetti began painting, in London, so many girls with very long necks that so many girls with very long necks began appearing in London. This principle could be applied perfectly to *Vogue*'s portrayal of ideal femininity on its covers.

In the earliest days of *Vogue* as a society gazette, the possibility had not yet surfaced that such preoccupations might contribute to the success of the magazine. *Vogue*'s covers, in consequence, were often characterless and perfunctory, leaning toward the academic school of art, with little tableaux entitled "Invitation," "Solitaire," "Chums—Engaged," or "Paddling Her Own Canoe." There was also the occasional art nouveau abstract design or blurry photograph of some society patroness.

Condé Nast changed all that. He knew that the single most important piece of artwork in a magazine was its cover. If the cover could be made seductive and intriguing enough, people would buy the magazine at the newsstand; and the economics of this kind of magazine publishing depended then, and depend now, largely upon the size of newsstand sales. Immediately abandoning photography and plunging into color, Nast experimented with all sorts of styles and periods of illustration, from ornate rococo scenes to Renoir-like portraits. By 1912 he had settled on at least one authentic *Vogue* cover artist. Her name was Helen Dryden and in 1912 she painted six covers, many more than any other artist. Dryden's early work was romantic, simple and posterish in style, and she was one of *Vogue*'s most prolific and successful artists for ten years. (Later, in response to the influences of the period, her work became more developed and subtle, filled with grace and movement.)

As an indication of Nast's belief in the importance of his artists and his covers, a cover credit line appears on *Vogue*'s contents page as early as October 1909. The artist is Gale Porter Hoskins, who was responsible on this occasion for a charming version of the *Vogue* emblem (a shepherdess stepping through the letter *V*), which was originated by Harry McVickar and frequently adapted over the years by other *Vogue* artists.

Masthead credits for covers then lapse until November 15, 1912, when they start appearing with regularity. That issue carried a cover of a splendidly posed eighteenth-century tableau of a masked harlequin and his rose-coiffured *amoureuse* by Frank X. Leyendecker, also destined to become one of Nast's favorite artists. The December 1 credit went to G. Wolf Plank, perhaps the most brilliant of the early illustrators, who continued to work for Nast for fifteen dazzling years. The Christmas cover, devoted to a turbaned lady with a holly wreath draped over her shoulders like a feather boa, was, suitably enough, by Helen Dryden.

By this time, Condé Nast's covers, displaying the most interesting decorative talent available in America, were regarded by the fashionable world as an education in taste. In the spring of 1914, at a charity Easter fete at the Waldorf Astoria, society posed in a series of *tableaux vivants* inspired by *Vogue* covers (Miss Beatrice Pratt and Mrs. Walter Stillman, for instance, mimed two Helen Dryden creations; Mrs. John L. Saulles and Mrs. Lloyd Aspinall reproduced covers by George Plank). In the winter of 1914, New York's Hotel Majestic opened a new restaurant called the Café Moderne. For its wall decorations, the café chose reproductions of *Vogue* covers, including work by Dryden, Plank, Leyendecker, and E. M. A. Steinmetz. And in 1918 paper bags with *Vogue* covers on them were sold for the benefit of the Red Cross.

The message of all these early covers is elegance, grace, with a tinge of exoticism. Women wear fantastical hats with trailing ribbons or curling plumes; their bodies are draped seductively on chaises lounges or swept up in a carpet made of stars of the Milky Way. They look pensively out of drawing-room windows at a large pale yellow moon; they pick fruit from brilliantly colored bowls or push a garden cart overflowing with daisies. There was movement, romance, and the most charming use of color in the decade's first covers, yet little artistic innovation. There was nothing to shock the American reader—no Nudes Descending Staircases along the lines of the art that appeared at the 1913 Armory Show. Nast's early covers depended on a certain Edwardian prettiness with overtones of the English Pre-Raphaelites and art nouveau fantasists such as Edmund Dulac, Arthur Rackham, and Alphonse Mucha. The women they immortalized were soft, feminine, mysterious, and a little perverse, given to aloof pursuits and secret smiles.

In an anniversary issue of *Vogue* in 1923, Nast praised three other artists as well as those mentioned: "Miss Claire Avery, whose delicate and charming sketches are familiar to all our readers; Miss Irma Campbell, who has drawn many changing silhouettes of the mode for us both in Paris and New York; and Mrs. Polly Tighe Francis because she has been with us many years, and because she draws fashions that are exactly what fashions should be."

Behind this gracious salute lay a vital key to the success of Nast's *Vogue*, for the elegance and aesthetic charm of the covers were only one aspect of the magazine's illustrative function. *Vogue* was specifically dedicated to imparting to its readers information about fashion—and that could be done only by the most careful rendering of the clothes that came out of the couture houses in Paris.

The fashion illustrations in Turnure's *Vogue* were stiff, tentative little things—an occupational hazard. Fashion artists were severely restricted by the condition of having to draw in most accurate detail every frill, seam, and buttonhole on the garment so that dressmakers around the country could copy it—and store buyers could know precisely what they were buying. Such a restriction almost totally prohibited any attempt at creativity on the part of the artist. In *Vogue*'s case, they were further hampered by the editor's acute lack of interest in the inert models that passed for fashion art. Harry McVickar himself was a skillful artist and could convey great grace and style in his pen-and-ink drawings. But he preferred to illustrate more masculine topics, full-page cartoons, and the occasional cover.

Nast saw that something had to be done about the fashion look of his magazine. Having witnessed the effect of Charles Dana Gibson's creations on the circulation of *Collier's,* between 1904 and 1906, when the artist drew one hundred pictures for him, he knew that a major impact could be made on *Vogue*'s fashion pages with the right artists. By 1909, the Gibson Girl was not only the foremost image of female perfection for Americans, but she had inspired, in a prefiguration of the media tie-ins so common later in the century, a whole industry of Gibson Girl shirtwaists, Gibson Girl skirts, Gibson Girl shoes, and even the Gibson Girl corset. Every girl in America wanted that cinched-in waist, those luxuriant curls swept up high, those tall collars, that long neck, that regal carriage, and that remote, supercilious, sexless smile. You could even wallpaper your room with the Gibson Girl's face repeated over and over and over. . . .

The trouble was that every other artist, it seemed, had been afflicted with Gibson's sensational vision. However hard each one tried, all the girls they drew for Nast's magazine turned out to look just like more Gibson Girls—only without the magic touch that be-

A version of the Gibson Girl drawn by Charles Dana Gibson in 1899—
healthy, unruffled, untouchable, wielding her golf club with unassailable
confidence.

longed to the originator alone. In 1910 and 1911 *Vogue*'s pages are haunted by the Gibson Girl's ubiquitous influence, dulled by the continued requirement of absolutely meticulous presentation of every dressmaking detail. By 1913 cover artists Helen Dryden, George Plank, and E. M. A. Steinmetz had been talked into occasionally doing some fashion work, but Dryden's and Steinmetz's efforts seem unconvincing, while Plank chose only the more exotic costumes to portray, which he could embellish with his customary imaginative flourishes. Meanwhile, a stream of other nameless artists continued to struggle with the unresponsive medium of nuts-and-bolts fashion drawing.

While Nast was pondering how to inject some life into his versions of the Mode, an exciting breakthrough had taken place on the other side of the Atlantic. It was spearheaded by Paul Poiret, the great French couturier, whose commitment to fantasy made him one of the most exotic and colorful figures of the late Belle Epoque. Poiret was a fantastical character who loved gold lamé, the Orient, and any kind of visual excess. He would appear at fancy-dress parties with his hair and beard painted gold; in the spring of 1911 he gave a party called the Ball of the Thousand and Second Night, at which all the guests came dressed as Persians, with himself as sultan, dressed in a pale gray quilted caftan with fur trimming and a white silk turban encrusted with jewels. His garden was decorated for the occasion with a painted awning by Raoul Dufy, and filled with pink ibis, white peacocks, and flamingoes. The highlight of the evening was the release of the sultan's favorite from a golden cage—this was his wife, Mme. Poiret, who pranced out in white-and-ocher chiffon harem pants, a gold lamé tunic, a gold lamé turban decorated with a great aigrette, and bangles on her wrists and ankles, all designed, of course, by Poiret himself.

His clothes idealized the female form in motion, a radical departure from the confining corsetry and constricted bosoms dictated by Edwardian fashion. Just as, in America, Isadora Duncan was seeking freedom from the tyranny of female costume in her floating, free-form dances, so Poiret demanded a new medium to express his sensuous, rhythmic creations. The old formal fashion plate could not remotely convey his dynamic vision. In 1908, he asked an un-known artist, Paul Iribe, to make for him an album of illustrations of his fashion designs. "He was an extremely odd chap," Poiret wrote of Iribe, "a Basque, plump as a capon, and reminding one both of a seminarist and of a printer's reader. He wore gold specta-cles, and a wide open collar, around which was tied rather loosely a scarf of the sort affected by Mr. Whitney Warren" (the famous American architect, who lived in Paris).

Iribe produced his plates by making ink drawings, which were then hand-colored by a time-consuming and expensive process known as *pochoir*—a form of hand-stenciling that created an effect of brilliant blocks of color with a bare minimum of detail. It was a perfect technique to express Poiret's fashions. Iribe introduced mo-nochromatic backgrounds to enhance the brilliant, unshaded col-ored areas of the clothes, which were modern and simple, falling in the sinuous lines that were the trademark of Poiret's work. Iribe was also the first artist who dared to show models with their backs turned to the reader.

This revolutionary way of presenting gowns reflected the dra-matic changes taking place in the haute couture. Breaking out of the corseted rigidities of the late Victorian and Edwardian Mode, couturiers like Paquin, Redfern, Doeuillet, and Vionnet followed Poiret's lead and both simplified and liberated the Mode. Paris taste was also deeply affected by the appearance of the Ballets Russes, who first performed before the French in 1909, and later returned to dazzle audiences in Paris and London with Fokine's innovative choreography and Bakst's and Benois's opulent fabrics and brilliant colors.

Poiret rightly claimed he had prepared the way. "I approached all colors from their peaks," he said in his autobiography, "and gave life to exhausted hues. Into the neurasthenic pastels, I hurled hell-bent wolves—reds, greens, purples, royal blues, orange, lemon." (As someone once said of Poiret, "If he did not dress an era, he certainly dyed it.") "But it was neither by returning life to colors nor by launching new forms," he continued, "that I rendered the greatest service to my epoch. It was by inspiring artists that I served the public of my time." In 1911, Poiret gave another un-known artist, Georges Lepape, the task of producing a second fash-ion album, *Les Choses de Paul Poiret*. Lepape was an even better communicator of Poiret's designs. He went further than Iribe—more flat blocks of color, impressionist backgrounds, white space, and highly theatrical poses for the models, who wore turbans, long, high-waisted dresses in mauves, lavenders, and purples, bobbed hair and languid expressions.

The appeal of these albums, with their opulently produced po-choir plates, was quickly appreciated by luxury-magazine publish-ers. Lepape was the artist chosen for the first of the new fashion journals that sprang up in 1912—*Modes et Manières d'Au-jourd'hui*. It was followed by *Le Journal des Dames et des Modes*, and toward the end of that year, the most famous of them all, *La Gazette du Bon Ton*, which appeared under the proprietorship of Lucien Vogel. Vogel was to play an important part in Condé Nast's career.

Lucien Vogel was a publisher, like Nast, not a fashion expert. His background had been in the publishing of high-quality art books, theatre albums, books of drawings. He also belonged to one of the most elegant social cliques in Paris at that time, many of whose members were artists—and it is these artists who became the back-bone of his *Gazette*. To ensure the success of his chic little publica-tion, he signed up a team of regular illustrators, whose talents have assured them a place in magazine history—Lepape, Charles Mar-tin, Georges Barbier, André Marty, Robert Bonfils, Pierre Brissaud, Paul Iribe, Bernard Boutet de Monvel, and later Benito, occasion-ally Erté, and Kees van Dongen. The original group of artists were known as the Beau Brummells or Knights of the Bracelet because, in characteristically self-conscious and stylized manner, they all wore bracelets.

In New York *Vogue* excitedly described them: "A certain dan-dyism of dress and manner which is a constant characteristic of a group makes them a 'school.' Their hat brims are a wee bit broader than the modish ones of the day and the hats are worn with a slight tilt, a very slight tilt but enough to give the impression of fastidiousness. Their coats are pinched in just a little at the waist, their ties are spotless and their boots immaculate. A bracelet slipping down over a wrist at an unexpected moment betrays a love of luxury."

To support these expensive tastes, fortunately, these dandies were obliged to produce a consistently high standard of work, which appeared in the *Gazette* over amusing little captions—another departure from the serious descriptive efforts of earlier journals. Provocative situations would be invented to enliven fashion titling, like "Ciel, Mon Mari!" for a particularly flirtatious evening gown.

Vogel, shrewd enough to ensnare such a talented group, also secured the sponsorship of seven of the most important couturiers in Paris for his magazine—Chéruit, Doeuillet, Lanvin, Doucet, Poiret, Redfern, and Worth. Their backing helped Vogel maintain the high-quality paper, printing, and artwork that he felt vital for the image of the *Gazette*. After all, as he recklessly announced, his magazine was "a showcase in which only the most luxurious examples of high fashion and the best of the decorative arts could be displayed, regardless of the cost involved."

Vogel was, in the words of Edna Chase, like a "dandified frog. He had round, protruding eyes and a chin lost in the flaring points of his exceptionally high collar. He also fancied lemon-yellow waistcoats, which he fondly believed gave him a British aspect." Nast probably met Vogel for the first time in 1914, when *Vogue* and the French couture got together to form the Protective Association of French Dressmakers. Vogel was one of the members of the syndicate. He spoke very little English, and Nast spoke no French, so their meeting can hardly have been inspiring; but it was to mark the beginning of a very important collaboration that lasted until Nast's death.

Nast's admiration for Vogel's *Gazette* knew no bounds. The French publisher's pursuit of quality at whatever the cost coincided with the standards Nast had set for *Vogue*. The work of Vogel's artists reflected the progress of the Mode in its more avant-garde forms, breaking with the old-fashioned tradition of illustration Nast himself had for so long been trying to eliminate. Moreover, these artists were participating in an extraordinary configuration of art and fashion that was taking shape in Paris, a fusion that occurs only once or twice in a century.

The couturier Jacques Doucet would collect Negro sculpture and cubist painting far in advance of their general acceptance. Paul Poiret would design the dining room of the ocean liner *Ile de France*. The fabric and dress designer Fortuny would construct a dome for La Scala, Milan. The newest and most modern dressmaker of them all, Chanel, would do costumes for the Ballets Russes.

And Bakst would draw a cover for *Vogue*.

Nast, like Diaghilev, provided a fuse that animated the artists' visions, and helped shape the modern movement.

The outbreak of the Great War offered Nast the involvement he was looking for. By 1915, paper costs, a falling interest in fashion, and the fact that many couturiers were not in Paris but at the front left the *Gazette* too weakened to continue. From 1915 to 1919 the *Gazette* ceased publication, and Nast harnessed its talent to his own publication. On July 15, 1916, American readers of *Vogue* learned for the first time of the artist Georges Lepape, who was profiled in the following issue with sensational costume designs for "L'Age d'Or des Bêtes," and "Les Maîtres de l'Heure," two French ballets created by a revue choreographer named Rip. "After the bewildering beauty of the Russian Ballet, we might have thought that our taste and our love of luxury in decoration would be forever dulled. M. Lepape has taken it upon himself to show us that the French taste is as discriminating as ever," wrote the profile writer, Jeanne Ramon Fernandez.

"And, by the way, who is Lepape that he suddenly springs upon Paris this rival to the Russian Ballet?" asked *Vogue* somewhat disingenuously. *"Vogue* will present to you in an interpretive article from one of its Paris contributors, the personality of this cleverly satirical painter-illustrator who dares to mock at modes in his fashion sketches and who in his ballet has incarnated bird and beast and metal with inimitable wit." In the same editorial, *Vogue* carefully paved the way for the appearance of the rest of Vogel's boys, including "the irrepressible A. E. Marty, one of that gay Beau Brummell group of Paris artists to which belong Lepape, Barbier, and Bernard Boutet de Monvel."

Lepape's first appearance on the cover of American *Vogue* was on October 15, 1916—a cover that was also reproduced the same month on one of the first-ever editions of the newly founded British *Vogue*. The debut was suitably dramatic—the cover portrayed a lady, her face almost hidden by a high fur collar and tricorne hat, enveloped in a red coat with a great flared skirt, huge fur cuffs and hem, standing on a checkerboard with her elongated umbrella pointing to what might be an olive branch. Behind her the dark storm clouds gather over France. In that issue Georges Barbier did some sketches of Geraldine Farrar as Thaïs, and in later issues he illustrated articles, one written by Roger Boutet de Monvel (Bernard's brother). Several examples of an early incarnation of Benito finish up the year.

The first of the modern French illustrators to appear in America was actually Erté, Russian by birth, who had apprenticed under Poiret as a dressmaker. His drawings, with their fabulously distorted figures and fantastic colors and backgrounds, guaranteed him recognition within the Bracelet set, and he did several fashion illustrations for the *Gazette du Bon Ton* before *Vogue*'s great rival, *Harper's Bazar,* scored the coup of presenting an Erté cover to America in January 1915. The artist did a few uncharacteristic drawings of window treatments, fruit arrangements, and other trivia for *Vogue* in 1916 before being put under exclusive contract by Hearst.

By 1917, Nast had his Beau Brummells regularly producing covers. But though he admired their fashion drawings in the *Gazette,* he was slow to put them to similar work in *Vogue.* American readers had to be introduced gradually to the radical new styles of illustration; American taste was more conservative than Europe's; and he and Edna Chase still held fast to his principle that fashion illustration must be, above all, informative. Also, another development was taking place that affected the way fashions could be portrayed—photography. By the beginning of the 1914–18 war, the technique of photography had reached a stage where it could reliably produce realistic reproduction of almost anything at all, as long as there was enough light. Photographs from Poiret, Doeuillet, Lanvin, Worth, Doucet, Jenny, and the other big houses began to pour into the New York office of *Vogue,* showing the most accurate representations ever dreamed of by an art director. Not only were they accurate, but they were also lifelike. Fashion illustration would never be the same. Now those stiff, formal drawings could be supplemented by living images. It was an entirely new toy for magazine publishers to play with.

Not that the photographs look so wonderful today. The models look almost as stiff as the drawings, and the outlines are blurred, gray, with little or no contrast or definition. As an art form, the medium was still in its infancy. It was to take another twenty years before a color photograph appeared on the cover of *Vogue.* But for the moment it relieved Nast of the continuing problem of rendering the Mode, and he concentrated on collecting a team of photographers who would make fashion come alive in America as successfully as the *pochoir* artists undoubtedly had in France.

After the end of the war, Paris revived. The *Gazette du Bon Ton* reappeared in 1920, with Vogel confidently declaring that "dress exemplified the spirit of its age," and that it was a "true document of its time." On this occasion Nast went through with his plan of producing an American edition, and in 1920 the first issue of the *Gazette du Bon Ton* appeared in New York. (The name had to be changed to *Gazette du Bon Genre* after four issues because the name *Bon Ton* was copyrighted by the S. T. Taylor Company.) The American edition ran the same plates as the Paris edition, but added American advertising. Nast charged $4.00 an issue, which may have seemed a lot to New York society, but seems a small amount today, even allowing for inflation, when one examines the exquisitely rendered hand-colored plates and the thick art paper on which the album was produced.

"We saw in America an opportunity to widen our field," the artist Benito remembers. "New York was very exciting for me. Some of my best friends were well-known artists and contributors to

*Vogue.* I had exhibitions organized at the Wildenstein Gallery, and we made money very easily, about $1,000 per drawing. I went back to France with a small fortune, and when my artist friends there saw me they all rushed to the United States to work there, too."

The profession was very competitive. Benito estimates that in the twenties there were at least six thousand working illustrators in New York, and over four thousand in Paris (compared with an estimated one hundred thousand in the United States today). *Vogue*'s art director, Heyworth Campbell, used to hold open house in his office every Friday so that artists could come in and show him their work. Vogel's French artists were *en pleine forme,* stimulated by the postwar explosion of energy in the decorative arts all over Europe. The style known as art deco, a largely French expression of skilled craftsmanship in luxurious materials and diverse functional and ethnic styles, was sweeping across the country and beyond. The French cabinetmaker Jacques-Emile Ruhlmann worked in exotic ebonies; Irish-born Eileen Gray used fabulous lacquers; in Vienna, Josef Hoffmann designed buildings encased in marble. The new style in furniture and decoration could be summed up in one word—"moderne."

And the modern look in fashion was long, long, long. Women's necks, fingers, legs, were transformed into fragile abstractions that emerged, drooping ever so slightly, from tubular gowns. Fabrics were soft and clinging, cut on the bias (Madeleine Vionnet's original invention), accentuating the elongated proportions of these new cubist goddesses. Chiffons, crepes, silks, Chanel's jersey swathed and draped the female form in graceful, luxurious cocoons. Wrists and arms twisted and coiled, extending seamlessly into long, thin cigarette holders; knees clung together in the hectic contortions of the chemise and the Charleston.

Artists like Lepape, Benito, Martin, and Barbier in France, Fish in England, and Claire Avery in America, had, as it were, been waiting, pens poised, for such a moment. Their drawings swirled and soared with the confidence of perfect expression as their women metamorphosed themselves into the sleek tubes, geometric shapes, and etiolated lines that characterized the new androgynous,

One of Helen Dryden's most elegant covers, her heroine in coils of rose-colored fabric, an amusing rose-and-turquoise hat, and a very unsentimental gray feather boa. The Chinoiserie mirror is a typical Dryden detail. *Vogue*, February 15, 1920.

The new art—Eric's impressionistic first cover, the model's head sketched in with the briefest of brushstrokes, her black glove dominating the pink and rose colors of the background. *Vogue*, November 10, 1930.

Georges Lepape's illustration of a red-and-gold lamé gown by Chéruit, resplendent, artful, decorative—but are there really no seams or fastenings? *Vogue*, January 1, 1923.

Benito's wonderfully elongated rendering of a silver velvet dress, trimmed with chinchilla, by Doucet—but how on earth does she pour herself in and out of it? *Vogue*, January 1, 1923.

sexually abandoned age. Even Helen Dryden portrayed modernism in her black-and-white fashion sketches. In 1920 Bakst did his cover for *Vogue*. In 1922, Chanel designed the costumes for Diaghilev's *Antigone,* with sets by Picasso. And in 1922, Nast launched six French artists in a new *Vogue* fashion series: each artist created a character (Françoise, Sophie, Sylvie, Rosine, Toinon, and Palmyre), to be portrayed each month in different clothes and situations, each in the individual style of illustration the artist favored. The title of this projected long-running serial was "The True History and Exploits of Six Parisiennes, Their Manners and Their Modes, Their Foibles and the Fables They Tell, Set Down Each Month for *Vogue.*" The artists were Benito, Brissaud, Lepape, Martin, Marty, and one new name, Mario Simon. Everyone was excited about the series, and about finally using the Beau Brummells for fashion reporting—what better proof could there be of the fusion between art and fashion than these new pages of *Vogue*?

"We swallowed them, hook, line and sinker," commented Nast later. "And, as a result, scored the first setback in the steady progress of *Vogue* since I had taken hold of the property. The trouble, soon obvious, was that this young group were chiefly interested in achieving amusing drawings and decorative effects—sometimes Japanese and sometimes eighteenth century; but they were bored to death by anything resembling an obligation to report the spirit of contemporary fashion faithfully—let alone to put seams and lines where they actually belonged."

The drawings are willful, wild, willowy, wonderful, but Nast was right. There was nothing in the way the clothes were represented to indicate a seam, a fastening, a tuck. Indeed they seemed hardly man-made at all, but surreal, otherworldly, triumphs of artifice, celebrations of the artists' imagination. So Nast was forced once again to return to basic principles—service before art. The gap between inspired and practical fashion drawing remained irreconcilable.

Nast was attacked in some quarters for a failure to keep in tune with artistic trends. "My critics at this time failed to realize that my decisions were not against a young movement of the day, but were decisions in support of *Vogue*'s mission in life—to serve those one

hundred and more thousands of women who were so literally interested in fashion that they wanted to see the mode thoroughly and
faithfully reported—rather than rendered as a form of decorative
art."

Mrs. Chase wholeheartedly backed him up. "I have never been
able to get up much sympathy for fashion artists who shrink from
clearly depicting the clothes they are sent to draw," she said
briskly. "If the great masters of old didn't think it beneath them
faithfully to render the silks and velvets, the ruffs and buttons and
plumes of their sitters, I don't see why it should be so irksome to
modern-day fashion artists to let a subscriber see what the dress she
may be interested in buying is really like."

Later, questions were raised about the exhilarating claim that art
and fashion had as gloriously coexisted in the pages of *Vogue* during the early postwar years as in the realms of music, drama, and
dance. Criticism concerned not the quality of the fashion art, but
the quality of the illustrators. Not one really great contemporary
artist was ever involved in Nast's fashionable publication. The influence of modern painters such as Toulouse-Lautrec, Braque, and
Matisse can be seen in the red-haired beauties of Iribe, the
sinuous lines of Martin, or the brilliant color splashes of Lepape—
but no museum has since collected the Beau Brummells' work. No
major painter of the period (with the arguable exception of Dali and
Tchelitchew) ever contributed to the *Gazette du Bon Ton* or to
*Vogue.*

There was, of course, Frank Crowninshield, who was renowned
for being in the artistic vanguard. In fact, so controversial was his
policy of publishing new French painters in *Vanity Fair* that, in the
August 1915 issue of the magazine, Robert Benchley wrote a piece
in which he bravely compared modern art to the work of a Montes-
sori eight-year-old, who could execute on his canvas—or on his
countenance—with some slight improvements in technique, that
post-impressionist masterpiece entitled "Absence of Mabel
Dodge." "The entire schools of Futurism and Post-Impressionism
could be turned over to the children to keep them out of still greater
mischief. They would get frightfully messed up of course, but think

of the ladies' portraits they could paint! Ladies with one yellow eye, and one green one, the green one somewhat smaller than its mate and at a somewhat trying right angle to it."

But even Crowny may have missed something. To be sure, he published Picasso and Braque in *Vanity Fair,* but his personal preferences were more modest. Despiau was his favorite sculptor, Segonzac and Marie Laurencin his favorite painters, and they made up the bulk of his own art collection. The only *Vogue* cover traceable to his influence was one by Marie Laurencin in 1923. These artists were pleasing to a certain taste and class, but the real maturity came later.

The restrictions of provincialism in France and America may have damaged the potential development of this type of magazine publishing. But the real explanation for the primacy of fashion over art in Nast's magazine remains the publisher's own sense of *Vogue*'s mission—faithfully and accurately to report the Mode. As for the covers, which were not constrained by such artistic limitations, Nast's policy was clearly expressed in 1926, when the *New York Herald Tribune* paid the following tribute to a *Vogue* cover:

> On the cover of one of those delightful magazines by which Mr. Condé Nast almost persuades us that style is an American invention, a lady recently rode a prancing steed. She sat side-saddle, clad in a habit of Victorian length, and cast upon the reader a glance of intense modesty. Nothing could have been more prim and conventional, save that as the eye looked close it discovered that the mount was a zebra, a neat black and white zebra, guided by scarlet reins. Examining yet more closely, the eye could descry the necks of three giraffes swimming across the middle distance.
>
> We have no means of knowing what, if any, symbolic meaning this lady possessed for Mr. Nast. Living in an age when a "Handy Book of Symbols" is standard equipment for every theatre goer, we should doubtless know at a glance the ancient and inevitable meaning of a zebra thus accoutred. But we suspect that Mr. Nast can take his symbols or leave them alone. . . . The point is that once in a while convention and novelty make a highly useful team.

Nast reprinted this editorial in his magazine (the cover was by Marty), with the following comment: "This editorial was read by *Vogue* with great interest and with great pleasure, because of its recognition of *Vogue*'s desire to promote all that is new in art (so long as it is inherently good and has the intangible quality of chic that characterizes all the material in the magazine), regardless of whether it belongs to the literal school of art or to the imaginative school—a school that can not be explained accurately through the medium of words."

Nast's revealing qualification of *Vogue*'s desire to promote all that is new in art indicates without a doubt where his loyalties lay. If Picasso or Matisse had produced the kind of work that seemed to him to contain "the intangible quality of chic" he looked for, then presumably he might have asked Vogel or de Brunhoff to invite them to do something for him. But his feelings about Picasso and Matisse were well known; and although Lepape, Brissaud, and the other imported artists did not fulfill expectations as fashion illustrators, they at least delivered enough chic covers to launch a Mode.

So in spite of falling into disfavor over their fashion renditions, the "Brummell lads," as Edna Chase called them, were allowed to continue letting their talents run riot on covers, with Lepape and Benito dominating the decade. When the requirements of fashion information were not at stake, their deviations from accurate reporting became assets.

Meanwhile, the hunt continued for responsible yet creative illustrators faithfully to render the Mode for *Vogue*.

Harriet Meserole, Douglas Pollard, Bolin, and Jean Pagès all put their names to some fine fashion drawings in the second half of the twenties. But the most important artist to emerge during that period was Carl Erickson, who signed himself Eric. He was a Swedish-American born in Wisconsin who was given to wearing bowler hats and bow ties and was invariably attached to Fez, his large brown poodle. His wife, Lee, was also an artist and writer, and the two lived for a great many years in Paris and reported on French fashion for Nast. Eric's appearance marks the end of the elongated, exaggerated look, and the end of fantasy and exoticism. His style also illustrated most appropriately the decline of the twenties.

Eric's work was realistic in an entirely new way. He used an impressionist brush to convey accurate proportions, and thick, simple outlines to communicate rhythm and movement. His style was economical and elegant, yet true to life—he, perhaps more than any other artist of his time, presented a genuine challenge to the achievements of photography, and redefined for a new generation the word "modernism." Eric also, more than any other of Nast's fashion artists, showed that it was possible to be both realistic and artistic without compromising either quality.

Eric's work habits were eccentric. He was usually half-drunk and swayed dreamily through the fashion sittings (he liked oysters and wine for breakfast), but he always produced good work—always starting with the model's eyes, then sketching the head, and finally the clothes. As he became established, a French artist, René Bouët-Willaumez, also began to do some innovative drawings for *Vogue* in Paris. He happened to have a style very similar to Eric's, which irritated Eric's competitive wife so much that Willaumez had to be removed to England for a while. In the thirties, an inordinate amount of paperwork flew between New York and Paris on the subject of the Ericksons, as Lee constantly demanded more portfolio work for her husband (illustrated travel stories, for instance), and complained about Michel de Brunhoff, editor of French *Vogue,* with whom she did not get on. (De Brunhoff, as we have seen, was ill equipped to cope with the hysterics and dramas that seemed endlessly to go on in the Paris office.) Threats to go over to the enemy, *Harper's Bazaar,* were constantly being bandied about by the contentious Mrs. Erickson, and Nast and Mrs. Chase put in a lot of hours smoothing ruffled feathers.

It was worth it. In 1941 Lucien Vogel told Nast that in a poll of the most elegant American and European women he knew, all agreed, as did Vogel, that Eric was by far the best artist appearing in the pages of *Vogue.* (Vogel, like Nast, had an unerring eye for changing styles.)

Eric, according to Nast,
combined a certain realism of detail (which was adequate, but perhaps not so legible as the blueprint style of real fashion reporters)
with incommensurably greater understanding and conviction in
portraying the spirit of today's elegance. This represented a victory
of realism over the decorative art on one side and over the lifeless
blueprint on the other side, and was quite in keeping with the fundamental and guiding decision made when I started to publish
*Vogue.*

Any new style of fashion illustration that can claim to be a potential successor of the present style must, in order to conform with
this fundamental decision, be a faithful and legible report of fashions, expressed in a manner which is pleasant, convincing, striking
(if possible), contemporary, and, above all, elegant. But mere novelty, or art value, or surprising "modernism" of such a style will
never, in my opinion, make it acceptable to our readers if it lacks in
any of the fundamental qualities required by the mission, the service, which is the foundation-stone upon which the *Vogue* formula
is built.

Another artistic accolade goes to Christian Bérard, known as
Bébé. A distinguished artist and stage designer in Paris, he was
brought into Nast's fold by Michel de Brunhoff, and although highly
temperamental, disorganized, and a drug addict, he produced some
fine drawings for *Vogue.* Bettina Ballard, an American *Vogue* editor
who worked with him in Paris, described him vividly: "Bébé usually
appeared about six in the evening set to work through the night. His
black beard was full of spaghetti and little active pets who lodged
there and he never dreamed of wiping his brushes any place but in
it. He had a slashing wit and the wickedest tongue in Paris, but he
could still draw more graphically than he could talk. He was ambi-
dextrous, drew equally well with both hands, and he'd pick up pen-
cils or brushes and before he'd finished describing a party it was
before your eyes on paper, the drawing room where it was held, the
women in their elegant dresses—the evening had come alive."

Bettina liked him more than Nast and Edna Chase did. His eccentricities were a little too flavorful for the latter to take—but it

was a coup to have him appear in *Vogue,* for his reputation in Paris at that time was enormous. (He was a protégé of Gertrude Stein's, and belonged to the neo-romantic school of artists that included Pavel Tchelitchew.) Bérard died young of his excesses, leaving a gap that only Eric could fill.

The *Gazette du Bon Ton* closed down in 1925. The days of deluxe hand-colored albums were over. The exclusivity and power base of the haute couture were beginning to give way to the ready-to-wear industry, with designers like Chanel democratizing the fashion industry with simpler, more practical clothes for women who were active, held jobs, and sought comfort instead of artifice. Photography responded to this new mood, and people began to get accustomed to the medium's visual generosity.

Nast knew what had happened. The "intangible quality of chic" that kept *Vogue* art modern, now, by the late twenties, required a new kind of realism, of practicality. As Benito worked on the new typefaces and bold headlines that would transform *Vogue*'s layouts, Nast was reexamining the styles of page illustration. Eric and Bérard were representatives of a new form of art that was immediate, realistic, making the resplendent follies of the Brummell lads—dare one say it?—*dated.*

The gradual change from the highly decorative, fanciful, and surreal drawings on the covers of the twenties to the more specific, detailed, photographic covers of the thirties illustrates Nast's progressive thinking—that the right covers for the contemporary mood were those that did not merely make the newsstands "blossom as a rose," as *Vogue* had put it in 1918, but told people something about the contents of the magazine. In other words, the cover was to become as important an agent of fashion information as the inside pages.

In 1932, the first color photograph—by Steichen—appeared on the cover of *Vogue.* It was of a woman in a bathing suit, holding a beach ball. The photograph was startling, it was brilliant, and it signaled the end of *Vogue*'s drawn covers.

In a March 21, 1936, memo, Nast analyzed *Vogue*'s covers for 1934 and 1935, giving figures for the newsstand supply, sale, and return of each issue. (This was a typical Nast exercise.) He added his own rating for each cover, and a brief comment on the magazine's newsstand sale. For instance, in 1934:

Jan. 1—Bruehl [the photographer]: Classed "B." This issue sold very well. This cover offers no poster value—unsmart, dull model. Supply, 47,447; sale, 36,187; % return, 24. [The cover by Bruehl was a color photograph of a model in Madras shirt and shorts reclining on the beach.]

Feb. 1—Huené: I classed this "A." Considering the season it did not sell well. Such good color and poster values should have sold better. Supply, 63,177; sale, 44,383; 30 percent return. [This was a color photograph by Hoyningen-Huené of a model wearing a pink-and-dark-blue hat by Suzy.]

In 1935:

March 15—Benito: I classed this "B." It sold poorly considering the season. I gave it the "B" classification because I thought it was bright, crisp in color and a little different. Supply, 64,427; sale 4,962; 30 percent return. [This cover showed a color sketch by Benito of a lady wearing a "blithe little peach-basket hat," in the words of the caption.]

July 15—Beaton: I classed this "B." It sold poorly. I gave this the "B" rating largely because it was different. This is always a poor seller. Supply, 40,210; sale, 26,218; return, 36 percent. [The cover showed a Beaton color sketch of a lady with a swept-up coiffure—"a headdress for festive nights when to be a different personality is the beginning of all adventure."]

For the two years, he gave only five *A*'s and twelve *D*'s.

These elaborate analyses indicate Nast's growing obsession with the influence of the magazine's cover. As newsstand sales continued to power his publications' profits, he grew more and more concerned with the effect of the "barker" or information value of his covers. It is impossible to speculate how well Helen Dryden or George Plank would have stood up under this scrutiny; but by the end of the twenties Nast was sure that frivolous charm and the essence of chic were no longer enough to sell the contents of *Vogue*.

By the mid-thirties, Nast's changed policy (or at least modified and refined policy) with regard to his covers had permeated down even to his most resistant staff. This is part of a memo, dated October 1938, from Crowninshield to Nast, dissecting the cover of a September issue of *Vogue* which had sold badly: "The trouble with the cover is that it simply means "art," or something arty, to every woman who looks at it. . . . Their psychological reaction would be purely one of art, not of dress, or fashion, or of a woman's desire to improve her appearance." (The cover, by Benito in his new, Eric-style incarnation, shows a black boy riding on a horse through a curtain as though on a stage. The horse and rider, depicted in thick, calligraphic strokes, wear mauve and purple plumes with gold jewelry.) Crowninshield, whose loyalty to art far outstripped his loyalty to fashion, must have been well indoctrinated to have made such criticism of the graceful Benito.

The memo prompted one from Nast which summarized his views on covers:

> You will recall that I have always advocated that a cover should serve as an eloquent barker in behalf of the show that goes on within the pages of the magazine, that it should be as functional as it can be made, and that our periodicals have maintained this policy quite religiously. A good example of the importance of this, you may recall, was brought about when we took over the *American Golfer,* abandoned the pretty face and pretty picture type of cover in favor of technical and innovative photographic golf-stroke covers, and thereby gained instantaneous increase in newsstand sales.
>
> This, incidentally, is the first evidence on record in my long experience where sales results can be definitely and unmistakably shown to have resulted from cover policy.

There were two conclusions that Nast drew from his elaborate analyses of covers—one was the importance of making the cover informative, and the other was the effectiveness of photographic covers. Throughout the thirties, Nast's art department built up an impressive amount of research data proving that the new color photographs of Steichen, Huené, Horst, and Beaton directly aided sales and lowered returns of the magazine, while costing not much more than drawings.

In 1930, Nast spent $101,000 on art and about $40,000 on photography. In 1933, he spent about $73,000 on art, and $60,000 on photography. By the end of the decade, the cost of photography far outstripped that of art.

For as well as selling power, photography offered something else—quality. Although *Vogue* had failed to exploit the genius of Picasso and Matisse, it took full advantage of the brilliance of its photographers. "I think greater quality was achieved through photography than through illustration," says Alexander Liberman, the artist and former art director of *Vogue*, who joined Condé Nast in 1941. (He is now editorial director of all the magazines.) "The reason was that an artist had to commit himself to reproducing a dress; a photographer was simply taking a picture of a beautiful woman. You can't ask Matisse to copy a dress pattern. Yet a photographer clicks the shutter and it's done."

In late 1936, an analysis of the sales of *Vogue* on the newsstand showed, beyond all doubt, that photographic covers sold better than illustrated ones. The contest was over. In 1938, eight covers were photographs (the number went up to twelve in 1939) and sixteen were artwork, by Bérard, Eric, Willaumez, Benito, Pagès, a surrealist named Pierre Roy, and Lepape. Lepape, the inexhaustible Georges, did his last cover for *Vogue* that year. He had worked for Nast for twenty-two years, producing over eighty covers and setting a standard of style and elegance that was never equalled. His last cover, on July 1, 1938, typical in subject matter, is strangely out of character in technique. It shows a woman in a long, gray quilted beach coat, with her back to the reader (as Paul Iribe had portrayed her so shockingly thirty years earlier), looking out to sea. The figure is represented in relief, giving a sharp, three-dimensional effect, with light and shade traced as though through the eye of a camera.

Perhaps Lepape was saluting the new visual convention that had finally replaced his own art and that of his braceleted colleagues. It was a sad but perceptive farewell to his great patron and publisher. Nast, relentlessly modern, now turned to the best young artists he could find to work their magic in the new medium.

# ELEVEN

# ENGLISH CHIC, SLAVIC CHARM, AND PARISIAN DRESSMAKERS

I f the story of Condé Nast's fashion artists is about the impact of cultural influences on the illustrative arts, the story of his photographers is entirely one of personalities—both in front of and behind the camera.

The first, mostly uncredited, photographs that appeared in *Vogue* were of society ladies at the races or yacht clubs, or of millinery, which for some reason was considered the most suitable subject for the camera. Photography in America at the turn of the century was not taken seriously at all: at one point in the 1890s the New York Society of Amateur Photographers speculated about the possibility of turning itself into a bicycling club. Most people, in both Europe and America, regarded photography as a passing fad, a scientific tool, or simply an invasion of privacy. The beautiful Comtesse Greffulhe, for instance, who was persistently pestered for her photograph by an infatuated Marcel Proust, spoke for most of her class when she told the American Proust scholar Mina Curtiss: "In those days, Madame, photographs were considered private and intimate. One didn't give them to outsiders."

But a group of photographers, led by the American Alfred Stieglitz, believed that there was more to photography than that. In 1902 in New York, Stieglitz, along with a young artist/photographer, Edward Steichen, portraitist Gertrude Kasebier, and Clarence H. White, formed the Photo-Secession Movement in an attempt to focus attention on photography as an art form. They exhibited their photographs alongside avant-garde European art such as Picasso drawings, Cézanne lithographs, and Matisse sculptures (this was long before such art was shown to the American public for the first time at the famous 1913 Armory Show), in order to make the point that their work, with its mysterious, soft-focus, allegorical style, could be justly compared with a painter's canvas.

Alfred Stieglitz was the undisputed father of this revolutionary movement. "He was photographing long before any of us," Edward Steichen said, "and many of his earliest prints have the fine simplicity and directness of the best work of the early masters. His famous photograph, 'Winter on Fifth Avenue,' taken in 1892, is still considered a masterpiece, and his studies of his wife, the painter Georgia O'Keeffe, have never been surpassed in sensitivity or beauty."

The attempt to make photography an art, like painting, was not supported by every experimenter in the medium. Indeed some felt that the success of the pictorial style retarded the growth of photographic technology. "High-speed film was available since the turn of the century, but for years it was used only in sports photography," wrote photographer Richard Avedon in an essay on the great French camera artist Lartigue: "As if there were some tacit agreement among photographers to remain within the provinces of painting in the hope of assuring their position as artists." (He might have added that high-speed film was also used for news reporting.)

While Stieglitz and Steichen were proposing a relationship between painting and photography at the Gallery 291 (named for the address on Fifth Avenue where the Photo-Secessionists exhibited their work), farther uptown Condé Nast was experimenting with photography as a medium to display fashion. Such fashion photography as there was originated in Paris, where the fashion came from—the models tended to be the wives of the couturiers or the distinguished personages who bought the clothes. The personages may have been distinguished, but the photographs that filled the pages of Nast's first *Vogue*s filled him with dissatisfaction. He felt sure that the banal backgrounds and dull portraits could be improved, that there was a more decorative function for photography than this.

His first notion was to ginger up the models by using actresses, or the most attractive society ladies, both enhancing their beauty and showing the rest of the world a romantic, evocative picture of how they dressed and lived. At first, this was no easy task, since resistance to photography remained strong. After all, those first attempts at photographic portraiture were not very *flattering,* lacking the cunning lighting, soft-focus lenses, and other devices in use today. The first actresses to appear modeling the Mode tended to be vaudeville or musical-comedy stars rather than serious stage actresses—Kitty Gordon and Grace George rather than Eleonora Duse. Moreover, these performers did not want to spend time on sittings, but demanded the photographer take his pictures in the theatre dressing room. As for Society, the first coup achieved by Nast, right after his takeover of *Vogue* in 1909, was a disaster. He had persuaded Mrs. Hermann Oelrichs and Mrs. William Greene Roelker, not to be photographed themselves, oh, dear, no, but to allow their chauffeurs to be photographed, beside their motorcars in Newport.

By a terrible mistake, the plates were published with the wrong captions, so Mrs. Roelker's Packard and chauffeurs in their mixed whipcord liveries were credited to Mrs. Oelrichs, while Mrs. Oelrichs's Renault and liveries of light gray cloth with black boots were ascribed to Mrs. Roelker. Mrs. Chase, *Vogue*'s fresh young assistant, bravely took the blame and confessed to her new employer. Nast, however, showed his true colors. "My dear, don't let it worry you," he reassured the nervous employee. "These things happen. You know what women are. Those two aren't speaking at the moment, so they'll be mad, but they'll get over it."

He was right. They were and they did, and they became two of the most photographed ladies ever to appear in the magazine.

The height of fashion illustration prior to 1914—on the left, a Martial and Armand gown of pink mousseline de soie, trimmed with pink satin ribbon; on the right, Doucet's gown of appliqué lace and panels of beaded and embroidered tulle. The thrillingly evocative poses were conjured up at the studio of Félix in Paris. *Vogue*, August 19, 1909.

Beginning in 1910, when Nast started to use more society portraits as well as fashion photographs, photographers began to receive credits in the magazine. The Campbell Studios, Ira L. Hill, Aimée duPont, and the International News Service were the most frequently used sources. Their work was embellished by decorated frames, oval cut-outs, and other illustrated borders known in the trade as "spinach." The Campbell Studios produced the most interesting effects—their backgrounds were more inventive, using mirrors, for instance. But in general, their efforts would not have supported Stieglitz in his campaign for the recognition of photography as art. Yet there was a powerful connection between Nast's and Stieglitz's worlds, a connection that was to prove brilliantly productive—they were both fascinated with the female form. Clarence White, Arnold Genthe, and Edward Steichen conveyed a new spirit of physical grace and elegance in portraits of female dancers such as Isadora Duncan and Ruth St. Denis, inspired by their uninhibited dress and movements. Meanwhile, in Paris, a photographer named Baron Adolphe de Meyer was finding similar inspiration in the Ballets Russes.

It was de Meyer who by the strangest of fates finally bridged the chasm between the visions of the Photo-Secessionists and the fashion images attempted in the pages of Nast's magazines.

The breakthrough came in 1913. The January 15 issue of *Vogue* that year opened with a startling portrait of Mrs. Harry Payne Whitney (née Vanderbilt), dressed in a darkly patterned Persian costume with a wide, stiff skirt and jeweled belt. Mrs. Whitney has a hand on her hip and her nose in the air in a pose of such hauteur that it was a wonder that the photographer did not collapse in fright. But the man behind the camera was de Meyer, who never collapsed before anyone, least of all a millionairess. The photograph, misty, alluring even in the midst of its remoteness, changed the face of society portraits.

Adolphe Meyer was born in Paris in 1868 of a German Jewish father and a Scottish mother. His father died when Adolphe (sometimes spelled Adolf) was young, leaving him a little money and some social connections, since by 1895 he had become a prominent member of London's fashionable Jewish set, led by Sir Ernest Cassel, banker and financial adviser to the Prince of Wales. The young de Meyer (the "de" was added at this time) took up photography at the instigation of his friend and patron, Lady de Gray, who was a friend of such photographable subjects as Sarah Bernhardt, Oscar Wilde, and the tenor Jean de Reszke. He also took flattering portraits of the Prince of Wales and of his wife, Princess Alexandra, as well as of the society women of the day.

In 1899, Adolphe, an uncloseted homosexual, married a former Paris dressmaker's model named Olga Caracciolo, whose social standing was enhanced by the fact that her godfather was the Prince of Wales (some said there was no need to add the "god"). It was a *mariage blanc,* and a great success. Their good looks, effete charm, and slightly mysterious origins suited perfectly the flavor of the period. Olga was given to wearing egret-feathered turbans and chinchilla coats, and was one of the first women to bob her hair. Adolphe held séances and seduced maharajas. Violet Trefusis (Mrs. George Keppel's daughter), using an old joke, called them Pédéraste and Médisante.

When the Prince of Wales became king, he contrived to obtain for the photographer the title Baron de Meyer so that he and his wife could be seated for the coronation. After the death of their protector, the king, Adolphe and Olga (having renamed themselves Gayne and Mahrah), betook themselves to Paris, where they encountered the Ballets Russes (de Meyer took some important photographs of Nijinsky, most brilliantly in *L'Après-midi d'un faune*), and then on to Venice, where they rented the Palazzo Balbi-Valier for a spell. Their hospitality turned the palazzo into a pleasure dome for transient decadents. In spite of all these extravagant distractions, de Meyer still found time to produce his unique brand of photographic composition (also thousands of snapshots and the occasional experiment in pornography), and such was his success that a show of his work was held at the Ritz-Carlton in New York in late 1912.

In spite of his social penchants, de Meyer wished to be taken seriously, and already had been recognized by Stieglitz with exhibitions in his 291 Gallery in New York. De Meyer evinced the greatest admiration for Stieglitz, and the two photographers corresponded frequently about their work. In 1903, de Meyer had visited New York and Newport, where he had been photographed by Gertrude Kasebier. It is probable, however, that Nast did not know about his work until the 1912 exhibition, although Edna Chase claims that it was she who first heard of him through the offices of her friend, architect and designer Weymer Mills, who gave him a letter of introduction to her. Nast was greatly excited by the innovative effects displayed in de Meyer's portraits and longed to capture the flighty photographer. History came to his aid.

When the European war broke out in 1914, de Meyer's enemies in London (of whom, not surprisingly, he had many) accused him of being (1) German, which he half was, and (2) a spy. Along with his wife, he was forced to flee to America. They arrived in New York penniless, homeless, and without the social support system on which they had so depended in London, Paris, and Venice.

Nast welcomed them enthusiastically and without delay signed de Meyer to the most generous contract anyone had ever offered a photographer. He was to take pictures for both *Vogue* and *Vanity Fair,* and for nobody else. Nast's terms for this exclusive contract seem laughable in today's terms—de Meyer was to be paid the princely sum of $100 a week, an indication of the regard in which photography was then held.

De Meyer was delighted, however, and soon his characteristic settings and lighting were decorating almost every issue of the two magazines. His talent and growing reputation rapidly broke down his sitters' resistance to the medium.

"Soon it became a certificate of elegance for a Newport aristocrat or a Broadway star to have her portrait, signed by de Meyer, in *Vogue,*" wrote his biographer, Philippe Jullian. "The Baron gave them all the aura of elegance bestowed by English chic, Slavic charm, and Parisian dressmakers. Mrs. Howard Cushing, Dorothy Gish, and the divine Lady Ribblesdale (once Mrs. John Jacob Astor) were his models; and through him all became part of the marvellous, vanished world of Edwardian balls and the Russian Ballet."

De Meyer, master of the halo light effect, photographs young bride Mary Pickford in the wedding dress originally worn by child-model Natica Nast.

For eight years, de Meyer's work dominated the pages of *Vogue* and *Vanity Fair*. Cecil Beaton later described the essence of his technique: "De Meyer's earliest photographs were taken under the influence of Stieglitz, with emphasis on sombre shadows and a somewhat aesthetic-looking subject emerging from a dark and fog-bound gloom. Then suddenly de Meyer found himself: the sun shone for him—and not only the sun, but the moon and all the stars. He used artificial light to make an aurora borealis. He discovered a soft-focus yet pinpoint-sharp lens which gave the required extra sparkle to shiny surfaces. He invented a new universe: a high-key world of water sparkling with sunshine, of moonlight and candlelight, of water-lilies in glass bowls, of tissues and gauzes, of pearly lustre and dazzling sundrops filtered through blossoming branches. He was able to reproduce the mystery of a Whistlerian nocturne by means of the camera."

Beaton's reference to a painter was not accidental. Stieglitz's efforts were finally being rewarded. By 1915 photography had gained a measure of respectability. That year *Vanity Fair* published photographs by Clarence White, Gertrude Kasebier, and Alfred Stieglitz, hailing them as exponents of the "new photography." Pioneer filmmakers were also exploiting the same soft-focus, moody, pictorial look, and films such as D. W. Griffith's *Intolerance,* with its flickering movements in intense light and shadow, introduced a wider audience to the camera's potential.

De Meyer's photographs could have been stills from Griffith's films; his triumph was that he showed that still photography could work magic, too, especially for the less-than-Whistlerian society matrons who posed for their portraits in *Vogue*. For the beauties who wore the great clothes of the day, he created fantasies of swirling, luminous femininity—even if, as Frank Crowninshield remarked, it meant putting a light bulb up your corsage. Nast's patronage of de Meyer gave fashion photography artistic legitimacy, a publishing achievement that transformed the photographic literature.

In 1922, seduced by what Mrs. Chase called a "heart-warming" salary, de Meyer went to work for William Randolph Hearst at

*Harper's Bazar,* the first of a series of defections to Hearst that were to haunt Nast's career. After he had trained his staff to the high standards of The Condé Nast Publications, it was a bitter pill to see them go and use their knowledge in the service of the only serious publishing rival he ever had to face. Nast and Edna Chase were deeply distressed by de Meyer's move, and the breach never really healed, in spite of de Meyer's later letters full of apologies and justifications—"My excuse, however, was that I had a lovely wife who was perishing in America—and that I had been promised Paris—Let's forget the past—it's all—so long ago!"

The move, however, was not a successful one for de Meyer, and he remained only about five years with Hearst. Nast might have gained a rueful satisfaction from that. The photographer was then in his fifties, and both he and his wife had succumbed to drugs, like so many displaced aesthetes who hovered on the fringes of the art world in Europe in the twenties. Opium and cocaine became their patrons, and as their grip on life became weaker, their one marketable currency—their ability to amuse—also dwindled. Wandering from Paris to Venice to Cannes, they picked up drifters like themselves, and became involved in seamy scandals. Olga died first— the woman whom de Meyer had immortalized in some of his best photographs over the years—and the inconsolable husband, already dabbling in spiritualism, took up the habit of communing with his beloved's ashes, which he carried about with him in a small box. (One day, it is said, friends mistakenly took this box for a cache of cocaine and began snorting Olga's dust.)

De Meyer returned to America in 1937 with a Tyrolean boy, Ernest, whom he introduced as his son. He went to Hollywood in an attempt to revive his photographic career, and wrote pathetic letters to Nast and Chase begging for work. The movie stars refused to sit for him unless he could guarantee the photographs would appear in *Vogue* or *Harper's Bazaar.* "I know how *you* would feel on the subject of my working—and you've given me to understand how Mr. Nast would feel," he admitted in a letter to Mrs. Chase. "I know you are justified—and he certainly is—but—so many years have passed. I know myself how I feel about wrongs which I have suffered from—having forgotten them long ago! Perhaps Mr. Nast has forgotten too? After all, I wouldn't interfere with any of your regular artists. . . . A picture here and there—occasionally—would help matters along tremendously."

His supplications fell on deaf ears. "Poor old de Meyer is back in America again," Chase wrote to Johnnie McMullin in June 1938. "He keeps writing me long and more or less reproachful letters because I do not see my way clear to having his work in *Vogue* again. I really would do anything in the world I could to help him, but I don't think it would be wise to put such dated material as de Meyer photographs in what we try so desperately to make a modern magazine."

De Meyer, reacting to the lack of interest in his work, defended his old skills against the new. "Photography outside of movies may have its uses for magazines and newspapers—as useful material, but it is commercially dead. There is a general excellence—in every country, the world over. So what's the use of struggling for unusual angles—which once seen are forgotten. Pay is indifferent and if one has a glorious past, it is stupid to jeopardize it going on when interest is waning for the sake of a few dollars."

Instead, de Meyer took to the lecture circuit, giving talks on famous women in history and the arts (the Empress Josephine, Elizabeth of Austria, Eleonora Duse), at $5.00 a ticket. He plucked up courage to write to Mrs. Chase, asking if Nast might lend his drawing room for one of these talks, for which he was asking a fee of $300—quite a lot in those days. Nast, not surprisingly, did not respond favorably to the idea, and de Meyer remained in California, eking out a living until he died, almost forgotten, in 1949, leaving Ernest, his faithful "son," the only survivor of a briefly brilliant but sadly unfulfilled career.

From Condé Nast's point of view, the timing of de Meyer's defection to Hearst turned out to be fortunate. After eight years of floating veils and haloed chins, it was surely time to move on to something else. Steichen, the modern master, was waiting in the wings.

Edward Steichen was born in Luxembourg in 1880, and grew up

in Milwaukee. He became interested in both painting and photography and came to New York in 1900 to seek out Alfred Stieglitz and the "painterly" photographers of the Photo-Secession movement. From 1906 to 1914, and again from 1919 to 1923, Steichen lived in France (it was during the first period that he became friendly with Rodin and photographed Clarisse Nast in his freezing studio), where he continued to paint as well as take pictures. During World War I he became a distinguished aerial photographer for the U.S. Army in France, attaining the rank of lieutenant colonel. This experience seems to have decided him to take up photography exclusively, for at the end of the war he destroyed all his canvases as a gesture of commitment to the camera. "So, in 1923," he related, "I went to New York for a prolonged stay."

> On landing in New York, I picked up a copy of *Vanity Fair,* which happened to have a page of portraits of photographers with a wonderful appreciation by Frank Crowninshield, the editor. . . . My portrait was in the center of the page with the caption, "The greatest living photographer," followed by the statement that, unfortunately, I had given up photography for painting. [Steichen's memory is faulty. The portrait is at the top right-hand corner.] So I wrote a letter to Crowninshield, thanking him for his gracious tribute to photography, but telling him that his information service was faulty, for I had not given up photography. On the contrary, I had given up painting and decided to devote myself exclusively to photography.
>
> This letter brought a prompt invitation from Crowninshield to meet with him and Condé Nast for lunch. They proposed that I work for the Condé Nast Publications as chief photographer. The work would be largely portraiture of prominent people for *Vanity Fair,* but Crowninshield wondered if I would also be willing to make fashion photographs for *Vogue.* He said they would not use my name with the fashion photographers, if I preferred. My response was that I had already made fashion photographs in 1911, for the magazine *Art et Décoration.* These were probably the first serious fashion photographs ever made. I also said that, if I made a photograph, I would stand by it with my name; otherwise I wouldn't make it. This pleased Nast, and we agreed in principle on the job.

A few days later the question of salary came up. When I stated what I thought would be a proper salary, Nast said that it was more than they had ever paid any photographer. I answered, "It was not *my* statement published in *Vanity Fair* that I was the greatest living portrait photographer." So Nast gave in.

Nast never gave him a contract, and Steichen could work for anyone he chose except Hearst (that included advertising).

The price was high, but he was worth it. *Vanity Fair* had nominated the photographer for the Hall of Fame as early as 1918, so the coup in ensnaring him was not to be underestimated. Steichen swept away de Meyer's unreal, filmy creations and replaced them with a sculptural, clean, pure realism. Not that he was very experienced, at first, in taking fashion shots. He himself describes his first attempt, which took place in Nast's apartment.

I had never made photographs with artificial light, but there was the Condé Nast electrician with a battery of about a dozen klieg arcs, wanting to know where he should put the lights. . . . Finally I realized I would have to do something about it, and I had him bank the lights all in one place and then asked for a couple of bed sheets. No one at a photographic fashion sitting had ever asked for bed sheets, but Carmel Snow, fashion editor of *Vogue* at the time, had a policy that a photographer should have whatever he required, and no questions asked. When the sheets came in, I lined up chairs in front of the electrician's lights and over them draped a four-ply thickness of sheets, so that when he turned on the lights, they didn't interfere with my model. The electrician was satisfied. I heard him say to one of the editors, "That guy knows his stuff." Applied to electric lights, this statement was as far from the truth as anything imaginable.

Of course, Steichen's use of artificial light soon became legendary. His lighting of models was exemplary in its simplicity and humanity, enhancing the look of the clothes while retaining a sense of real life. Nast once said to him, "Every woman de Meyer photographs looks like a model. You make every model look like a

Steichen's artistry with his favorite model, Marion Morehouse, enhances this cloth-of-gold gown veiled with white chiffon by J. Suzanne Talbot. *Vogue,* May 1, 1925.

woman." Most of Steichen's work for Nast was done in the twenties, when women were uninhibited, relaxed, down-to-earth, no longer the dreamy romantic icons of the Belle Epoque. Condé Nast had once again chosen the right person at the right time. It also suited Steichen, who had fallen out with Stieglitz over the latter's pro-German attitude during the war, to prove that photographs could be art in the pages of fashion magazines just as well as on the walls of a museum. (Although Stieglitz's position was not entirely rigid. When de Meyer wrote to him in 1940 seeking justification for having done so much fashion work, Stieglitz assured him, "No, you have not prostituted photography. Anyone who may say that or may have said that does not know what he or she is talking about.")

In 1936, thirteen years after his signing with Nast, Steichen wrote a quick, hand-written note to Edna Chase that shows his feelings: "Dear Edna, The May 1st *Vogue* is tops. For swank—novelty—variety—human interest and cash value—All hail to you all, Devotedly, Steichen."

But a year later, the colonel (as *Vogue* editors sometimes called him) decided he would retire. "Fashion photography had become routine. . . . I found the advertising becoming more and more artificial and I disliked some of the approaches to it that were developing. Among these were the sex appeal approaches designed to sell lotions or cosmetics. . . ."

Nast wrote Steichen a letter on his retirement, in which he said:

Though your work for our publications over so long a period of years did not bring me into the same daily contact I had with Edna and Frank, I always felt that you, as well as they, were, in a true sense, founders of this business. . . . You have helped us daily, during all those years, as few men have ever helped us, and, what is more, you were always there, if I lifted the telephone, ready to co-operate with us in all of our problems.

I remember, as if it were yesterday, our luncheon together at old Delmonico's, when I first tried to seduce you into becoming a professional photographer, at the expense of your career as a painter. What a fortunate thing for me that you were weak and surrendered to my solicitations! I believe that that luncheon did more to further the art and progress of photography in America than any other single event or agency in the past quarter century.

Nast had his facts endearingly wrong about that meeting, but his judgment of its impact was sound enough. He continued to take the greatest interest in Steichen's work, and when he came across one of Steichen's Sandburg heads, published in *U.S. Camera* in 1940, he wrote a little note congratulating him. "It makes me sad that they are not being published in the December 1939 issue of *Vanity Fair!*" he added wistfully.

While the "cunning colonel" was changing the face of *Vogue* in New York, a young Russian-born photographer was becoming the talk of Paris—George Hoyningen-Huené (another baron, which nobody minded). Main Bocher, the American who was then fashion editor of French *Vogue* and who later became a couturier, recalled that Hoyningen-Huené once came into the office for the purpose of selling the magazine on the work of the avant-garde photographer Man Ray: "But from George's conversation I felt very strongly that he himself had a great interest in photography and might be led into doing the pages I felt *Vogue* needed."

Hoyningen-Huené became one of Nast's favorite photographers, although his temperament was as explosive as gunpowder. "He would walk into a sitting late, take one withering look at the models standing nervously in the dresses he was to photograph, turn to the editor in charge, and say, 'Is this what you expect me to photograph?,' snap the cameras a few times, and walk away," remembered *Vogue* editor Bettina Ballard. "Everyone was terrified of him."

*Vogue*'s Paris studio became well known among photographers, with artists such as André Kertész occasionally dropping in to do some free-lance work for the magazine. Any new talent in town would want to see and be seen there.

England managed to throw a major talent into this international pantheon—Cecil Beaton, who started his *Vogue* career as a writer and illustrator in 1926. The Bloomsbury-ish editor of London *Vogue*, Dorothy Todd, noticed Beaton's photographic efforts in a

Hoyningen-Huené's exquisite jewellike composition sets off Mainbocher's Chinese blue-and-white floral-printed crêpe tunic and skirt. *Vogue,* April 15, 1934.

show and invited him to photograph some of the poets and writers living and working in Cambridge, but his biggest early break was photographing Edith Sitwell, whose medieval gothic face was a perfect foil for Beaton's fanciful imagination. It was these photographs that came to the attention of Mrs. Chase on a talent-hunting trip to London. She at once invited him to New York.

Beaton arrived in New York for the first time in the winter of 1928, bearing, "still wrapped in its cocoon of pink veiling, the Kodak camera, the spidery tripod, the rather tarnished nets and silver tissues, the crumpled lengths of Burnet cottons, and the badly cracked American cloth, which formed my backgrounds"—the poignant props of his photographic career.

When he had been working for *Vogue* for a few months, Mrs. Chase one day asked him who did his developing for him. "Oh, Mrs. Chase," he said, "Ninnie [his old nurse, who still lived with the Beaton family] does it for me at home, in the bathtub." Frank Crowninshield was a great admirer of Beaton's work, declaring that Steichen, de Meyer, and Beaton were the *only* photographers. "But it's so amazing that you can do things like this with a toy camera."

Condé Nast was also fascinated by Beaton's primitive equipment. Although he often admired the results, he found frequent opportunities to criticize, too, the mottled or gray effect of the photographs when they had been enlarged for publication in the magazine. "What we want is color!" he would say. "This is so flat and gray. There's too little contrast and no definition."

Finally, Nast came out with what was really bothering him. "It's all very well for you to take pictures with a snapshot camera," he told Beaton, "but you've got to grow up! Don't you realize you're giving yourself so much unnecessary trouble by not having good technical equipment? Now you've got to go off and buy yourself a big camera to take pictures on an 8 by 10 plate."

Beaton resisted this advice, complaining that with such an enormous camera he would not be able to climb up ladders. "At any rate," Nast insisted, "the pictures you take on the ground will be better." Nast was supported in this by his art director, M. F. Agha, a Turkish-born multilingual artist newly imported by Nast from his failing office of *Vogue* in Berlin. Agha had very strong views on design and layout, and he wrote, in his idiosyncratic English, a letter to Beaton in 1929 about the difficulties they were experiencing in reproducing his photographs. "I think that all these defaults are due to the fact that you are using a small camera, and submit your photographs to too great enlargements that makes the grey surfaces to lose consistency, and sometimes makes the figures look muddy. . . . Mr. Nast likes your photographs very much for their qualities of charm and good composition and is very anxious to see you improve their technical qualities."

According to Beaton, Nast did not offer to buy him the new camera everyone was urging on him, so the photographer, disgruntled, bought one himself, and went off to photograph stars in Hollywood. For the first few sittings he cursed Nast for lumbering him with the monstrous new equipment, but he soon saw that the effects he could achieve far outstripped those of his trusty folding Kodak. When he returned to New York, he was an enthusiastic convert.

Beaton cleverly saw that the wisest course for him to take in his career was to be as different as possible from Steichen, the "almighty photographer," as Beaton called him. "Whereas Steichen's pictures were taken with an uncompromising frankness of viewpoint, against a plain background, perhaps half black, half white, my sitters were more likely to be somewhat hazily discovered in a bower or grotto of silvery blossom or in some shades of polka dots." Beaton spent much of his time photographing Ina Claire, Gertrude Lawrence, Beatrice Lillie, and his other illustrious subjects in Condé Nast's drawing room at his new apartment, 1040 Park Avenue—"with the Chinese paper which came from Haddon Hall, in his mirrored dressing rooms where I was always so impressed to see each day fresh bunches of lilies of the valley in the mirror vases, in his salon with the Coromandel screen, Savonnerie carpet, and French drawings, or in his English-walnut library."

After his success in New York, Beaton went on to Paris, where he began to take pictures in the stimulating atmosphere of the *Vogue* studio. George Hoyningen-Huené took an interest in the young photographer, and introduced him to the new Rolleiflex camera. "It's a most simple and useful little machine. The negative is just big enough to enlarge to almost any size. I'll get you one if you like." So Huené got Beaton a Rolleiflex and the two photographers went to Africa together in early 1930. Huené also introduced the young Englishman to Jean Cocteau, who was smoking opium, at which point, Beaton later remarked, "I considered that adult life could reach no higher."

Beaton's photographic career blossomed under Nast's regime, in spite of what Beaton regarded as the over-stringent rules of camerawork that Nast imposed. "All the pictures published had to be of the highest standard of technical perfection. However, in spite of my genuine admiration for Steichen's work, I felt that his influence had gone too far when, after an extremely strenuous afternoon's work converting the studio into a luxurious white bedroom (I had mounted a ladder with my camera to photograph Gertrude Lawrence in a bed as light and airy as whipped cream and had remained for one hour on the ladder exposing dozens of plates while Miss Lawrence gave a histrionic performance between the flowered sheets), I was told that the photograph was not considered publishable because in the foreground was a vase of lilies seen out of focus."

Beaton's work, so different from Steichen's, harked back to that first master of romanticism, Baron de Meyer. De Meyer had been Beaton's earliest idol. "It is he who too often persuaded me, in almost every studio picture I take, to give a dazzle to the hair by placing a brilliant lamp above the sitter's head." Beaton's baroque backgrounds and lighting became his trademark. He loved exotic props—massed flowers, screens, draped chiffons, and later surrealist effects such as the use of theatre props for backgrounds. By the beginning of the thirties, *Vogue* was using Beaton in an almost unceasing stream of elaborate compositions—so much so that by 1933 the Paris office was complaining that there was altogether too much Beaton in *Vogue*: "He is not doing anything new and the fussy pictures are not of the times," wrote Bettina Ballard to Edna Chase.

Beaton's greatest coup was to be the official photographer at the engagement and wedding of the Duke of Windsor and Mrs. Simpson. Condé Nast believed so strongly in the newsworthiness of the event that he decided to devote six pages of American *Vogue* to the engagement photographs (an extravagant commitment to a non-fashion feature, and contrary to the advice of British *Vogue,* who felt the whole thing was in poor taste). It turned out to be one of Nast's wise business decisions, since the issue sold out everywhere across the country in a matter of days.

Beaton also continued to send *Vogue* amusing social notes and diaries of his travels to New York, London, Paris, and Hollywood, accompanied by clever, satirical sketches that entertained his readers. His sketches were so amusing that sometimes he was called in to illustrate other people's articles, and it was one of these assignments that caused a major scandal and nearly cost him his photographic career.

In the February 1, 1938, issue of American *Vogue,* which hit the newsstands about a week earlier, Frank Crowninshield published one of his periodic essays on New York life. This one was entitled "The New Left Wing of New York Society."

In the past year or two a new kind of confusion concerning [New York] society has become general, due to the appearance of a newly formed, colourful, prodigal, and highly publicized social army, the ranks of which are largely made up of rich, carefree, emancipated, and quite often, idle people. Furthermore, the morale of this new social battalion is in many respects at variance, not only with that animating the more conservative West and South, but also with that of older and more traditional society in New York itself. . . . The burden of all the publicity [engendered by this group] has been to one effect: namely, that society here has become, not only democratized, but disintegrated; that all the old rituals have broken up, and the old barriers broken down; and that, to be more specific about it, three hundred or more fashionable people have become so intolerably fed up with what they thought the pomp, stuffiness, and retarded tempo of traditional society, that they seceded from it, en masse, and created an integrated and per-

Beaton's eye was never better than in this cunning placement of the Duchess of Windsor so that the ornamented French dresser gives extra meaning to the striking Mainbocher gown. *Vogue,* June 1, 1937.

fectly functioning social cosmos of their own. . . . This colourful social group has now everywhere become known as Café Society, for the reason that so many of its activities—daily and nightly— take place in our better-known cafés and night-clubs.

Typical Crowninshield stuff, in short, and apart from its interest in marking the official debut of that much-disputed phrase, "café society," nothing to get agitated about. In order to enliven the piece, Cecil Beaton was asked to provide his usual light and witty drawings as a decorative border, which the artist duly did. As was customary, Beaton added tiny details in writing to the illustrations, such as shop signs, newspaper headlines, book titles. Often the writing was so small that it was indecipherable. On this occasion, it would have been better so. For in two places on the right-hand page of his illustration to Crowninshield's piece, and bearing no relation to the piece, Beaton had referred to "kikes." On a drawing of a Western Union telegram are the words "Party darling Love Kike." The second place is on the page of an illustrated journal as the caption to a photograph: "M. R. Andrew ball at the El Morocco brought out all the damn kikes in town."

The writing is minuscule. The unsuspecting eye would never catch it. Apparently at least one *Vogue* editor did see it, however. Margaret Case, *Vogue*'s society editor and a great friend of Beaton's, told him to alter the lettering before it was printed. "Let someone else do it," Beaton replied. "I wash my hands of the whole thing." His tone was of one who was used to having his work altered by editors and who had become exasperated with tiredness and overwork. The article was published, and somebody (nobody to this day knows who it was) tipped off the one person most likely to appreciate it—Walter Winchell.

Winchell, familiar to his *New York Daily Mirror* readers as a fierce anti-Nazi, inserted a long item in his January 24, 1938, column: "The Feb. issue of Vogue, the mag, contains some hidden anti-Semitism! . . . A magnifying glass is necessary to detect it in Cecil Beaton's lettering for Frank Crowninshield's article on New York society on page 73. . . ." Winchell then proceeded to spell out the offending issues. Beaton had also microscopically written: "Why is Mrs. Selznick such a social wow? Why Mrs. Goldwyn etc. Why Mrs. L.B. Mayer?" and Winchell punctiliously included this in the anti-Semitic package.

That was all, but it was enough. Phone calls flooded *Vogue*'s New York office in protest, from Nast's most distinguished friends such as Bernard Baruch, to the smallest fashion accessory distributor. The department stores were appalled. Seventh Avenue was outraged. Condé Nast's most important advertisers threatened a boycott. It was a body blow to the Nast publications.

Condé Nast had to do something, and do it fast. Moreover, he had to do it without the help and advice of his most trusted colleague, Edna Chase. She was vacationing in Nassau when the storm broke.

On the day the Winchell story appeared, Nast issued two statements. The first read in part: "Had I known that the lines existed in the illustration or had any of my staff known of their existence, the drawing would have been discarded, as the suggestion in it is wholly contrary not only to my publishing policy but to my private views, personal friendships and relationships.

"Of this issue of *Vogue,* 280,000 copies were printed. 150,000 had been shipped before I knew of these lines. Of the 130,000 not yet shipped, the page referred to has been reprinted with the objectionable lines stricken out."

The second statement added: "Mr. Beaton and I were both agreed that the matter was of such gravity that an exchange of views was desirable. As a result of our interview, Mr. Beaton tendered his resignation as a contributing photographer and artist on the staff of *Vogue* and I have accepted his resignation."

Behind those words lay a costly exercise. The reprinting of the page, the excision of all Beaton's work in upcoming issues, the canceling of innumerable fashion sittings, were all expensive to accomplish. But it was the only adequate gesture Nast could make, and he made it with admirable dispatch.

The story, and Nast's actions, were widely reported in the press in New York and London. The gossip columnists loved the story, adding tidbits such as that Beaton had sent a special bound copy of that issue of *Vogue* to Goebbels, who was arranging jobs for Beaton with a Berlin magazine; and that he was being called the "Heillustrator." But Nast's role, and his personal efforts at apology, were well received. Many observers, including photographers, admired his swift action and forthright stand. Condé Nast may have lost a lot of money over the unpleasant affair, but he gained immeasurably in prestige. "This incident was only another occasion on which your integrity was so completely affirmed," *Vogue* correspondent Johnnie McMullin wrote to him. "From all sides, I hear of your great courage and ultimate triumph over adversity in this affair."

What got into Beaton remains a mystery. He was in Hollywood when he did his illustrations, and at the time, both in Hollywood and New York, there was an unspecific but recognizable atmosphere of anti-Semitism, particularly in the higher echelons of society. This prevailing mood, at its height in the late thirties, affords a context within which Beaton's aberration appears slightly less wild. He wrote to Edna Chase in Nassau in melodramatic terms:

> You may, by now, have heard of the terrible thing that has happened to us this week. How a wretched little foible which was not even intentional or conscious for more than a split second, should through a chain of unfortunate circumstances have developed into something so serious that we have all been staring at ruin at much too close quarters. . . . Of course the regrets for the whole blunder are limitless and each day seems to bring further blows raining down onto our unhappy heads but my chief sorrow is for Condé who apart from all monetary losses has through force of circumstances been made to suffer one of the most unhappy weeks of his career. . . . I am spending a few days asleep in the country as the telephone, letters and panics of the Monday and Tuesday have reduced my nerves to a state in which only a murderer can find himself.

To Edna, then, he explained it as a "wretched little foible." To some, he said it was a joke. To others, and this was reported in the press, he said he had wanted to put something over on the company. Johnnie McMullin concluded that it must have been more stupidity than wickedness—"The only other alternative is that, like Hitler, he had begun to think himself omnipotent."

In April 1938, beginning to feel the financial pinch, Beaton asked Nast to review his case. Condé replied:

> Several months have elapsed, and, in fairness to you, I have given it very careful thought and have discussed the situation at some length with other publishers, but in spite of my warm friendship for you and my full appreciation of your splendid work as an artist, I deplore the fact that I do not feel that I can ask you to rejoin our staff.
>
> Although I am ready to believe that you have no really anti-Semitic feelings and that what you did had no more significance in your mind than a foolish prank, nevertheless you chose, most disastrously for all of us, to play a prank in such a way that you plunged me, as a publisher, into a political situation completely out of character with *Vogue* and entirely at variance with and distasteful to my own feelings.
>
> In spite of the extraordinary volume of publicity which the incident brought forth, I would gladly have accepted your apology had the joke been turned against me personally. But, as a publisher, I cannot condone this jibe which puts me in the position of sponsoring a cruel and offensive fling at a problem upon which the attention of the whole world is at present riveted.

Beaton also attempted to duck the banishment by assuming the boycott only applied in the United States. He returned to England after the uproar and promptly began bombarding the London office of *Vogue* with ideas for photographic sittings—the Duchess of Gloucester, for instance, had graciously consented to be photographed by the great Beaton, and was it all right for him to go ahead? The word came swiftly back from New York—no. (Beaton made out all right, however. Agha saw him in September 1938 at the Café Royal in London, "where the boys foregather. He was fluttering from one table to another and had a very deep tan complexion and rather heavy mascara on his eyes. Otherwise he feels all right, I understand, and is doing some work for the *Tatler,* photographing British celebrities.")

It was three years before Condé Nast again published any work by Beaton, and on that occasion the photographer wrote to thank him. "I should be very interested to know," he added, "if you heard reverberations from the row of three years ago—or whether the upheaval of the world has put the matter in truer perspective. . . ." This does not sound like the expression of a politically sensitive man, or indeed of a remorseful one. The incident remains an unpleasant stain on the character of the photographer, and a painful experience for Nast, whose personal abhorrence of the affair was quite genuine: as he pointed out to his outraged advertisers, he had welcomed with delight the marriage of his daughter, Natica, to Gerald Felix Warburg, of the distinguished banking family, in 1933.

The loss of Beaton put severe pressure on *Vogue,* for as the Paris office had so grumpily observed, his contributions made up a considerable amount of the editorial pages in the middle thirties. Moreover, *Vogue*'s other major photographer, George Hoyningen-Huené, had also departed in a storm of temperament, leaving an unwelcome vacuum.

This particular *crise* had happened in the summer of 1934, when Huené's contract was being renegotiated. Agha had flown over to Paris for the sensitive discussions, and over a lunch at a restaurant at which Horst was present, Huené became so enraged by a remark of Agha's that he overturned the table in his face. The ensuing row reverberated across the Atlantic. Margaret Case, visiting Paris to cover the Paris openings, wrote a personal letter to Mrs. Chase one night at midnight in bed, to explain what had happened: Huené had agitatedly told her,

> Agha was the wrong person to deal with me. If I leave it's Agha's fault. Agha said Condé wanted to chastise me, that I was a naughty boy! No one has ever chastised me, and I don't intend to let them start now." I said, "For Heaven's sakes, George, no one is trying to chastise you. They are simply trying to talk a little sensible business

to you. You have received nothing but wonderful backing and generosity from the organization—You have the finest studio of its kind in the world, plenty of holidays, huge success, money, everything—why do you make life so difficult," etc. etc. (I beg of you do not tell anyone, not even Condé, that he said that about Agha. Agha has been the best sort of an ambassador and I would hate to have Condé hear that I quoted this crazy remark of George's to you. A man like he might take it seriously. . . .)

Yesterday I was asked to lunch with Cecil [Beaton], Horst and George. Our Cecil acted in a very loyal and dignified way. At the table George announced, "This, my dear Margaret, is a resignation lunch. Drink to it!" Up to then I do not think Cecil knew about the situation. He seemed terribly surprised and we pretended it was a joke. Then George said something very unkind about Condé, and coolly and with scorn. Cecil said, "I think Condé is grand, I could not admire him more than I do for what he has done and what he is. I think you are silly to give up your studio. What do you intend to do?" "I have no plans, no plans—perhaps I will starve—perhaps I will work for *Harper's*," etc.

In spite of Mrs. Chase's personal intervention, Huené this time kept his word and went over to the other side, Hearst's *Harper's Bazaar*—another bitter blow. (Beaton's loyalty to Nast was ironic considering the catastrophe that was later to shatter them both.) Yet Huené's defection, like de Meyer's, was turned to Nast's advantage. On this occasion the opportunity fell to a young German photographer, Horst P. Horst.

Horst had come from Germany to Paris to study architecture under Le Corbusier in the late twenties. In 1930 Agha met him in Paris and suggested he try taking photographs in the *Vogue* studio. Horst objected that he had never taken a photograph in his life. "I went to the *Vogue* studio," he recalls, "and there was an assistant there who knew all about lighting and the exposures and all the techniques. I just posed the girl and bravely clicked the shutter."

Soon Horst was clicking the shutter with less bravery and more skill. He photographed Janet Flanner, the Paris correspondent of *The New Yorker,* in the pose of the *New Yorker* dandy, with a monocle, and she was so pleased with the result that she wrote about it in her column. Nast, quick as usual to notice the mention of new photographic talent, invited Horst to come to New York. In 1932, the young photographer arrived, and Nast hired him at $60 a week.

After a few months, Nast asked Horst to come into his office. All around the large room were Horst's photographs—including all the rejects. Nast went over them with Horst, one by one, commenting, criticizing. "He gave Horst a two-hour lecture on the aesthetics of photography and the general rules of good business behavior," was how Agha described it later to Mrs. Chase. According to Horst, at the end of this difficult interview, Nast said, "I suppose you think you're as good as Steichen." To which Horst replied, "If I thought I couldn't become as good as Steichen, I'd never have started." Nast, irritated by this expression of arrogance, told Horst shortly after that he was fired. "He was preoccupied with his divorce," Horst said later. "He was not himself." (He was also, although Horst did not know it, deeply involved with his disastrous financial affairs.)

Horst left the next day, in spite of Agha's entreaties. He returned briefly to Paris, made a trip to Africa, then finally resumed work in the Paris *Vogue* studio with George Hoyningen-Huené.

After Huené's abrupt departure in 1934, Horst was suddenly the golden boy in New York again, and in 1935 he was invited to do the Paris collections for American *Vogue,* thus starting a new and harmonious relationship with the New York office that lasted long after Nast died.

Mrs. Chase, ever on the alert for the sensitive egos of her artists, wrote Edward Steichen a careful letter about Horst's permanent return to America in late 1935 (which was precipitated by visa problems in France). "I feel sure that the question will arise in your mind as to what extent Horst's presence here may affect the amount of work which you do for *Vogue*," she wrote. "I have a feeling that we are often pressing you into sittings which do not really interest you, but that you do them because you know our needs—and not because you find them stimulating or exciting. Also, because we have had so much space to cover and because of the exigencies of our budget, we have often asked you to take more things at a sitting

than you have wanted to do. With Horst here, I think we could eliminate some of this kind of work, make the actual sittings easier, and
get more exciting and distinguished ideas for your assignments."
(Nast, as always in tune with his editor's thinking, noted on a draft
of this letter, "In my opinion, you have presented the case very ably
to Steichen. I think it will be a very helpful letter.")

Horst, whether aware of these ripples or not, put his own stamp
on *Vogue*'s photography during the thirties. His work was more romantic than Hoyningen-Huené's, more flamboyant than Steichen's.
He paid a great deal of attention to the setting, perhaps influenced
by his architectural training. He used famous modernist designers
such as Jean Michel Frank to design his backgrounds. "My first
pictures were loaded with background," Horst wrote in his book,
*Photographs of a Decade.* "I was continually dismantling palaces,
hauling in small forests and entire hothouses meant to enhance but
really crushing the little woman in their midst. Finally I realized the
incongruous effect and began a series of strong black compositions
that made a big inky splash on the magazine page, blotting out
everything else. This went so far that one day a *Vogue* editor produced during a sitting a little flashlight—'just for the dress,
please.' "

Nast always liked his photographers to be experimental. Two in
particular, both making surprising appearances in the commercial
field, contributed extensively to *Vanity Fair* and *Vogue* from the
beginning of the twenties through the thirties: Charles Sheeler,
whose work as a painter outshone his rather undistinguished portrait photography for Nast; and Man Ray, an important figure in the
French avant-garde, who used to call his surrealist pictures for Nast
"photograms," "shadowgraphs," or "rayographs."

There were more arbitrary additions to the roster of photographers. Condé Nast once invited an attractive, leggy girl called Toni
Frissell to join *Vogue,* and decided to start her off as a caption-
writer. This was quickly recognized to be a mistake (she could not
spell, for one thing), so she was encouraged instead to take society
snapshots at the parties and events of the season, an occupation for
which she was much better suited, since she had excellent connec-

Horst at his most architecturally alluring. The model draped beside the intriguingly broken-stringed harp wears a pink tea-gown by Lanvin; the highlighted model is in blue crêpe by Molyneux. *Vogue*, April 15, 1937.

tions and went everywhere. Frissell soon became interested enough in photography to wish to be taken seriously, and began working on fashion shots as well as her social coverage. Nast, pursuing his interest in her, used to visit the studio when she was working: she describes one day when, pregnant by her husband, F. M. Bacon, she was lying on the floor to achieve a more interesting camera angle, and noticed a beautifully creased pair of pants and perfectly polished shoes close to her nose.

"What are you doing down there?" Condé asked.

"Well, I'm interested in the way it looks from down here. I see things in my own way," she replied defiantly.

Her visual experiments may have amused Nast, but they did not reassure him as to her photographic skills. Agha had little time for Frissell's talents, and when in 1934 she requested a large raise— from $2,400 a year to $3,600 a year, which meant *Vogue* would have to use about ten times as many of her photographs as they normally used—Agha strenuously objected. "I do not think *Vanity Fair* can help the situation," he commented. *"Vanity Fair* should publish only the work of people who are excellent art-photographers; therefore, in my opinion, there is no place in *Vanity Fair* either for Frissell or, in my opinion, for Beaton."

Frissell, however, was kept on, bravely fighting for recognition in a field which supported almost no other women. There were, of course, women photographers, but few worked professionally in the magazine business. A story, in *Vanity Fair* in 1935, makes the point: Toni Frissell had been commissioned to go to Washington to take an informal photograph of "one of those well-groomed, well-mannered South American diplomats."

His unnamed Excellency reported that he could give no more than fifteen minutes to the sitting, so Miss Frissell sent her butler ahead, by morning train out of New York, to put the requisite equipment in readiness before she arrived. When she herself reached Washington in midafternoon, she was greeted at the door of the embassy by a very elaborate Latin-American flunkey. At first, he did not quite catch her name, and it looked as though she were going to have a great deal of trouble gaining an entrance. Her own servant, by the way, was nowhere in sight.

"Pardon, Madame—the name?"

"Miss Frissell," she repeated carefully. "Miss Frissell—by appointment with His Excellency. I believe my man came some time ago."

"Ah! yes, Madame," he answered, motioning apologetically for her to come inside. "This way," he indicated, after removing her coat. "Mr. Frissell, the photographer, is already here. Just now, His Excellency is entertaining him upstairs."

Frissell's tenacity was rewarded in a way that she herself could hardly have foreseen. In the late thirties, when Steichen had retired, Huené had defected, and Beaton had resigned, photographers for the Condé Nast publications were a little thin on the ground, and her contributions became extremely valuable. Furthermore, Frissell's work took on a new significance at that time, for reasons connected with the development of photographic technique. She had always been accustomed to taking her snapshots outdoors—on the ski slope, on the beach, on horseback. These action shots were, by the end of the decade, replacing formal studio fashion photographs in every magazine in the country. Frissell, quite unconsciously, was spearheading a revolution, an irony worthy of at least a shrug from the scornful Agha.

André Durst was the last photographer of note to work for *Vogue* before Nast's death. He was a protégé of Huené's, and after the latter's abrupt departure and Horst's disappearance to America, Durst became the Paris studio's main photographer. Bettina Ballard described his work: "He took Dali-like photographs of elegant women standing in a desert with such surrealist props as a rope twirling around one of them that zoomed off into space . . . [He was] the first photographer to translate a surrealist feeling to fashion photography."

Once more a reference to painting—but this time painting of a very different order. The wheel had come full circle. There was no doubt in anybody's mind now about the connection between photography and painting. (Or vice versa; scholars are quick to point out, for instance, the impact of Dora Maar's war photographs on Picasso's art, and in particular on his 1937 masterpiece "Guernica.") There was no doubt in anybody's mind either about photography's effectiveness as a communications tool—newspapers and magazines were committed to photography by the end of the twenties. Least of all was there any doubt about photography as a respectable medium. By the early thirties photography had become so chic that *Vogue* published a feature entitled "9 Society Amateurs behind Their Cameras," including Mr. and Mrs. William Paley, Tilly Losch James, the Hon. David Herbert, and Mrs. Sigourney Thayer.

Condé Nast had greatly accelerated the acceptance of the medium. In a way, he created a profession. By giving photographers a public forum for their work and promoting them consistently in *Vogue* and *Vanity Fair,* he gave them a wider audience and bestowed social acceptability upon them.

Most people, if they thought about it at all, believed that Nast was simply an astute collector of photographers for his magazines. Only the inner circle of his staff knew the truth—that as well as being a patron of some of the most talented artists working behind the camera, this conventional, decorous man was also ringmaster to a mad circus that he personally trained, directed, and disciplined according to his personal vision and private standards, and that it was out of this strict school that some of those photographers' finest work was produced.

# TWELVE

# THE RINGMASTER

However turbulent Horst's start with Condé Nast, the photographer would, after his difficult employer's death, pay him a handsome tribute: "No other publisher has ever demonstrated a courage comparable to the late Condé Nast. Photography owes him an incalculable debt. In the early days of *Vogue* and *Vanity Fair*, it was he who persuaded Baron de Meyer and Commander Edward Steichen literally to *create* fashion photography. . . . Indeed, there is not one significant contemporary name in photography that has not appeared on the pages of the Nast magazines. And until the day of his death Mr. Nast remained creatively restless, always foreseeing inevitable change long before anybody else, always demanding—and getting—new results from old artists, always seeking out young talent and giving it rich and unpredictable opportunities."

Nast's contribution to the look of *Vogue, Vanity Fair,* and *House & Garden* has generally been assumed to have been minimal. He was a businessman, an advertising expert, a statistician, went the *on dit*—what he knew about art and layout could have fit into one of his natty custom-made shoes. He himself was heard to say on more than one occasion, "I am merely a glorified bookkeeper." This, it can be said with confidence, was excessive modesty. The evidence shows that his interest, involvement, and artistic judgment in visual matters were just as influential as his financial and promotional directives. Horst's tribute, though perhaps a surprise to some, was no exaggeration. He spoke only of photography, but his words could as well apply to the total look of Nast's publishing empire.

Condé Nast's interest in the visual side of his magazines went back to the beginning. If he was going to produce a commodity that was to represent the best of everything, its quality had to be beyond reproach. Mr. Vanderbilt would never consent to be photographed outside his mansion or Mrs. Stuyvesant Fish at a private ball if the portrait appeared on scruffy paper, poorly reproduced, inartistically composed.

His first move on the artistic front was at the end of 1909, when he appointed Heyworth Campbell to be art director of *Vogue*. *Vogue* had not had an adequate art director since Harry McVickar departed. Campbell was an accomplished illustrator who contributed many of the best designs that *Vogue* had used over the years to decorate its pages. On Mrs. Chase's somewhat apprehensive recommendation, Nast took him on full time to direct the layout of the magazine. In 1923, on the thirtieth anniversary of the founding of *Vogue,* he wrote a few words of praise to his first art director: "His keen sense of decoration and proportion and his almost instinctive appreciation of every form of beauty have given to the editorial pages of the magazine an individuality and distinction that are wholly his own. His make-up of the *Vogue* pages, that is to say, the skilful handling, assembling, and arranging of type, photographs, and drawings, has created a style for magazine pages which has been widely followed or more or less adopted by other magazines, not only in America and England, but in the capitals of Europe as well."

Heyworth Campbell was an attractive man who kept a bottle of gin in his desk drawer (a habit he sustained during Prohibition), and if anyone on the staff didn't feel up to snuff, he'd gladly offer a thimbleful. The thimblefuls he offered himself were more often tumbler-sized, which later became a problem, but he and Nast between them set the style for *Vogue* which lasted until the late twenties.

Frank Crowninshield had his own personal say in preparing *Vanity Fair*'s layouts. "He'd take a pencil and indicate how big he wanted a picture, how many columns of type he'd like, how big a headline—and, presto, the page would come out looking beautiful," Jeanne Ballot, his secretary and assistant, said.

(The author Paul Gallico, one of *Vanity Fair*'s favorite writers, volunteered a different version of how the magazine was put together. He insisted that all the editorial work was done by Jeanne, "a French secretary who had a bang on her forehead, a rosebud mouth, and enormous blue eyes, and who was always alluded to as 'Baby.' " It was Baby, he maintained, who really got out the magazine, simply by collecting an odd assortment of ideas and bon mots that had dripped from the staff while they were imbibing cocktails, playing backgammon, or lunching. Baby would then paste all such literary miscellanea on a dummy, along with any other articles and photographs that happened to be lying around—and send her mixed grill to the bewildered printer.)

For thirteen years, Heyworth Campbell directed the art department in an accomplished manner, but by 1923, in spite of Nast's generous tribute to his old colleague, the magazines, in particular *Vogue,* badly needed a face-lift. It was during that same year that Steichen first started working for Nast's publications, and he at once put his finger on the problem.

"A picture editor or art director on a fashion magazine is faced with having to tell the same story year after year," he pointed out. "All he has to present are photographs of the newest fashions. To make the pages appear different, he has to secure variety somehow." Steichen added that at the time of his arrival, he regarded the layout and presentation of both *Vogue* and *Vanity Fair* as "namby-pamby, meaningless, and conventional." Strong words, but both Nast and Crowninshield knew he was right. Campbell had been brought up in the old school, when decorative drawings, modest headlines, classical type, and dense blocks of print suited well enough a genteel society gazette; but this was hardly the style to express the innovative, liberated flavor of the twenties. Nast needed the eye of a new talent who would give to his magazines the geometric, functional, modernist look that Jacques-Emile Ruhlmann, Jean Michel Frank, and Josef Hoffmann had brought to furniture, lighting, and the architectural elements of interior design.

At about the time the style that became known as "moderne" was being launched on an unsuspecting public at the Paris Exposition of Decorative and Industrial Arts in 1925, Nast asked Benito, whose elegant art deco goddesses and cubist heroines had begun to transform *Vogue* covers, if he would work on a completely new layout for the inside pages of the magazine. If *Vogue,* the acknowledged arbiter of fashion, did not mirror the aesthetic spirit of the age, then Nast was betraying every principle upon which he had become so amazingly successful.

Benito, under a series of three-year contracts with the Nast publications, used to go back to Paris at the end of each period in order to reacquaint himself with that vibrant center of art and fashion. On one of these trips he took with him Nast's assignment and worked on it in Paris, finally drawing up a dummy that was printed by the fine French printing firm of Draeger Brothers.

Part of Benito's dummy is in the form of a letter to Nast, in which he explains why his magazines were successful for so long. "Aside from good management, they have been successful because their typographic appearance suited exactly the taste of the elite; they developed in a time when it was fashionable to copy the 18th century style; types, passepartouts, frames of pictures, vignettes, etc., everything has been in imitation of the 18th century."

Benito then cautiously ventures that the infatuation with the eighteenth century seems to be coming to an end, and that the trend is toward modernism in all its forms. Ornate Louis XV drawing rooms with paneling, gilt chairs, and chandeliers are passé—in their place is the spare, architectural purity of the modernist style. "This admitted, I started to make a general survey of modern typography."

Benito's dummy incorporated a typeface entirely new to American eyes. It approximated Gothic—unornamented letters without serifs. (The serif is a decorative stroke used in classical lettering.) Sans serif, a twentieth-century typeface with no ornamentation of any kind, was a favorite of the Bauhaus in Germany, whose faculty members had broken away from traditional styles of art and design, and whose progressive graphics matched Benito's ideas for typographical innovation. America, still dedicated to typography that was eighteenth century in origin (Bodoni and Cheltenham, for example), could not provide the modern look Benito required.

Benito's layout was also revolutionary: heavy black lines under the Gothic headings; extravagant use of white space; illustrations in the spare, economical, Brancusi-influenced style of the day. "I have chosen," he wrote to Nast, "from what already exists, what seemed to suit the new spirit of the activities which we are supposed to represent. . . . Some of its expressions would stir anyone to enthusiasm—an enthusiasm that has a delicious gasp in it."

The artist proceeded to summarize his efforts for Nast in an essay on modern aesthetics, printed in the stark, futuristic typeface: "Let us realize that we are living at a time when for the first time, thanks to machinery, we are living in effective collaboration with the pure geometric forms. Le Corbusier writes [on] architecture, but his reasons are applicable to all forms of art. Modern aesthetics can be explained in one word: machinery. Machinery is geometry in action. . . . The setting up of a magazine page is a form of architecture, it must be simple, pure, clear, legible like a modern architect's plan, and as we do a modern magazine we must do it like modern architecture."

Nast found much to agree with in this statement, being a fervent supporter of clarity, legibility, and modernity himself. He looked at the dummy with, no doubt, a "delicious gasp" of enthusiasm, and paid Benito $5,000 for his work, a generous sum. He also offered him the art directorship of *Vogue* (after Heyworth Campbell finally resigned in 1927), thus giving the ultimate seal of approval to Benito's radical suggestions. Benito turned him down. "I don't want to have to go to the office every day," he said. Benito had made a lot of money working for Nast, and he wanted to go back to Spain and become a landowner and care for his vineyards and bulls for the rest of his life. So in 1928 he left New York and went to Madrid (only to return two years later when the Crash divested him of most of the hard-earned dollars that were going to fulfill his dream).

Nast was in a difficult position after Benito's departure. He had in his hands a blueprint for change—and nobody to direct its passage to reality. Enter M. F. Agha.

A more unlikely figure could hardly have been imagined. His full name was Mehemed Fehmy Agha. He was born in 1898 of Turkish parents in the Russian Ukraine and, at the time Nast found him, he was working in Berlin as an artist on the rapidly sinking German edition of *Vogue.* The young Turk had originally started his career as studio chief for the Dorland Advertising Agency in Paris, whose chief executive, Walter Maas, was in charge of starting up the new German *Vogue.* Maas, impressed by his artistic and photographic work and also by his internationalism (Agha spoke Russian, German, French, Turkish, and English), sent him to Berlin, where Nast, having arrived to see if he could stem the magazine's demise, immediately sensed talent. "After I had passed a few days in Berlin," he said, "I began seeing more and more of [Agha's] work. There were so many evidences in it of order, taste, and invention that I began thinking of him as a possible Art Director for our American periodicals. Before leaving Berlin, I spent a morning with him in discussing type, engraving, illustration and layout. It was at that conference that my opinions underwent a singular psychological change with regard to Turks in general, and Russian Turks in particular."

Frank Crowninshield, who was present in Berlin on this occasion with Nast, described Agha's arrival in New York in 1929: "He spread out in so many activities that it was almost a matter of awe and wonder. There was, in fact, but one living entity to which his growth could be compared. I allude to the heart of that famous chicken which, at the Rockefeller Institute in New York, annually, amazingly—and with nothing but bouillon to nourish it—so increases in size and power that only the most constant and ruthless

pruning prevents its covering the furthermost corners of the inhab-
ited globe."

Agha, known as Dr. Agha (not for medical reasons; his doctor-
ate was in political science, which Germans would have considered
justification for the title, and which perhaps affected the highly political content of the *Vanity Fair* covers he later selected), had
black, tightly curled hair, a Cupid's-bow mouth, a monocle, and a
splendidly guttural accent. He was attended to at home by his Si-
berian wife, Claudine, and a very large, very black butler, whom
Benito longed to paint but never dared ask. The girls in the office
called Agha the Terrible Turk. When he first arrived, he was given
a single room in the offices of *Vogue,* but very soon he occupied
two, then four, then six. Nast rapidly gave him the art editorship not
only of *Vogue* but of *Vanity Fair* and *House & Garden* as well. "A
little like his twin at the Rockefeller Institute," Crowninshield said,
"he spread out so rapidly that an additional floor had to be engaged
in the Graybar Building in order to prevent his bulging out of the
windows, growing through the roof, or occupying the elevator
shafts and ladies' rooms."

Agha quickly set to work to transform the layouts and picture
presentation of the three magazines under his charge. He banished
italic typefaces. He changed the shape of headlines. He made a bold
use of white space. He placed photographs asymmetrically on the
page. And in 1929 he introduced sans-serif type to the pages of
*Vogue* and *Vanity Fair.*

These changes are generally thought to have sprung unassisted
from Agha's exotic head. In fact, Agha followed almost exactly the
blueprint that Benito had drawn up in his dummy a few years earlier—precisely as Nast had asked him to do. For Nast was utterly
committed to this new look, however much opposition it might
meet, and he had secured Agha's cooperation when they began
working together. The publisher knew the continued success of the
magazines to a large extent depended on the commitment to modernism.

In August 1929, Nast wrote a letter to Benito in Spain, saying,

This rendering of Dr. M. F.
Agha, made for a trade
design publication,
scrupulously conveys
the art director's acute
Napoleonic tendencies.

"I hope you are pleased with the gradual change in the *Vogue* make-up, which changes I think are, at least in their general lines, on the scheme that you had in mind. Dr. Agha will probably soon begin to change the make-up of *Vanity Fair*. I should be very glad to hear from you telling me what you think of the progress we are making with respect to *Vogue*'s make-up. You can speak to me quite confidentially, for, if you do not desire it, I shall not show your letter to Dr. Agha."

Benito's response was reassuring; he thought Dr. Agha was doing his job very well.

(Nast continued to have the greatest respect for Benito's talent. Soon after Benito came back to New York in 1930 to recoup his losses, he did a cover—of a woman running along a beach with a greyhound—that became one of Nast's favorites, probably because it combined the exaggerated grace of Benito's best art deco work with a more realistic style that prefigured the illustrations of Eric, *Vogue*'s most important artist in the late thirties and the forties.)

Nast, Agha, and Benito were satisfied with the new make-up of *Vogue*. *Vogue*'s readers, however, were not so sure. In fact, word soon reached Mrs. Chase that her readers were distinctly unhappy with the alarming new visual challenges presented by their beloved magazine. The editor inquired whether Dr. Agha really had to persist in these offensive practices. "We must not go by the letters or the opinions of a few persons to whom we can speak," Nast said firmly, "but rather, to use our own judgment." Agha agreed. "It is a good thing to try to show everybody that we are still alive and leaders in the field of typographic mode. We have been the first on the market to produce this kind of Germanic type for the machine setting, and all the others are following us." But Agha had more to say. A shrewd political operator as well as a clever art director, he had quickly caught on to Nast's mania for statistics, and exploited numbers as well as his employer did when it suited his cause, as in the case of Mrs. Chase's troubled readers. ·

"The new types that belong to the same Sans-Serif family as our new Intertype Vogue are very extensively used by the advertisers of the class publications," he cunningly argued. "42 percent of all the advertisements in *Vogue* and 41 percent of the advertisements of *Harper's Bazaar* use this kind of type. If we take the professional typographic publications in which there are advertisers, by which we can judge the success of the new types, the figures are even higher, 46 percent for the *Printer's Ink* and 45 percent for *Advertising and Selling*." Nast was in ecstasy. Mrs. Chase was silenced. The sans-serif type stayed.

Agha's experiments sometimes went slightly too far. He introduced *Vanity Fair* to headlines and captions without capital letters, a style to which some of *Vanity Fair*'s readers might already have become accustomed through exposure to the work of E. E. Cummings. Indeed Cummings, who had been a regular contributor to *Vanity Fair* since 1925 (not, however, in lower case) and who was married to the ex-wife of *Vanity Fair* artist Ralph Barton, may well have been promoting lower case to the magazine's editors for years. Whether through the poet's influence or not, headlines without capital letters were apparently quite acceptable in *Vanity Fair* when Agha instituted them; but when the art director ordered a whole issue of the magazine without one capital letter appearing in it, readers were so exercised that he never repeated it. (Cummings's connection with Condé Nast's publications continued; in 1932, after divorcing Anne Barton, he married Marion Morehouse, Steichen's favorite fashion model and much photographed in *Vogue*.)

Although he was experimental in design, Agha was quite puritanical and refused to pass photographs or illustrations that smacked of sex. Horst once took a picture of a model dressed in a white chiffon evening gown, stretched out on a silk quilt on the floor, with one arm thrown in languid abandon over her brow. The Terrible Turk rejected it.

Agha had a sharp, ironic wit and a finely tuned sense of the absurd. In 1933, when photography was becoming fashionable, he concocted a story with George Hoyningen-Huené for *Vanity Fair* entitled "The Man Behind the Camera":

Is it true that "the camera cannot lie," or is it rather that "the man behind the camera" makes the dumb apparatus interpret reality in his own way? Here is *Vanity Fair*'s contribution to the controversy: seven portraits of the same lady, Mme. Lucien Lelong, taken by the same artist, Baron Hoyningen-Huené, in the manners of different masters of photography. Huené has brilliantly imitated the stately composition of D. O. Hill, the twisted pathos of de Meyer, the flowery chaos of Beaton, the masterly simplicity of Steichen, the dissolutions of Man Ray, and the dermatology of Lerski [a photographer who favored close-ups]. He also made one portrait in his own manner. Does the lady look the same when pictured in different techniques? Does the style of the photographer obliterate the personality of the sitter? Is photography Art?

Condé Nast had something to do with that piece. He had a favorite story on the subject with which Agha was familiar. A famous Fifth Avenue photographer had invited Nast to visit his studio to look at his latest photographs. Nast politely admired the exhibition and then said, "And what a clever idea to show nothing but different versions of the same girl!" "What do you mean, the same girl?" demanded the photographer in irritation. "These are the portraits of the beauties in Flo Ziegfeld's chorus, all twenty-four of them."

"Which may or may not prove the truth of the old saying," Agha added, "that an artist always produces a likeness, not of the sitter, but of himself."

Agha was widely respected in the business, but he was also acid-tongued and inclined to extreme cynicism. His approach to art was almost that of an anthropologist—he was curious as to how things were done, by what kind of people, reacting under what kind of pressure, but remained himself entirely the objective observer. He could admire execution, but never content. The graphic arts were not really important; the artists who worked for him were mostly prima donnas, to be tolerated at best, rejected, or ignored. He was once described as "the man who knew too much to like anything." He gave his life to improving the look of Nast's magazines, but there was always the sense that, deep down in his Turkish-Russian soul, there lurked a profound distaste for the whole business. "Personally," he admitted once, "I might be inclined to [the view] that a fashion magazine's conception of beauty, elegance and taste might

be insipid and nauseating, but I firmly believe that a fashion magazine is not the place to display our dislikes for these things."

Nast adored Agha. He said he had found in him "a man with
whom I could not very well assume the role of teacher since he had
assumed that role himself after relegating me, politely, to the
dunce's corner where, apparently, he thought I really belonged."

The two men got along famously. Nast could scarcely have differed more from Agha in background or temperament, but as was
often the case with the self-effacing publisher, he responded instantly to Agha's flamboyance, acerbic wit, and cynicism. Once
again, as with Frank Crowninshield, he could play the role of
protégé. The working relationship, however, was more balanced
than that word implies. Allene Talmey recalled an occasion in the
late thirties when she had done a very elaborate photographic session with the Aquacade at the World's Fair, involving 150 people in
the picture, with dancers making patterns and the Olympic Star at
the top. "It was hard work with Bruehl [the photographer], but the
final pictures were beautiful. Dr. Agha looked at them in his Pasha-
like way and said, 'It is impossible.'

"I immediately burst into tears, which I didn't do normally,
grabbed the photographs and said I was going to show them to
Condé. I rushed in and said, 'Condé, look at these photographs.' He
looked at them by the window and said, 'It must be a double page
spread.' And there was Agha listening. All he said was, 'That's just
what I told her.' But of course Condé knew what had happened."

When Alexander Liberman, now editorial director of all the
Condé Nast magazines, first joined *Vogue* in 1941, he was put to
work on some layouts of illustrations by Pagès. At the end of the
week, Dr. Agha called him in and said to him, "Well, I'm terribly
sorry, you're really not good enough for *Vogue*." So, unbeknownst
to Nast, Liberman was fired that Friday.

Meanwhile, it had been arranged for him to meet the publisher
the following Monday. So the artist arrived on Monday at Nast's office, and they had an interesting conversation about magazines, Liberman's past in Paris, Lucien Vogel, for whom Liberman had

worked, and so forth, and Liberman showed him a Gold Medal diploma he had won for magazine production.

"Well," said Nast, "a man like you must be on *Vogue*."

"Dr. Agha never said a word, I never said a word, and that's how I started on *Vogue*," Liberman said later.

Agha was often autocratic and intolerant on his own, but he never put himself in an antagonistic position vis-à-vis Nast. He was far too clever.

"The day an art director is stronger than the editor is a bad day for the magazine," Nast once told Carmel Snow. He may have relinquished to Agha his role as teacher, but he never relinquished his authority.

Nast and Agha spent hours and hours discussing layouts, photographers, and "Is photography art?" Agha would tell Nast about the latest technological developments in photography, such as the 1933 introduction of infrared photographic plates by Eastman Kodak. "These plates give the pictures a very striking and eerie appearance," he told Nast. "The landscapes look almost like snow scenes with dark skies and light-colored trees. I thought it would be fun to photograph somebody's gardens in that manner. I know that such a thing was never done in any general publication and only a few photographs of that kind were shown in the photographic papers."

But their most profound understanding was inspired by their common vision of the role of *Vogue,* the most sensitive of the magazines to art and layout. In 1937, Cecil Beaton asked for a return to less realistic photography in *Vogue.* "I think the startling lighting and meticulously modern photographs now leave us as cold as the modern windows of the best fashion shops. Not even the people in the street are bouleversé by the white backgrounds and cubistic forms any more."

Agha responded swiftly and uncompromisingly to this suggested change in style. "It really means denying everything *Vogue* stands for. *Vogue* readers want to see elegant backgrounds and furniture and smart ladies gracefully wearing smart dresses against these backgrounds. This is really the role of a fashion magazine. The technique of the presentation of this material can be changed—the ladies do not always have to have tea or be arranging flowers—but deliberate distortion of the posing, lighting and photographic printing in order to produce deliberately ugly, elegant effects, I feel, is absolutely a wrong thing to do. . . . I think that what [Beaton] is trying to do now is to deny everything *Vogue* has worshiped for so many years—to substitute ugliness for beauty, dowdiness for elegance, bad technique in photography for the good technique which we spent so many years trying to develop."

Nast had said almost the same thing a few years earlier when he saw the disastrous results of the impractical fashion illustrations cooked up by the *Gazette du Bon Ton* boys. "Mere novelty, or art value," he said then, "or surprising 'modernism' of any new style of fashion illustration will never, in my opinion, make it acceptable to our readers if it lacks in any of the fundamental qualities required by the mission, the service, which is the foundation-stone upon which the *Vogue* formula is built."

The *Vogue* formula, to which Nast returned over and over during his career, depended on service—the imparting of fashion information to his readers as efficiently and clearly as possible. He believed, therefore, that *legibility* was the fundamental principle behind every editorial decision. "Legibility," he told his staff, "is the first essential of good editing—it demands clear writing, the logical organization of written or illustrated material, photographs or drawings that clearly fulfill their mission, informative titles and sub-titles properly displayed. The necessity for legibility applies uniformly to all the various kinds of editorial material. The editor who makes his periodical readable and satisfactory to its subscribers must achieve legibility on a dozen different fronts. Sloppy editing that defeats legibility on any one of these fronts puts the reader to extra work to discover what, in text or picture, the publication is getting at. The editor succeeds in achieving legibility only when he protects the reader from even momentary doubt as to the meaning of whatever kind of editorial material he is offering his reader."

To this end, throughout his career, Nast would meticulously

measure the position of titles and artwork on the magazine's page. If a line, caption or illustration was off by a fraction of an inch, according to his blueprint, the page would have to be reset. However inventive the art director wished to be, Nast's ruler would be the final arbiter. Naturally enough, these regulations invariably drove the art department into a frenzy.

Yet this was not all. Nast also continually peppered his editors with memos, noting legible or illegible work, either in his own or other periodicals. These two examples were addressed to Frank Crowninshield in 1933 and 1935:

> I was much interested in the article "The Tale of a Bear" in the March 4th issue of the *Saturday Evening Post.* It contains observations and facts that I was keenly anxious to read but, notwithstanding my genuine interest, I simply could not struggle through the article.
>
> Without eliminating any material of importance, this manuscript could have been cut 30 percent; perhaps even 50 percent.

The second one also concerned brevity:

> You will remember that, on a number of occasions, I have spoken of the great value of brevity—of the importance of purging articles of their "fluff"—and I have told you of the publishers' belief that one of the reasons why *Collier's,* after ten years of failure, has become successful, is by following this policy of conciseness.
>
> In connection with this, I offer for your reading a story in the April 15th issue of *Collier's,* which is completed on one page.

(*Collier's* went into a slight decline after Nast's departure, which he must have found somewhat gratifying.)

Nast's knowledge of literature was limited, although he loved to write himself and wrote considerably better than he talked. He would closet himself in his office for hours on end composing the memos, letters, and directives that mark the course of his career. His criticisms of the features in his periodicals were usually on the level of legibility attained, not on literary content. He rarely read a book, and entrusted much of the literary side of his periodicals to Frank Crowninshield and the continual parade of clever young women such as Dorothy Parker, Clare Boothe Brokaw (later Luce), Helen Brown Norden (later Lawrenson), Marya Mannes, Millicent Fenwick, and Allene Talmey who over the years took up residence in his offices. He knew what was good all right—the literary contributions in his magazines attest to that—but his writers escaped the full force of his attention.

It was to his photographers that he stressed most often and most urgently his principle of legibility. There were several reasons for this. One was his primary interest in photography as a medium for imparting fashion information. Another was his painful experience with fashionable illustrators such as Brissaud, Marty, and Lepape, who drew beautiful women in beautiful clothes without giving *Vogue* readers the faintest help in copying the dresses for themselves, or any confidence at all that they knew what they were ordering if they ordered the dresses directly from the couture house. Photographers, in Nast's view, manifested precisely the same tendencies toward artistic license and creative excess. Lastly, many of them genuinely needed direction.

One of the more revealing facts about Nast's photographers was that most of them were something else before Nast employed them. Steichen was a painter/art-photographer, de Meyer a society dilettante, Beaton a writer and illustrator, Horst an architectural student, Hoyningen-Huené an illustrator, Charles Sheeler an artist, and so forth. Nast believed that their innocence of the medium would ultimately prove a strength, even if it meant waiting out their mistakes as novices. (In 1938, when André Durst was a newcomer to the *Vogue* roster in Paris, there was some discussion as to whether or not he was up to snuff. Michel de Brunhoff pointed out that many of the photographers who had successfully developed had started off disappointingly, and he included Horst and Huené in that category.) Nast liked to take them on as tabulae rasae, ready to receive the Word. His two-hour lecture to Horst in 1932 may not have gone down very well at the time, but it did not affect Horst's respect for Nast later. (Beaton once said he would never want to work for *Harper's Bazaar* because he would not get the criticism he so valued from Nast.) Indeed all the great photographers who worked for Nast were constantly being criticized, analyzed, exhorted, and instructed by the ringmaster. Here is one of Nast's critiques of the cover of *Vogue*'s September 15, 1940, issue—a dress by Hattie Carnegie, photographed by Horst:

> The basis of the beauty of this unusually graceful and charming dress was the manner in which the sash was draped. The scheme of draping was a new idea and the main feature of the dress. Obviously, then, an adequate report of the dress required that the photograph should show how the sash fell from the waist down the length of the living model to the floor.

Nast then pointed out to his editors how completely the photograph failed to report these high points, and that, moreover, it had not even the virtue of being in itself a beautiful picture:

> The right arm was so placed that it covered the waist, thereby obscuring the fall of the sash. In addition, a table had been placed in front of the figure, which not only obscured the fall of the sash along the length of the legs, but distorted the one bit of the sash that was left to view. The awkward position of the left arm produced a pose that was not only ugly in itself, but pulled the whole dress out of shape. Moreover, the props themselves were confusing; not only were they of no value to the composition, but they were positively distracting because of their overwhelming effect on the model.

Poor Horst took the brunt of the attack on this occasion, but no photographer escaped the eagle eye. John Rawlings was lambasted for two photographs in the December 15, 1941, issue of *Vogue* in which "the accessories consist of monstrous statues, of consoles and wooden scrolls, placed in the foreground, completely killing the dresses. They not only distract attention, but imprison the model and in some parts are so aggressive that they merge with the model, thus creating general confusion." In another photograph by the wretched Rawlings, "the sword of the statue on the left attacks the right arm of the woman, and the hand of the statue on the right seems about to seize her upraised arm." And in another, "the column to the left seems to be resting on the lady's neck and shoulders, forcing her into an unnatural position."

Rawlings was rapped for a further series, about which Nast grumbled, "There is as much confusion and action in these pages as you will see in a Kilkenny cat fight! I refer to the columns, vases, statues, men in the background in pointless positions, restlessly designed floors and walls. We have a combination of elements that distract the attention which should be centered on the models wearing the clothes."

Not that the publisher wanted total starkness and monotony of background. "For example, a room with beautiful furniture and charming decoration, an architectural detail, a landscape, a building—any background picturing luxurious surroundings can add to the impression of the beauty of a dress." (Agha could have written that.) "But the use of such backgrounds requires judgment and taste in their selection, a painter's sense of composition, and above all, a realization that the prime object of the photograph is to report the dress accurately and to bring out its distinctive characteristics or its utility. I am beginning to think we shall be obliged to appoint a censor whose sole duty at all sittings will be to accomplish simplicity by eliminating backgrounds and accessories of every nature—furniture, ornaments, decoration and architectural details—that are distracting and unnecessary."

This was the publisher-as-editor speaking, and he did not mince words. People remember the familiar, if awesome, sight of Condé Nast leafing through dummies of *Vogue* and tearing out page after page that failed to meet his strict specifications. His decision was final: every picture had to be passed by him.

It was not only the look of the photograph that mattered, of course. It was where the picture was placed on the page, where the title was positioned, how many inches the margin measured. There was to be no exception to the rules.

By the middle thirties, photographers began to chafe under

Nast's strict regime. Largely owing to the development of new, light, flexible cameras such as the Leica, the Rolleiflex, and the Hasselblad, and the introduction of increasingly high-speed film, photography had discovered a new identity, light-years away from the formal studio portraits Nast favored; the perfect "action shot" was the goal all avant-garde photographers now sought to achieve.

A new kind of magazine publishing was born out of these technological breakthroughs with the debut of *Life* in 1936. Although *Life* is often called the prototype of photojournalism, the title should justly go to *Vu,* a newsmagazine created in Paris in 1928 by the brilliant and versatile Lucien Vogel. Vogel, after the death of the *Gazette du Bon Ton,* turned his attention to politics, and *Vu* became a mixture of politics, news, and fashion, presented in an entirely new form of photographic reportage. (It was here that Alexander Liberman got his training; he became art director, then managing editor of *Vu.*) Under Vogel's somewhat eccentric editorship, the magazine's political views soon were discredited; but when *Life* was on the drawing board, the people involved came to the *Vu* office in Paris to see how it was put together.

*Life* was the triumph of Henry R. Luce, publisher of *Time* and *Fortune,* whose wife, Clare, had worked as managing editor of *Vanity Fair* before her marriage. (*Life* was actually Clare Boothe Luce's idea in the first place, and she had originally submitted the idea to Nast.) Luce once described what photojournalism meant, using the great *Life* photographer Alfred Eisenstaedt as an example: "Eisie showed that the camera could deal with an entire subject—whether the subject was a man, a maker of history, or whether it was a social phenomenon. That is what is meant by photojournalism." By whatever definition, it was the perfect technique—instantaneous, emblematic, capturing a moment frozen in time—to communicate the new political forces that were beginning to dominate the world as Germany, Spain, Russia, and the Depression-racked countries of the West grappled with violent social change. The superrealism of Eisenstaedt's camera captured images of political symbolism that encapsulated better than any words the darkening mood of the decade.

Nast's photographers could not fail to be aware of these dramatic developments in their field. Horst in particular objected to Nast's rigid adherence to the cumbersome old cameras that produced eight-by-ten-inch pictures, instead of the new light equipment; he claimed that his large studio portraits in their meticulously measured white frames reeked of the dated standards of a bygone age. People pointed to *Harper's Bazaar,* which, under the editorship of Carmel Snow, had secured the services of the brilliant Hungarian photographer Martin Munkacsi. His exuberant, lively, energetic action fashion shots, displayed in startling layouts by art director Alexey Brodovitch, were to be copied by generations to come, and injected a new sense of realism into the pages of Nast's rival publication. It was said that Nast, with his authoritarian views, was beginning to lose his touch.

Henry Luce believed that people should be photographed the way they lived, the way the reader could relate to them, and suddenly Toni Frissell's pictures for *Vogue* began to look different. In spite of her less-than-impressive reputation within the company, Frissell's action snapshots of people outdoors, on the move, prefigured the use of exotic locations in Africa, Iran, and Morocco by fashion photographers in the later part of the century. She, like Munkacsi, brought a breath of fresh air to fashion, reflecting the new image of women as active, healthy, sports-loving people instead of static icons, closeted in overstuffed interiors. When the war started, Frissell, not surprisingly, became a very successful photographer for *Life.*

Nast, ever conscious of changing trends in fashion, finally began to abandon his devotion to the eight-by-ten-inch studio shot. He was to a certain extent persuaded by Henry Luce, with whom he had many animated debates on the subject of commercial art photography versus photoreportage. The issue of how the public reacted to indoor and outdoor photography for fashion continued to exercise the two publishers throughout the latter part of the thirties, and in June 1941, Nast decided to put it to his readers: *Vogue* ran a contest in that issue to decide once and for all which the readers preferred.

Escape from the studio—Toni Frissell's earthy outdoor shot of white linen slacks and red-and-white sweater from Peck & Peck brings realism to fashion sittings. *Vogue*, April 15, 1939.

Two photographs were shown, side by side, one on each page: on the left, a studio photograph taken by Horst, of two models in evening gowns, leaning against a Directoire love seat; and on the right, the same two models and evening gowns photographed outdoors, on the beach, by Toni Frissell, lit by the sun and blown by the wind. The readers were invited to write in, stating their preference. The results were surprising. Over three quarters of the respondents chose Horst's studio photograph. It was not what Nast had expected, having by now committed himself to the outdoor shot. "We must have asked the question wrong," he muttered to an amused Horst. Lucien Vogel, past master of the artistic fashion plate, suggested a more valid reason: "Since the models were in evening dresses, the average reader finds the studio photographs more natural, both on account of their setting and the lighting. On the contrary, the photographs taken outdoors seem artificial. The average reader is quite rightly disturbed by the incongruity between the evening dresses and the settings, lighting effects and poses in the outdoor photographs."

Despite this reactionary response from readers, Nast as usual preferred his own judgment to the opinions of others, and pressed on with outdoor fashion photography, urging all his photographers to strive for more realism, relaxation, and informality in their pictures. One of the last letters he ever wrote was to the photographer/writer Lee Miller (later the wife of Roland Penrose), who had sent him some recent samples of her work in London. The note, dated August 17, 1942, a month before he died, reads: "The photographs are much more alive now, the backgrounds more interesting, the lighting and posing more dramatic and real. You managed to handle some of the deadliest studio situations in the manner of a spontaneous outdoor snapshot." This was a change of tune indeed for the old studio champion. But then Nast's nerve never failed when it came to endorsing a trend.

So *Vogue*, perhaps, is owed a place in the history of photojournalism along with *Life*, even if Toni Frissell's and Lee Miller's fashion shots bear little comparison to the poignant historical documents of Alfred Eisenstaedt. Or do they? Nast's photographers al-

ways encompassed more than a passing picture of the Mode. In his lifetime, just as the division between art and fashion was blurred by such cultural phenomena as the Ballets Russes, for which Chanel designed costumes, so fashion photography became not only a commercial medium, but also an attempt to view the world, and women in particular, in a heightened, inventive, even prophetic way. Anatole France once wrote that if he wanted to know about life a hundred years hence, he would look at a fashion magazine—it would tell him more about future humanity than novels, histories, or philosophies. "The greatest fashion photography is more than the photography of fashion," Susan Sontag asserts. "The abiding complexity of fashion photography—as of fashion itself—derives from the transaction between 'the perfect' (which is, or claims to be, timeless) and 'the dated' (which inexorably discloses the pathos and absurdity of time)." Steichen, Hoyningen-Huené, Man Ray, and Horst were all involved in this transaction, and the *Vogue* studios in Paris, London, and New York provided a forum for their complex commentaries. "We never felt we were just taking a photograph," Horst says. "We were making a record of our time."

Nast put this record before the public. He knew what a fashion magazine should—and could—do; he knew how his artists should express that function; and he wielded his critical and analytical authority over them so that they would achieve this goal. He was looking for the ultimate in fashion communication—to record the perfect. The results are the stuff of history. The extent to which Nast's passion and drive influenced not only his own magazines but magazines the world over, and not only in his lifetime but for decades to come, would probably have amazed those who observed the stiff, dapper figure, usually accompanied by a beautiful young girl, stepping out cautiously at openings, parties, and other social events in New York in the twenties and thirties. A glorified bookkeeper? No, rather, a modest Medici, directing a modest art to its finest achievement.

# THIRTEEN

# PARKS AND
# PICTURE PALACES

In addition to the highest-quality editorial work, art, and layouts, there is another element involved in a publication of distinction—fine printing. When Condé Nast bought *Vogue, Vanity Fair,* and *House & Garden,* they were all printed by regular commercial printers. Not surprisingly, the quality of these printers' work was not up to the standard of excellence Nast required. For several years he suffered their efforts on his behalf—efforts often diluted by strikes and other difficulties. His major printer suffered a crippling strike in 1918, and left New York City in 1921, shortly afterward going bankrupt. Nast decided he must be his own printer.

In 1921, strongly supported by his vice-president and business manager, Francis L. Wurzburg, who had joined the company a year earlier from a job in advertising, Nast bought an interest in a small printing press in Greenwich, Connecticut, called the Arbor Press, owned by Douglas C. McMurtrie. When Nast's principal printer went broke, the Arbor Press was given the responsibility of taking on the entire printing of the Condé Nast publications.

The Arbor Press had been built in 1919–20 on a partly rocky, partly swampy site in Greenwich, adjacent to the Boston Post Road. Nast decided to remodel this unprepossessing plant into something more suitable for the printing press of his three quality publications, so he turned to two of the most distinguished landscape architects of the day, Guy Lowell and Ferruccio Vitale, to transform it for him. This they did, to the tune of something over $350,000, which in 1921 was an astonishing sum of money.

The plant was expanded to about 300,000 square feet of floor space, and completely modernized. It was a complex and costly exercise. Nast had to bring in new equipment and train skilled craftsmen, in addition to enlarging the buildings. After the installation of a spectacular amount of new machinery, it was found the plant could accommodate more magazines than those owned by Nast, so in later years *The New Yorker, Field and Stream, Scientific American, Modern Photography, Mademoiselle,* and other high-class publications were also printed there, making the press quite profitable for a time.

Nast's first printing presses were common names in the printing industry, standard equipment for magazine printing—flat-bed, sheet-fed single-color Miehles, single-color U.P.M.s (United Printing Machinery), and two-color Babcocks. Flat-bed presses, into which the sheets were fed horizontally, were efficient only for small production; guaranteed to produce better-quality printing, they took a long time in the process. (Mass-market magazines were printed on rotary presses, which worked at speed.) Nast's flat-bed presses could deliver only about 1,200 sheets per hour. *House & Garden*'s circulation in the early twenties was about 100,000, and it took two weeks, with men working day and night, to complete the run. But the higher ink viscosity, greater gloss, and sharper definition provided by the flat-bed technique gave Nast the look he wanted. New press and administration buildings were added in 1923, and in time the composing room was full of the most modern linotype machines, stocked with Dr. Agha's beloved sans-serif type.

The external appearance of the plant was also given a dramatic face-lift, for Condé Nast's business, after all, had to do with the aesthetics of appearance. Guy Lowell and Ferruccio Vitale went to town on their employer's lavish budget. Nast had bought twenty-two acres on one side of the Boston Post Road, to which he added eleven acres on the other, so that the road cut through the middle of the property. The architects designed semicircular driveways each side of the road. In this circle, sixty full-grown elm trees, the finest in New England, were planted. All kinds of shrubs, ferns, trees, and flowering plants were brought in to decorate the grounds. Cascading fountains and gorgeous flower beds dazzled travelers along the road; sculpture imported from Italy gave a timeless flavor to the formal gardens. Local weddings were held under the statue of Cupid in the Georgian Love Temple garden.

Nast overlooked no details in his search for perfection. He caused the telephone and telegraph wires along the Post Road to be buried underground so they would not mar the landscape. He also put up cedar lamp posts with specially designed lights along his stretch of the highway. In front of the main building was a great lawn, impeccably kept by a staff of gardeners. The building was modernized with a skin of glass and industrial pine floors. The park itself required an endless supply of plant and flower specialists; the landscaping was not fully completed for six years.

Lew Wurzburg, Nast's hard-working and thorough executive, had personally supervised the beautification project and went to Italy himself to select the sculptures that decorated the gardens. But according to Edna Chase, even he eventually began to panic; as Nast poured more and more money into the landscaping, Wurzburg muttered, "It ought to be into *equipment* that would bring something back." But Nast wanted perfection, even in his elms and topsoil. It was the look of the thing that counted, and in its departure from conventional industrial design, the Greenwich press was revolutionary. People seeing it from the road often wondered if it was a college campus, until they saw the imposing engraved stone columns on each side of the highway, announcing, *"Vogue, Vanity Fair, House & Garden,* the Condé Nast Press."

Psychologists may argue about the effects of environment on workers, but in its forty-five years of existence, the Greenwich plant suffered only the briefest of strike actions by the employees who worked in this agreeable park. In late 1923 the compositors and pressmen struck to make the plant a union shop. A court injunction restrained the strikers from further picketing, and although on that occasion sand was thrown at the presses and a few other violent incidents were reported, things soon returned to normal, and continued that way until the thirties. In the wake of the Wagner Act, the plant became fully unionized in 1937.

In 1924 *Vogue* officially announced the move to Greenwich: *"Vogue, Vanity Fair* and *House & Garden* . . . announce the transfer of their executive and publishing offices to the Administration Building of The Condé Nast Publications, Inc., Greenwich, Conn. The circulation, accounting, purchasing, make-up, research, and pattern-factory departments are included in the transfer." The editorial and advertising departments remained in New York. The Pattern Building was added in 1927, the electrotype foundry in 1931, and the web press room in 1937. The installation of two- and five-color web presses meant it was possible for the first time to produce quality printing at high speeds.

By the late twenties, the Condé Nast Press had become renowned for its technical excellence. The press regularly published books of typefaces and lists of new types as they were incorporated into the printing operation at Greenwich. A 1929 copy of the *Condé Nast Type Book* shows its deluxe origins; the book is handsomely bound, with heavy gold lettering on the cover, signifying its biblical standing in the eyes of its readers. When Benito in 1927–28 initiated the typographic changes that Agha later incorporated into linotype, he said, "For the time being with the material at hand, there is no fear that any other publisher could get closer to modern tendencies without falling into the grotesque." He then added, with great prescience, "I can see only one danger of our losing first place, and that is in our mechanical process. 'Rotogravure' will eventually replace typography, but after looking into this, I do not believe that it is yet suitable for a magazine like ours." (The magazines finally went over to rotogravure thirty years after Nast's death.)

The glamour factory—outside, a grand tower and the west formal garden (with Georgian Love Temple); inside, the most modern printing machinery.

In 1931, a *New York Times* editorial paid tribute to Nast's pioneering efforts. Entitled, "A Tribute to Printing," it read in part:

> For years Americans have been going abroad to learn about color processes and typography. They have been despairingly saying that the Europeans order these things far better, that the most expensive and complicated foreign machinery has, when transplanted, failed to produce the results obtainable on home soil. Part of this was "defeatist" psychology; part of it was true, but the April issue of *Vanity Fair* should dissipate this publication inferiority.
>
> The April issue of *Vanity Fair* is a distinguished product, both in printing and in color effects. The two-tone portrait reproduction and the four-color printing process have been perfected to a point not passed in Europe or elsewhere. Apart from the format, and from the editorial layout (which has been revised and definitely bettered), *Vanity Fair* is a delight to the eye of the expert and of the reader. . . . The clean-cut, readable print has just the strength and delicacy for which the publisher, through experimentation, has been striving.

Nast was inordinately proud of the plant, and invariably took even the grandest visitors to see it. A photograph in *Vogue,* taken by Toni Frissell, of Princesse Guy de Polignac and the Comte de Roussy de Sales at the Condé Nast Press in 1934 indicates its importance in the eyes of its owner. In the late thirties, Benjamin Bogin, then manager of the Greenwich division, remembers, Condé brought his young daughter to the press for the first time. "As we drove past the entrance, he gave her a little nudge and pointed with a proud flourish to his name engraved on the stone columns."

The plant held annual dances, which Nast always attended, mixing with the printers and dancing with their wives, who always hoped to get to dance with him and were thrilled if they did. At one of these parties a local policeman went up to Nast and said, "Mr. Nast, I was a state trooper and once I stopped you for speeding on the Post Road, and when you told me who you were I let you go with a warning." Nast laughed politely, only later confessing that he had never driven a car in his life, "but I didn't want to hurt his feelings." (The imposter was subsequently guessed to be an employee known for reckless driving—and a quick imagination.)

The New York staff was much impressed with the new plant, to which it was connected by six direct telephone lines. "The copy room," Jeanne Ballot recalls, "was permanently linked with a gentleman called Mr. Gackstetter. For years we talked to Mr. Gackstetter over the phone. We never saw him—but we felt we knew him intimately. He caught all our mistakes, and we wheedled him into fixing a lot of unfixable things—like scratching in commas on the plates, or changing an *e* to an *a*.

"One day, Mr. Freeman, managing editor of *Vanity Fair,* suggested that we write a memo of thanks to Mr. Gackstetter for his tender care, with every proof error we could think of in it. He was very polite about the memo—but I don't think he found it very funny. He probably thought we were just making our usual mistakes."

The printing plant, which set the type, printed and bound the sheets, then mailed the magazine to subscribers and shipped them to newsdealers, allowed Nast to achieve the high-quality printing he so ardently desired. He now had the finest paper and the finest presses. It was natural that he also looked for the finest engravings of his artwork. Engravers (the people who transferred the illustration onto a copper plate for printing) varied greatly, both individually and within the various companies. Technological developments in color photography in 1926–27 accelerated Nast's decision to buy his own engraving plant. One of the first to realize the immense potential of new color-engraving techniques, in 1928 he bought a photoengraving company in New York City that was to become a center of experimental color photoengraving, as well as giving him control over the quality of all his engravings for the magazines. Nast, at this time at the height of his financial success, was eager to plough back some of his enormous profits into printing technology.

The Condé Nast photoengraving plant was a pioneer in the production of four-color engravings, and demanded new skills from craftsmen, who had to be specially trained, from photographers, who had to use color in a new way, and from engravers, who had to make color separations of the photographs through red, blue, and yellow filters (the fourth color was black), and etch four separate copper plates for printing. In 1931, Anton Bruehl, a German-born Australian recognized as one of the leading exponents of color photography, became the partner of Fernand Bourges, head color technician of the Condé Nast Engravers. Bourges had developed a process for creating color separations whose quality could not be duplicated by any other means until the introduction of Kodachrome by Eastman-Kodak in 1935; so for four years Condé Nast controlled the most exciting new photographic technique in the world.

On September 18, 1931, Agha made an agreement with Bruehl, the photographer, and Bourges, the developer, about the price of the color photographs they made for the Nast publications:

Mr. Bruehl will be paid a bulk price per sitting for his arrangement and lighting of the color composition that Bourges has to photograph [i.e., rephotograph on plates for color separations]. His charge for this work will be $100 per sitting instead of $150 that he charges for black and white sittings. This concession is due to the fact that all the plates and prints are made by Bourges, and not by Bruehl, and also to the fact that Bruehl is willing to collaborate with us in this interesting new medium.

We must not forget that color photography is a very difficult thing, and it is impossible for Bruehl and Bourges to take more than two or at the outside three subjects a day. Therefore if we plan, for instance, two pages, on which four different pictures are used, it is possible that the photographers will have to spend two days in making them, and in this case it will be counted as two sittings.

Our arrangement with Bourges is different from Bruehl's. Bourges cannot be paid per sitting because his work is directly dependent on the number of subjects. He has to make eighteen plates for each subject (positives, negatives, and color transparencies, etc.), and naturally, if we put three subjects on a page, it makes his work just three times as difficult as for a photograph that is given a full page size.

Bourges is very anxious to give us all the possible facilities, but he thinks he will be losing money if he takes less than $100 per subject, and that on the condition that he has no less than ten sittings a month.

Agha finally estimated that color artwork would cost Nast an average of $300 a page, as compared with $1,000 a page paid by *Ladies' Home Journal* to their color photographer, Nickolas Muray. Agha added that this information ought to be kept secret, for obvious reasons.

The agreement was satisfactory, and the first color photograph dazzled readers of the issue of *Vogue* dated April 15, 1932. The subject matter was relatively modest—a spring table-setting, with a peach-pink and pale green tablecloth, light purple walls, and some rather muddy yellow primroses, daffodils, and tulips, in a big white frame. The photographic credit read: "Bruehl-Bourges Photo— Condé Nast process." More color photographs followed, and by the end of the year Mrs. Chase was writing a letter of congratulation to the two photographers for their success. Bourges thanked her, adding, "At present I am building a new apparatus which I believe will help us considerably in making color separations of fashions, etc."

Emboldened by these efforts, Nast entrusted Steichen with *Vogue*'s first photographic color cover, which appeared in July 1932. It is a sensational picture of a woman wearing a red bathing suit, sitting cross-legged, holding a beach ball above her head and looking down as though to throw it. The light is intensely dramatic and sculptural, with golden highlights on the model's skin contrasting with the brilliant blue background sky and clear red bathing costume and ball. The only other color accent is white, for the model's belt, swimming hat, sandals, and a striped section of the ball. The lettering of the word *Vogue* is also in white. Simple and clean, in Steichen's inimitable fashion, this extraordinary picture was the first of a series of brilliant covers produced through the Condé Nast process. They stand as a landmark in the history of photography.

The credit for this first photograph was given to Steichen without reference to the Condé Nast process. This was a concession to Bruehl, who insisted that "Condé Nast Engraving" should be mentioned only under photographs taken by Bruehl. He wanted the impression to be given that if people wanted Condé Nast engravings for their color photographs, they had to order them from Bruehl himself. This was a typical Bruehl move: he was an emotional and insecure man, constantly suffering from outraged feelings over imagined insults and slights from the Nast organization, always feeling he was being rejected in favor of Steichen, Horst, and so forth. The problem came to a head in 1936, when Bruchl refused to do any more work for Nast, saying he was not given enough important assignments, that everybody despised him, and that he never wanted to be a photographer anyway, he hated photography, and his real ambition was to be a sailor. Agha managed to soothe the nautical distemper on that occasion, but the relationship was never an easy one after that. In spite of these difficulties, Bruehl's contribution to *Vogue,* and to color printing, did not go unrecognized.

In 1935, Nast published an oversized brochure about his color work entitled "Color Sells," to encourage advertisers to plunge into the "new art," as he called it. In this handsome document, he pays tribute to the leaders in printing technique who produced such outstanding results in color reproduction. As well as extensively praising Bruehl and Bourges, he names the Condé Nast Engravers, Inc., the Condé Nast Press, the Louis deJonge Company (for paper coating), and two other companies who were deeply involved in Nast's personal and financial crisis during the Depression—his paper supplier, Crocker, Burbank & Company, and his ink supplier, the International Printing Ink Corporation. "It may truly be said," the brochure declared, "that the new art of color photography was launched in the editorial pages of *Vogue, Vanity Fair* and *House & Garden.*"

In September 1932, another printing breakthrough occurred: the first bleed page ever to be seen in a magazine appeared in *Vogue.* (*Harper's Bazaar* made it two months later.) Not only was it a bleed page (i.e., the photograph ran to the edges of the page instead of being "framed" in a white margin, as had been the custom), but it was in color. A right-hand page showed ten types of new fabric on the market, in colors ranging from apple-green to beige; the reader then turned the page to discover a double-page spread of fifteen fabric samples, with a woman's hand resting on top of them. The right-hand page bleeds on three sides, leaving a white margin at the bottom where a tiny credit reads, "Bruehl-Bourges Photo— Condé Nast Studios." The double-page spread has no margins at all. It is an arresting series of photographs, and marks the beginning of what was to become the most common form of photographic reproduction in magazines.

The high-speed color camera was responsible for the final important breakthrough during Condé Nast's lifetime, this time in *Vanity Fair*. In September 1935, Steichen took a color photograph of the corps de ballet at the Radio City Music Hall. He took the photograph with a thousandth-of-a-second shutter synchronized with flashbulbs—a novel technique made possible by the just-perfected high-speed camera.

What makes Nast's efforts all the more remarkable is the period in which these developments were taking place. Again and again, Nast committed himself to progressive technology at a time of drastic financial retrenchment for most businesses in the United States. To produce a bleed page, wider paper had to be fed into the presses, which meant two things: that new presses had to be built to receive the wider paper, and that there was a greater amount of paper waste—and when paper was as thick and heavily coated as Nast's stock, this was a very expensive proposition. Nast's photographic bills were also skyrocketing. Before 1914, the photographs he used were often free gifts from press agents of the theatre, ballet, sports, and so forth. The big photography studios charged $4 per print for their society portraits. By the late thirties, Nast was spending over $200,000 a year on photographs alone, not counting engraving costs. Photographers themselves, who once charged $20 a sitting, by 1940 could charge as much as $1,000. Color doubled the cost—one of Bruehl's color pages cost $300 in 1935, as opposed to $150 for black and white, and that was for the sitting alone. A set of four-color engravings at that time cost about $250, compared to $2,500 today.

Nast's perfectionism with regard to the appearance of his magazines bordered on the obsessional. The obsession could be safely indulged in when times were prosperous, and until the 1929 Wall Street Crash, his pursuit of innovations and improvements in printing technology was generally received with enthusiasm. (Even editors, however, occasionally crumpled under Nast's pressure. "But Mr. Nast, the average reader will never notice," an editor once wailed in protest over a niggling pictorial detail. "I will," snapped back the publisher.)

But the Crash was to divest Nast of his fortune, and with it, his independence. His obsessions then looked like arrant irresponsibility to the bankers and accountants who were struggling to save his publications from bankruptcy after 1929. They saw no reason to support Nast's continued experiments in photography during the Depression; they could not begin to appreciate his interest in quality printing and new color-engraving techniques in the worst years of the slump. It is to Nast's credit that, in spite of overwhelming pressure, he continued to fight for the standards attained by the Greenwich press, and it is a tribute to his judgment that the press survived this time of economic drought and continued operating long after his death.

The old buildings at Greenwich still exist, but the fountains and Italian statues have long been replaced by factory developments and the rose gardens and herbaceous borders by a condominium. Nothing else remains but the two stone columns on each side of the Post Road, which still proclaim the names of Nast's magazines. These columns, quaintly left standing in the midst of the suburban sprawl like a pair of forgotten guests at the end of a party, are not much of a monument, compared to William Randolph Hearst's San Simeon; but if Hearst left a more visible memorial, Nast left a publishing record that his only serious rival in the magazine business never matched.

# FOURTEEN

# THE DEFECTORS

There was only one competitor in the magazine world as far as Condé Nast was concerned. His name was William Randolph Hearst. There were other contenders in the field, to be sure, the most important being Cyrus H. K. Curtis, whose eleven-story office building in Philadelphia was made entirely of white marble shipped from Maine and boasted stained-glass windows executed by Louis C. Tiffany and a mosaic mural by Maxfield Parrish. Magazine publishers evidently have a penchant for monuments. Curtis's *Ladies' Home Journal*, under the editorship of Edward W. Bok, was the first women's magazine to reach a circulation of a million. But Nast did not care for large circulations. The mass market did not interest him. Only when William Randolph Hearst bought *Harper's Bazar* in 1913 were the battle lines drawn.

*Harper's Bazar* was one of four periodicals owned by Harper and Brothers. (The others were *Harper's Magazine, Harper's Weekly,* and *Harper's Young People.*) Originally, it was a weekly, and a typical summary of its contents appeared thus in 1893:

Fashion: The Bazar's facilities are unsurpassed. It anticipates changes in the Mode.

Worth Models. Sandoz and Magniant constantly furnish beautiful designs for the Bazar from Worth Models, for carriage, promenade, dinner, reception and evening toilets.

The Pattern-Sheet Supplement enables women to cut their own garments at home, and is indispensable to the *Modiste*.

Serials will be written by Walter Besant and Edna Lyall.

Short Stories. By Mary E. Wilkins, Marion Harland, Harriett Prescott Spofford and others.

Cooking and Serving. Useful receipts in great variety will be prepared by competent writers.

Embroidery and needlework will be frequently illustrated by Candace Wheeler and Mary C. Hungerford.

Special Features. "At the Toilet," by Christine Terhune Herrick. "Color effects in the Garden," by Candace Wheeler. Olive Thorne Miller writes of domestic pets.

At this point in its history, its orientation toward the family and what Harper and Brothers called "the home circle" was entirely different from the upper-class appeal of *Vogue*. In 1901, the magazine was converted into a monthly and limped along rather ineffectually until 1913, when Hearst took it over.

Hearst was fifty in 1913, and worth millions of dollars in newspapers and real estate. His first venture into magazines had been in 1904, when he started an American version of an English magazine called *The Car* that had taken his fancy in London. The first women's magazine to enter his empire was *Good Housekeeping*, which he bought in 1911. This was also a mass-market magazine, devoted to service articles and fiction. But *Harper's Bazar* was another matter altogether. Hearst was determined to produce a worthy competitor to *Vogue*, a seemingly modest ambition since he had almost unlimited funds at his disposal. In 1913 the battle lines were uncompromisingly drawn when *Harper's Bazar* advertised itself as "the first magazine published *for* women of the upper class; the others are published *at* them." At this point *Harper's Bazar*'s circulation was better than *Vogue*'s—65,000 as opposed to 30,000. (In

1916, both magazines were neck and neck with circulations of 100,000. By 1918, the *Bazar* had dropped back to 85,000; it stayed in second place until the mid-thirties.)

Hearst was not above using his own publications in the effort to undermine his rival. In September 1923, the following news item ran in Hearst newspapers in New York and across the country:

#### VOGUE GIVES UP IDEA OF LONDON EDITION

Condé Nast, editor and owner of *Vogue,* has abandoned his attempt to establish *Vogue* in London, and has sold the English edition of *Vogue* to the publishing House of Hutchinson & Company. . . .

In this connection, it is interesting to note that all attempts to establish English editions of American editions have not failed. The English edition of *Good Housekeeping,* owned and published by William Randolph Hearst, has become in two short years the leading women's magazine in England. . . .

Of course the whole story was nonsense. This was Hearst at his most scurrilous and irresponsible. Nast's response was to buy a full page in the trade journal *Printer's Ink* a week later, reprinting the Hearst newspaper item, with a very terse comment:

This story, which appeared ONLY in the Hearst newspapers throughout the country, is absolutely false. I have not sold, and am not contemplating the sale of British *Vogue* to anyone. Condé Nast.

There is no record of any other such public-relations attempt by Hearst to demoralize Nast. It was the kind of cheap trick Nast would never have contemplated. But he was up against a tough enemy. Hearst soon found that the most effective way to upset the Nast organization and give strength to his own was by grand larceny. Since so much of the success of *Vogue* could be attributed to its artists, advertising people, and editors, Hearst would appeal to the vulnerability of Nast's personnel. It turned out to be a highly effective policy.

One of Hearst's earliest coups was the signing of a ten-year exclusive contract with the brilliant *Gazette du Bon Ton* artist Erté, whose first cover for *Harper's Bazar* in 1915 must have sent a few frissons through the art department at *Vogue*. In 1916 *Harper's Bazar* presciently published the first Chanel dress to be seen in America—a "charming chemise." So there were some publishing firsts quickly claimed by Hearst. But it was the employee thefts, spectacular, painful, and continual for a period of over twenty years, that did the most profound damage to Nast's organization.

The first to go was Baron Adolphe de Meyer, in 1922, persuaded by Hearst's primary and usually irresistible lure, money. Since de Meyer's uniquely stylish photographs had been the hallmark of the early *Vogue*s, his departure was a severe blow. A decade later the equally distinguished photographer George Hoyningen-Huené rushed off to Hearst in a fit of pique after a row with Dr. Agha in Paris. Heyworth Campbell, the founding art director of Nast's *Vogue*, turned up at *Harper's Bazaar* in the middle thirties. Hearst's people even attempted to shake Edna Chase from her desk at *Vogue*—at double her salary, of course.

But by far the most serious of all the defections was that of Carmel Snow. She was a protégée of Edna Chase's, enthusiastic, a hard worker, and blessed with a flair for fashion. Nast, also taken by the bright Irish girl, taught her to write captions and titles. He saw her potential and spent a lot of time with her, buying her clothes, taking her to Newport and for weekends in the Adirondacks. Carmel insisted that there was never anything romantic between them, but that he simply wanted her to drink in the atmosphere of the *Vogue* world, which was a far cry from her unpretentious and rowdy Irish background. She started working for *Vogue* in 1921 and was made fashion editor in 1926. So closely did she work with Nast and Chase that the staff used to say that Edna was Condé's wife and Carmel his mistress. Carmel was to find her role in this ménage à trois less and less comfortable as time went on.

By the late twenties there were four *Vogue*s, American, French, British, and for a short while, German, and Edna Chase was editor in chief of all of them. This meant that she had to spend more and more time abroad, and in the spring of 1929, after much agonized discussion between Nast and Chase, it was decided to give Carmel Snow the post of New York editor of *Vogue*.

Carmel Snow was by this time married, with a growing family. She also had a brother, Tom White, of whom she was very fond. In 1929, Tom White went to work for Hearst, a fact that made Nast distinctly uneasy.

"Edna," he said, "I have a feeling that Tom will eventually want Carmel to go over to Hearst, and I don't think she should be with us unless she's under contract. As a matter of fact, I've suggested it to her."

"What did she say?"

"She was indignant. She said nothing would induce her to work for Hearst, she wouldn't dream of it, and she gave me her word to that effect." Nast never forgot her demonstration of outrage.

That was in 1929. In 1932, in the midst of the Depression, Mrs. Snow went into the hospital to have her fourth baby. Nast went to see her as usual and to say good-bye before leaving for Europe.

Later that week, having waited until Nast was halfway across the Atlantic, Carmel Snow called Edna Chase to the hospital and announced that she had decided to go to *Harper's Bazaar*.

Mrs. Chase was stunned. "We had given her the title of editor of American *Vogue* and it was my expectation that when I retired she would take over my duties and become the editor in chief of the three publications. She was fully aware of the keen rivalry between *Vogue* and *Harper's Bazaar* and she was now throwing over all that we had built together over the years to go to work for the man who, Nast felt, had tried assiduously and continually to undermine his property and bribe away his best people."

Mrs. Chase tried every means at her disposal to make her change her mind. She said that Nast could match any money Hearst offered. She asked her at least to wait till he returned from Europe. She even wheeled in Leslie, Nast's ex-wife, who was staying at 1040 Park at the time. Carmel was godmother to Leslie and Condé's daughter, Leslie, born in 1930, and Mrs. Chase thought the mother's presence might arouse some sense of conscience in the treacherous editor. But Mrs. Snow was adamant. She was doing it for her family, for easier working hours (*Bazaar* was a monthly), for the challenge.

With a heavy heart, Edna sent a cable to Paris with the news. Nast was shattered. In his distress, he sent for Harry Yoxall in London to come over to Paris to see him, and for the second time in his life, he got well and truly drunk. Yoxall had to put him to bed.

Nast did not speak of the matter after that, but he never forgave his Carmel. He forbade his elder daughter, Natica, ever to speak to her. Once, when he saw Horst talk to her at a party, he went up to him later and asked him never to speak to her again.

Mrs. Snow's side of the story sheds a different light on the whole affair. "When I was approached by Mr. Hearst's representative and invited to become the fashion editor of *Harper's Bazaar,*" she explained, "I honestly believed that Condé would be glad to be relieved of the burden of my salary, which, for those Depression days, was considerable. The salary I was offered was exactly the same, the title was less important. But since Mrs. Chase had already proposed that I be demoted to society editor, I felt that I was no longer necessary to *Vogue.* These are facts which *Vogue* partisans have never mentioned."

There is no doubt that friction between Mrs. Chase and Mrs. Snow had developed over the years. Mrs. Snow chafed at her subordinate position, and although both Nast and Chase had promised her Chase's job, it seemed less and less likely that Edna was ever going to relinquish it. (In fact she did not do so for another twenty years.) Carmel Snow was as brilliant an editor in her way as Mrs. Chase was in hers, and a clash was inevitable.

Mrs. Chase never got over it. About four years after the defection, Mrs. Snow offered an olive branch to her former editor in chief by inviting her to dinner. Mrs. Chase's answer shows the extent of her feelings:

> Thank you for your kind invitation to dine on Friday. I wish I could accept, but the old relationship that existed between us was so made up of our long years of work and play together that when

you threw that all aside in order to build up the property of the man who had been our meanest rival, you killed in my heart an affection and a faith that nothing but your own words could have destroyed.

Our friendship was not built on trivialities, Carmel, it was welded from the joys and struggles of mutual accomplishment and a common interest. I still feel too keenly the sorrow of this whole situation to be able to see you in the old familiar way.

I often think of you and the children and I hope they are all well. In my heart I do you the justice to believe that you too have suffered.

In 1945, at a luncheon with a new young editor named Rosamond Riley (now Rosamond Bernier Russell), Mrs. Chase began to speak of Carmel Snow, and as she talked, Rosamond Riley was astonished to see tears suddenly begin to course down the cheeks of the tough old editor and businesswoman. By then Carmel Snow had been gone thirteen years.

On the business side, another damaging defection that took place at the same time as Carmel Snow's was that of Paul MacNamara, advertising manager of *Vogue*. An aggressive Irishman, MacNamara had learned the highly successful Nast method of advertising and promotion straight from the horse's mouth, and his knowledge of its strengths and weaknesses made him a most dangerous opponent. Nast must have found this a painful loss to bear.

As soon as Carmel Snow took over *Harper's Bazaar,* the impact was felt throughout the fashion world. She had learned from Nast and Agha the importance of layout, and one of her first coups was the hiring of the brilliant Russian architect and designer Alexey Brodovitch (who had been to see Agha at *Vogue* a year earlier) as her art director. At the same time, having watched Nast's photographers at work—particularly Steichen, with whom she had become close friends—she was on the lookout to build up her own stable. She quickly found two who were to change the face of the *Bazaar,* and by implication, *Vogue*—Martin Munkacsi and Louise Dahl-Wolfe.

Munkacsi was a Hungarian who had arrived in New York speaking hardly any English. While *Vogue*'s photographers were still constructing artful interiors in the studio for their fashion sittings, Munkacsi took his new high-speed Leica and photographed women outside, on the move, in action. "Just snapshots," commented Nast when they first appeared in *Harper's Bazaar.* "Farm girls jumping over fences," sniffed Edna Chase. But Munkacsi's stimulating images prefigured the energy, naturalism, and vitality that has dominated fashion photography ever since.

Louise Dahl-Wolfe went first to *Vogue,* as most artists and photographers did, to show her work to the famous Dr. Agha. Not in the best of health at the time, she cannot have appeared very prepossessing to the critical eye of the Turkish cynic, for in his summarizing memo to Nast which accompanied her portfolio, he wrote, "This work has definite possibilities, but it's by a middle-aged woman who probably won't develop much farther." By a wicked stroke of misfortune, this memo remained attached to the portfolio when it was returned to the photographer.

Shortly afterward, Miss Dahl-Wolfe's innovative work, particularly in color, was enhancing the pages of *Harper's Bazaar;* Agha had delivered her into the hands of Carmel Snow.

Mrs. Snow also took a fancy to the impressionistic art of Bébé Bérard, the eccentric French scenic designer and artist whose fashion drawings were usually produced with the aid of drink or drugs. His work was different and charming, although Hearst hated it.

*Harper's Bazaar* secured exclusive use of Bérard's talent until George Hoyningen-Huené had his famous spat with Agha in 1935 and rushed off to Carmel Snow. In retaliation, Mrs. Chase stole away Bérard and signed him up jubilantly for *Vogue.* This kind of competitive exclusivity was not without its problems, however. In late 1938, a publishing crisis arose over the proposed publication in *Harper's Bazaar* of a series of "modern master" paintings, one of which was a portrait of one Madame Larivière painted by Bérard. On hearing this news, telegrams flew across the Atlantic from Nast, with JUPITER, NERO, and other code words for the Hearst organization scattered throughout the messages like expletives. Nast insisted the reproduction be banned from the *Bazaar*'s pages, since Bérard was now Nast's exclusive property. Fury reigned at Bérard's

Carmel Snow, all
hauteur and authority
in this photograph by
Richard Avedon—a
fitting rival to Edna
Woolman Chase.

A new look in layouts
at *Harper's Bazaar*,
created by art director
Alexey Brodovitch and
photographer Martin
Munkacsi, inspired by
Carmel Snow.

betrayal. Michel de Brunhoff rushed to the defense of his artist. It was not his fault—Bérard had simply painted the portrait: what happened to it afterward was the Larivières' business. However, since it was well known that Carmel Snow would never pass up an opportunity to seduce Bérard back into the fold, this seemed yet another Machiavellian move on her part. When Nast finally persuaded Bérard and the Larivières to demand the portrait's withdrawal, the *Bazaar* had already made the color plates for its reproduction, so Carmel said Nast could have the plates for the rather excessive sum of $850. De Brunhoff, who was mediator in these negotiations, cabled Nast for instructions. Nast told de Brunhoff to buy the plates: PREFER GIVING CONSENT RATHER THAN HAVING CARMEL WORKING ON BERARD IN PARIS, he cabled back.

Luckily, Bérard died of drugs and dissipation before Carmel could get her hands on him again after that. But it had been a close thing.

Hearst, the newspaper man, was often able to beat Nast in newsgathering coups. Probably the most irritating one concerned both magazines' obsession with Mrs. Wallis Simpson in the middle thirties. In May 1936, a full year before Cecil Beaton published his triumphant photographs of the future Duchess of Windsor in *Vogue*, *Harper's Bazaar* smugly presented to its readers "the most important American in London," Mrs. Wallis Simpson, in photographs by . . . George Hoyningen-Huené.

All the artists and photographers knew of the intense rivalry between Hearst and Nast and exploited it ruthlessly in their demands for more money, more work, more trips, more portfolios, more admiration, more love. It was a powerful weapon and they knew it. Nervousness about Carmel Snow's poaching skills led one French *Vogue* editor to write to Edna Chase in 1933 about their precious new artist Eric: "Unless we sometime soon give Eric something besides straight fashion pages the *Bazaar* will hear some of his talk and give him promises of portfolios with travel. . . ." Mrs. Snow's powers seemed to them at times to be positively witchlike: "Mrs. Snow appeared on Saturday at Augustabernard's. We all spoke very politely but slightly uncomfortably. I wish I could stay until Mrs.

Snow leaves for I would like to know what she is going to do—she might work on Eric. . . ."

On the other hand, artists would be penalized for working for one magazine rather than the other. Lucien Vogel once asked Edna Chase if she and Frank Crowninshield might not like to show some of the work of the artist Drian, who was having an exhibition in New York at the time. "I feel very reluctant to give Drian any publicity because he has been entirely identified with the *Bazaar*," Mrs. Chase replied. "Although I think his original things extremely interesting, I am not very keen about exploiting the art exhibitions of the *Bazaar* artists." And in the late thirties, when someone asked her if she might not like to use Erté, since he was no longer under exclusive contract to Hearst, she found the idea absurd. She never used Baron de Meyer again either, although he wrote long, pathetic letters to her from California begging for work. Such artists were tainted, in her view, forever.

The seductions continued throughout Nast's lifetime, increasing greatly in bitterness after the Carmel Snow affair. The bait was always the most reliable one—more money. Rumors endlessly flitted along the *Vogue* corridors about editors in New York and Paris being wooed by Hearst's people, so much so that Mrs. Chase once asked Nast whether she should try to find out if they were true. "I am not much impressed by the story of these delicate flirtations with any member of our staff by Carmel Snow and the Hearst organization," Nast said stiffly. "It has been my experience over many years that when they want anyone, you don't hear delicate purrings from the cat or the organization but that they soon go after whomever they want definitely, vigorously, openly, and with large bait."

Hearst's aggressive campaign of luring away Nast's staff seems not to have been reciprocated to any great extent. Mrs. Reginald Fellowes, for instance, briefly worked for the *Bazaar* in Paris in the mid-thirties. On finding herself bored, she asked the *Vogue* people if they might not give her something more interesting to do at *Vogue*. She was delicately told that there was a convention between Hearst and Nast that they did not engage each other's employees. Even if Hearst had broken the agreement by engaging Carmel

Snow and others, Nast wished to uphold it. The only real anxiety engendered by Mrs. Fellowes's request was that her departure would leave a gap in the *Bazaar* organization that they would no doubt seek to fill by enticing away yet another *Vogue* editor. . . .

*Harper's Bazaar* was not the only weapon Hearst used to undermine Nast. *The Smart Set,* founded in 1890, started as a society journal. In 1914, George Jean Nathan and H. L. Mencken bought it and turned it into a literary magazine with writers familiar to *Vanity Fair* readers, such as Aldous Huxley, Ben Hecht, Michael Arlen, Gilbert Seldes, and Donald Ogden Stewart. However, its circulation never rose above about 22,000, and in 1924 the two editors began a new magazine called *The American Mercury,* leaving *The Smart Set* to find its way into the acquisitive hands of William Randolph Hearst. In 1928 Hearst sold it, then in 1930 bought it back again and attempted to turn it into a legitimate competitor to *Vanity Fair,* hiring Arthur Samuels of *The New Yorker* to edit it. But demand for such magazines was rapidly diminishing as the Depression took hold, and *The Smart Set* folded.

In 1925, in another attack on Nast's upper-crust constituency, Hearst bought *Town & Country,* founded in 1846. This magazine was more country-oriented and less sophisticated than any of Nast's three publications, but it also appealed to the rich, aspiring middle class, and it became a respectable contestant.

In December 1933, Hearst purchased *House Beautiful* and combined it with *Home & Field,* presenting new competition to *House & Garden,* which was not doing particularly well, for obvious reasons, during the early Depression years. To meet this situation, Nast strengthened the editorial and trade staffs of *House & Garden,* allotted more pages for black and white and color photographs and inaugurated a Trade Supplement and other promotional activities. *House Beautiful* found itself in the same position with relation to *House & Garden* as *Harper's Bazaar* had vis à vis *Vogue*—good, but not quite good enough.

In spite of Nast's continued supremacy, the threat of Hearst never left him, not for one minute. Hearst cast a shadow over almost every policy decision of Nast's publications. In 1936, for instance, after *Vanity Fair* had folded, the question was raised among the senior staff whether to take the line "incorporating *Vanity Fair*" off the cover of *Vogue*. MacDonald DeWitt, Nast's lawyer, said on that occasion: "I think the risk of Hearst taking advantage of anything which might be claimed to be abandonment on our part of the title *Vanity Fair* is too great to warrant any weakening of our position." The phrase "incorporating *Vanity Fair*" remained.

Any chance Nast found to show his superiority over Hearst was seized upon. In 1935 he noted that *Fortune* magazine had made an investigation of the reading habits of 3,955 women in the New York *Social Register* and 1,460 in the Chicago *Social Register*. *Vogue* was found to have 653 readers in the *Social Register* group, compared to 361 who subscribed to the *Bazaar*. This was exactly the kind of statistic Nast most appreciated. (After all, it resembled the claim he had made at the very beginning of his ownership of *Vogue*.)

In the thirties, with Carmel Snow at the helm of *Harper's Bazaar* and every magazine fighting for a diminishing pool of readers, competition was particularly fierce. In a significant policy move, *Harper's Bazaar* began to publish quality fiction. Later, Nast said, "When *Harper's Bazaar* began to give so much space to highly paid fiction (fiction being the most powerful of all circulation-builders), I thought that it would soon outdistance *Vogue* in circulation. Many years have passed, and this result has not come about."

At no time did Nast underestimate the *Bazaar*'s potential; he was always using it as an example for possible improvements to *Vogue*. A case in point was the famous 1940 *Vogue* cover showing a Hattie Carnegie dress, which Nast felt failed properly to represent the dress. On this occasion he had no hesitation in handing the palm to his rival. "It so happens," he told his editors, "that *Harper's Bazaar* has reported the same dress, also in full color, in its September 15th issue. In the *Bazaar*'s photograph reporting this dress will be found proof of the soundness of my criticism. So far as the dress itself is concerned, without entering into a discussion of the background, the *Bazaar*'s photograph avoids the many faults of *Vogue*'s. In a word, the *Bazaar* reports the dress—*Vogue* doesn't."

In the last year of his life, Nast compiled a vast memorandum on his editorial policies. It was an exhaustive study, really a summary of a lifetime's publishing experience. It fell to Lew Wurzburg to voice the fears expressed by many of Nast's by now well-indoctrinated staff: "It would be worth many thousands of dollars to the Hearst organization," he said, "if this memorandum should fall into their hands and they should apply its philosophy to *Harper's Bazaar.* I hope, therefore, that you limit its distribution to your important and trustworthy editors, particularly if they are going to be allowed to take the memorandum out of the office."

In spite of their rivalry, there were some intriguing similarities between William Randolph Hearst and Condé Nast. Hearst, like Nast, had only a nominal father and a dominating mother on whom he depended. Hearst was also a chronically shy man, compensating for the affliction by courting headlines, encouraging sensationalism, and leading an excessively public life that ultimately led to his pursuit of the presidency. Like Nast, he inspired great loyalty in his women employees, notably Annie Laurie and Louella Parsons, but lacked the ability to make mature friendships.

Hearst was ten years older than Nast, and like his competitor, he had a taste for younger women. In 1903, when he was a day under forty, he married Millicent Willson, a beautiful young girl of twenty-one. He also turned his honeymoon into a social occasion (perhaps both these men doubted themselves when facing their young brides alone). While Nast summoned family and friends to Nassau and Palm Beach, Hearst, sailing for Europe on the *Kaiser Wilhelm II,* reserved extra staterooms for his great friend Governor James L. Budd of California. (When Budd failed to show up, Hearst quickly substituted Fremont Older, editor of the *San Francisco Bulletin,* and his wife.)

In later years, when Hearst had taken up with Marion Davies, Millicent Hearst became a good friend of Condé Nast's and was often seen at his parties in New York or in Sands Point, where they were neighbors. (There was nothing provocative in this. Mrs. Hearst remained a loyal supporter of her wayward husband, and Nast would never have discussed their publishing rivalry in her presence.)

In the high twenties, William Randolph Hearst owned twenty-two daily papers, fifteen Sunday papers, seven magazines in the United States and two in England, including *Cosmopolitan, Good House-keeping, Hearst's International,* and *Harper's Bazar.* His profits were built largely on mass-market publishing. Although Hearst gave Nast a run for his money in the quality field, Hearst's preferred formula was cheap sensationalism for editorial content, and cheap quality for production. While Nast, it might be said, invented class publishing, Hearst invented the popular press; and on the basis of these innovations, both garnered great wealth.

Hearst was as lavish in his spending as Nast. The castles in Europe and America that Hearst filled with treasures and the generosity he was wont to extend to privileged employees reflect a response similar to Nast's own response to becoming a millionaire several times over. They both enjoyed their money. They both suffered in consequence.

After the Crash, Hearst's empire collapsed almost as dramatically as Nast's, and on a much larger scale. By 1937 Hearst was nearly bankrupt and, again like Nast, was forced to give up financial control of his company. It went to Clarence Shearn, a senior lawyer for the Chase National Bank (Nast's onetime banker), holder of some of Hearst's notes. Hearst's total debt came to $126,000,000. He had to close newspapers, sell his art and his houses, watch his world crumble practically overnight, but he still fired off telegrams in his customary fashion to the newspaper and magazine editors who served him, criticizing, complaining, commenting. Maintaining the illusion of control seems to be the only acceptable position for ruined magazine publishers.

Ironically, the end of the thirties saw an upswing in both Nast's and Hearst's fortunes. The war saved them both, although security came sooner for Nast than for Hearst. *Vogue* finally showed a respectable record: in 1938 an advertising dollar spent on a full page bought 109 readers in *Vogue* as compared with 100 in the *Bazaar* and 55 in *Town & Country*. After all the storms, Nast still lived at 1040 Park Avenue. And Hearst was still king of San Simeon.

Hearst once invited Edna Chase and her daughter, Ilka, to his California castle for a weekend, which showed a certain amount of broad-mindedness on his part. (Ilka had become a good friend of Marion Davies.) They were given a suite in one of the guest houses, "simple Renaissance dwellings," as Ilka described them, "rich in tapestries and rare objects, built to shelter eight or ten in luxury."

Throughout the weekend, the Chases were amused to note that Edna, though by far the oldest and most distinguished woman there, sat neither on Hearst's left nor on his right at dinner, but somewhere below the salt. "What I am dying to know," Mrs. Chase later said, "is whether it was malice or just an original form of *Bazaar* etiquette." This, however, was the only indication of controversy that occurred. Conversations throughout the visit between the two great rivals remained entirely on the level of trivialities, which indicates the extent of feisty Mrs. Chase's self-control. W. A. Swanberg says in his biography of Hearst that Hearst was upset by Ilka Chase's representation of him in her memoir, *Past Imperfect*, as a somewhat sinister person who looked like an octopus. But surely Hearst must have known that a certain residue of hostility was to be expected between the Chase family and their host. After all, an apocryphal but illuminating story that went the rounds of the *Vogue* staff in 1938 shows that Hearst himself was not immune to the passions of rivalry.

Apparently Carmel Snow decided to hire a French noblewoman to add *ton* to the *Bazaar*. Her choice settled upon the Marquise de Vogüé, of all names, and this proposal was duly cabled to Hearst. Hearst, who received the cable without all the little attendant dots and accents, and having probably never heard of the distinguished house of Vogüé, thought somebody was making fun of him and nearly burst one of his remaining blood vessels. The project was hastily dropped, and the choice fell instead upon Anne de la Rochefoucauld, who was exceedingly unpopular but whose name did not lend itself to emotional outbursts.

Condé Nast certainly never went to San Simeon, nor did William Randolph Hearst ever attend a party at 1040 Park Avenue. Natica, however, remembers going to a fancy-dress ball given by Hearst. And when *Time* magazine published a fierce attack on Hearst in 1939, Nast received no pleasure from it. He believed it was both unfair and irresponsible to attack an old man, even one who was still so powerful.

By that time, Nast could afford to be generous. Whether Nast's obsession with Hearst was paranoia or good business sense, the fact is that despite all the defections and talent raids, *Harper's Bazaar* never beat *Vogue* in advertising ratings. Before the departure of Carmel Snow, there was no contest. In 1925, the *Bazaar* received only 36.3 percent of the combined linage of the two magazines. At the beginning of 1929, *Vogue* led women's magazines in monthly advertising with 118,088 lines. *Ladies' Home Journal* came next, with 87,865 lines, followed by *Good Housekeeping,* with 75,977 lines. *Harper's Bazaar* came fourth, with 69,334 lines. In the general magazine category, *House & Garden* led in 1929 with 89,020 lines, followed by *Town & Country* with 80,011 lines. *House Beautiful* had 48,750 lines, and *Vanity Fair* 44,748 lines.

Throughout the thirties, *Vogue* never let *Harper's Bazaar* quite catch up (except in circulation for a few years), although *Town & Country* came out ahead of *House & Garden.* Two new magazines, *Fortune* and *Esquire,* appeared at the top of the advertising lists, and these two remained there through the end of the decade.

At the end of 1942, the year Nast died, the monthly advertising linage ran as follows:

*Vogue* 60,634 lines (circulation 223,475)
*Ladies' Home Journal* 54,531 lines
*Harper's Bazaar* 47,624 lines (circulation 203,025)
*Mademoiselle* 46,970 lines
*Good Housekeeping* 37,201 lines
*Glamour* (Nast's new entry) 13,013 lines

In the general category:

> *Fortune* 101,622 lines
> *Esquire* 77,869 lines
> *Town & Country* 36,687 lines
> *House Beautiful* 25,819 lines (circulation 327,267)
> *House & Garden* 23,350 lines (circulation 243,119)

Nast was not home free with all his publications, but his beloved flagship, *Vogue,* remained untouchable. For twenty-nine years, *Vogue* had carried more advertising space than any other magazine in the women's field. That was a statistic Nast must have cherished.

In two respects, however, William Randolph Hearst thumpingly defeated his longtime competitor. Although ten years older, he survived Nast by nine years, dying at the age of eighty-eight in 1951, and leaving, in contrast to his ruined rival, a personal estate of $59,500,000.

# FIFTEEN

# A SPLENDID MIRAGE

In April 1926, *Vogue* presented the first in a series of articles in letter form, "written for the benefit of those who have an interest in society, its inner workings and outer forms." The letters were written by Madame de Style to her daughter, Madame La Mode, and the first one was "On the Subject of How to Launch a New-comer into Society."

"I think I should begin it in some summer watering-place," Madame de Style advised. "One is much more apt to become friends with the leisure classes when they are almost at leisure. Don't you feel the truth of that?"

Indeed, *Vogue* readers did. Their leisure was becoming more pleasurably leisurely every year as the stock market bounced and spiraled its way heavenward. Not that *Vogue* would ever let them get away with anything *too* relaxed. "Don't make the mistake of thinking up a lot of girlish printed frocks for sitting about on the rocks when what you really needed was a tweed skirt and sweater," Mrs. Chase admonished her vacationing ladies, "and don't think that the tweed skirt and sweater will do you particular credit at the casino in the afternoon. And above all, don't be underdressed or over-undressed." On this occasion, the editor in chief exhorted in vain. For the most exciting thing to happen to leisure in the twenties was Sunburn, and most people, enthusiastically undressing to expose their once-protected flesh to the sun's rays, exhibited a leathery glow that had previously characterized only the less privileged classes.

*Vogue* also had something to say about the less privileged classes during this feverish period. "To get the best out of servants these days may be difficult," the magazine allowed. "A firm rule is needed, but also a ready appreciation of good work and a generous desire to make them as happy and comfortable as possible. Those who have not always had servants don't understand this." How the wives of the nouveaux riches, poring over *Vogue* in their Fifth Avenue mansions, must have quailed at this stern reproach from their mentor.

Servants, to be sure, had always exercised *Vogue* readers to a most alarming degree. As far back as 1910, advice on servants was a regular feature, such as this piece in December 1912, suggesting suitable Christmas presents for the servant's hall: "In planning gifts for the servants, practicality and fitness should be the first consideration, but not, as is so often the case, the only ones." The article then goes on to suggest a Persian paw set ("furs always appeal to a woman, no matter what her station in life") for $14.75, or a black serge dress "that will prove an acceptable present to a maid of any station." (Price, $10.50.)

But by the twenties, how to deal with one's servants had become a major problem. It seems, however, that *Vogue* had little sympathy for the new breed of employers who were so filled with insecurity about their domestics. In April 1927, a four-page manual appeared, with illustrations, describing how to dress your servants so as to keep them as happy and comfortable as possible. It contained the following remarks: "The question of the proper clothes for a butler and of liveries for footmen is little understood today; for the old aristocracy is losing them, while the new plutocracy is acquiring them all unknowing of any tradition about their attire. . . ." (Would those poor little wives of the plutocracy *never* be allowed to forget?) The article then generously threw out some crumbs of advice: "A butler in a very smart house might wear a morning, or cutaway, coat, while superintending the work of his men and attending his own duties up to one o'clock. With it, he would wear the striped trousers and high waistcoat which would make part of his costume when he waited at the table . . ."

Not that *Vogue* could be accused of ignoring the plutocracy altogether. In 1926, the magazine published a highly topical series of articles on Florida, mecca of the plutocrats, center of speculation fever. "To believe in this miracle called the Florida boom, to credit the story of riches made in that land of Arabian nights, and to share the Floridian optimism about the future, one has only to motor from Palm Beach along the shore road to Miami Beach and see the city for the first time from the causeway. . . . The experience is never to be forgotten, and, while it is veritable pandemonium, it is the pandemonium of a new and prosperous world that nothing can 'down.' "

Indeed, so determined to wax lyrical about this new millionaire's paradise was our correspondent that when tackling the local Seminole Indians ("an odd people"), he managed to find their clothes a positive inspiration for *Vogue:* "They are more like something Bakst might have designed for the Russian Ballet than the expected costume of the American Indian." What imagination! What chic!

But then everything looked chic to *Vogue* in those days (chic being the new definition of the Mode for a swiftly changing, arriviste society)—cubism, Campbell's Soup, Pierce Arrows, Newport, Katharine Cornell, Jean Michel Frank, belted frocks, Paul Whiteman's orchestra, brimless hats, Mrs. Robert Goelet, yellow morning rooms, Vionnet sports dresses, Eugene permanent waves, suntan, poems by Iris Tree, and New York, of course, the shimmering city— "The crowding of Fifth Avenue with motors flashing in the sun, the tumult of the smart restaurants, the anguished haste of dressmakers and modistes, and the sandwiching of picture exhibitions and special matinees for the illuminati between luncheons at Marguery's and first nights of the luscious and glittering summer reviews . . ."

*Vanity Fair,* meanwhile, was instructing its readers on the new fad for Negro blues singers (by Carl Van Vechten); the Black Bottom (danced in the photographs by Ann Pennington); the films of D. W. Griffith; and what to give an Intellectual Lady for Christmas ("Is Art Divine? Then delight her with an Austrian water-color painted by Sweibruck. Is she thrilled by the Modern School? Then give her a modernistic piece which covers the table but is also a pillow cover . . ."). In March 1927, *Vanity Fair* published an item that could only have been written in a period when people felt everything, forever, was going to be a matter of superlatives:

> *Vanity Fair* is about to make an enforced hegira to a new habitat. The growth of the periodical, during the past few years, is our excuse for seeking a slightly more pretentious maisonette. Our new thirty-story abode—the Graybar Building—lies situate on Lexington Avenue, between 43rd and 44th Streets. Once installed there, the Editor's desk will become an integral part of the Grand Central Station, being distant by only two hundred feet from the engine of the 20th Century Limited. The Graybar is the largest office building in the world. 12,500 people will daily find sanctuary in its 1,200,000 square feet of floor space, while 60,000 visitors will use its thirty-five elevators. Best of all, our secretary—a fastidious and leisurely luncher—will have direct (and roofed-over) access to four excellent restaurants—the Belmont, the Biltmore, the Commodore and the Roosevelt. . . .

In that same issue, the Cunard Line (*Aquitania, Berengaria, Mauretania*) boasted about its cosmopolitan food and deft English stewards; Alexander Woollcott wrote on censorship in the New York theatre; Charles Stuart Street described the new game of contract bridge, which, "like a conflagration, is sweeping over our clubs and drawing-rooms"; a photograph of Edith Wharton appeared under the title, "Our Most Distinguished Ambassador to Europe"; and Steichen's latest design in silk, a match-box pattern, was photographed. (This photograph cost the magazine $130—very expensive. A Charles Sheeler photograph of the three leading actresses in *The Constant Nymph* cost only $33.) Aldous Huxley published a piece on morality, and the five people nominated for *Vanity Fair*'s Hall of Fame were Dr. Adolph Lorenz, "because his experiments in the cure of infantile paralysis have been extraordinary"; Benedetto Croce, "because he founded the modern school of the philosophy of scientific criticism"; M. Carey Thomas, "because she is one of the greatest American educators, and President Emeritus of Bryn Mawr College"; Harold Ross, "because he spent his youth leaving the staff of practically every newspaper in the country . . . and finally because, although born in Aspen, Colorado, he is now Editor in Chief of *The New Yorker*"; and Carl Van Vechten, "because, as an authority on music, cats and Harlem, he tranquilly refutes the acid theories about dilettantes." The back page advertisement was for Steinway pianos, "the instrument of the immortals," with Alfred Cortot as immortal endorser (prices, $875 and up).

Benito did a cover for this issue which brilliantly encapsulated the spirit of the time: a man in a top hat, white tie, and holding a monocle, stands behind a woman with sleek jet-black hair, wearing a red, purple, and white jacket, a red and white art deco bracelet, and holding a mask. Their necks are impossibly long, their lips impossibly red; their faces are shadowed in the cubist mode, their eyes night-blue slits of jaded sophistication.

In an essay on Charles Lindbergh, John Lardner has described 1927 as "the perfect year for the perfect feat. It was the apex of the era, chronologically and emotionally. It was an epoch of noise, hero worship, and the sort of 'individualism' which seems to have meant that people were not disposed to look at themselves, and their lives in general, and therefore ran gaping and thirsty to look at anything done by one man or woman that was special and apart from the life they knew." Lardner was referring to Charles Lindbergh's historic flight from New York to Paris in May of that year. Everyone worshipped Lindbergh; they also worshipped anyone who was making money, particularly those who made astronomical sums of money, whose stories filled the newspapers. Business was revered; some of his staff thought that Condé Nast should be President.

In 1927 the publisher was fifty-four. He was rich. He was famous. He belonged to the Racquet and Tennis, Piping Rock, Tuxedo, Knickerbocker, Dutch Treat, Riding, National Links, and Deepdale Golf clubs. He was in the *Social Register*. He was a well-known figure at Newport, Aiken, Southampton, and in Paris and London. He was seen almost every night with a different girl at an opening, exhibition, night club, or cabaret. He was named one of the Ten Best-Dressed Men (though he confessed to Helen Lawrenson that he had worn the same dinner jacket for ten years).

For Condé Nast, as for many people, the decade's history was written in numbers. He saw the company's earnings rise from $241,410 (after taxes and depreciation) in 1923 to a high of $1,425,076 in 1928. *Vogue* circulation rose from 16,853 in 1909, when he bought it, to 138,783 in 1928. *Vanity Fair* started in 1913 at a circulation of 12,855 and rose to a high of 84,646 in 1928. *House & Garden* jumped from 67,055 in 1920 to 131,780 in 1928. Throughout the twenties, *Vogue* led all the other competitive magazines in advertising pages. In 1928, *Vogue* had 159,028 pages to *Ladies' Home Journal*'s 97,574, and *Harper's Bazar*'s 83,454. *House & Garden* also led the other magazines in its field—in 1928, *House & Garden* claimed 105,724 pages to *Town & Country*'s 90,876, and *House Beautiful*'s 56,630. During the four-year period 1924–28, the earnings of the combined Condé Nast Publications rose from $454,000 to $1,425,076—an increase of 213 percent.

Vogue Patterns also continued to make healthy progress. In 1920 the Pattern Service made a profit of $11,640. In 1928 its profit was $150,360. The Condé Nast Press, regarded in the industry as one of the greatest success stories of all, expanded its volume of business from $380,935 in 1921, when it started, to $3,450,255 in 1929, making a profit, after machinery depreciation, of $388,900.

So successful was the printing business, that in 1927, as we have seen, Nast committed himself to an extensive enlargement and modernization program for the Greenwich plant, involving a capital investment of $2,044,000 over the four-year period 1928–32. Another expense incurred was the folding of German *Vogue,* which, with other minor expenditures, brought the capital outlay for the four-year period to $3,000,000—a figure that could easily be covered, it seemed, by the continued success of the company as a whole.

Nast was also amassing a personal fortune at a comfortable rate. In 1927 he bought a vast mansion in Sands Point, Long Island, with porches, terraces, formal gardens, a tennis court, an oval pool with an ivy-covered bathhouse, and land stretching down to Long Island Sound. With typical attention to detail, he subjected his new estate to the most extensive remodeling. Nast tore down and reconstructed the pool several times over, adding landscaping and drainage until it was just right. The total cost of remodeling the estate came to something like $750,000, a large sum even in those days.

This house became the venue for parties and a haven for house guests, particularly visitors from Europe. Harry Yoxall, who used to stay there on visits from London, remembered there was always something faintly amateurish about the running of the household. "None of the luggage turned up in our rooms, I recall. And when we played bridge after dinner, the butler was so eager to clean up ashtrays that you couldn't concentrate on the game. It was as though they had all been hired for the night." Shades of Gatsby, Yoxall felt. Nast's perfectionism competed with his inexperience in such large-scale hospitality. But Sandy Key, as Nast's daughter Natica named the place, was never less than glamorous; and in those days when swimming pools were still a rarity, his was one of the biggest and grandest anyone had ever seen.

Nast's European offices continued to flourish. The publisher spent most of his summers in New York, London, and Paris, traveling on the great ocean liners, "packed," as *Vogue* said, "with the smart world." He was accompanied by trunks, cases of documents, and gifts, like an Oriental potentate on a grand tour of his dominions. In both capitals he entertained lavishly, only inhibited in Paris

The front lawn and lily pond at Sands Point, Condé Nast's last great palace, bought too late for him ever properly to enjoy it.

by his inability to speak the language (Frank Crowninshield usually accompanied him and solved that problem).

In London he would take a suite at the Ritz with two bathrooms. After a day at the office he liked to take a piping hot bath in one, and then plunge into the stone-cold water waiting for him in the other. (Having two baths was also, needless to say, a welcome convenience for any lady companion invited up to his suite late at night.) After this physical restorative he would rest for half an hour, sometimes taking a massage, then put on white tie and tails for the evening's entertainment.

Harry Yoxall used to watch his employer's social progress in London with interest and admiration, for he knew that Nast was an astonishingly hard worker and, however late the evening, would show up at ten the next morning and work through till long after dark the following night. "On nights when he had no party to go to, I was kept at the Ritz after dinner in his private sitting room till long after my suburban train had left. On one occasion, I remember, we were thrashing out a particularly difficult problem, and by the end of the evening we still had not resolved it. The following day he was to leave for Paris, so he asked me to join him for breakfast. I duly did, and still discussing things, I accompanied him to Victoria, and then on the train to Dover. With matters still not settled to his satisfaction, Nast urged me to continue on with him to Paris. 'I can't,' I told him. But he truly expected me to travel with him to the ends of the earth, if necessary, until he was satisfied that the right decision had been made."

After these grand sprees in Europe, Nast and Crowninshield would come back with trunkloads of presents for the staff—Chanel necklaces, tiny beaded purses, silk scarves, fancy metal French belts. Nast once gave Jeanne Ballot a big square of brocade—gold and maroon, bordered by eight inches of gold lamé. "I had no idea what it was, and asked John Bishop, who said he thought it was a piano cover. Then Mr. Nast came into our office and modelled my present. It was an evening wrap. The square folded over at the top, you wrapped it round you like a cocoon, clutched it together, and the result was pure glamour."

Nast always took great pains with his presents. Presenting them was the kind of thing that tended to embarrass this shy man, so the gifts were often given with extraordinary elaborateness, and usually indirectly, so that nobody need feel awkward about accepting his generosity in person. A typical example came early in his ownership of *Vogue*. One Christmas he sent Edna Chase a box of candy. Her daughter, Ilka, happened to open it to eat one of the chocolates and discovered in the frilled paper cup a twenty-dollar gold piece. "I flew to the box," Mrs. Chase related. "Under each chocolate was a gold coin, to the amount of five hundred dollars." Nast had also written a note: "This box of candy is a little Xmas token of Miss Vogue's appreciation of all you have done for her, and as a further token of appreciation she has instructed Mr. Beckerle, beginning with January 1st, to place you on the roll at $7,500 a year. Sincerely, Miss Vogue, by Condé Nast, sec."

By the twenties, the gifts were more extravagant—triple-gold Cartier rings in an office party raffle; $10,000 tucked into the bottom of a box of golf balls (a leaving present for Heyworth Campbell); glorious baby clothes for a junior advertising assistant's new baby; theatre and opera tickets in abundance for everyone. In spite of this lavishness, Nast always found a way to do it without ostentation. He liked to invite the staff to swimming parties at his new house in Sands Point. One of the girls who attended a party with Jeanne Ballot was *Vanity Fair* staffer Agnes Geraghty, who was an Olympic swimming champion. Jeanne Ballot described what happened: "Mr. Nast held up a $20 gold piece and announced that there would be a race across the pool between Jeanne Ballot and Agnes Geraghty. Like Cassius, I plunged in—just as Agnes reached the other side of the pool. A lovely way for him to give Agnes $20."

Lew Wurzburg, who at the time was building a new house in Bronxville, was with Nast one day when they saw a set of handsome antique dining-room chairs that Wurzburg admired greatly, but which were far too expensive for him. The following Christmas, the Wurzburgs were astonished to see a truck pull up outside their house. Out of it came the eight antique chairs. "It was the only time I saw my father cry," his daughter, Elinor, said later.

One of the most graceful of all his complicated efforts at gift-giving is contained in this letter to the one-and-only Edna Chase, written with typical self-deprecation in 1928:

> Dear Edna,
> Fact No. 1: I am a very rich man. Fact No. 2: Your devotion, industry, and very amazing intelligence have been a very great factor in accomplishing Fact No. 1. Fact No. 3: Having achieved great wealth at a time of great age I find some difficulty in spending my money. Fact No. 4: I have found one expenditure that will give me supreme pleasure and that will compensate for my bald head and my trials and tribulations in accomplishing this wealth. Fact No. 5: I have set aside $100,000 which I want you to use for embroidery on the house you are about to build on Long Island.
> Gratefully and affectionately, Condé.

(Edna Chase had married, in 1921, her second husband, an affable Englishman named Richard Newton, who seems to have taken his wife's career and devotion to Nast in his stride, as well as the financial largesse heaped upon her. Unfortunately, she had drawn only $25,000 of the $100,000 Nast gave her for her new house in Oyster Bay when the Crash came and "the rest," as she said, "vanished like fairy gold.").

Although Nast grew richer and more famous as the decade progressed, he continued to maintain his informal relationship with his staff, becoming, if anything, more avuncular as he got older. He had always believed in the open-door policy with the company—quite literally; his office door was always open. His concern for his employees went further than simply presenting them with pretty baby clothes or giving Christmas parties. He used to talk to them cheerfully in the corridors, find out what they were doing, how they were getting on. It was not unusual to find him standing behind you—particularly if you were a pretty girl alone in the office. On one occasion, a young typist was trying to type a Roman numeral on a manuscript she was working on. It was giving her a hard time. Suddenly she heard a helpful voice over her shoulder: "Try the capital I," said Condé Nast.

On another occasion, talking to a sixteen-year-old girl who worked in the mail room, he found out something that distressed him very much. She told him that she lived in Riverhead, Long Island, and that since she had to do the first mail of the day, she had to get up at 5:30 a.m. in order to get to work on time. Since she also had the last mail delivery at night, she always got home very late. Allene Talmey was in Nast's office shortly after he had made this discovery, and overheard him on the phone to one of his executives. "He was white with anger," she recalls. " 'Why in the hell didn't you know she had the last delivery so got home late?' he demanded of the poor fellow at the other end of the phone. 'It's outrageous. It must be changed at once.' "

Such anger could only come from a very kind heart.

Perhaps Nast's most relaxing moments occurred on the golf course. He played regularly, keenly, although he never became a great player. "The amount of time I've played with professionals, I could have bought the best golf course there is," he once ruefully said. Yet typically, he was as happy to play golf with members of his staff as with the pros or the fashionable types from Newport or Tuxedo Park. On the golf course, his staff would continue to call him Mr. Nast, although he urged them to say "Condé." On one occasion, he was playing in a tournament with Edward McSweeney, one of his advertising men, who, as usual, addressed him throughout the game as Mr. Nast. At the final hole, Nast missed the drive. Turning to his colleague, he said, "What did I do wrong?"

McSweeney, in the heat of the moment, replied, "You forgot to put your fat ass into it."

Without batting an eye, Nast said, "Now do you know me well enough to call me Condé?"

There were, however, rules. The golf course was one thing, but in the office Nast could not stand disrespect from his staff. Going up in the elevator with a business colleague, he was greeted by a smart young salesman who said, "Good morning, Condé." Nast said nothing until they had left the elevator. "Who was that impertinent person?" he asked. He was told it was one of his star salesmen. "Fire him," Nast said.

When he threw his office parties, he invited everyone—the stockroom people, the messengers, the typists, the editors, and right on up. (According to Carmel Snow, the *Vogue* girls used to squabble about what they would wear to these occasions. "I'm going to wear my red Chanel—you'll have to wear your white.") Nast and Crowny often used to attend parties given by the staff, even seedy ones down in Greenwich Village. At one of these, an employee remembers, "We were milling about in the kitchen and there was Mr. Nast. I don't know who brought him. The hostess saw him and cried, 'Why, Mr. Nast, you're drinking out of a jelly glass.' And he was, and he was enjoying it."

This tendency to unpretentiousness could go to extremes. His business lunches were as often as not held at the Automat (his favorite) or Thompson's, a cafeteria near 42nd Street. (The *Vanity Fair* lunchers would have had the vapors at such a suggestion.) "You won't believe it," he'd say, "but the coffee here is better than the Waldorf's." Or, "This is the best hot chocolate you can get anywhere." His lunch companions would eye him suspiciously, but would down whatever it was with polite resignation.

Nast genuinely preferred the simpler things of life, but one suspects he could also be a tease. Once, after a long working dinner with Harry Yoxall in New York, Nast took him to a prizefight at Yankee Stadium (which Yoxall found exceedingly boring). Afterward, he asked if Yoxall would care for a "Black and White." This was during Prohibition, and after the ordeals he'd been through, Yoxall's eyes lit up at the thought of a nightcap. Nast solemnly conducted him into a drugstore and ordered two dishes of chocolate and vanilla ice cream. "He lapped his up like a schoolboy," said the rueful Englishman.

In contrast, Nast's own parties grew in size and sophistication, particularly after 1925, when Nast (with Crowninshield in tow) moved into the thirty-room penthouse on Park Avenue. It is perhaps a comment on Nast's exalted social cachet at this time that the real estate agents of 1040 Park took a full page in *Vanity Fair* to announce that Mr. Nast had purchased a large apartment in the building. "Go and do thou likewise," the advertisement then urged—rather tastelessly, perhaps, to our modern eyes. The apartment was designed especially for him and decorated with the extravagant opulence decreed by his old friend and adviser Elsie de Wolfe. Under her guidance, he built a collection of furniture, paintings, and rugs that dazzled the eye. In this, as in all his projects, perfection was the key word, and between the two of them, they just about achieved it.

Nast once bought a pair of Louis XIV candelabra in Paris, for which he paid a great deal of money. When the treasures arrived in New York, some doubt was expressed as to their authenticity. Nast promptly instituted an investigation, which was to last two years; lawyers checked the Paris dealer's background and the candelabra were carried about from country to country, collecting expert opinions. Nast could not rest until he knew the answer. Finally, it was decided that they were indeed fakes and the Paris dealer had to refund the money.

Elsie de Wolfe installed Savonnerie rugs, grisaille walls, Nattier, Schall, and van Huysum paintings, Louis XV and XVI furniture, and a Chinese wallpaper that was originally found in the attic of Welbeck Abbey in England and then adorned the ballroom of the mansion of the Marquis of Anglesey in Wales. Nast so appreciated the results that he did not change one thing in the seventeen years he lived there.

Everyone hoped to be the recipient of one of the exquisite invitations that arrived in the mail boxes of New York's beau monde. After all, Nast was the one who had broken convention by inviting Mrs. Vanderbilt and George Gershwin to the same party, so almost everyone in the world could justifiably hope to appear on one of his meticulously kept lists. Parties for Helen Wills, Lady Diana Cooper, Mary Pickford, Ferenc Molnár, Beatrice Lillie, Lord Birkenhead; all-male parties to show movies of the Tunney-Dempsey fight; a theatre party in honor of a Loretta Young opening night; after-the-opera suppers for Grace Moore; a friend's debutante party; the Condé Nast office party; parties for guests whose names are now long-forgotten—people of all sorts came to Condé Nast's apartment in those years, many of them, like Jay Gatsby's guests, paying him "the subtle tribute of knowing nothing whatever about him."

The apartment was a fitting background for the glamorous people who came there. It provided endless fodder for the gossip columns. It was also a fitting background for his magazines. Throughout the twenties, the penthouse at 1040 Park was in almost constant use, not only for dinners, cocktails, and buffets, but also as a studio for the photographers of *Vogue* and *Vanity Fair*. Steichen, Sheeler, and the rest of Nast's stable knew the glittering interior of that apartment as well as they knew their cameras. After 1926, any studio portrait in *Vogue* or *Vanity Fair* may well have in its background a detail expressing Elsie de Wolfe's decorating flair—which was precisely, triumphantly, the point. Condé Nast's apartment was a stage set for his magazines, and the parties were animated versions of their pages. *Vogue* and *Vanity Fair*—Nast's publishing jewels—had finally come to life.

The faces pressed against the glass would have been surprised to learn that the fabled Mr. Nast was often ill-at-ease as host of these gatherings; that he forgot the names of his guests and even of his friends and had to be prompted by colleagues; that he shook hands as stiffly as he danced, and preferred to play bridge in some quiet room. They would have been confused to learn that Mr. Nast liked nothing better than to have Uneeda Biscuits and a glass of milk for lunch at the office, or a working dinner at the Automat. They would have been astonished to see the famous magazine proprietor sitting at a soda fountain lapping up chocolate ice cream. That such a well-known, sophisticated man-about-town was actually uncomfortable in the glittering social world into which he had catapulted himself smacked of an unlikely morality in those artificial, hedonistic days.

Not that Nast himself could have analyzed the malaise. Was he not having fun? He went out with everyone, from opera singers to flappers. The quantity and elaborateness of his social engagement diaries were the stuff of myth to his staff. His personal secretaries spent many overtime hours keeping them properly collated, both at his office and at his home. Mothers warned their debutante daughters, who had been lucky enough to land the most desirable job in the world on *Vogue* or *Vanity Fair,* to watch out for Mr. Nast. He was known to be not safe in taxis. Some of the more conservative members of society, who had always regarded him as an upstart, felt he was a philanderer and a corruptor of morals. After all, if he allowed a caricature of the great J. P. Morgan wearing his underpants to appear in one of his journals, what could be said in favor of the man?

Edmund Wilson, who worked at *Vanity Fair* in the early twenties, called Nast the glossiest bounder he had ever known, and accused him of "obnoxious vulgarity," which shows how poor a judge of character the prim young author was in his assessment of a rather lonely man's attempt to make sense of his wealth and transform it into affection. Nast was never glossy, and he was never vulgar. Now in his mid-fifties, he was a shy, inarticulate man who looked like a Victorian banker. The matrons need not have worried. The debutantes were embarrassed, or giggled at his approaches, and went out with him once, then found excuses. He was never ungentlemanly, never offensive. He had simply created a setting that perfectly mirrored the style of the times, a style that it was his business to know and represent accurately in his magazines, but a style whose superficiality and speed ran strangely counter to the man's true disposition.

This was the supreme irony of Condé Nast's life. He had worked with fanatical intensity, attention to detail, and great natural talent to escape a mediocre Midwest background and become a millionaire. He had assimilated the feelings, interests, and desires of a rich, privileged elite in order to provide them with the correct images of fashionableness, and to feed the aspirations of those yearning to compete. In so doing, as though by osmosis, to all appearances he had joined that elite. Even if he was not quite one of them, the Van Rensselaers, the Goelets, the Iselins, and the Biddles who greeted him in Newport felt that his charm, elegance, and worldly success in large part made up for lack of lineage.

It was at this lofty point that he began to experience social vertigo. Self-deprecation was a symptom. "I'm just a glorified book-keeper." "With full, accurate and prompt figures anyone of reasonable intelligence can run a publishing business." His cheap meals were another. His loyalty to ice cream and other childhood pleasures, such as amusement arcades, was another. The sense of distance he communicated at even the gayest of his **parties** indicates most poignantly his dissociation from the world he had so assiduously cultivated for over thirty years.

It was in this mood of dislocation that he embarked upon a romance that swept him crazily to the shores of that grim, unforgiving decade, the thirties.

There is no doubt that the tightly laced matrons of Old New York (the Tabbies, as society columnist Cholly Knickerbocker called them) purred pleasurably over their Sèvres teacups when news of Condé Nast's second marriage hurtled down the Fifth Avenue grapevine. It was 1928, the publisher was fifty-five years old, and he was proposing to wed a girl almost young enough to be his granddaughter.

There had been women enough through the years since the separation and divorce from Clarisse. But this one was different. She was not just another young society beauty, fledgling actress, or New York sophisticate. She was pretty, funny, unspoiled, and came from the Midwest (Lake Forest, Illinois). Her name was Leslie Foster, and June 19, 1928, was her twenty-first birthday.

Her parents had known Nast since the early days of his marriage to Clarisse. At the age of eight, little Leslie had been dandled on the rather stiff knee of the publisher.

They met again in 1927, when Leslie was nineteen, in Nassau, where her parents had taken her as a reward for going through a business and typing course in Chicago. The Fosters noticed Nast at another table in the hotel dining room and invited him to join them. After a little conversation, Nast turned to Leslie and said, "Do you have a beau here?"

Leslie shook her head, laughing, saying she had only just arrived.

"Well," Nast said eagerly, "may I be your beau?"

That was Nassau.

Shortly after, Leslie Foster arrived in New York. After a brief stint at Macy's, she switched to a job on a fashion trade journal for Seventh Avenue. There she met *Vogue* editor Carmel Snow, who took a fancy to her and invited her to come and work for *Vogue*. Leslie accepted.

She had discreetly been seeing Condé since her arrival in New York. When he heard she had taken a job on *Vogue* he was horrified and begged her not to take it. But it was too late. For eight awkward months she worked for *Vogue*, while the staff gradually sensed that something more than usual was going on between their boss and his young protégée. One day, Nast went into Mrs. Chase's office and said rather sheepishly, "Er . . . Edna, on that routine form thing, about Leslie Foster's background and experience and age . . . er . . . let's not send that up to Greenwich. I mean, why should they know how young she is?"

But of course everyone knew precisely how young she was. She was the same age as Nast's daughter, and the same age as Nast's son's fiancée, Charlotte Babcock Brown. The whole thing was absurd.

For the first part of 1928, Leslie wrestled with its absurdities, calling it off, calling it on, writing letters, loving him. In the summer of that year, after waiting until Condé was setting off for Europe, she wrote him a letter in which she said she could not go on with the affair. As soon as she had sent it, she desperately regretted it. Condé, equally in despair, wrote her back from Europe proposing marriage. She accepted at once.

It was a love match all right, but an impossible one. When Reggie Vanderbilt, aged forty-three, married nineteen-year-old Gloria Morgan in 1923, the scandal had rocked New York to its foundations. This was five years later, but things had not changed. Natica, who had moved out of her mother's apartment to live with her father at 1040 Park, was being asked to share the place with a young woman her age whom she was expected to address as stepmother. Coudert Nast, who was preparing for his wedding to Charlotte in

December, was about to be upstaged by another wedding—his father's. The Fosters could not bear to contemplate their daughter's future. Edna Chase finally took Leslie out to dinner at the Cosmopolitan Club to try to dissuade her from going through with the marriage.

On December 7, 1928, Coudert and Charlotte were married at the home of her parents at 40 East 38th Street. Condé's wedding present to them was a co-op on East 72nd Street and a personal gift of $500 to his new daughter-in-law. He also gave a large reception for them, so large that the list of guests took up almost two full columns of *The New York Times*. They spent their honeymoon in the southwest and Mexico, and afterward in Nassau.

On December 28, 1928, Condé Nast and Leslie Foster were married quietly at the winter home of the bride's parents in Aiken, South Carolina. The marriage came as a surprise to almost everybody, including Natica. She remembers visiting the new country house in Sands Point with her father, accompanied by "this strange young blonde woman who kept rushing about, playing the phonograph and trying everything out," little knowing that the house was being prepared for this stranger. When Condé left to get married, Natica was still in the dark; he left her a note under her door with the news. The event was very informal, with only close friends and relatives present (including, of course, Frank Crowninshield). The couple spent a few days in Miami before sailing for Nassau on the S. S. *New Northland*.

An unfortunate incident with the press marred their stay in Florida. Nast, aware of the news potential of his marriage, had attempted to remain incognito, but Miami customs officials discovered his secret when he tried to obtain papers for passage to Nassau. It was revealed gleefully that the couple had been traveling under the names Mr. and Mrs. Charles Foster. Poor Condé. Such efforts at concealment already contained the seeds of disaster.

In Nassau they joined Coudert and Charlotte, also on honeymoon. That meant all the Nasts except one were in Nassau. Charlotte, another young bride, realized with amusement that as a married woman she could now chaperone Natica, although they were almost the same age; so she invited her down to join the various Nasts. "It was great," Natica said drily. "Mrs. Nast, Mrs. Nast, and Miss Nast. Life was a song."

After the initial awkwardness, life for a while *was* a song. Leslie was the beautiful, gay, and amusing hostess Nast had always dreamed of. She adored him, and he looked after her as he would a precious creature, taking control of her deportment, her hair, her clothes. He liked lavishing his wealth on her (she was prettier than Mrs. Chase), although her tastes were not as extravagant as he might have wished. On a visit to London on her own, shortly after her marriage, Leslie booked into her usual small hotel, where Elsie de Wolfe and Johnnie McMullin found her. They were appalled at her modest surroundings.

"You are now the wife of a very wealthy man, Leslie," Elsie told her. "You must live accordingly. Move at once to the Ritz and get a maid. I have already picked out the pearls I feel Condé should give you."

The newly married couple traveled to Paris, where Louis Nast refused to meet his young sister-in-law. They went to Berlin to investigate the problems of German *Vogue*, and suffered together the strange customs of the Germans. Leslie remembered one party given in honor of the American publisher and his young bride. It was a luncheon at a country club outside Berlin, with many of the press barons of Germany in attendance. After the cocktail hour, a pair of doors was thrown open to reveal the buffet lunch table. "Everyone rushed like animals to the table, leaving us totally alone in the cocktail room!"

They laughed a lot over that. They also laughed at Condé's story of being invited to a business lunch in Berlin with another German press magnate. When he arrived at the cloakroom he was asked to take off his clothes. Nast thought it was a joke, but the lunch date turned out to be taking place in a nudist business club. He was the only one who failed to undress. Nast, like his wife, had a lively sense of the absurd, but neither of them was sorry to leave Germany—and the shredded hopes of German *Vogue*.

Condé Nast's young second wife, Leslie, undertaking various marital duties: playing a serious game of backgammon (top), meeting Clare Boothe Luce (above left), and taking a stroll outside 1040 Park Avenue with her step-daughter (but sister in friendship), Natica.

For a while, in those carefree spring and summer days of 1929, Nast was happy. New York, as Fitzgerald put it, whispered of "fantastic success and eternal youth . . . my splendid mirage." Nast bought a new Rolls Royce to celebrate his marriage, and with boyish enthusiasm suggested to Leslie that it would be fun to go to the dock to watch the shiny new toy being unloaded. Unfortunately, the car was not correctly strapped in and they gazed in awe as it crashed on the dock in a thousand pieces. Never mind. What could be more amusing? In the summer of 1929 you just ordered another one.

After the marriage, Leslie stopped working at *Vogue* (until the Depression, *no* young lady continued to work at *Vogue* after marriage) and found time on her hands. Nast worked hard and kept late hours, and the apartment was awfully big for her to wander about in. (Frank Crowninshield had moved out in 1927, after Leslie had appeared on the scene.) Domestic duties were less than demanding, since 1040 Park Avenue had for years been organized for its bachelor owner with streamlined efficiency. Since there was even a man hired for the sole purpose of checking ventilation at parties, it was hardly likely that the young Mrs. Nast was going to find herself vastly busy in her new role as homemaker.

Leslie became lifelong friends with Natica, after a sticky beginning (they were almost the same age, yet one was the other's stepmother), and they spent a lot of time together. Condé would come home and listen benignly to their chatter, treating them both as his daughters, rather than one as his wife. This, oddly enough, seemed to draw the two girls even closer together and they had a lot of fun, but it did not make an already difficult marriage easier. Leslie turned her considerable energies to the decorative arts, and did some work for Contempora Ltd., an organization that employed European artists to design industrial objects and fabrics. It kept her connected to her husband's work, and also gave her something to do. So did becoming pregnant.

In early 1930 she gave birth to a daughter, Leslie. But by that time her husband was rarely home in time to give either of them much attention. He even neglected to place an announcement of the new arrival in the newspaper, a striking oversight on the part of this punctilious social archivist.

For by 1930, everything that he cared about most in the world, except his family, had fallen apart.

# SIXTEEN

# END OF THE SEASON

In April 1928, Condé Nast bought a controlling interest in the Park-Lexington Corporation, which owned Grand Central Palace and the adjoining Park-Lexington Building—a property that covered the entire block from Park Avenue to Lexington Avenue between 46th and 47th streets. Its valuation was set at $9,600,000. Grand Central Palace was an exhibition hall, where motor shows, flower shows, and furniture exhibits were held. It also boasted, on the top floor, a miniature golf course—the current craze of the social set. It would be frivolous to suggest that those avid golfers, Condé Nast (who, incidentally, also bought a magazine called *The American Golfer* that year) and Frank Crowninshield merely wanted access to that golf course; although it was, to be sure, marvelously convenient to their offices. But in those dollar-happy days, to buy a whole building in order to do some putting was not the most outrageous idea anyone had ever contemplated.

In a statement after the purchase, Nast said that the Palace would be continued as an exposition center, although its general scope would be widened. With this deal, Nast was continuing his progress, begun with *Vogue*'s international editions and the Greenwich press, along the heady path of expansion. After all, by that time he was personally worth something like $8 million—a fortune ripe for exploitation.

Shortly after the purchase of the Park-Lex Corporation, Nast was traveling in the elevator with a *Vogue* salesman who congratulated him on buying Grand Central Palace. Nast thanked him and said, "Well, you know, sometimes when you've succeeded in one business, you succeed in something else. I just hope that's the case."

He could not have been more wrong.

Nast believed in experts, whether it was Frank Crowninshield telling him about Marie Laurencin or Tommy Armour showing him the perfect golf swing. If an expert told him something, that expert must be right. He considered himself an expert in the publishing of deluxe magazines and a partial expert in photography, but he did not consider himself remotely an expert in the field of finance.

Yet in the mid-twenties everybody was an expert in the field of finance. People became bond salesmen right out of school; even one's hairdresser discussed the latest stock offerings on Wall Street. *Vogue,* sensitive as usual to the national madness, published on April 27, 1929, an editorial composed entirely in the language of a stock-market report: "The market leader, Chanel, always a good indicator of chic, held her place, while such reliable names as Paquin, Louiseboulanger, and Patou rallied with sharp advances. Conservative investors showed active buying as always in Chéruit and Lanvin. The spectacular rise of Augustabernard can be compared only to that of General Motors and Radio last summer . . ." and so forth. This two-page "market letter," illustrated by Jean Pagès, showed several sophisticated ladies in chairs watching the Big Board, on which were listed the major dressmakers, with fashion forecasts ("sudden drop," "fluctuating," "good returns," and so forth). It is all most clever and amusing, but its implications, perhaps illuminated by hindsight, leave the reader faintly uneasy. Could the values of the stock market seduce a nation so completely without some kind of retribution?

Condé Nast, seduced like most people, began to take an interest in finance, and started to look for the best experts in America to instruct him. He did not have to look for long. After all, they were the very people he dined with, entertained at his parties, stayed with at Newport, wrote about and photographed for his magazines. He knew their wives, visited their houses, listened over brandy and cigars to their tales of fortunes being made at the blink of an eye on the crazy market.

A group of these gentlemen happened to be closely connected with the stockbroking firm of Goldman, Sachs & Company. One was Waddill Catchings, its president, and another was Harrison Williams, whose main claim to fame, apart from his millions, was his wife, Mona, an exotic beauty who once hung her Christmas tree entirely with ermine tails, and who was one of the most photographed women in *Vogue*. ("It can hardly be said that Mona Williams lives simply," Mrs. Chase once remarked, "yet her native flair for extravagance is disciplined, without vulgarity, and that is no commonplace achievement.")

These men, his chums, told Nast it was absurd, in these booming times, to retain The Condé Nast Publications Inc. as a private company. (The stock was owned mostly by Nast himself, with his ex-wife Clarisse, Lew Wurzburg, Edna Chase, and Frank Crowninshield as additional stockholders.) They said he could make money, lots of it, if he went on the Big Board. *Everybody* was doing it.

In March 1927, it was announced that Goldman, Sachs & Company and Shearson, Hammill & Company had bought a substantial common stock interest in Condé Nast Publications Inc. This offering, it was added, would not involve any change in the control of the company. A few days later, a public offering of 320,000 common shares of The Condé Nast Publications Inc. was made by Goldman, Sachs, at $28.50 a share. On admittance to trading on the Curb, they sold at up to $32 a share on dealings of about 8,000 shares. In May of that year, a quarterly dividend of 50 cents a share was declared. Nast himself retained 201,200 shares.

It was a fabulous year. By the end of 1927, nine months after going public, Nast saw his stock almost double, the share price rising to a high of $53. Earnings had risen to $3.62 a share, with a net income of $1,213,903. In 1928 the situation looked even better. Net profits rose to $1,425,076, equivalent to $4.43 a share.

On April 5, 1928, the day Nast's splendid first annual report was published, a *New York Times* headline read: STOCKS DROP, MONEY 16 PERCENT; MARKET NERVOUS. It was a momentary frisson of the earthquake to come. But Nast was not nervous. He was in the hands of experts. "Bankers know about these things," he assured Edna Chase.

Edna was very nervous indeed. For in 1928 Nast borrowed $2,000,000, with no collateral save his own note, from the Equitable Trust Company, to buy into the newly formed Goldman, Sachs Trading Corporation. It was a conglomerate—fishing interests, salt mines, copper, corporations—and all clients of Goldman, Sachs were asked to buy stock. Waddill Catchings had personally told his friend Nast that this was a great investment. For a while it seemed he was right; the stock split two for one and then split again and made many investors millionaires overnight.

That Christmas Nast married Leslie Foster.

In January 1929, the future looked even rosier. Employees of Condé Nast Publications were admitted to stock ownership, and of more than 900 employees, 345 subscribed, for 3,458 shares of common stock, at a price of $80. (Stock had already been offered to some of them in lieu of a Christmas bonus in 1928.) As the year continued, Condé Nast stock continued to rise.

Frank Crowninshield, with his usual nose for sniffing out the social preoccupations of the time, wrote a prophetic piece for *Vogue* as 1929 reached its apogee:

> If one were asked to name the most striking single difference between the society of New York at the moment and the same society a few years ago, one might reasonably answer, "Higher gambling." Higher risks, higher stakes, higher hazards are in the air, and this follows naturally from the constantly increasing prosper-

ity, extravagance and adventurousness . . . of the American people. . . . Everywhere the pace is faster, the love of risk greater. This love of risk has been extremely well exemplified by recent adventures in the stock market. Where two years ago there were ten speculators, there are twenty today. Where investors bought bonds, they now buy common stocks. Where the public bought cheap motors, they now buy high-priced cars. Risk is in the air in all walks and classes of society.

Even cautious, meticulous, analytical Nast had caught the fever. He had just married a beautiful young wife. He owned a huge block of New York real estate. He had recklessly spent at least $750,000 on remodeling his vast new estate at Sands Point. His stock-market investments were soaring. Early in 1929, honeymooning in Palm Beach, he invited down a dashing young Russian émigré who worked on Wall Street, called Iva Sergei Voidato-Patcévitch. Nast had taken an interest in him, and was thinking of hiring him. When Patcévitch arrived, Nast told him that Goldman, Sachs stock had just gone up to $300 a share.

"I think I just made six million dollars," he said. "I'm a very rich man."

"Sell it, Condé," said Patcévitch.

But Nast, like so many others, was in too far to draw back. The wise advice of Patcévitch, who shortly afterward joined the company as Condé Nast's personal assistant, did not outweigh the expertise of Waddill Catchings, who gave no such warning. The publisher hung on.

And the stock went on rising. All that summer he was riding high. The market quadrupled. Condé Nast stock went up to $93, paying $2 a share. Gross revenues from the company came to $10,251,000. Nast at one time was reliably reported to be worth, on paper, $16,000,000. In the last days of the summer of 1929, the talk from Southampton to Bar Harbor was all the same—how much higher could the market go? Waddill Catchings, Harrison Williams, and Condé Nast shared in the atmosphere of elation. "If Harrison is worth $800 million now, how soon will he become a billionaire?" was the sort of agreeable speculation that hung lazily over the conversation during those hot August weekends.

On October 29, 1929, the stock market collapsed and millions of fortunes were wiped out in a matter of hours. Goldman, Sachs stock went down from $400 to $5. The Equitable Trust Company, to whom Nast owed $2,000,000, went under and was absorbed by Chase Securities (later the Chase National Bank). Business for the combined Condé Nast Publications plummeted. Condé Nast stock nose-dived from a high of $93 down to $4½.

The publisher was ruined. Not only had he lost his controlling stock, but it was almost worthless.

His first thought was for his publications. Three months after the Wall Street collapse, in December 1929, he persuaded his bankers to sell him a three-year 6 percent note issue of $2,000,000. "I decided on this financing because I was, naturally, uncertain as to what might be the length and seriousness of the oncoming depression, and wanted to be in a position not only to liquidate the remaining capital expenditures for the printing press equipment, but I wanted also to be in a financial position to continue to manage these publications in accordance with their tradition, in a manner that would give full value to our readers and advertisers." (He wrote this in 1932, when he was looking for $1,000,000 to refund the remainder of this issue.)

Nast was either courageous or mad, according to whether you were an editor or an accountant. In 1927 he had embarked on an ambitious enlargement and modernization program for the printing plant, which in 1930 he was still not prepared to abandon. True to his word to keep the magazines going in the style to which his readers had become accustomed, in 1931 he introduced the first color photographs into the pages of *Vogue, Vanity Fair,* and *House & Garden.* This dramatically improved the appearance of the publications, demonstrating to the publishing industry the brilliant potential of quality color printing, and proclaiming once again Nast's position as leader in the field.

In the autumn of 1930 and again in the spring of 1931, Nast also undertook broad prestige advertising campaigns, taking out full-page advertisements in newspapers and magazines—media-buying on an unprecedented scale. These two major campaigns, which were launched at the beginning of the most severe depression America had ever known, cost the company approximately $500,000.

Nast, at this time, was sure he could avert disaster. In March 1930, he told Edna:

> Business for the combined publications is off about five percent in January and twelve percent in February. Most of the wise men in Wall Street and in the business world seem to think that the depression will not be a bad one, considering the seriousness of the stock market debacle, nor a very long one. They look for an upturn in business before the end of six months. This may be true but I don't think anyone knows a damn thing about what is going to happen. If they have the wisdom to point out the future business for this coming year that same wisdom should have enabled them to forecast the crash, yet even such institutions as J. P. Morgan and Company did not know it was coming. Certainly I don't know enough to form my own opinion and I have no respect for the wisdom of the wise men but, as I am generally optimistic, I think we should do fairly well.

So Nast had finally and painfully lost his faith in the experts and their fashionable wives; but he had retained faith in himself, and in his ability to run his magazines in the way he knew best, in the way that had been so remarkably successful. Ironically, it was now that the experts began to claim their pound of flesh. They might have lost their power over his mind, but they were busy gaining control over his soul. Like Faust, he was about to pay for his hour of glory.

In December 1930, it was announced that Sidney J. Weinberg, a senior partner of Goldman, Sachs & Company, had been elected a director of The Condé Nast Publications Inc. This short news item marked the beginning of the Mephistophelian nightmare. It meant that the control of the magazines had passed from Condé Nast into the hands of the bankers. It was a blow from which the publisher never fully recovered.

In 1931, shareholders of the Goldman, Sachs Trading Corporation charged the corporation officers, including Waddill Catchings, Harrison Williams, and Sidney Weinberg, with illegal deals, improper investment of funds, and other illegal activities. The shareholders' losses were enormous. There was no way they could possibly recoup their investments.

Nor could Nast. He watched in impotent despair as his mounting debt, plus his cherished stock, passed from hand to hand in the complicated realignments made after the Crash. Chase Securities, which had taken over the debt, was sold to the Blue Ridge Corporation, a subsidiary of the Shenandoah Corporation, which Harrison Williams owned. (The Shenandoah Corporation, in turn, was a part of the ill-fated Goldman, Sachs Trading Corporation.) In 1930, Nast's trusty adviser, Waddill Catchings, became chairman of the Shenandoah and Blue Ridge Corporations, thus controlling his friend's fate. But in early 1932, Floyd Odlum, president of the Atlas Utilities Corporation, became a director of Goldman, Sachs. Odlum, an independent operator who made money selling short in the Crash, also at that time bought a controlling interest in Blue Ridge. Thus after two years of musical chairs involving Catchings and Williams, Nast's debt ended up in the hands of Floyd Odlum and the Blue Ridge Corporation. The figures were awesome: in 1932 Nast owed Blue Ridge $4,800,000, with collateral of 160,000 shares of Condé Nast Publications common stock.

Nast had one avenue to recovery—to continue publishing his magazines successfully. Yet now that avenue was closed to him. His fate was governed by a handful of businessmen who knew nothing about publishing class publications. For four years, the publisher's struggle to wrest back control from these men, some of whom had been his closest companions on the golf course and in smoking rooms from Newport to Oyster Bay, became the obsession that overrode all others, wrecking his marriage, his health, and finally, his spirit.

From the first, they failed to understand him. He insisted on continuing to modernize the printing plant, in spite of the fact that the

company's business was suffering acutely from the Crash and subsequent jittery financial climate. He was determined to launch an
expensive and radical advertising campaign when figures showed
that advertising revenue for the combined publications was sinking
rapidly—from $6,028,900 in 1929 to $4,929,600 in 1930, down
another $1,417,800 in 1931, and down another $1,166,800
in 1932. The accumulated loss in advertising from 1929 to 1932
was $3,683,900, making a loss in profit to the company of
$1,220,400.

The annual report for 1930 announced a net income of
$1,789,850, equivalent to $3.27 a share on the common stock; in
1931, the net profit was $370,459, equivalent to $1.18 a share.
That year, no dividend was announced, owing to the prevailing conditions in general business, although, Nast bravely declared, "the
corporation continues to operate at a profit." In 1932, the company's net loss was $63,907.

The publisher attempted to show that in spite of the bad figures,
the publications had been—and could still be—on the verge of a
great increase in earnings. The bankers were not impressed. Why
should they be? They thought he was spending far too much money.
They did not understand why it was necessary. Why bother with
color printing when it was so expensive? Why cling to quality paper
when cheaper stock was easily available? Why worry about perfect
photographic reproduction when a change to something less than
perfect would surely not be noticed by the average reader? Nast
even continued to give parties, inviting Waddill Catchings and Sidney Weinberg to meet the staff and see why the occasions made
good business sense. The bankers remained unconvinced. They
thought his extravagance was incomprehensible, unbusinesslike,
untenable. It was the classic clash between quality and the check-
book.

At one point his old friend and adviser Waddill Catchings decided that Nast himself must go. The financier was, however, prepared to make an offer to Mrs. Chase that she could not refuse, if
she would stay on and keep things going. Edna was the wrong person to try that line on. She told Catchings bluntly that if Nast went,

she and all the staff would go, too. He would be left with an empty shell. It was as simple as that.

So Nast stayed. But his position was wretched. Every month the Goldman, Sachs people would meet with senior members of the Condé Nast organization and discuss ways to save money, cut costs, and make the magazines more profitable. The meetings were not comfortable. Edna Chase was frostily polite. Lew Wurzburg was a defeated man, having lost everything, including the trust of his employer, in the Crash—for Lew had been in the thick of the stock-market action, urging Nast on, one of his "experts." (Nast never respected Wurzburg after that, although Wurzburg later made some of his money back.) Only Frank Crowninshield of the senior staff emerged relatively unscathed. In 1929, at the height of the market, when Condé Nast shares had reached their peak, Crowninshield had quietly sold his stock. This did not, as might be imagined, help relations between the two men—but Nast was preoccupied with only one thing, and that was to regain control of his company. Nothing else mattered—not old friends, not his magazines, not even his pride.

Dear Mr. Crocker,

I have always believed in and endeavoured to adhere to the philosophy that where a man and his work do not speak for him, little can be gained by any speech-making he may do for himself. On my return to New York, after each of my visits to you in Fitchburg, I have hung my head in embarrassment, if not in shame, when I have reflected on the hours that I talked to you and your associates about the great things that I had done, was doing, and could continue to do! However, I think I am putting the case conservatively when I assure you that, in these two meetings, I talked more about myself than I have in the 30 years I have been in business. You have been so very kind and considerate in so many matters, I am sure you will realize that this seeming boastfulness is not a habit, but merely a part of this particularly difficult situation . . .

Charles T. Crocker was the president of Crocker, Burbank & Company, of Fitchburg, Massachusetts, manufacturers of fine paper. Crocker was one of the two major suppliers of the paper on which all Condé Nast's publications were printed. Nast owed Crocker a great deal of money, which he could not pay. Moreover, Nast wanted to continue to use Crocker's fine paper, in spite of his bankers and in spite of his debt. Moreover, Nast also wanted Crocker to help him get his stock back.

Hence Nast's imploring visits to Fitchburg, attempting to borrow money, defer debts, persuade Crocker to help him out. There were many letters of appeal, many speeches, more visits to Fitchburg. Nast attempted to woo the paper manufacturer with invitations to chic social events in New York, boxing matches and the like. Crocker would not be moved, but in conjunction with Nast's other paper supplier, Perkins, Goodwin & Company, he bought some stock, subject to repurchase, which helped just a fraction. In 1932, Crocker, no doubt weary of Nast's persistence, suggested that he borrow money from the newly formed Reconstruction Finance Corporation. "Our case," replied Nast with what dignity he could muster, "does not come within even striking distance of any of the clauses under which the RFC are empowered to offer assistance."

The publisher refused to give up. On the contrary. After this series of rebuffs, Nast suggested to Crocker that, if he could not persuade his company to enter into some financial assistance program with The Condé Nast Publications, he make Nast a personal loan of $1,500,000, with interest paid through Condé Nast stock. Aware that this sounded an unpersuasive deal, even to his ears, Nast hastily promised further financial rewards—through the sale of his Sands Point property, for instance. "I have what I think may fairly be stated to be a reasonable chance of selling this property," he pleaded. "It is presently occupied, under a year's lease expiring this coming April, by Louis F. Reed, Jr., who is son-in-law of Arthur G. Hoffman, the Vice President of the Great Atlantic and Pacific Tea Company." Reed had apparently expressed an interest in the property, and Nast told Crocker that he had placed a price of $600,000 on the property—a sum less than the cost of Nast's extensive improvements to the house prior to 1929. How had the mighty fallen.

October 7, 1932.

Dear Mr. Nast,

We have gone over your recent proposition rather carefully, but feel that it is impossible for us to make you any personal loan . . .

C. T. Crocker.

This caused Nast only to intensify his feverish efforts. His employees were persuaded to sell back their stock to the company—at an appreciably higher price than the current market value. A group of Nast's friends attempted to create a consortium to buy back Nast's stock from Blue Ridge. In the last days of 1932, another crisis hit: December 15 was the date of the refunding of the $2,000,000 notes raised by Nast in 1929. In September, the company requested holders of the notes to exchange them for first-mortgage 6½-percent gold bonds of the corporation and cash. At that time there was $1,000,000 of the notes outstanding. By December, 75 percent of the notes were deposited under the offer. The final 25 percent were paid by three of Nast's business colleagues: The International Printing Ink Corporation, Perkins, Goodwin & Company, and Crocker, Burbank. Mr. Crocker had finally come through.

It was not enough to achieve Nast's main goal, but it was a crumb, and he wrote a grateful letter to Crocker at the end of 1932. "This has been a tremendously difficult year for all of us. It has been a year to tax to the core any man's physical and nervous energies. Your cooperation in subscribing to the bonds that were left over, and your extension of the repurchase date bought by the Crocker, Burbank Company were, of course, life-saving acts to this company."

Poor Condé. He was indeed taxed to the core, with little relief in sight. The notes were saved, but the company still belonged, lock, stock, and barrel, to the Blue Ridge Corporation and Floyd B. Odlum. At the beginning of 1933, as well as owning Nast's collateral stock, Blue Ridge owned 6,000 shares outright, constituting control of The Condé Nast Publications, which at that time had 314,000 shares issued and outstanding.

Floyd Odlum was perfectly well aware of Nast's effort to buy back his stock, and indicated that he would be willing to resell to Nast his note at the valuation placed on it in the Blue Ridge portfolio when he took over control—namely, $1,250,000, or $6.25 per share.

In May 1933, Nast explained to the long-suffering C. T. Crocker that he would very much like to take advantage of Mr. Odlum's generous offer, and therefore would Mr. Crocker consider lending him $500,000, which, with $500,000 from Perkins, Goodwin and $250,000 from the International Printing Ink Company, would add up to the requisite $1,250,000 to pay Mr. Odlum for the shares?

> Dear Mr. Nast,
> We definitely state our inability to meet the financing ideas you have presented. Our concern is represented by endeavours of the proper manufacture of *paper* . . .
>
> C. T. Crocker.

These perpetual supplications and rejections must have deeply offended Nast's fastidious nature, and the fact that he continued the appeals for at least four years indicates the extent of his obsession. He had no life apart from his magazines. If they were taken away from him, his existence was futile.

During this time, however, he continued to live, to all outward appearances, as he had before the Crash. The parties, though severely reduced, continued to make gossip headlines. Grace Moore, Lady Mendl (Elsie de Wolfe), Cecil Beaton, George Gershwin, Helen Wills, and Princess Nathalie Paley continued to be guests of honor at Nast's famous Park Avenue penthouse in the early thirties. Helen Brown Norden, to whom Nast had confided his bankruptcy ("I lost my shirt in Goldman, Sachs," he told her), found it puzzling that he still entertained so lavishly, particularly when some of the guests were people like Harrison Williams, to whom he owed millions. In fact, it was perfectly in keeping with Nast's philosophy. He had to keep the show on the road, for the sake of the magazines.

The show must go on—impeccable as always in white tie, Condé Nast receives Elsa Maxwell's pearls of wisdom while his magazine empire collapses in ruin.

One of the themes he had always stressed to his creditors was that his magazines stood for something more enduring than the trivialities of momentary fame or fashion; that the name *Vogue* was synonymous with quality and style; and that the Condé Nast publications represented a way of life that even the Depression could not entirely destroy. He was not going to compromise that image at any cost. He must continue to convey that sense of promise and optimism his magazines had always stood for, however humiliating the private negotiations to which he was subjected with Mr. Odlum and Mr. Crocker.

There was an element of wisdom in Crocker's last rejection slip, however, that Nast would have done well to observe. His compulsion to sort out his financial affairs was seriously distracting him from the business with which he had originally made his fortune, magazine publishing. The constructing of documents with financial statements, capital expenditure programs, fixed asset positions, consolidated balance sheets, letters of appeal, arguments, special pleading—the documents with which he hoped to convince people that he was worth helping—left him little time or energy for the work he had once so loved—the photography, layouts, models, headlines, the matériel of *Vogue, Vanity Fair,* and *House & Garden.* In 1931 and again in 1932, his staff had taken a 10 percent pay cut. Photographers and artists had readjusted their prices to accommodate the company's difficulties. They were all anxious to help, and continue to keep alive his quality publications. But Nast had withdrawn into a mountain of desperate paperwork. He was sequestered, day after day, in his now-sealed office. During 1933 he even asked Dr. Agha to take over the selection of photographs for *Vogue,* formerly one of Nast's happiest functions as publisher.

"You have obligations to the business," Edna Chase told him urgently, watching her beloved employer lose touch more and more as the months went on, "which you should be most concerned to fulfill and if you do fulfill them, and there is anything like a reasonable recovery in business, you have every prospect of becoming a millionaire again. I know that unless you can soon bring yourself to give your *undivided* attention to the business, it will be too late."

In one area of his life, it was already too late.

Nast could not keep his marriage going while experiencing such stress. A crisis was inevitable. He had married his young wife in the mood of excitement and unreality that swept the country in 1928 and 1929. With his empire dispersed, so were his dreams. Sapped by the ordeals he had to endure in his business life, he could no longer muster the energy or confidence to be a proper, caring husband. In his demoralized state, he grew increasingly distressed by the difference in their ages, and he saw in the cold light of the new world that the marriage had been a hopeless miscalculation.

By an unfair stroke of fate that it is tempting to interpret symbolically, in February 1931 Nast entered New York's Presbyterian Hospital for a prostate operation. It was as though the Crash had deprived him, in one great gesture, of all his manhood. Not that his wife, Leslie, complained. She loved Condé dearly, and suffered greatly for him during his reverses, assuring him that the money had never meant anything to her and that they could happily survive in a simpler way as a family with their baby daughter. But Nast felt sure it was all over. He urged her to leave him and marry someone more suitable, specifically naming Major Rex Benson, a polo-playing Englishman attached to the British Embassy in Washington, who had discreetly been paying court to the young Mrs. Nast. "Marry him. He will make you happier than I can," he told his wife.

Reluctantly, sadly, persuaded only by his entreaties, Leslie Nast agreed to divorce him. The divorce took place very quietly, and few people knew about it. She married Rex Benson in November 1932, in London.

Another departure marks this period—Carmel Snow's defection to Hearst. It could hardly have come at a worse time.

But as hope continued to ebb away, and as Nast's dreams of once more being his own master faded, help came from an unexpected quarter. Some of his friends, including the financier Bernard Baruch, had heard of his difficulties and attempted to help him by forming a syndicate to buy back his shares. These efforts met with little success, but in 1933 news of his struggle reached the ears of a new and more likely benefactor, the British press magnate Lord Camrose.

Camrose, chairman of Allied Newspapers and Amalgamated Press, Ltd., was a friend of the merchant banker Leo d'Erlanger; and Leo d'Erlanger was the husband of the young Texas beauty whom Condé Nast had helped choose as a model for Jean Patou's first American collection in 1924, to whom he had sent baskets of food when she was struggling to make ends meet as an actress, and to whom he had finally given a job on *Vogue*—Edwina Pru. D'Erlanger knew about Condé's many kindnesses to his wife, and on hearing of his troubles decided to approach Camrose.

In England, the Condé Nast publications looked healthier than they did in the United States, where in 1933 the company's net loss was $501,187. British *Vogue* had not suffered nearly as seriously from the Depression as her American sister. In fact, the French and British operations showed an increase in profits from $14,000 in 1933 to $88,000 in 1934 (the profits belonged largely to British *Vogue*, thanks to Harry Yoxall's successful development of double numbers of the magazine with the *Vogue Pattern Book*), and they were even able to lend the American company $100,000, a tidy sum at that time.

On the strength of these figures, and in an extraordinary spirit of friendship, Camrose looked favorably upon the *Vogue* business, and after a preliminary sortie to examine whether he might not simply buy the British company as a separate operation, in January 1934 he agreed to lend Nast $1,000,000 with which to repurchase the majority of the shares owned by Blue Ridge. Of these, 171,000 shares were placed under option to Camrose, leaving Nast in possession of 40,000, for which he paid nothing. Moreover, he was granted the right to purchase an additional 40,000 shares at a price later to be agreed upon (a right he was never able to exercise). Camrose, with d'Erlanger as banker, also provided Nast with $300,000 working capital.

None of these extremely generous transactions was made known to the public. It was considered a gentleman's agreement, with all sides remaining silent about the bailing-out of Condé Nast. The promissory note of $4,800,000 was purchased from the Blue Ridge Corporation by Vogue Studios, Inc., whose stockholders were Coudert Nast, Natica Nast, and a minor, Leslie Nast. The shares were put into a voting trust called Nast Limited, 1 New Bond Street, London, England, and in the required annual statement of ownership published in *Vogue*, shareholders of Nast Limited were discreetly listed as Condé Nast, William Berry, James G. Berry, and Edward Iliffe, Daily Telegraph Buildings, Fleet Street, London, England. (William Berry was the family name of Lord Camrose, James G. Berry was his brother, Lord Kemsley, and Edward Iliffe was their colleague, another press baron.) Within the Condé Nast office, Camrose was given the code name, BARROW, to maintain secrecy. Nast wrote to his old and loyal correspondent Johnnie McMullin, then in London, asking him not to say anything about the deal, both from his point of view and from d'Erlanger's: "On several occasions [Leo] has said that what he had done was wholly a personal matter; that it was not the firm's transaction; and that he preferred, therefore, not to have the name of d'Erlanger mentioned."

Not the least relieved of Nast's colleagues when he heard the good news was Charles T. Crocker. Boxing matches and chic parties in New York had never appealed to him, and the file of begging letters from the publisher had become increasingly painful to look upon. "I regard the arrangement as highly satisfactory," Nast told his crusty creditor, "and will permit me to work out the company affairs with highly successful publishers who know the business, instead of with bankers who are ignorant of it."

It was a happy enough solution. Barring the thing Nast desired most—the repossession of his company—the arrangement with Camrose, who was geographically distant and who left him a reasonably free hand, was the most tolerable regime that could have been devised. He was not his own man—he never would be again—but in the eyes of the world, Condé Nast was still Condé Nast, proprietor of *Vogue* and *Vanity Fair*, arbiter of taste, host of glamorous parties, *homme du monde*. His promise to his constituency had not been broken.

# SEVENTEEN

# ALL IS VANITY

At the beginning of 1935, the newly incarnated publisher might have had reason for a faint glimmer of optimism. *Vogue* actually made a profit in 1934 of $19,927. His other magazines managed to reduce losses; both *Vanity Fair* and *The American Golfer* were helped by liquor advertising, illegal during Prohibition and now a greedy space-buyer again.

Unfortunately, in spite of these mildly encouraging figures, 1935 turned out to be a disastrous year for advertising for every periodical in the country. Only *Vogue*'s revenue rose—up 14 percent from 1934. But *House & Garden*'s dropped off 26 percent; *The American Golfer*'s, 23 percent; *Vanity Fair*'s, 39 percent; and the company still had outstanding debts in every direction.

Lord Camrose, like the bankers before him, thought Nast continued to exhibit extravagance and impracticality. Camrose owned newspapers such as the London *Daily Telegraph,* a bastion of sobriety and conservative taste; Nast's insistence on the aesthetics of publishing seemed a somewhat rarefied ideal in the prevailing conditions.

Nast, against the ropes, sent Camrose countless memoranda and charts about profit turnarounds, advertising expenditures, circulation prospects, and so forth, which so utterly confused His Lordship that they were sent to Harry Yoxall in the London office to be interpreted. Under all Nast's eager paperwork lay serious problems, and Camrose was not about to let them remain unsolved under his proprietorship.

The most vulnerable magazine was *Vanity Fair*. However brilliant the editorial material, the figures at the end of the year had always been poor, and after 1934 there was no more indulgence to be squeezed out of its overextended owners. The world had changed since *Vanity Fair* first resounded under Frank Crowninshield's baton in 1914. Then, and in the subsequent postwar years, the younger generation was swept up in a kind of reckless sangfroid that to some extent dissipated the sense of waste and loss caused by the millions of deaths in what seemed afterward to be a pointless war. In Europe, dada and surrealism were the extreme expressions of this mood, which *Vanity Fair*'s quirky satirical style matched perfectly, and which intoxicated a provincial but prosperous class of America's young, exposed for the first time to a genuinely liberated culture.

But by the 1930s, *Vanity Fair*'s appeal to a fast-living, iconoclastic metropolitan set had faded in the eyes of its advertisers, who expressed their disfavor by allowing the issues to get thinner and thinner as the decade progressed. Crowninshield had never cared for advertising, nor did he stoop to hustling for it now. He believed the magazine was immortal.

Not that *Vanity Fair* remained totally unaffected by the changing political climate. In 1930, a beautiful young blond woman called Clare Boothe Brokaw joined the staff, after a typical poaching-from-*Vogue* act on the part of Crowninshield. The manner of her hiring was typical Condé. He met her at a party, where she expressed interest in coming to work for him. According to Margaret Case Harriman, who wrote a profile of Clare Boothe Luce (she married Henry R. Luce in 1935) for *The New Yorker* in 1941, Nast at the time did not think she was serious. "I thought it was just one of those momentary exuberances, a sudden notion she'd soon forget. I told her I was leaving for Europe the next day . . . and suggested she go around and see Mrs. Chase. I was counting on Edna to get me off the hook. Clare was a very pretty girl, you know." However, the next day, Clare Boothe Brokaw arrived at *Vogue,* found an empty desk, and started work. A few weeks later, she was formally hired.

Clare Brokaw quickly took the measure of Condé Nast's empire, and apparently liked what she saw. According to Margaret Case Harriman, "Condé later told me with a nervous chuckle that Clare, only a few months after she went to work on *Vanity Fair,* came to him and offered to buy a controlling interest in Condé Nast Publications."

Condé did not sell. Instead, Mrs. Brokaw turned her energies to *Vanity Fair,* by inventing such departments as "We Nominate for the Hall of Oblivion," which caused much merriment and controversy until Nast lost a $50,000 contract for the Condé Nast Press to print *Dance Magazine* because its publisher, Bernarr Macfadden, was unfortunately a successful nominee for Oblivion. After that, Nast insisted on seeing all the names before the page was published, thus removing the essential element of noncensorship, and the page was finally dropped.

In addition, Mrs. Brokaw, with the support of *Vanity Fair*'s managing editor, Donald Freeman (who was also in love with her), brought a much stronger political slant to the magazine. Walter Lippmann, Alva Johnston, Drew Pearson, John Maynard Keynes, John Gunther, George E. Sokolsky, and John Hemphill became regular contributors, and articles on war reparations, Hitler, Hindenburg, and Hoover were all familiar leads to issues. Covers and cartoons became relentlessly political, the Mexican illustrator Covarrubias showing his brilliance with ferocious caricatures of Mussolini, and the Italian artist Garretto catching Hitler to perfection. The radical artist George Grosz, after fleeing Germany in 1932, also came to work for *Vanity Fair.* The elegant fantasies of Fish and Benito seemed dated memories.

The politics reflected the mood of the time but put a jackboot into the flighty and frivolous heart of *Vanity Fair,* from which it never recovered. Crowny began to lose interest, concentrating on the art and satires, leaving the political material to the new generation of editors. In late 1932 Donald Freeman was tragically killed in an automobile accident at the age of only twenty-nine. By January 1933 Clare Boothe Brokaw was managing editor. In her first issue, William Harlan Hale published a story called "The Germans Are Marching Again." The photographs accompanying this piece were small black-and-white snapshots laid out in a style that was previously thought suitable only for newspapers. People, even readers of *Vanity Fair,* had come to expect the new technique provided by technological developments in photography—"instant history" at the click of the shutter. People wanted visual news. Could *Vanity Fair* adapt to the times? Should it?

In 1931 Nast asked Clare Brokaw and her colleagues at the magazine to come up with an idea that would give *Vanity Fair* a new formula and attract advertising once more. "He did not ask Crowninshield," she said, "who was much too devoted to the formula of the magazine as it existed, and who insisted it must just go on as it was."

Mrs. Brokaw wrote a long memorandum suggesting Nast buy *Life* magazine and turn *Vanity Fair* into a picture journal. (The old *Life* was a humorous magazine patterned after British *Punch.*) "My memorandum recommended to Condé that he buy the magazine, which had just folded and whose title could have been purchased, as I remember, for about $17,000, and that he change *Life* into a picture magazine. On the strength of this memorandum, I was asked by Condé to make a dummy with Dr. Agha and the Bruehl brothers, photographers who worked for the Nast publications. A dummy was prepared under my direction, with the artwork done under Dr. Agha's direction, and it was submitted to Condé."

For a while Nast toyed with the dummy, and it almost became an insert in *Vanity Fair,* but the idea collapsed. The truth of the matter was that Nast, totally preoccupied with refinancing his debts, was not prepared to commit himself to a venture that was, after all, a major break from his tried and true method of publishing maga-

One of *Vanity Fair*'s last great political cartoonists, Garretto, designs a cover of brutal relevance a few months before the magazine's demise. *Vanity Fair*, August 1935.

zines. Mrs. Brokaw's magazine was to correspond roughly to the French picture magazine *Vu*, Vogel's early and successful contender in the newsmagazine field. Nast, burned by the stock-market experts, deeply demoralized, and filled with uncertainty, withdrew into the only world he had successfully penetrated, the women's market.

Meanwhile, Clare Brokaw met her second husband, Henry Luce, and persuaded him to publish a picture magazine, which was, of course, *Life*. Some time after its debut, Luce was sued by the Bruehl brothers, who in 1932 had produced another dummy, which they had sent to Luce. "This led to a lawsuit," Mrs. Luce related, "in which the Bruehl brothers sued *Life* for $5 million for having plagiarized their dummy. The suit collapsed when I produced my file, with the original prospectus for *Life*, which had been made some time before they made theirs." Luce's *Life* made its first appearance in November 1936; and, as the world knows, it turned out to be one of his most spectacular successes.

The only venture Nast was prepared to contemplate in order to save the faltering *Vanity Fair* was one in a familiar field—a beauty magazine. In 1934, he worked for months with desperate intensity on what was called the Arden project, a secret plan to change *Vanity Fair* into—*Beauty*. The business staff was asked to produce countless statistical tables for projected circulations, color pages, editorial pages, and so forth, in Nast's characteristically thorough method of procedure. But the statistics did not encourage him to undertake this new proposal.

"An appraisal of the various factors which had to be taken into consideration in deciding whether or not to go on with the project of converting *Vanity Fair* into a beauty magazine convinced me that its inauguration at this time would be unwise," he wearily told Lord Camrose in October 1935. "It has been decided to postpone the launching of the new beauty magazine until September, 1936, in the meantime continuing the publication of *Vanity Fair* and preparing the way for *Beauty* by presenting in the forthcoming issues of *Vanity Fair* more editorial features of interest to women."

He justified his decision by the slump in advertising that was taking place throughout the industry in 1935. "I reasoned that if periodicals of established prestige as advertising mediums were having such a struggle for volume of advertising, a wholly new project would find the going very heavy."

Regardless of the unfavorable business conditions, it was surely the height of folly to suppose that *Vanity Fair* could be transformed into a women's beauty magazine, and the fact that it was so seriously considered indicates both the desperation of his efforts to keep *Vanity Fair* from going under, and also his sadly diminished business judgment at this stage in his career.

Throughout 1934 and 1935, Nast attempted to strengthen *Vanity Fair* by instituting more and more stringent budgets. What they spent on articles and artwork seems pathetically small now—$19,839 for the month of February 1934, for instance, a figure pared down to $16,680 for the same month a year later. And even these sums came in under budget, as Frank Crowninshield was at pains to point out to his anxious publisher. In May 1935, Crowninshield explained, "As you will see, we were *under* budget, by $375, in February; and *under* our budget, by $1,500, in March. Furthermore, those two months, we spent $4,800 less than we spent during the same two months of last year."

In October 1935, Nast took out to lunch a young writer named Allene Talmey, who had recently sold an article to *Vanity Fair* and had previously worked for *Stage* magazine.

> Condé asked me what my ideas were for *Vanity Fair,* if I were managing editor. "Mr. Nast," I said, "I would have to think about it." So two weeks later, I called him with some suggestions, which he asked me to write down for him. "No," I said, "I'll tell you in person." So he invited me to lunch.
>
> We lunched, and I told him the various suggestions. Then Condé said, "Miss Talmey, will you be my managing editor?" So I said, "Yes." He said, "How much money do you want?" I said I would think about it. Then he said, "Why don't you write it down on a slip of paper, and so will I." So we both wrote our sums down on slips of paper and handed them to each other. I had written $75 a week. So had he. We were both enchanted with this.

The managing editor of *Vanity Fair* at the time of this enchanting luncheon was Nast's mistress, Helen Brown Norden (later
Lawrenson). When Allene Talmey arrived to take up her post as
managing editor on November 18, 1935, Helen Norden still held
the job. "Condé hid me for two weeks until he fired her." And the
reason he fired her was that he was merging *Vanity Fair* with
*Vogue*.

Crowninshield is said to have felt that Nast did not do enough to
try to save his beloved magazine. This story shows that even as late
as November 1935, Nast was still prepared to take on new staff in
hopes of keeping it alive.

In December 1935, the *Vanity Fair* staff was told that the magazine, with its March 1936 issue, would be merged with *Vogue*.

"Lessening advertising patronage now accorded to periodicals
like *Vanity Fair*," the announcement said, "has made the publication of it as a single publishing unit unremunerative." At the end of
December 1935, *Vanity Fair*'s circulation was under 90,000; the
circulation of *Vogue* was 156,000.

The news was greeted by the staff with the utmost despondency.
How could the magazine that proudly declared it would enable you
"to ignite a dinner party at fifty yards" be extinguished? How could
the magazine that had published the finest writers, artists, illustrators, and critics in the world for twenty years be put to rest? People
got drunk. Nast promised he would find them all jobs, except for
Helen Norden, whose departure saved the company her annual salary of $6,000. ("How do you fire a girl you know you're in love
with?" asked Allene Talmey. "He must have known she wouldn't
mind—and she didn't.")

Frank Crowninshield was the most *bouleversé* of all. For him it
was a profound personal loss, the end of everything. After the
merger, he went to Boca Grande and sent a wistful note to Helen
Norden, saying, "I came here for six weeks rest after forty-five
years of the publishing business. We had fun, didn't we, despite the
worries and fears?" They did have fun, a kind of fun that could
never be recaptured, and certainly not at *Vogue*, under Mrs.
Chase's eagle eye. Crowny was given the title of editorial adviser to

*Vogue* in matters of literature, criticism, and art. It was not a happy role. There had always been a certain amount of friction between him and Edna Chase. This new state of affairs hardly ameliorated their relationship. During his tenure as consultant, he issued a memo which, although funny, could hardly have elicited much mirth from the editor in chief of a publication so different from *Vanity Fair:* The memo was entitled, "The Smell of Our Publications." "It is really impossible to read the current issue of *Vogue,* which I received yesterday, without a slight feeling of nausea. I enclose a copy of Smell Exhibit A . . ."

The merger itself was contrary to all Nast's instincts about publishing—people bought a magazine for a specific reason, and if you altered its content you diluted the interest, fragmented the readership, and thereby lost the advertising. He culled *Vanity Fair* as carefully as possible for its most *Vogue*-ish material—the first merged issue, March 1, 1936, contained *Vanity Fair* writers George Jean Nathan (on Renoir), Marya Mannes (on "Night Life in New York," with illustrations by Vertès), and Paul Gallico (on women fencers).

"We feel confident that this richer *Vogue* will please *Vogue's* readers," Nast said in a nervously reassuring publisher's note: "And although it may not completely fill the place of *Vanity Fair,* we hope that this larger and more varied *Vogue* will give *Vanity Fair's* readers a sense of being at home in its pages."

It was unlikely. Shortly after the merger, so the story goes, an elderly New York club member, finding himself unable to lay his hands on a copy of *Vanity Fair,* irritably ordered a club servant to bring him the current issue at once. "Why, that's a female magazine now, sir," stammered the servant. "We just throw it away as soon as it comes in." Like the praying mantis, *Vogue* had devoured its male mate.

The effect on *Vogue's* circulation was immediately apparent. For the year March 1, 1936, to February 15, 1937, *Vogue* enjoyed an average newsstand sale increase of 14,000 copies, from an average sale of 41,000 with 29 percent returns (unsold copies from the newsstands), to 55,000 with 23 percent returns. Nast was quick to point out, however, that part of this increase was due to *Vogue*'s already rising circulation in its own right (based on previous years' figures), and part to the improving economic situation. In fact, only 4.8 percent of *Vanity Fair* readers renewed subscriptions to *Vogue* after their subscriptions to *Vanity Fair* expired. This may have seemed gloomy news to the old *Vanity Fair* people, but Nast, although disappointed, knew precisely the reason why. It merely confirmed his view, many times expounded, that readers showed a high degree of selectivity with respect to the periodicals they bought.

"To expect *Vanity Fair* readers, who had never seen in it so much as a single page of women's fashions, to find a substitute for it in a magazine which was giving over 80 percent to women's fashions, just didn't make sense. *Vogue* could not expect a high renewal percentage from former *Vanity Fair* readers unless the editorial formula of *Vogue* was so fundamentally changed as to destroy its former essential aim and purpose." And no one, least of all Nast, was going to tamper with that.

The death of *Vanity Fair* can be attributed to several causes. The most obvious one was the climate: although in the thirties the political content of its editorial space was greatly stepped up by Freeman and Brokaw, in the opinion of many observers that change sounded its death knell. For *Vanity Fair* could never be altogether lured out of the dining club and onto the hustings. *Time,* Henry Luce's upper-crust newsmagazine, which as early as 1927 had a circulation of 136,000, provided the hard-nosed news reporting and journalism that politically awakened citizens wanted. *Vanity Fair* carried too much dilettante baggage to compete. Belles lettres were no match for National Socialism.

In addition, other magazines had sprung up to erode *Vanity Fair*'s constituency. *The New Yorker,* in particular, became the alternative glossy magazine aimed specifically at the metropolitan area—a leaf out of Nast's book that worked brilliantly. *The New Yorker,* printed, ironically, at Nast's Greenwich plant, was now publishing Dorothy Parker, whom Nast and Crowninshield had fired for an anti-Ziegfeld review, and Robert Benchley, who had resigned (with Robert Sherwood) in protest. These were damaging losses.

The final financial blow was the introduction of *Esquire* in 1933. Before that date, a quarter of *Vanity Fair*'s income came from menswear advertising. *Esquire* rapidly stole most of that away—plus most of *Vanity Fair*'s best menswear artists—running eight to twelve pages of men's fashions per issue to *Vanity Fair*'s two. In 1936, the year of the merger, *Esquire*'s circulation was almost 500,000, a fabulous publishing success. When *Vanity Fair* folded, it was number ten on too many advertisers' lists.

Two years later, Nast wrote to his longtime men's fashion and society columnist, Johnnie McMullin: "Now I scold myself very bitterly. I believe that had I in the early days an appreciation of the importance of what you had started in your Well-Dressed Man department for *Vanity Fair* and of the intelligence with which you were developing this idea, *Vanity Fair* might have been saved for us because that appreciation would have led me to keep you on the job here. After all, what *Esquire* did ten years later, you really started in *Vanity Fair*."

Frank Crowninshield would never have agreed with Nast about that. "Darling," he once said to Edna Chase when she urged him to give more space to the Well-Dressed Man department, "a gentleman *knows* how to dress."

Ironically, it was in a sense the success of Nast's own philosophy that ultimately made *Vanity Fair* redundant. His belief in class publishing—fashion magazines for fashion readers, golfing magazines for golfers, and so forth—had become a publishing axiom by the middle thirties. *Vanity Fair,* however, was in the position of catering to a mixed, not altogether definable class, a world, in the words of Elizabeth Janeway, "that dinged and donged along by itself and did not have to be held together by anxieties and categorical imperatives and value judgements." *Vanity Fair*'s brilliant writing, splendid photography, and witty illustrations could all have been siphoned off and placed in specialized journals—the writing in

*The New Yorker,* men's fashion in *Esquire,* political cartoons in one of the newsweeklies, photography in *Life,* perhaps. *Vanity Fair* offered quality in all these departments to an eclectically-minded intelligentsia. But by this time, advertisers wanted specialization, not eclecticism—Nast's marketing genius had, in this case, boomeranged.

Nast also lost another magazine during this difficult period—*The American Golfer,* which the publisher, a passionate golfer himself, had bought in the expansionist days of 1928. Using his usual technique, he stripped the magazine of any material irrelevant to golf, and the magazine's circulation immediately rose. But by 1935, its revenues, too, had dropped drastically, and its staff joined *Vanity Fair's* in receiving termination notices. Operating losses on the two publications for 1935 came to more than $250,000.

The third patient was *House & Garden,* the publication most deeply affected, apart from *Vanity Fair,* by the Depression, with advertising revenue dropping off at a faster rate even than that of *The American Golfer.* Nast was loath to diagnose its sickness as terminal, however. "*House & Garden's* loss in earning power since 1930 is due wholly to the demoralization of the building and decoration industry to which its pages are devoted," he said. "It still holds a leading position in its field editorially and as an advertising medium, and it is reasonable to expect that it will regain an earning power of $250,000 a year on the recovery of the building and decoration industry."

In the twenties, *House & Garden* had no real competition except from a weak *House Beautiful* and a rarefied *Arts and Decoration.* Unfortunately, when William Randolph Hearst's *House Beautiful* entered the arena at the end of 1933, *House & Garden's* editors and advertising staff failed to meet the challenge, and Nast's magazine continued to decline. Nast dismissed some personnel, hired a new advertising manager, Charles Whitney, former advertising manager of *House Beautiful* (one of Nast's few pilferings from Hearst), and a new architectural editor.

Nast also considered a change in pricing. He was intensely sensitive to shifts in the magazine marketplace, and had not failed to no-

tice the astonishing success of *Esquire,* which was selling over 150,-
000 copies on the newsstands at a price of 50 cents a copy, as opposed to *Vogue* and *House & Garden,* which were both selling
50,000 or less at a price of 35 cents. He considered remodeling
*House & Garden* along the lines of *Esquire* (more color, more editorial pages, for instance) and selling it at a higher price, with the expectation that it, too, could raise its newsstand sales. In the end, he
decided against it. "If it were a failure, a retracing of our step might
be impractical and, therefore, the property might be irretrievably
hurt."

He made the right decision. By the late thirties, *House & Garden*
had again become a relatively healthy member of the combined
publications. Nast began promoting double numbers of the magazine (two separately bound units, each with its own cover, the second featuring a special subject), which became enormously
successful. He also urged "How To" sections on *House & Garden*'s
aesthetically inclined editor, Richardson Wright, and Dr. Agha, the
art director, both of whom abhorred the idea. (Agha thought *House
& Garden* was one of the ugliest magazines in existence. "It is a
runner-up in this respect with *Life* magazine, and the ugliness of
both magazines is due to the same reason—'idea' editing, to the
exclusion of 'visual' editing.") When circulation again improved,
they had to admit Nast's wisdom. "Practicality is its future," the
prescient publisher insisted.

Affairs in Europe also demanded Nast's attention. In 1934,
French *Vogue, Jardin des Modes,* and the Dorland Advertising
Agency, Paris and Berlin, had reduced their combined losses from
$55,000 in 1933 to $8,500 in 1934. The combined French and
British operations showed an increase in profits from $14,000 in
1933 to $88,000 in 1934. These gains were drops in the ocean, but
they offered the only notes of cheer on the balance sheet.

French *Vogue* had always been a loser, but a serious problem was
looming with *Jardin des Modes,* which was both losing money and
making excessive demands on Michel de Brunhoff, whom Nast
needed to concentrate on *Frog.* Edna Chase urged him to drop *Jar-*

*din* completely. (She had always, right from its inception, been jealous of *Jardin*'s influence over French *Vogue*.) "If you go on with it, you may very easily lose a number of thousand dollars more and then decide to close it out after all, and if you do succeed in keeping it going, I don't see enough money in it to risk the loss of the little momentum French *Vogue* is now gaining. If you drop *Jardin,* it would not be very damaging to the Nast prestige, but if French *Vogue* failed, I think it would be."

On this occasion Nast finessed her advice, but saw to it that Lucien Vogel took over the major responsibility for editing *Jardin,* leaving de Brunhoff to hold up the wavering fortunes of *Frog.*

In spite of these preoccupations, faced while Nast was still attempting to establish a working relationship with Lord Camrose and was still under great pressure from creditors and noteholders, the publisher embarked on one new venture in the thirties that proved to be as enduring as his former successes. It had been observed that the Vogue pattern business was suffering badly from the Depression, the reason being that a Vogue pattern cost as much as $2.00, and competitors were bringing out much cheaper versions. Yet the pattern business in general was thriving, as it obviously would in times of economic hardship, when women could not afford ready-made, store-bought clothes. A young friend of Frank Crowninshield's, Mary Reinhardt (later Lasker), suggested that Nast bring out a cheaper line of patterns, modeled on the clothes of Hollywood movie stars.

So in 1932 Hollywood Patterns were born, with Mary Reinhardt as sales promoter, and were distributed to chain stores around the country instead of to exclusive *Vogue*-assigned outlets. It was Nast's first foray into the mass market, and in spite of his lack of enthusiasm ("He never had anything to do with them," Mrs. Lasker remembered), the experiment worked. The *Hollywood Pattern Book* was so successful that, seven years later, it became a magazine in its own right, with a new title, *Glamour of Hollywood*, with Alice Thompson as its first editor in chief. The wheel had come full circle for Condé Nast, for it was out of his successful development of the Home Pattern Company into a fashion catalogue in the distant past of 1904 that his plans for *Vogue* as a fashion publication had begun to take shape.

"Entertainment is Hollywood's business," ran Nast's announcement of the new magazine in February 1939,

> but its byproduct and most powerful magnet is glamour. Working in splendidly equipped laboratories, Hollywood fashion designers and make-up artists have perfected the science of giving screen actresses their maximum of appeal.
>
> Recognizing Hollywood's importance as a disseminator of fashion, beauty and charm, *Glamour* has been created to interpret that fashion, beauty, and charm in terms of the average woman's daily needs. By revealing how the movie stars achieve their particular appeal, the new magazine will satisfy a great and heretofore unsatisfied demand for authentic beauty and fashion news from the film world—the demand of the thousands of women, the young in particular, who are eager to learn the fashion and beauty secrets of the Garbos, the Dietrichs, and the Crawfords. . . . Differing widely from the scores of fan magazines now being published, *Glamour* is planned to do for Hollywood what *Vogue* has done so magnificently for Paris and New York.

*Glamour of Hollywood,* Nast's last entry into the field of magazine publishing, was introduced three years before he died, when he was sixty-six—a time when most people would be considering retirement. Nobody could say he lacked courage. *Glamour* was of a very different order from his familiar "class" publications, and there were those who said he did not understand the mass market and would fall flat on his face. It was the last test of his publishing expertise, and although he had taken little interest in Hollywood Patterns, he spent much of the last three years of his life refining, justifying, and exploring the *Glamour* formula in the light of a lifetime's experience.

It is interesting to examine the procedures Nast instituted to develop *Glamour.* Nothing more clearly shows his painstaking thoroughness, his extraordinary instincts, and his prophetic qualities as a publisher, even at this late date in his career.

When *Glamour* was entering its second year, Nast spoke about his concept of mass-magazine publishing, and its relation to his new baby:

No periodical has ever ridden to success on its own strength. No periodical published in the United States has, within itself, the power to stimulate a sufficiently broad interest on the part of its readers in some subject, to develop for itself an adequate circulation. Granting this to be true, it follows as a matter of course, that the greater the strength and universality of the power on which a publisher hopes to ride his publication to success, the quicker will he gain his periodical's circulation. Publishers in America, whether or not they have worked this thing out theoretically, as I have, have followed the theory in practice because every one of them, during the past forty years, who was after a big circulation, has chosen some "outside" power to put back of his magazine; I mean such power as human nature's universal interest in fiction. . . . *The Saturday Evening Post, Collier's, The Ladies' Home Journal,* the *Woman's Home Companion,* may let their editors dabble in this or that interest, but from 40 percent to 60 percent of their space is always given over to fiction.

Prior to the advent of Mr. Luce, news subjects were thought to be exclusively within the province of the daily newspaper. Luce thought differently and has ridden his publications into an extraordinary success by putting back of them the power that is found in the interest of human beings in the news of their fellow human beings. . . .

Now, within the past score of years, there has arisen an instrument that has generated an interest-arousing power, a publicity power, paralleling that of the newspapers. I mean the moving picture industry. Each week, in the United States, 85,000,000 entrances are bought to the moving pictures. Any power big enough to develop a concentration and universality of interest that will bring 85,000,000 people together weekly, evidently is an extraordinary power.

Once more, Nast had proved his astute business sense. The eleventh issue of *Glamour* achieved a newsstand sale of 200,000—an unusual achievement, justifying Nast's supposition that such a quick and broad success achieved by a periodical with a Hollywood orientation, not broadly advertised, and with its first six issues very hastily edited, might portend a circulation of half a million or more.

His prognosis was correct. A year later, approximately 250,000 copies were sold of the March-April 1941 issue, with returns of between 17 and 20 percent, a very low percentage indeed. Returns for the previous year, 1940, had averaged only 35 percent; the figures were remarkably encouraging.

Nast, however, was not satisfied. He suspected that the potential for *Glamour* was far greater than he had estimated, considering the figures and what he regarded as the limitations of the magazine. He felt that the connection with Hollywood was too restricting; he also felt that the women to whom they were addressing the magazine could encompass the career girls currently being attracted by *Mademoiselle,* Street & Smith's highly successful publication that had first appeared in 1935, and whose subtitle read, "A Magazine for Smart Young Women."

Nast decided he must study the makeup of *Mademoiselle*—its features, how many pages they absorbed, and what percentage of the total book they represented. He noticed that one-third of *Mlle* (an abbreviation, pronounced "Millie" by the staff) was devoted to clothes and shopping, one-third was divided between social life and careers, and one-third was given to features. "The college girl, which was the magazine's build-up, now only accounts for a little over 2% of the space," he observed. "All the other features are crowded into the last third of the magazine." He immediately took this mix and asked his advertising manager to draw up a new proposal for page disposal in *Glamour,* so that the magazine would have a better proportion of personal features.

Concerned to capture some of the career-girl readership, he asked Frank Crowninshield, in his role as consultant, for his opinion. Crowny, not surprisingly, was soundly for the upgrading of the magazine. "The point is really that we must, in the girls who are shown in *Glamour,* aim, first, for a little higher order of breeding; second, a higher order of intelligence; and third, a higher degree of usefulness in the fabric of society. As it now is, outside of the fact that some of the women have succeeded in the movies, they are, as a lot, mediocre and inconsequential."

Nast was inclined to agree. "I believe," he said, "that style is as important in less expensive clothes as it is in those in the higher price level." He then suggested that it might be wise to announce to the readers of *Glamour* that its editor was now (from May 1941) to be Miss Elizabeth Penrose, former editor of British *Vogue,* and that Miss Penrose had at her hand all the fashion information gathered for *Vogue.*

In April 1941, eighteen people gathered at 1040 Park Avenue for a *Glamour* editorial meeting to discuss these questions. They included Mrs. Chase, Frank Crowninshield, Dr. Agha, Lew Wurzburg, Lucien Vogel (who had been forced to flee Paris when the war broke out and was now serving as a consultant to Nast in New York), and Betty Penrose, *Glamour's* new editor. The following items were raised, as recorded in the detailed minutes of the meeting:

(1) The Hollywood tie-up: "I do not feel that we should throw out Hollywood completely," Nast decided. "I think we should use it when it suits our purpose."

(2) Covers: "My thought is that we would use Hollywood stars for covers when it serves our fashion purpose, but we should not be committed to publish a Hollywood star on every *Glamour* cover."

(3) Movie reviews: "I am against these reviews because they are always out of date. Whatever is said to the contrary, whenever a movie gets to a certain place, the local paper reviews it." (A vote was taken on this issue: eight voted to drop movie reviews, seven voted to retain them.)

(4) Pictures of movie stars in their homes: "I am sure that there is widespread interest in such features," declared Nast.

"But these features have been very monotonous," objected Dr. Agha.

"That has been due to bad editing—too much similarity in pose, et cetera. I am as certain about the general interest in the pictures of the lives of the stars as I am of anything in the publishing business, but whether we can do *good* features of this sort is the question."

(5) Fiction: Nast had always been interested in this subject. "I have been greatly impressed by the fiction in *Mademoiselle.* I have been against using fiction in our magazines because all the other magazines like the *Post* can pay big prices, and, therefore, I thought we could not compete. *Mademoiselle,* however, has disproved this. . . . It never raised the circulation of *Bazaar,* but we have before us this success of *Mlle,* and I think it is a subject that is worth looking into. No magazine that has devoted itself wholly to fashion has been a great success. The *Ladies' Home Journal, Woman's Home Companion,* et cetera, given only about 10% to fashions—*Mlle* has devoted only a very little space to fashions. That's why I wanted to use Hollywood as an outside interest to supplement fashions in *Glamour.*"

(6) Crowded pages: "It started as a theory on my part, but it is no longer theory. Each time we have tried it we have redeemed a property or subject that was down and out. I notice with great pleasure that *Glamour* is filled with crowded pages in the new issue. Each of these pages will be circulation builders."

These remarks drew great opposition from the advertising people, however, who said that advertisers did not like them. "The buyers place orders in proportion to what they think their credit is to be." Their complaints included that the clothes illustrated could not be seen, and that the impact of the individual item was lessened. Moreover, the stores did not buy articles shown in a crowded spread.

"I don't care about this," Nast said. "I am thinking of the reader and I know that it will build up circulation. It has built up *House & Garden*'s circulation beyond belief. . . . These magazines are to give information—they are service magazines—if you give a woman 5 hats to choose from she is not going to be as satisfied as if she had 20 hats to pick from."

(7) A subtitle on the cover (copying *Mlle*): Many of those present

Condé Nast's newest entry, with a cover photograph by Rawlings—
the issue that made a newsstand sale record. *Glamour*, August 1941.

at the meeting had suggestions for a subtitle, ranging from "Young Fashions for Young Incomes," to "The Way to Fashion, Beauty and Charm on a Budget."

"We should think up a statement that would say that all the fashion information of the great fashion-gathering organization of *Vogue* is at the disposal of *Glamour*," urged Nast. "We should drive home the point that not only are these clothes inexpensive, but they are smart."

Crowninshield thought there should be some connection in the subtitle with the Condé Nast publications: "We want to get the co-operation of the big people. We want to get Benchley to write, and so forth. Such people would far rather write for a Condé Nast Publication than they would for a book called *Glamour*. Why not say—I don't know just how to say it—'A Condé Nast Publication—publishers of *Vogue*'?"

Members of the staff objected to that, saying that some people were frightened of *Vogue*, or that they would confuse the two magazines.

"You think that the readers will think that *Glamour* is another *Vogue*?" asked Nast. "I should think that a look at a half-dozen pages would take care of this. What I want to stress is that we will make a great mistake if we only play up inexpensive clothes. We must say that there is style back of our expensive merchandise. That is what I want to accomplish and I know no better way than a connecting-up with *Vogue*."

The staff were split on the issue; finally Crowninshield suggested putting the subtitle, not on the cover, but on the contents page. All agreed to this solution, and the meeting was adjourned.

Most of Nast's publishing talents are displayed in the brief summary of this editorial meeting. His sense of what *Glamour*'s readership wanted is unerring, from the canceling of movie reviews to the insistence on features showing movie stars in their homes. His ability to analyze the competition and take from it what could be useful (as he did with *Harper's Bazaar*) is well demonstrated here. (The fate of *Mademoiselle* turned out to be ironic: in 1959, Street & Smith was bought by The Condé Nast Publications under its new owner, the Newhouse organization. So *Mademoiselle,* so often held up by Nast as the model of the competition to *Glamour,* finally became a Condé Nast magazine.) And most surprising of all is his enthusiastic support of an entirely new form of layout—crowded pages. For most of his life, Nast had insisted on the clean white page, with one or two large photographs, framed in white margins to the most meticulous measurements, as the preferred look for his magazines. Now he was cheerfully advocating what some critics could only have described as a mess—five or more items of fashion merchandise spread about the page in a seemingly random fashion, so that the reader's eye was attracted this way and that, until she settled on what interested her. Today, this is one of the most successful forms of magazine layout, but in those days it was very novel, and coming from Nast it was positively heretical. Considering his advanced age and chronically cautious temperament, such foresight and clairvoyance into the minds of his readers (in this case, twenty-year-old working girls), is remarkable.

In September 1941, Nast wrote to his son, who was by then in the Army: "We gave the American News Company [his newsstand suppliers] 330,006 copies of the August issue of *Glamour* and sold 90 percent of them—10 percent return, as you probably know, is a remarkably low percentage."

That issue had as a subtitle on its cover: "For Young Women—the Way to Fashion, Beauty and Charm." On the contents page was written: *"Glamour,* Published by The Condé Nast Publications, Publishers of *Vogue, House & Garden, Vogue Pattern Book,* British *Vogue."* There were several crowded pages, several shots of movie stars wearing fashions, six college and career articles, no movie reviews, and no fiction. The Nast touch had worked again—but it was to be his last flourish.

# EIGHTEEN

# TWILIGHT OF THE MODE

In November 1936, Roosevelt carried every state except Maine and Vermont in the presidential election. It was enough to exacerbate Condé Nast's already too-high blood pressure. "I would rather they picked someone out of Bellevue than have that man re-elected," he imaginatively remarked. It was the first occasion Nast was known to have taken up a political position on anything.

His magazines remained tactfully aloof from the matter. The only one to carry political material in any recognizable way was *Vanity Fair,* whose most radical statement had appeared as early as June 1932, written anonymously for the magazine by John Carter (a member of the State Department who usually used the pseudonym Jay Franklin). It was entitled "Wanted: a Dictator!" and it said: "Representative Government has collapsed before the clamor of special interests. The American people can give no mandate before November, and the situation is critical. We must declare an immediate truce on party politics and create, legally or *illegally,* an emergency organization, if the executive power is to rescue the national finances and the national credit from the nerveless hands of a lobby-ridden Congress. The alternative is chaos."

This was signed "The Editors," showing how strongly the magazine was behind it. (All except Clare Boothe Luce. She said later that its publication had caused her to threaten to resign.)

It was not only *Vanity Fair,* of the Condé Nast publications, that was expressing admiration for dictators in those years. In June 1933, *"Vogue*'s Eye View of the Mode" was trilling away in excitement at a favorite political leader of the moment: "Those people in the photograph at the left are gazing down at the New Rome: a Rome resurrected by Mussolini from glorious ruins to glorious life; a city bathed in mysterious floods of light, where the policemen wear white piqué gloves and hats, where the Opera has all the pre-War Vienna glitter of jewels and uniforms (the Fascisti black shirt is starched for evening!); and where the noblewomen emanate the splendour and dignity of the palaces they inhabit . . ."

As for Hitler, *Vogue* was thrilled to present to its readers in August 1936 the great man's country retreat, Haus Wachenfeld, at Berchtesgaden: "German, jumbled, and gemütlich . . . On the side of a mountain, the chalet has a suburban neatness, with a sun porch and canaries, and its rooms, a cozy podge of clocks, dwarfs, and swastika cushions. Nothing at Wachenfeld suggests the 'agitated simplicity' of his Berlin home, the constant exercise of his power as governmental art dictator. (He is the author of the classic comment: 'There exists no art except Nordic-Grecian.')"

In spite of these masterpieces of political insight in *Vogue*'s pages, Hoovervilles, Roosevelt's bonus army, and the other symptoms of a restive world in America and in Europe were dealing Nast's publications a blow more lethal than anything since the beginning of the century. In a climate where the need for bread replaced the need for breeding, the raison d'être of his magazines was at risk. The grand society of taste and style that he had designed, drawn up, and populated for his advertisers and readers was dwindling to a point somewhere on the East Coast where the blue eagle of the National Recovery Act and the WPA programs had failed to penetrate.

Not that his financial condition suffered under the New Deal. There was a moment in the middle of the decade when things seemed suddenly much better—what Malcolm Cowley has identified as "The High Thirties." The Dow Jones industrial stock averages had risen by 200 percent—from 59.93 at the end of 1932 to 179.90 at the end of 1936. In 1936 The Condé Nast Publications Inc. showed a profit of $471,363, compared with a loss in 1935 of $208,167, and Nast told his stockholders: "The important developments affecting the company's operations for 1936 were the great increase in circulation and in advertising enjoyed by *Vogue* and *House & Garden;* increase in sales of Vogue and Hollywood Patterns; improved business, particularly in the last half of the year, for the company's manufacturing unit, Condé Nast Press, and the discontinuance of two of its unprofitable properties, *Vanity Fair* and *The American Golfer."*

This little triumph was a hollow one, however. The truth was, Condé was tired. The Crash had wiped out his enthusiasm. He was unsure about the survival of his properties. The changing political situation filled him with doubts, splintered his resolve. The ringing words with which he had once pronounced the infallibility of his publishing methods were reduced to tentative justifications and explanations:

> Heretofore, from the early days of the building [of the magazines] and subsequently—whether in days of plenty or want—I have built and maintained these properties by pumping into them such editorial values and exploiting them with such propaganda as my publishing judgment and experience told me the situation called for. When long-range expenditures . . . have been determined upon, I have felt so sure of their soundness that often they have been made, I confess, without my being very sure of [the magazines'] ability to finance them. . . . I realize now, in view of existing circumstances, that I can no longer adhere as rigidly as I have done in the past to what I might call my long-range policy.

Although Lord Camrose was providing financial support, things were not the same. Carmel Snow had gone. Steichen had gone. Hoyningen-Huené had gone. *Vanity Fair* was dead. Frank Crowninshield's spirit was quenched. Edna Chase was nearly sixty and getting tired. Even the old faithful Lew Wurzburg had lost his authority. People said *Harper's Bazaar* was looking much more exciting than *Vogue*. The parties at 1040 Park continued—for Ina Claire, Lady Patricia Ward, Eve Curie, Laurette Taylor, Edwina d'Erlanger, Lord Kemsley, Elsa Maxwell, Geraldine Farrar, and Clare Boothe Luce, among others. Occasionally the old gaiety returned, but not very often. In 1937 Nast gave a supper dance for the opening of Mrs. Luce's play, *The Women* (which starred Mrs. Chase's daughter, Ilka), and out of 902 guests invited, 602 came. The notation of attendance beside these figures reads like an apology: "66 percent—very bad, stormy weather." To be sure, the system of party analysis Nast had perfected so long ago still functioned. But the secretaries did it mechanically, without curiosity. The fun had gone out of the lists and breakdowns, just as the fun had gone out of the parties themselves, despite the repeal of Prohibition—perhaps, in some small way, because of it. Every day now, it seemed, was very bad, stormy weather.

Nast was also plagued by family problems. His little daughter, Leslie, lived with him during term time, and went to school in New York; she lived with her mother and stepfather in England in the holidays. Also living at 1040 Park for some of the time was Peter Nast, Coudert's little boy, about the same age as Leslie, whose mother, having divorced Coudert in 1933, was living in Mexico. It was at this point that Clarisse, who had married a stockbroker named Victor Onativia, reentered the picture; she was to dominate much of Nast's personal affairs for his last years.

The main problem was Peter, who was an unhappy, disturbed little boy—for obvious reasons. His mother was abroad, and his father was under the influence of Clarisse, who insisted Peter should not be sent to his mother. The boy's other grandmother, Mrs. Donald Brown, although friendly and well-meaning, was also difficult and demanding. Coudert, who had been with the National Guard ever since his Harvard days, was called up in 1940 and thus forced to leave these two women and his father to fight over his young son. (Coudert, a successful lawyer, became a general in the U.S. Army and was buried at Arlington National Cemetery with full military honors on his death in 1980.)

There were violent arguments over the boy's schooling. Clarisse insisted he be taken out of a school where he had seemed, for the first time, to settle down, because his religious education, she felt, was inadequate. The letters exchanged between Condé and Clarisse over their grandchild were acrimonious, with Clarisse accusing her former husband of interfering when he objected to the child's being removed from the one place he had apparently begun to enjoy. Coudert tried to keep the peace by writing pathetic remonstrances to his mother: "You have read into Dad's actions motives and influences that were not there . . ."

Coudert's own situation was not exactly simple. In 1937 he married for the second time—a midwestern girl named Julie Ensley, who had psychiatric problems and spent much time in the Menninger Clinic. Julie was unable to cope with her own life, let alone take on Coudert's or Coudert's son's problems. On one occasion in 1940, when Coudert came home on leave and Julie was allowed out of the clinic to spend Thanksgiving with him, it was thanks to Condé that they were able to celebrate at all—he thoughtfully sent a turkey to the melancholy couple.

Nast was an attentive and loving grandparent. "Peter is a handsome youngster," he wrote to Coudert. "It is a pity to have this appearance marred by his protruding teeth. . . . I am going to take advantage of your permission and have Dr. Waugh take a look at them." He wrote Peter letters at school to cheer him up: "You know my breakfast menu—I drink a little tea, eat a little toast and honey and large mouthfuls of the *New York Times*. When I was eating the *Times*, I took a bite of the weather reports and learned that at 11:30 there was to be a half hour shower of turtles . . ."

If he agonized over the poor little boy, little Leslie was the light of his last days. He took the greatest interest in everything about her, including her clothes, ordering boxes and boxes to be sent to the apartment and asking women friends to advise on her wardrobe. He hired a series of governesses for her, French and German (just as Clarisse had done for their children). Sometimes the governesses were horrible, such as the one who made Peter eat mustard as a punishment for not eating his supper, and another who was so beastly that little Leslie confided in George, Nast's chauffeur and the conduit between father and daughter ("It never occurred to me to tell my father," she said later). Nast was mortified, as any parent would have been, and the governess was gone the next day. (Nast, who had always sought the unpretentious, grew to rely on George more and more in his last years. They communicated more freely than Nast had probably ever done with his society friends. The publisher had always loved cars, although he had never learned to drive, and their conversations as George drove at top speed, egged on by Nast, from Sands Point to New York or from New York to Newport must have been some of the few truly relaxing moments Nast knew in the two or three years before he died.)

Clarisse nagged, wrote letters, visited the apartment endlessly, causing trouble. When she came to 1040 Park to visit Peter, she was so allergic to little Leslie's presence that the child had to be taken out of the apartment. (Big Leslie had apparently had the same effect. "Has That Woman been in this room?" Clarisse would demand, stiffening like a panther about to spring.)

Nast suffered these scenes with patience. He always answered her letters, explaining, soothing, smoothing out resentments, trying his best to protect both Leslie's and Peter's future. In his old age he was finally becoming the father he had never had himself. There was just enough time. Leslie remembers his taking her on trips by train to Pinehurst, North Carolina, and to Boca Grande, Florida, sometimes with Uncle Frank in attendance—"beautiful old trains, with drawing rooms, it was very exciting." At 1040 Park, Leslie used to eat her supper on a tray, with the governess. Then Nast came home. "He'd have a rest in his big bed before going out to dinner, and I used to get into bed with him and he'd read to me." He was stern with her about only one thing—posture. He made her

Life with father: Leslie poses with dogs for Lusha Nelson (opposite page, above), attends a party at 1040 Park Avenue (opposite page, below), and listens agog to one of Uncle Frank Crowninshield's outrageous tales.

pay attention to her walk. He also, in characteristic fashion, re-mained dedicated to pulchritude. "This was our only area of dis-agreement," Leslie remembers. "I had two best friends; one of my best friends was extremely pretty and elegant, but my *best* best friend was rather plain and dumpy-looking. It was always the pretty one that he wanted me to play with."

In the summer, when Leslie was in England with her mother, Nast often visited them on his trips to Europe. There was such manifest affection between father and mother that little Leslie often wondered why they had divorced.

Illusions, however, were becoming harder and harder to hold onto, as political events tumbled over each other with increasing ur-gency in 1937 and 1938. Only at Elsie Mendl's opulent Versailles apartment did life seem *almost* as amusing and inconsequential as ever. French *Vogue* editor Bettina Ballard recorded the conversa-tion at one of Lady Mendl's glamorous luncheons in September 1938:

> Someone asks if anyone at the table has ever known a Czechoslo-vakian? One man admits his valet is of that nationality—but hardly worth fighting for. No one seems to know why France gave her word to protect a country with so many unknown people in it—why not forget this word? Sir Charles [Mendl] explains patiently that if you sign a check, it is a little bit difficult to deny your signature. Johnny Fauçigny-Lucinge says that Bonnet told him that if Hitler holds to his bluff, France will end by accepting a plebiscite of the Sudetens. Elsa Schiaparelli says she knows there won't be a war—just by instinct. Elsie Mendl says there is going to be a miracle. Diana Vreeland says it is all chemical—that Hitler is a madman during the full moon and is capable of any extremities at that time. Everyone thinks of the very big moon that will come up in a few hours. A faded beauty adds another coat of powder and says that Anthony Eden and Laval gave Italy to Germany. Someone remem-bers how people in the streets of Paris got down on their knees when President Wilson passed. Lady Castlerosse is very annoyed with the whole business because she has a new house in Venice and how can she go to Venice if there is a European war? Mrs. Douglas

Fairbanks is very glad she is just plain Mrs. Fairbanks with an American passport. Kitty Miller knows that nothing will happen before she finishes her fittings and sails off to New York.

Not even Hitler could fly in the face of such confidence, and Mrs. Gilbert Miller no doubt secured her Paquins and her Lanvins in time for the spring season in New York; but a year after this luncheon, Bettina Ballard was one of the few editors left in the Paris office of *Vogue*. Michel de Brunhoff was waiting to be mobilized— Bébé Bérard and Benito had already departed for war. Those chic black shirts that the adorable Fascisti wore starched for evening were already démodés.

Nast sent de Brunhoff a cable at the outbreak of war which read: "We are about to be cut off from each other. I know that you will have to make vital decisions. This is to tell you that I approve in advance every decision that you will make in the name of Condé Nast Publications."

Armed with this supportive message, de Brunhoff braced for one of the biggest decisions he ever had to make. When the Germans occupied Paris, they announced that French *Vogue* and *Jardin des Modes* would be allowed to continue publication, under German control, of course. De Brunhoff, not enamored of this offer, played for time. One of the Germans' conditions involved the presenting of documentary proof that the Nast publications had "no Jewish capital or attachments." De Brunhoff was also asked to furnish a biography of all the staff he intended to work with. As the negotiations continued, it became clear that de Brunhoff was not going to be able to satisfy his German masters, and he finally decided to liquidate the business. Thus *Frog* escaped the Hun in a heroic act of self-immolation. (De Brunhoff's stand was particularly courageous in view of the collaborationist atmosphere pervading the French publishing industry generally during the Occupation.)

Of the French *Vogue* family, Lucien Vogel, whose newsmagazine, *Vu,* had demonstrated distinctly anti-Nazi leanings, was forced to flee Paris with his family, and lived in New York until the liberation of France. Solange d'Ayen, the aristocratic and beautiful fash-

The publisher at his happiest—a typical working lunch with Iva Patcévitch (right) and Michel de Brunhoff, photographed by Lusha Nelson in 1937.

ion editor (to whom Poulenc once dedicated a song) was imprisoned briefly in 1942, but suffered much more deeply when her husband was deported and died in Belsen on the eve of its liberation in 1945. Her nineteen-year-old son, who had insisted on enlisting when he heard his father had been taken to Germany, was killed in an army truck accident while his father was still in prison. (He may never have known about his son's death.) Michel de Brunhoff's son, another nineteen-year-old, was shot by the Gestapo in 1944. De Brunhoff himself survived the war, and was in charge of the first post-liberation issue of French *Vogue,* which appeared in January 1945.

British *Vogue* survived the Blitz under the firm direction of its editor, Elizabeth Penrose, who came to *Glamour* in 1941, leaving the British editor's chair to Audrey Withers. "Our policy is to maintain the standards of civilization," the magazine declared. "We believe that women's place is *Vogue*'s place. And women's first duty, as we understand it, is to preserve the arts of peace by practicing them, so that in happier times they will not have fallen into disuse. British *Vogue* found this to be true in the dark years of 1914–1918, during which it was born and throughout which it mirrored women's many-sided activities, so, once more, we raise the 'carry on' signal as proudly as a banner."

In fact, British *Vogue* did well during the war. Paper-rationing caused a cut in the number of pages and the circulation, and soon advertisers were clamoring for a place in the restricted space; and readers, who were deprived of all other forms of glamour, were ready to pay 7/6 for secondhand copies of the magazine (which then cost 1/6).

In 1941 a serious setback occurred when a bombing raid destroyed the warehouse, with a loss of 350,000 patterns and 450,000 of the cheap do-it-yourself knitting leaflets that Harry Yoxall had started. Luckily, the prescient Yoxall had kept duplicates of all the master patterns, plus one of each cutting machine, in the basement of his Richmond house, so they never went out of production.

During these years of crisis, Yoxall felt Nast never fully sympathized with the staff of *Brogue*. *Vogue* in America was again in financial difficulties and Nast, now in his late sixties, seemed less and less able to deal with adversity. His mind appeared closed to the hardships of the London office. "He was concerned only with the financial losses to the parent company that the war would be causing," Yoxall said. "He tried to persuade me that I should cut all salaries by at least 10 percent. I asked him what he proposed to do in New York and was told that the U.S. was at peace and he could do nothing." Under Mrs. Chase's direction, however, he supported various efforts, including a fund to help those members of the British staff who had lost homes in the air raids, and the dispatching of CARE parcels from the New York office.

Before Pearl Harbor, *Vogue* paid as much attention to the European war as was justified by its effect on the Mode. "What Paris women wear in war time," for instance, described "turbans, berets—no silly hats; Schiaparelli's blue wool suit for nocturnal 'alertes'; and Madame Lanvin's black tweed case to carry a British gas mask." Eric, the fashion artist, sketched clothes entitled "In the Ritz shelter—'abri' outfits by Molyneux and Piguet." In 1940, *Vogue* published letters from British and French correspondents, describing what was happening abroad:

> My little house is crammed with people; soldiers turn up unexpectedly from Dunkirk and need places to rest for a few days. Only the big news placards are in print now, and they just say LATEST WAR NEWS. The new bits are marked in chalk on slates or written in blue pencil on paper—because the news changes so quickly . . . [Lady Stanley, London].

> More than ever, American help means everything to us and American generosity is absolutely wonderful. . . . To us, on the borders of the Seine, and not so far from the battle, loves, lives, and belongings have lost every kind of meaning. There is only one aim—succeed . . . [Duchesse d'Ayen, Paris].

> Paris seems as safe a place as any—and what does it matter now about furniture and silver and treasures? Clarita de Forceville fled

her château in a pig-merchant's wagon with several old women, leaving everything behind her. Madame de Marenches left millions of francs' worth of rare furniture, tapestries, and silver when she abandoned Rotoirs . . . [Thomas Kernan, Paris].

Biarritz this moment is a strange sight—so many Rolls Royces, maids, valets, and dogs gathered together under so few roofs. This hotel has a list of people that reads like the "Grande Semaine" at Deauville in the old days. Certainly these rich fashionables gathered here will never live like that again . . . [John McMullin, evacuated to Biarritz.]

We try to look at each sentence and imagine how it will read in the face of all the disasters that may happen before it sees the light of day . . . [Audrey Withers, London.]

Condé Nast, ever vigilant, began to enquire whether *Vogue*'s war features had a deterrent effect on sales. Nobody could find any evidence that they did. His war-consciousness was fanned by the arrival of a new editor at *Vogue,* Millicent Fenwick. She had started work in 1938 as a young divorcée, desperately needing funds to provide for her children. Nast, as always, had been kind to her. When the war started, she became war editor, provided war features, and sold war bonds. Mrs. Fenwick took Nast to task for allowing himself to be photographed with René de Chambrun, Laval's son-in-law, and objected that a party given by Miss Anne Morgan for de Chambrun, who became the Vichy French ambassador to the United States in late 1940, was appearing in the pages of *Vogue.* "Condé was totally open to these suggestions and quickly changed his attitude to the collaborationists. It just had not occurred to him."

Nast also accepted Mrs. Fenwick's insistence that personality captions should include the person's war work, if any. She also remembers the occasion when a Swiss gentleman arrived to see Mrs. Chase with some fashion drawings he wanted to sell. Mrs. Fenwick was brought into the meeting since she spoke French and could translate for the visitor. Since Paris fashion was by this time nonexistent, *Vogue* was desperately short of designs, and urgently needed editorial material. Mrs. Chase asked the Swiss visitor some searching questions about payment, which was to be sent to Switzerland, and it soon became clear that something was wrong about the deal.

"Where will the money end up that we send to Switzerland?" she asked.

"Why, to us," the gentleman answered.

"Yes, but where? Who made the designs, to whom is the payment going ultimately?"

"Well," said the Swiss reluctantly, "he is in Paris, actually."

Mrs. Chase drew up her tiny frame to its full height. "I would rather publish *Vogue* with blank pages than send one cent to support the Nazis," she declared. Nast was by now in agreement. His antennae had picked up the mood of the country, and American interest in the European battleground led him to say in April 1941: "All my study has made me think we must be watchful, very watchful. We must not allow people to think of *Vogue* as a really frivolous periodical, unaware of the serious challenges that have been going on in the life, interests and psychology of women."

A year later Edna Chase emphasized this new note in her address to the Fashion Group of New York. It was entitled "Morals—a Realistic Inventory for the Fashion Industry": "Fashions do not die because of wars," she told them briskly.

> Many of the best of them are covered by war's necessities. . . . Today, we want to take the folly out of fashion, but not the charm, the taste, and the becomingness. We shall have to begin to think more about value now, *real value*. . . . We are not going to be so easily satisfied with surface effects.
>
> Certainly, since the war, the attitude of people in England has changed enormously, and I think it will change here too. Over there, they have acquired a very different outlook—and, with it, they have attained a freedom, a mystic quality; they seem truly to have found their souls.
>
> I think the spiritual rebirth the British people have undergone is one which we, too, must undergo. . . .

As *Vogue* began to take the folly out of fashion, it also introduced a new note of nostalgia into its pages, much of it created by Frank Crowninshield. As early as 1925 he had begun to tell sad tales about the death of kings, such as this one, prompted by the demolition of some of New York's great Fifth Avenue mansions: "To old New Yorkers, the real melancholy of the situation comes, not from the fact that the houses are soon to crumble into dust, but that the old and well-ordered social fabric, the old philosophy of fashionable living (which Society, in the nineties, had embraced as a creed), has itself crumbled and vanished utterly from view. In place of a society restricted to a few hundred people of good breeding, we now have a social fabric mounting into the thousands, most of whom have inherited no very definite traditional creed of conduct or behavior."

By 1940, Crowny's writing, like rare perfume, lingered long and caressingly over the fabulous Mrs. Rita Acosta Lydig, the 1913 Armory Show, the vanishing skills of the toastmaster, the art of Charles Dana Gibson, and the shining stars of vaudeville. "Strange how the memory can be tapped; how, at the beck of sights and sounds in themselves fleeting and fragmentary, figures and voices, long since forgotten, appear as if by magic, throw off their veils, and . . . live again."

For Crowninshield, like Nast, found the modern world changed beyond recognition, quite apart from the war, which was changing everything. To read about Rita Lydig, with her 350 pairs of shoes, 87 coats, 48 swan-necked blouses, 17 lace underskirts, "exhibiting in her box at the Metropolitan," as Crowninshield wrote, "a little artfully, her fabulous back, and surrounded by such diplomats, artists, and notables as were in vogue at the time," was like listening to an old song that had once been the theme of a long-lost love. To read his descriptions of Gibson's extraordinary reign—"all of his young people were perennially in love; in love on the bridle-path, at the dinner table, on the beach, at the opera, and in the ballroom"—was like coming across a faded, yellowing invitation whose engraved surface still gleamed faintly if you held it under the light.

In September 1942, the month of Nast's death, Crowninshield

published a piece entitled, "Newport—Those Days, This War," in which he described how Newport, taken over by the Navy, had changed since the days when "Mrs. William Astor ruled over society with an iron hand, and when she was not only acclaimed the Mystic Rose of the Patriarchs' Balls, but was actually the indubitable Queen Bee in New York's busiest social hive. That was the era of sailor hats—for men and women alike; of frilly parasols, and of the Renoir type of dresses; of boned, high collars and stiff-boned corsets; of beguiling bustles—although they were already vanishing from the mode; of elegantly gloved hands and wrists; of buttoned boots and of shirtwaists which, a little improved upon, were later to be affected by Charles Dana Gibson's attractive young heroines." Now, with the Navy installed, Crowny related, "hamburgers, as delicacies of the table, have replaced terrapin. Gold plates have had to make way for self-service trays; banquet halls for snack bars. The words 'champagne,' 'caviar' and 'Napoleon brandy,' though still pleasing to the ear, are never so much as whispered. Stakes at bridge, towie and backgammon have tumbled mightily, while the Country Club, after fifty years of ritualistic restrictions, has become a public, dollar-a-round golf links."

There would be no point now in Nast's asking an editor who had returned from a weekend in Newport, "What were the chauffeurs wearing?" There were no chauffeurs left; they had all gone to the war. Those at the wheel in Newport were drivers in military uniform. Even if there were a few old retainers left behind, nobody would care any longer. The bright days were gone when work was play and the magazines were real life.

The folly had surely gone out of fashion. "The Breakers" now housed a public air-raid shelter.

Work remained, as it always had, Nast's solace. He became an obsessive memorandum writer, dictating page after page of philosophy, analysis, breakdown, and more analysis. The tone of these memos became more and more long-winded and testy. He would call attention to something he had heard or read, and urge his editors to take some meaning from it. In 1940, for instance, gossip columnists and photographers were obsessed by a former debutante,

Brenda Diana Duff Frazier, and featured her over and over again in their stories. "The young lady is gifted with no outstanding qualities of mind or beauty," Nast told his staff, "yet she has been so built up by the newspapers that when she gets into circulation she stops everything except buses. In the command of public interest, she holds her own with royalty, public figures or distinguished socialites. A guest at a recent wedding, at which Brenda Frazier was a bridesmaid, told me that for once the customary pursuit of the bride by the photographers was abandoned for snaps of Brenda. This became so evident that everyone was embarrassed.

"Again I urge a careful reading of the newspapers by the editors so that they may be informed accurately as to which personalities and events are being featured by the newspapers."

Nobody could accuse Nast of not carefully reading the newspapers. He worked harder and harder, nights and weekends, struggling with figures, statistics, covers, Brenda Frazier's latest appearances. Sometimes his judgment remained sound, and his old instincts alert. Allene Talmey complained to him about squabbles between editors and the art department and said, "We are becoming increasingly afraid, and timid, mainly because we are constantly menaced with the threat, 'Mr. Nast won't like it.' So far, whenever I have fought back and taken the issue to you, I have found that you did like it." And the ones he liked were the original, dramatic layouts rather than the "ugly, dry ones" presented by the art department.

But more often, his ceaseless exhortations were irrelevant or redundant. And with this compulsive behavior came a distinct character change. Even Edna Chase was aware of it. He became irritable, brusque, querulous, autocratic. "He ignored the opinions even of men like Lew Wurzburg, his vice president, and MacDonald DeWitt, his legal adviser," Mrs. Chase said. "His own judgment, indeed, became a kind of obsession with him. Everyone else's was poor. Occasionally he and I would talk together, but the old wonderful confidence in each other, the frank disagreements, adjusted and easily forgotten, the feeling of oneness were gone."

He was urged to take rests, take a holiday, ease off, relax. Some

The succession in a rarely assembled group photograph outside the Paris office. From left to right: Alexander Liberman, Nina LeClerc, Michel de Brunhoff, Edna Chase, Iva Patcévitch, Thomas Kernan, Despina Messinesi, Rosamond Bernier.

of the senior staff, alarmed by his manner, began to look for someone to take over the reins, or at least attempt to help him slow
down. The man Nast was most willing to work with at that time was
Harry Yoxall, and in the summer of 1939 Yoxall sailed to New
York on a six-months trial basis, acting as Nast's personal assistant.
"I soon saw I was dealing with a changed man and a very difficult
one; I was also uncertain of how I should be accepted, not only by
the New York staff, coming in from abroad over their heads, but
also by American advertisers, and how at the age of forty-three I
could make a new social life in America, despite the fact that I had
an American wife."

With the signing of the German-Russian pact Yoxall decided to
go back at once to England, where he put the office on alert for the
war to come. Nast did not object. He was as irritable with Yoxall as
with everyone else.

In 1941 he began to have dangerously high blood pressure, and
an oxygen tank was installed in his office. His secretary, Mary
Campbell, who was also a trained physical-education teacher, knew
how to nurse him, and did so with the utmost discretion. Nobody
knew about his illness. In staff meetings in his office, Wurzburg or
Chase would say something that annoyed him, and suddenly his
color would alter and he would get into a rage and dismiss everybody. As soon as they had left the room in dismay, he would sum-
mon Miss Campbell to administer oxygen to him in his private
bathroom.

It was a sad sight for everybody to witness. Only Iva Patcévitch
was let into his confidence in late 1941, when Nast's doctors told
him he had a serious heart condition. Patcévitch was made to promise not to tell anyone. Nast did not want to be pitied or treated as an
invalid. He wanted to keep a grip on things to the very end, particularly since he felt the organization was not up to the standards he
had once achieved for it. Throughout 1941 and early 1942 he continued to bombard his staff with long, increasingly rambling memos.
They became altogether impossible for the staff to cope with. "In
looking through the recent issues of *Vogue,*" one started, "I believe

I ought to call your attention to certain mistakes which are too often repeated . . ."

The memo was *sixty-seven* pages long.

"He was in a terrible state of mind in the last months before he died," said Patcévitch. "He did nothing but dictate memos. He was attempting to write an appraisal of every member of the staff before he died."

This was Nast *in extremis,* the overtired, precision-calibrated mind shuffling and reshuffling his affairs in a desperate caricature of a lifetime's thoroughness, determined to cover every angle, so that things would be in perfect order for his departure.

In December 1941, the month America entered the war, Nast went into the hospital. He described it later in a letter to Coudert: "I was taken to the hospital late one evening and the doctor, expecting the development of pneumonia at any moment, was ready with all the necessary paraphernalia, oxygen tank, etc. I have been more completely out of circulation both as respects the office and the outside world than ever before in my life. I did not even take telephone calls." Even to his son, he kept up the subterfuge about his ailment. Pneumonia, an ear infection—those were the stories the office was told.

In fact it was a heart attack, and it was serious. But Nast would not, could not, stop.

There were parties still to be given. In March 1942, he organized a birthday party for little Leslie and Peter at 1040 Park. "The plan for the party is as follows," he instructed. "The children are to lunch at their own home, come to 1040 at about 1:40, where they will be taken to the movies and afterwards come back for supper at the apartment." Always the conscientious host, he warned Peter's grandmother, Mrs. Donald Brown, "I am not attempting to get an even number of boys and girls."

By May 1942, he had given, since leaving the hospital, five dinners, three cocktail parties (one for the tenants of 1040 Park), and the birthday party for the children.

There were also pretty girls still to be courted. Even at this late date, a new young face in town ignited the old carnal spark. In the summer of 1942, at a party with Frank Crowninshield, Nast met Rosamond Riley. She had recently arrived from Mexico, and Crowny first noticed her at the party as she discussed, with evident knowledge and authority, the work and pre-Columbian art collection of the Mexican artist Covarrubias, who, of course, had been a favorite contributor to *Vanity Fair*. Once more stepping into their old roué double act, Crowny and Condé bore down upon this unusually intelligent young female and, as they had done so many times before, invited her to work for *Vogue*.

Rosamond Riley at the time was taking a typing and speed-writing course near Grand Central Station, and had no interest whatsoever in working for *Vogue*, which Condé thought somewhat eccentric. Undaunted, he began to invite her out.

"He would sometimes take me out to dinner after my course, which was in the evening. He liked to pick me up in his limousine, but it would have blown my cover at the typing school so I insisted he park it round the corner so nobody would see me."

He took her back to 1040 Park, that enormous, glittering mise-en-scène, whose empty rooms must have seemed cavernous to the young visitor, and haunted to the lonely old man who lived there. And then, Rosamond remembers, the "automatic pounce" would occur, which she felt was for him a moment of transition, set apart from daily life, a distraction from the burdens of his business, and easy for her to check.

Something else remained in her mind from these brief summer evenings with Condé Nast. When he started in on his obligatory advances, he would first turn aside to take a pill. It was the kind of thing a very young girl would think funny and sad all at the same time. (She had no idea, of course, of the extent of his debility.)

In April 1942, he sent a memo to Mrs. Chase that read in part:

> You will recall that last September I sent you a binder containing two years' covers of *Vogue*, together with sales figures for each issue, so arranged that the effect of each cover on the sale of its issue could be easily studied. In the memorandum which accompanied these exhibits, I asked for your opinion on the reasons for the

good or bad influence on sales of special-issue subjects, different types of covers, cover barkers and positions of barkers on covers. . . . I am sorry to say that, with the exception of Miss Daves and Dr. Agha, I have had no response from any of the editors to the request I made nearly seven months ago.

In July, he wrote to Coudert: "We are cutting drastically all along the line and are entertaining the hope that we may be fortunate enough to suffer no greater harm than to have our 1941 profits of $268,000 wiped out."

In August, as his financial difficulties increased, Nast's spectacular house at Sands Point, on which he had lavished so much attention and money and where he had spent so little time, was taken over by the Brooklyn Trust Company. Mary Campbell said that she was quite certain this single event hastened the end. (The house was later demolished.) Also in August, he tore himself away from his compulsive paperwork to visit little Leslie, who was in summer camp in Vermont. He perhaps sensed that it might be the last time he would ever see her.

In September, he had another heart attack. It was thought that climbing a hill in Vermont during his visit to his daughter had contributed to the condition. This time, the doctors insisted he stay in bed. In mid-September, Frank Crowninshield told Edna Chase that Nast was upset because she had not replied to a long letter he had written to her. Mrs. Chase expressed surprise—she had not received any letter, only the rambling memos that continued to reach her office. It turned out that Nast, addressing the envelope himself, had simply written her name and, as the address, "Long Island." Mrs. Chase finally found the letter, which contained the usual hectoring essay on the problems that beset his magazines and the failure of the editors to improve. But toward the end, his mind turned to more personal matters: "Now I have become aware of the fact that the memos issued by me from time to time during the past year offended you," he wrote. "I didn't realize to what extent until you told me the other day that my recent memo on covers had killed your interest in *Vogue*." Nast then revealed the magnitude of his mental torment as he felt his strength ebbing away:

> Edna, we have been a great team. I believe I have been a wide-awake and intelligent publisher, but I am the first to admit to myself, and to acknowledge to the world, that without you I could never have built *Vogue*. We have built this great property together. Let us, together, see it through the present crisis or those that may come after.
>
> I am carrying a very heavy burden. I seem to have no interest in life but seeing these properties through. Whether I am to break under this ordeal I do not know. But I do know that I ought to be free from any unnecessary or added burdens. Your feeling—I think unjustified—is, for me, a crushing load. It would certainly make life considerably happier for me if I felt that you would, in no way, resent this letter. It is written, dear Edna, in the hope that no more barriers will ever arise between us.

Edna, overwhelmed, sent a note back by messenger:

> Dearest Condé,
> You sent your letter to Long Island but omitted the name of the town. Finally it was returned and I have received it. I am so busy now that I cannot undertake an answer but some day I will try to tell you, quite unemotionally, how I feel about things and why. In the meantime please know that neither memos nor age nor any other thing can destroy the abiding love I have for you now and always. I shall come to you in a few hours. Edna.

She did. Shortly after receiving this tenderest of billets-doux Nast was reunited with his old companion. Lying propped up in bed, wearing a shawl that she had given him, he held the hand of the woman who would have come to him at any hour, anywhere, throughout their life together. It was the final consummation of a union that had lasted longer and meant more than the most binding of marriages.

A few days later he was dead.

Condé Nast died at about noon on Saturday, September 19, 1942, at 1040 Park Avenue. He was sixty-nine years old. The funeral was held in the Roman Catholic Church of St. Ignatius Loyola (with a little help from Mary Campbell, a convert to Catholicism through the offices of Fulton Sheen). So Nast was buried in the Church into which he had been born. His pallbearers included his closest publishing colleagues, the visibly grief-stricken Frank Crowninshield, MacDonald DeWitt, Richardson Wright, Iva Patcévitch, Frank Soule (head of the advertising department), and friends from the world he had been identified with for so long, including Bernard Baruch, Henry R. Luce, Harrison Williams, Frank L. Crocker (a lawyer in the Gloria Vanderbilt custody case), Herbert Bayard Swope, and Gilbert Miller.

Eight hundred friends and business associates attended the funeral, including four hundred present employees of The Condé Nast Publications—and one prominent former one. Walking up the aisle of the church, Edna Chase was staggered to see the small, white-haired figure of Carmel Snow on her knees, saying her rosary. "She knew what Condé had felt toward her," Mrs. Chase wrote later. "I wondered what was in her heart at that moment."

The coffin rested at 1040 Park Avenue before its journey to the Gate of Heaven Cemetery in Pleasantville, New York. It was placed in the center of the drawing room, a beautifully proportioned room decorated in celadon colors—pale greenish-blue walls and blue silk upholstery, where once "a hundred pairs of gold and silver slippers had shuffled the shining dust." It was flooded with light from the terrace and filled with the flowers Nast had always placed there for entertaining. "Over the coffin," Natica recalls, "I put the best banquet cloth, which was a sheer, shimmering silver over pale yellow; and on top of that, a handful of bouvardia—a fragrant little white flower—tied with ribbon, from his children.

"The employees of the press came down in buses and I received them in the little library at the end of the ballroom, with other guests. Flowers of tribute were massed in the hall." Coudert, alas, was absent; he heard of his father's death over the radio in the Pacific. The rest of the family, with Iva Patcévitch, his wife, Nada, and

Mary Campbell, went with the cortege to Pleasantville, where Nast was buried next to his mother.

The press saluted his career in their columns. Henry Luce's *Time* said: "For a generation he was the man from whom millions of American women got most of their ideas, directly or indirectly, about the desirable American standard of living."

*The New York Times* said: "Mr. Nast's magazines are distinctly 'class' publications. They are the embodiment of his ideal of a qualitative rather than a quantitative product and of his purpose to publish magazines which are authoritative in their field."

*Vogue,* feeling no need to restate what the staff knew so well about his principles, merely said: "The qualities which we—his associates and friends—felt in him most strongly were his complete approachability and understanding. His door, like his heart, was always open."

On the evening of Nast's death, Mary Campbell handed Iva Patcévitch a letter. It was dated May 9, 1942, four months earlier:

Dear Pat:

When Mary gives you this you will be acting President of the Company. I would have told you my plans but I couldn't. Mary will convey my messages to you and Barrow. I am turning the management of the property over into your hands. I suggest you appoint Mary your personal assistant. Unofficially she has served me in that capacity for the past year and has demonstrated her value.

It is a hard and difficult road ahead. You have proven your loyalty, integrity and business ability. I am confident that you will ably continue the outstanding leadership of our periodicals and push them to even greater prestige and brilliance.

Good luck and my deep gratitude to you, dear Pat, for the many things you have done for me.

Affectionately yours,
Condé

With this little note, the succession, over which Nast had tortured himself so much in the last years of his life, was secured. It caused a few raised eyebrows—Patcévitch was young (forty), Russian, and relatively unknown in the company—and at least one shattered expectation, that of Lew Wurzburg, who had served Nast faithfully for over twenty years. He never recovered from the disappointment. But as usual, Nast's choice turned out to be *à point*. Although the fortunes of the publications were shaky at the time Patcévitch took them over, in a few years the new president had steered the company into calmer waters, ensuring its survival.

For Nast, that was the only thing that mattered. Nowhere is this more clearly shown than in the revelation of his personal estate, which was left in three equal shares to his three children.

At his death, Condé Nast owned 7,900 shares of common stock in The Condé Nast Publications, Inc., valued at $17,775.00. He owned 1066.49 shares of stock in the Park-Lexington Corporation, valued at $1,066.49. He also owned 300 shares of the Caledonia Mining Company, estimated as valueless. He possessed 500 U.S. Savings Bonds, valued at $75 per 100. In checking accounts and cash, he had approximately $3,000. The total value of his estate came to about $21,600.00.

The debts were no less shocking. Apart from taxes, estate duties, and creditors (which included Jack & Charlie's "21" and Tiffany & Company), Nast owed $3,645,277.17 on the promissory note assigned to Vogue Studios in 1934, plus $1,914,149.51 unpaid interest (at 6 percent) on that note. He owed Northern Allied Newspapers (advertising representatives) $100,134.78, and Nast Limited $17,218.00.

What the publisher must have suffered as he chatted lightly to Princess Nathalie Paley over a glass of champagne at one of his parties hardly bears thinking about. To live so long under the weight of such crushing debts while presenting to the world the face of prosperity would have tested the skills of Janus. What an American finale.

When the estate was settled in December 1948, its value had increased, with the sale of stocks, redemption of bonds, and so on, to $52,708.90. Not counting the over $5 million in business debts from the Great Crash, Nast personally owed $68,385.96.

The three heirs liquidated Vogue Studios, Inc., and applied the proceeds to the huge Blue Ridge debt, which was taken over by The Condé Nast Publications corporation. The other debts, to Northern Allied and to Nast Limited, which had arisen through Nast's personal borrowing in order to meet the stock options of his employees, were also absorbed by the company.

There was one other source of income—the symbol, in a sense, of everything Nast had created.

In January 1943, Parke Bernet auctioned off the contents of the famous penthouse at 1040 Park Avenue. It was a three-day sale, expected to realize a sizable sum, considering the distinction of the collection and general interest in the publisher. Both Frank Crowninshield and Elsie de Wolfe wrote introductions to the catalogue. But the timing was fatal; with the world at war, neither professional dealers nor the general public were in the mood to buy. The auction was a disaster, with treasures being knocked down for a fraction of their true worth. Six Hepplewhite carved mahogany chairs, for instance, sold for $630; a Chien Lung black-and-gold screen for $410; a landscape by Jean Frédéric Schall for $4,400. The total proceeds of the sale came to $101,362, a gratifying reminder for moralists of the transience of worldly possessions, and of the irrelevance of fine furniture, paintings, silver, and porcelain when human survival is at stake.

The apartment itself remained empty, unsalable, abandoned by history. It was rented for a while and then finally broken up into smaller units. That great sweep of rooftop entertaining space was lost forever.

Condé Nast would surely have smiled rather than grieved. He had never sustained any serious illusions about his position in life, or about the inherent value of the world he had so successfully bought and sold. In that last summer of 1942, during the hot July evenings with Rosamond Riley, he would look around the vast, treasure-filled apartment and say to her, with a sort of wry amusement, "I used to own all this." He would bring out the albums of photographs of the famous parties—the socialites, the actresses, the musicians, the artists, the writers, the models, some of them household words still, others already consigned to oblivion; postcards of Newport, Sands Point, Paris, London; newspaper clippings about openings, nightclubs, golf tournaments, horse shows, ocean voyages—showing her the detritus of his past like a small boy displaying his trophies.

"Think of it," he said to her, his eyes bright for a moment. "Here I was, just a boy from St. Louis, and Edna Chase a Quaker from New Jersey. Between us, we set the standards of the time. We showed America the meaning of style."

No *Vogue* caption-writer could have summarized it better. Condé Nast, meticulous to the end, had perfectly composed his own epitaph.

# CODA

When Condé Nast died, his magazines were already recovering from their decline. At his death, the company shares were quoted at 2¼. One year later, they had risen to 8, and by 1947, to a high of 14.

Frank Crowninshield, Nast's great friend and colleague, died on December 28, 1947, at the age of seventy-five. Tributes referred to his great taste, his courage, his editorial brilliance, his wit, and his capacity for friendship. *The New York Times*'s glowing obituary ended thus: "There will never be anybody quite like Frank Crowninshield again. The mold is broken."

Edna Woolman Chase died on March 20, 1957, six days after her eightieth birthday. She had served sixty-two of those eighty years on *Vogue*, a devotion matched only by her loyalty to, and admiration of, the man who had picked her out and named her editor in chief in 1914. "It was our mutual love for *Vogue* that united us," she once declared. After Nast's death, she was alone for the first time, but she never gave up. As her magazine said: "She stimulated, demanded, searched forever for the best there was—and then demanded better than that."

Lord Camrose died in 1954, and his son, Michael (Baron Hartwell), continued running the company until 1958. He then sold his Amalgamated Press, which included The Condé Nast Publications, to the Daily Mirror Group under Cecil King.

Iva Patcévitch, armed with a clause in the original agreement between Camrose and Nast which stated that the Condé Nast stock could be repurchased within a six-month period after any sale of Amalgamated Press, went to London to meet Cecil King, the man who might be the new owner of the company and officiator at the unlikely marriage between the *Daily Mirror* (a mass tabloid) and *Vogue.* The meeting was not a success. Patcévitch returned to the United States bent on finding a buyer for the company, and in March 1959, S. I. Newhouse, of the newspaper chain, said he would take a controlling interest. Newhouse later became the sole stockholder, thus removing the company from quotation on the stock exchange.

Under this disposal, *Vogue, House & Garden,* and *Glamour* were launched into a new era, the triumphant witnesses of Nast's genius and his toil. Today, still under the artistic and editorial guidance of Alexander Liberman, *Vogue* has a circulation of well over a million; and *Vanity Fair,* perhaps the brightest jewel in Nast's crown, is about to be reintroduced as a magazine to a new generation of readers. Forty years after his death, Condé Nast's spirit lives.

# NOTES

Except where otherwise indicated, all references to *Vogue* mean American *Vogue*.

Except where otherwise indicated, all advertising linages come from *Printer's Ink* and all circulation figures are from the *Ayer Directory of Newspapers, Magazines & Trade Publications.*

Abbreviations:

CNA—the Condé Nast Archives, c/o The Condé Nast Publications Inc., 350 Madison Avenue, New York, N.Y. 10017

*AIV—Always in Vogue,* by Edna Woolman Chase and Ilka Chase, Doubleday & Company, 1954

## PRELUDE: "THIS IS A CLASSY JOINT"

CNA provided me with most of the information about Condé Nast's parties, including the breakdowns. Some details came from an interview with the artist Benito, and additional material from an article he wrote for his local Spanish newspaper in Valladolid.

The building had been designed: interview with Andrew Alpert, architect

Wonderful copy, all in all: *Vogue*, August 1, 1928

"What is charm to an American?": Paul Poiret, *My First Fifty Years*, V. Gollancz, Ltd., 1931

"You may say": Interview with Millicent Fenwick

"The parties of Condé Nast": F. Scott Fitzgerald, *The Crack-Up*. New Directions, 1945

Groucho Marx was overheard: Helen Lawrenson, *Stranger at the Party*, Random House, 1975

once in Paris: interview with Harry Yoxall

Once, at the notorious Quatre-Arts Ball: Grace Moore, *You're Only Human Once*, Doubleday, Doran & Co., 1944

"while in his blue garden": F. Scott Fitzgerald, *The Great Gatsby*, Scribner's, 1925

"It was a time of escape": John Lardner, *The Aspirin Age 1919–1941*, Simon & Schuster, 1949

## CHAPTER 1: A TIDIER GARDEN

My main source for this chapter was Carl Wittke's *William Nast, Patriarch of German Methodism*, Wayne State University Press, 1959. Additional material came from interviews with Mrs. Gerald F. Warburg and Lady Benson. Details about the Benoist family and the mansion, Oakland, were provided by the Affton Historical Society, St. Louis, Mo. 63123.

Freudians may see: interview with Dr. Richard Wallace

## CHAPTER TWO: FIGURE JIM

Information about Nast's Georgetown career came from *Tradition in Turmoil*, a document celebrating the 75th anniversary of the Georgetown College Student Council. Mrs. Gerald F. Warburg also helped me. The main source for Nast's work at *Collier's* and at the Home Pattern Company was CNA. The changes in the economic status of women are discussed in Sheila Rothman's *Woman's Proper Place: A History of Changing Ideals and Practices, 1870 to the Present*, Basic Books, 1978. Three books provided me with information about the history of magazines: Frank Luther Mott, *A History of American Magazines*, Belknap/Harvard University Press, 1957; James Playstead Wood, *Magazines in the United States*, Ronald, 1971; and Theodore Peterson, *Magazines in the Twentieth Century*, University of Illinois Press, 1956.

"You know perfectly well, Condé": *AIV*
Early in 1899: ibid.


## CHAPTER THREE: THE REQUIREMENTS OF CLASS

*AIV* provided me with much information about the early days of *Vogue*.

"Social prominence": Mrs. John King Van Rensselaer, in collaboration
  with Frederic Van der Water, *The Social Ladder*, H. Holt & Co., 1924
"It's this way, you see": Edith Wharton, *The House of Mirth*, Scribner's,
  1905
Mrs. Van Rensselaer gleefully tells: Van Rensselaer, *Social Ladder*
"ushered in by the sale": Frank Crowninshield, *Vogue*, January 1, 1923
"Harry McVickar, who belonged": Walter G. Robinson, *Vogue*, January
  1, 1923
"A very odd thing": *Vogue*, July 5, 1900
"more than one": Van Rensselaer, *Social Ladder*


## CHAPTER FOUR: CLARISSE COUDERT, SOPRANO

Much of the background information about Clarisse Nast came from interviews with Mrs. Gerald F. Warburg, Lady Benson, and The Hon. Mrs. Mark Bonham Carter.

"Slender, suave": Marie Stark, "It's Nice Work If You Can Get It," unpublished ms., circa 1940
Clarisse's grandfather: interview with Ferdinand Coudert
On July 22, 1897: *The New York Times*
Paris, in 1906: Judith Cladel, *Rodin*, Harcourt, Brace & Company,
  1937
The photographer's name: One of Steichen's portraits of Clarisse appears in his book, *A Life in Photography*, Doubleday, 1963. Two
  others are in the collection of the Museum of Modern Art, New York.
Her first inspiration: *AIV*

"Well, it looks just like": Stark, "It's Nice Work"
"There was a little girl": ibid.
"turning the pages": *AIV*
Some of her most effective efforts: *Vogue*, March 1, 1919
"It took real guts": Harford Powel, *Advertising & Selling*, August 1, 1935
On one occasion: Stark, "It's Nice Work"
At that time: *The New York Times*, October 22, 1914

## CHAPTER FIVE: "WHAT WERE THE CHAUFFEURS WEARING?"

Condé Nast's transformation of *Vogue* is largely documented in CNA.

For a few months: *AIV*
"Oh, good," Nast would say: interview with Paul Bonner

## CHAPTER SIX: WAR À LA MODE

My sources for the history of fashion were *Mirror, Mirror: A Social History of Fashion,* by Michael and Ariane Batterberry, Holt, Rinehart, & Winston, 1977; and *Ready-Made Miracle,* by Jessica Daves, G. P. Putnam's Sons, 1967. Except where otherwise noted, all the material on Edna Woolman Chase came from *AIV*.

"She had emerald-green eyes": interview with Lydia Sherwood McClean
"You have a very fine pen": interview with Marya Mannes
"At last I have gotten around": CNA
"I have taken one look": ibid.
"The cloche is": *Vogue*, March 1, 1924
*"Vogue*—surely as sophisticated": *Vogue*, February 15, 1926
"One notices": *Vogue*, March 15, 1924
"the under one of tweed": *Vogue*, January 1, 1922
When Mrs. Chase met her daughter: Ilka Chase, *Past Imperfect*, Doubleday, Doran, 1942
"As I see the function of *Vogue*": CNA
"Dearest Condé": CNA
A witty, energetic and strong-willed lady: Frank Crowninshield, *Vogue*, January 1, 1923

Benjamin Sonnenberg, who once said: Geoffrey Hellman, *The New Yorker,* April 8, 1950

"Everyone leaned forward": Emily Post, *Vogue,* December 1, 1914

## CHAPTER SEVEN: "THE COCKTAIL WITHOUT A PADLOCK"

Much of the information about Crowninshield's background came from Geoffrey T. Hellman's profile, "Last of the Species," in *The New Yorker,* September 19 and 26, 1942. Jeanne Ballot Winham provided me with many stories about Crowninshield and *Vanity Fair.* CNA was the other main source.

"I remember trying": Frank Crowninshield, *Vogue,* September 15, 1940

"Mr. Crowninshield": Jeanne Ballot Winham, "Very Innocent Bystander," unpublished ms.

"Why not spend your summer": Helen Lawrenson, *Stranger at the Party,* Random House, 1975

One of Crowninshield's favorite diversions: *AIV*

A typical Crowninshield evening: interview with Allene Talmey

"A trait in F.C.": Condé Nast, quoted in *The New Yorker,* February 14, 1948

He confessed it himself: Frank Crowninshield, *The New Yorker*

He would sometimes show: interview with Ewart Newsom

Helen Lawrenson tells: Lawrenson, *Stranger at the Party*

"We are not going to print": *Vanity Fair,* January 1916

*Vanity Fair* was signaling: Crowninshield, *Vogue,* January 1, 1923

"Do you, sir": *Vanity Fair,* June 1917

"I find that I really need": Jack London, *Vanity Fair,* September 1914

"God must have loved": Harford Powel, *Advertising & Selling,* February 16, 1933

"As a people": Richardson Wright, *House & Garden,* October 1925

## CHAPTER EIGHT: THE GRAND TOUR

Except where otherwise noted, information for this chapter came from CNA, *AIV,* and interviews with Iva Patcévitch and Harry Yoxall.

"We sat in the meadow": Vita Sackville-West to Harold Nicolson, September 24, 1926 (courtesy Victoria Glendinning)

"*Vogue* was snobbish to a degree": Alison Settle in an interview with Linda Blandford, *The Observer* (London), July 1, 1973

Leone Blakemore Moats: Alice-Leone Moats, *Town & Country*, October 1978

De Brunhoff was happiest: Bettina Ballard, *In My Fashion*, David McKay Company, 1960

"De Brunhoff would write things down": ibid.


## CHAPTER NINE: DROIT DU SEIGNEUR

My main sources for this chapter were CNA, *AIV*, and interviews with Iva Patcévitch.

"Crowninshield had faintly amoral": Edmund Wilson, *The Twenties*, Farrar, Straus and Giroux, 1975

"Around 1922": Geoffrey T. Hellman, "Last of the Species," *The New Yorker*, September 19, 1942

"I had been sent to Exeter": interview with Ewart Newsom

"In spite of his not very attractive": Wilson, *The Twenties*

"They probably thought we were fairies": Helen Lawrenson, *Stranger at the Party*, Random House, 1975

"He believed that all women": Diana Vreeland, *Vogue Poster Book*, Harmony Books, 1975

"a type of modern woman": St. John Irvine, *Vanity Fair*, July 1920

"After a day like this": Marie Stark, "It's Nice Work If You Can Get It," unpublished ms., circa 1940

He divided his women employees: interview with Allene Talmey

"I brought with me": interview with Benito

"Stylishly dressed": L. L. Calloway, letter to the author

His devotion to the singer: Grace Moore, *You're Only Human Once*, Doubleday, Doran & Co., 1944

"Well, Gracie": ibid.

"I came three thousand miles": Lawrenson, *Stranger at the Party*

she wanted him to be a lawyer: Stark, "It's Nice Work"

"Condé had a book of exercises": Lawrenson, *Stranger at the Party* "yet another boring date": interview with Lydia Sherwood McClean

"He had no hubris": Lawrenson, *Stranger at the Party*


## CHAPTER 10: GIRLS WITH LONG NECKS

Except where otherwise stated, information for this chapter came from *The Golden Age of Style,* by Julian Robinson, Harcourt, Brace, Jovanovich, 1976; *Fashion Illustration,* Introduction by Pauline Ridley, Rizzoli, 1979; *The Art of Vogue Covers, 1909–1940,* by William Packer, Crown Publishers, 1980, and from *AIV.*

Having witnessed the effect: Frank Crowninshield, *Vogue,* November 1, 1940

Just as in America: Elizabeth Kendall, *Where She Danced,* Alfred A. Knopf, 1979

"He was an extremely odd chap": Paul Poiret, *My First Fifty Years,* V. Gollancz, Ltd., 1931

"I approached all colors": ibid.

"We saw in America": interview with Benito

"We swallowed them, hook, line and sinker": CNA

"My critics at this time": ibid.

Eric's work habits: Bettina Ballard, *In My Fashion,* David McKay Company, 1960

In the thirties, an inordinate amount: CNA

"combined a certain realism of detail": ibid.

"Bébé usually appeared": Ballard, *In My Fashion*

In a March 21, 1936, memo: CNA

"The trouble with the cover": ibid.

"I think greater quality was achieved": interview with Alexander Liberman


## CHAPTER 11: ENGLISH CHIC, SLAVIC CHARM,
## AND PARISIAN DRESSMAKERS

Much of my information about the history of photography came from the *Vogue Book of Fashion Photography 1919–1979,* Simon & Schuster, 1979; and *Ready-Made Miracle* by Jessica Daves, G. P. Putnam's Sons,

1967. Except where otherwise stated, letters and business documents about photographers came from CNA.

"In those days, Madame": Mina Curtiss, *Other People's Letters,* Houghton Mifflin, 1978

"He was photographing": Edward Steichen, *Vogue,* June 15, 1941

"High-speed film": Richard Avedon, *Diary of a Century—Jacques Henri Lartigue,* Viking, 1970

"My dear, don't let it worry you": *AIV*

Yet there was a powerful connection: Elizabeth Kendall, *Where She Danced,* Knopf, 1979

Adolphe Meyer: biographical information from Philippe Jullian, *De Meyer,* Alfred A. Knopf, 1976

"De Meyer's earliest photographs": Cecil Beaton, *Vogue,* April, 1976

Edward Steichen was born: Edward Steichen, *A Life in Photography,* Doubleday, 1963

"Fashion photography had become": ibid.

"He would walk into a sitting late": Bettina Ballard, *In My Fashion,* David McKay Company, 1960

"still wrapped in its cocoon": Cecil Beaton, *Photobiography,* Doubleday, 1951

"It's all very well": ibid.

"Whereas Steichen's pictures": ibid.

"It's a most simple": Cecil Beaton, *Selected Diaries 1926–74,* Weidenfeld & Nicolson, 1979

"I considered that adult life": ibid.

"It is he who too often persuaded me": Beaton, *Photobiography*

"Let someone else do it": Cecil Beaton, letter courtesy Hugo Vickers

"I went to the *Vogue* studio": Horst P. Horst, *Photographs of a Decade,* J. J. Augustin, 1944

"I suppose you think": interview with Horst

Condé Nast once invited: interview with Toni Frissell Bacon

Nast, pursuing his interest in her: anecdote in Margaretta K. Mitchell, *Recollections: Ten Women of Photography,* Viking, 1979

"one of those well-groomed": *Vanity Fair,* April 1935

"He took Dali-like": Ballard, *In My Fashion*

## CHAPTER 12: THE RINGMASTER

Much of my information about Dr. Agha came from *AIV* and from interviews with Benito and Iva Patcévitch. Some of the photographic history is contained in the *Vogue Book of Fashion Photography 1919–1979,* Simon & Schuster, 1979.

"No other publisher": Horst P. Horst, *Photographs of a Decade,* J. J. Augustin, 1944

Heyworth Campbell was an attractive man: interview with Jeanne Ballot Winham

"He'd take a pencil": ibid.

Paul Gallico: quoted by Frank Crowninshield, *Vogue,* March 15, 1945

"A picture editor": Edward Steichen, *A Life in Photography,* Doubleday, 1963

Nast asked Benito: interview with Benito

"Aside from good management": dummy courtesy of Mrs. Raphael Semmes

"I don't want to have to go": interview with Benito

"After I had passed a few days": Condé Nast, *P/M Magazine,* New York, August-September 1939

"He spread out": Frank Crowninshield, *P/M Magazine*

"We must not go by the letters": CNA

"42 percent of all the advertisements": ibid.

Horst once took a picture: interview with Horst

He had a favorite story: Horst, *Photographs of a Decade*

"Personally, I might be inclined": CNA

"a man with whom I could not very well assume": Condé Nast, *P/M Magazine*

"It was hard work with Bruehl": interview with Allene Talmey

When Alexander Liberman first joined: interview with Alexander Liberman

"The day an art director": Carmel Snow, *The World of Carmel Snow,* McGraw-Hill, 1962

"These plates give": CNA

"I think the startling lighting": ibid.

"Mere novelty or art value": ibid.

"Legibility is the first essential": ibid.

He rarely read a book: interview with Allene Talmey

Michel de Brunhoff pointed out: CNA
Beaton once said: interview with Horst
"The basis of the beauty": CNA
Vogel, after the death: interview with Alexander Liberman
*Life* was actually: interview with Clare Boothe Luce
"Eisie showed that": Alfred Eisenstaedt, *Witness to Our Time,* Viking, 1966
Horst in particular objected: interview with Horst
"We must have asked": ibid.
"Since the models": CNA
"The greatest fashion photography": Susan Sontag, *Vogue,* September 1978
"We never felt": interview with Horst


## CHAPTER THIRTEEN: PARKS AND PICTURE PALACES

Except where otherwise stated, information about the Greenwich Press came from CNA and from interviews with Benjamin Bogin.

But according to Edna Chase: *AIV*
"For the time being": Benito dummy, courtesy of Mrs. Raphael Semmes
"The copy room": Jeanne Ballot Winham, "Very Innocent Bystander," unpublished ms.
"But Mr. Nast": interview with Iva Patcévitch


## CHAPTER FOURTEEN: THE DEFECTORS

Except where otherwise noted, information for this chapter came from CNA; *AIV; The World of Carmel Snow,* by Carmel Snow, McGraw-Hill, 1962; and W. A. Swanberg, *Citizen Hearst,* Scribner's, 1961.

She even wheeled in Leslie: interview with Lady Benson
In his distress: interview with Harry Yoxall
In 1945, at a luncheon: interview with Rosamond Bernier Russell
"simple Renaissance dwellings": Ilka Chase, *Past Imperfect,* Doubleday, Doran, 1942

## CHAPTER FIFTEEN: A SPLENDID MIRAGE

The material in this chapter concerning Edna Chase was drawn from *AIV*.

"To believe in this miracle": *Vogue,* February 1, 1926
"the perfect year": John Lardner, *The Aspirin Age, 1919–1941,* Simon
    & Schuster, 1949
Nast tore down: interview with Iva Patcévitch
"None of the luggage": interview with Harry Yoxall
"On nights when": ibid.
"I had no idea": Jeanne Ballot Winham, "Very Innocent Bystander,"
    unpublished ms.
"I flew to the box": *AIV*
"Mr. Nast held up": Ballot, "Very Innocent Bystander"
"It was the only time": interview with Elinor Wurzburg Lawrence
"Try the capital I": letter from Rosalie Zimmermann to the author
"He was white with anger": interview with Allene Talmey
"Good morning, Condé": interview with Ewart Newsom
"We were milling about": letter from Rosalie Zimmermann
"You wouldn't believe it": interviews with Iva Patcévitch and Allene
    Talmey
"He lapped his up": interview with Harry Yoxall
"Go and do thou likewise": *Vanity Fair,* June 1924
 Nast once bought: interview with Iva Patcévitch
"obnoxious vulgarity": Edmund Wilson, *The Twenties,* Farrar, Straus &
    Giroux, 1975
"Do you have a beau here?": interview with Lady Benson
"It was great": interview with Mrs. Gerald F. Warburg
"Everyone rushed": interview with Lady Benson
"fantastic success": F. Scott Fitzgerald, *The Crack-Up,* New Directions,
    1945

## CHAPTER SIXTEEN: END OF THE SEASON

Except where otherwise noted, information for this chapter came from
CNA, from *AIV*, and from interviews with Iva Patcévitch.

"Well, you know": interview with Ewart Newsom

"If one were asked": Frank Crowninshield, *Vogue*, September 14, 1929

"Marry him.": interview with Lady Benson

## CHAPTER SEVENTEEN: ALL IS VANITY

Except where otherwise stated, information for this chapter came from CNA and from interviews with Iva Patcévitch.

"I thought it was just one of those": Margaret Case Harriman, *The New Yorker*, January 4, 1941

"Condé later told me": Margaret Case Harriman, *Blessed Are the Debonair*, Rinehart and Company

"He did not ask Crowninshield": interview with Clare Boothe Luce

"Condé asked me": interview with Allene Talmey

"I came here": Helen Lawrenson, *Stranger at the Party*, Random House, 1975

"Darling": interview with Ewart Newsom

"that dinged and donged": Elizabeth Janeway, *New York Times Book Review*, October 30, 1960

"If you go on with it": *AIV*

"He never had anything to do with them": interview with Mary Lasker

## CHAPTER EIGHTEEN: TWILIGHT OF THE MODE

CNA and *AIV* provided much of the source material for this chapter, with added information from Lady Benson, Mrs. Gerald F. Warburg, The Hon. Mrs. Mark Bonham Carter, Alexander Liberman, and Harry Yoxall.

"I would rather": interview with Mrs. Ian Wilson-Young

She said later: interview with Clare Boothe Luce

"Our policy is to maintain": *Vogue*, September 1939

"My little house": *Vogue*, July 15, 1940

"Condé was totally open": interview with Millicent Fenwick

"Where will the money end up": ibid.

"To old New Yorkers": Frank Crowninshield, *Vanity Fair*, October 1925

"Strange how the memory": Frank Crowninshield, *Vogue*, July 1, 1942 "exhibiting in her box": Frank Crowninshield, *Vogue,* April 1, 1940

"all of his young people": Frank Crowninshield, *Vogue*, November 1, 1940

 "He would sometimes": interview with Rosamond Bernier Russell

"Think of it": ibid.

## CODA

Information for this coda came from CNA, Harry Yoxall, and Iva Patcévitch.

"There will never be anybody": *The New York Times*, December 30, 1947

"She stimulated, demanded": *Vogue*, April 15, 1957

# INDEX

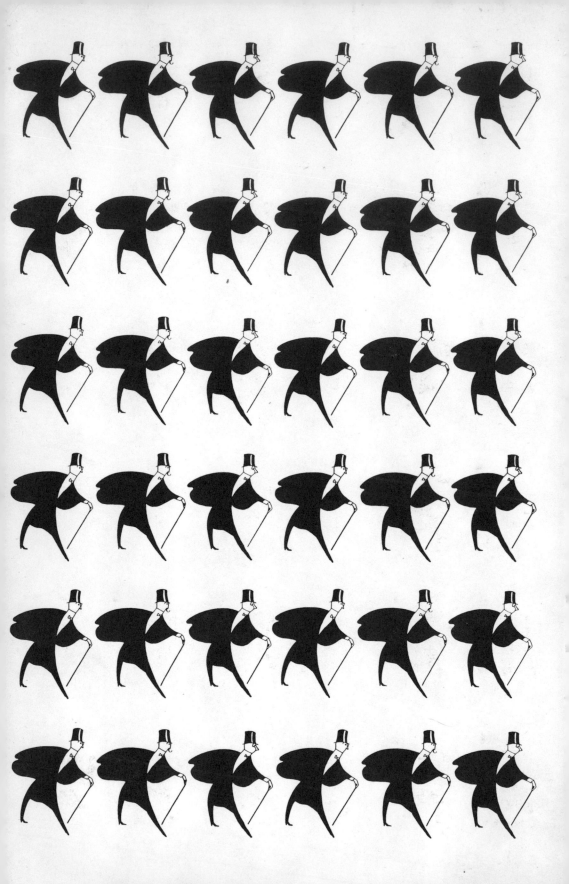